A LAST HEIR OF RE'VALL NOVEL

Little Voltain

Saphira's Story

KAREN THROWER

This is a work of fiction. Names, characters, places, and incidents are products of the author's imagination or are used fictitiously and are not to be construed as real. Any resemblance to actual events, locations, organizations, or persons, living or dead, is entirely coincidental.

World Castle Publishing, LLC
Pensacola, Florida

Hardback ISBN: 9798248837687
Paperback ISBN: 9798891265325
eBook ISBN: 9798891265332
First Edition World Castle Publishing, LLC, March 3, 2026
http://www.worldcastlepublishing.com

Cover: Cover Designs by Karen
Editor: Karen Fuller

CHAPTER 1

ARDENRY: 19 YEARS AGO

Mother Lily Voltain ran through the streets of Ardenry, eyes blinded by tears. She had to get to her sister's house; it was the closest place she could think to go that was safe. She dashed between people and carts, almost twisting her ankle as she stepped in a hole. But she couldn't stop. She couldn't slow down, not now. Lily reached Oakenwald St. and prayed she could keep running. Number twelve came into view, and she squeezed the rock in her pocket as hard as she could, prying Lavinia would notice her own rock heating up. Lily ran up the stairs, and banged on the door.

"Please!" She cried, "Let me in, please hurry!" She banged on the door until it opened a moment later.

Lavinia stood in the doorway, her eyes in shock. "Lily what's wrong?" She pulled Lily inside and locked the door behind them. Lily threw her arms around her sister, shaking, feeling as if she'd hyperventilate. Lavinia held her tight, running her hand down her sister's long hair.

"We'll go home." Lily looked up and saw Lavinia's husband, Rysden with the children standing by the fireplace. The now five-year-old twins looked scared, and Kaythen was worried.

Lavinia nodded. "I'll send you a message later." He cast a spell, and the four of them disappeared, leaving the sisters alone.

"I'm sorry I forgot the children would be with you," Lily cried.

"Don't you worry about them," she led her sister to the chairs and sat her down. "What happened?"

CHAPTER 2
FIRST TASK

Saphira slowly walked around her room, checking things off her list. "Shirts, pants, socks, underclothes, dagger and sheaths, boots, brush, gold sack, waterskin, bed roll, cloak. That's it, I guess." She had been packing all day and was finally ready. The only thing left to do was tell her family.

"Saphy, dinner!" Her mother called out.

"Coming!" She quietly made her way down the stairs and saw her parents at the table. Her mother, Lily, was pouring them some sweet wine, and her father, William, was putting the plates out. Saphira walked up behind her mother, but she didn't notice and yelled for Saphira again.

"Saphy, are you—" Lily turned and gave a little startle, "Oh!" She chuckled, "Sorry, honey, I didn't hear you." Saphira smiled and sat down. She loved sneaking up on her family; no one ever heard her. Her brothers called her 'little sneaker' when she was a kid because her favorite pastime was sneaking up and scaring them. Sometimes Christopher still called her that, and she knew Foster would as well if he were home. But he left almost four years ago to travel the world. Saphira remembered how sad her parents were in the days after Foster left, and knowing she was about to do the same thing, made her feel like there was a lead weight in her stomach. Saphira took her parents' hands over the table as her mother prayed over the nightly meal.

"Blessed Otto, thank you for this meal with family. We truly appreciate our time together. Please keep an eye on our son and brother, Foster, while he makes his way in the world. Thank you for this day and your love." Saphira felt the blessing, and a small, sad smile pulled at her lips. Her mother blessed their dinner every night, and Saphira knew she'd miss hearing it. The thought of her name being added to the nightly prayer was both heartwarming and sad.

Saphira took a sip of her wine while her father began cutting his chicken. "So, how was your day, Saphy?" He chewed his bite with a smile.

Here goes nothing, she thought. "Pretty busy actually," she said, putting the glass down.

"Oh yeah, what did you do?" She watched her father eat his meal. He looked happy and knew his smile was about to disappear.

"I packed." Both her parents suddenly looked up. The sound of their cutlery clinking against the plates cut the silence, and she tried to bravely look into their hurt eyes.

"Why were you packing Saphira?" Her father's voice was quiet, and she fought hard to keep her lower lip from quivering as she cleared her throat.

"I want to travel like Foster, like you did. I want to go to Ardenry and find a group."

Lily gently laid her hand on Saphira's shoulder. "Is there nothing to keep you here? I thought you and Miles were getting along rather well these days."

She shook her head and sighed, "I've thought and prayed about it, Mom, and I feel my destiny lies outside of Raventree. I bet there are a lot of groups who could use my skills. Besides, I don't love Miles, he's more like a trusted confidant." Saphira knew her mother and Lord Giles had hoped one day she would be interested in either of his sons. And while Miles came close, they weren't right together.

"There's a lot more to being a rogue than sneaking Saphira," William said. "Groups expect you to do dangerous things like pick traps and poisoned locks." He leaned over and laid his hand over hers. He had a look on his face that Saphira wasn't sure she had seen before, like he was afraid. "You'll have to kill people, Saphy. Are you prepared for that?" She knew very well what was expected of her. She had spent many nights in the taverns of Raventree listening to all kinds of stories from the traveling sneakers. Nothing ever stirred her like dreaming of going out into the world and making a fortune using her natural-born talents. Her own parents traveled for a time as well, and she knew they both took lives, even her mother did, but to a lesser extent. It was something she had thought about frequently, if she could take a life. She always assumed it was one of those things you wouldn't know how you'd react until you were in the moment.

"I know what will be expected of me." She looked between her parents. "I've thought about this a lot. I must go. I'm restless here, Papa. I want to go out in the world and make a name for myself."

Her mother leaned over and gave her a hug. "I know you've felt restless for a while, Saphira, and if you feel going out into the world will make you happy, I give you my blessing. But promise me, you'll learn all you can about traps and locks before you join a group." Saphira knew her mother wouldn't fight her on her decision and smiled against her shoulder. But she was right, Saphira needed more practice with locks. She could pick any door in the house and a few in the castle, but that was it. Ardenry would be the perfect place to learn and grow her skills.

"I promise Mom, I'll learn quick."

"You do learn quickly, baby." Lily sat up and kissed her daughter's forehead.

But her father was not so easily swayed. "Now, Sweets, I don't know about this." Her father still looked apprehensive as his eyes moved between them.

"William, she is a grown woman now, and if she feels her place is out there, then who are we to stop her?"

Saphira spoke up with her best argument. "Besides, Foster was the same age when he left."

William was still visibly stunned. "But…you're my baby girl, you can't leave." His voice was still quiet, and Saphira vowed not to cry at her father's sentimental words.

Lily gave a little chuckle. "William, really, do you think Foster was any less my baby boy when he left? Our children are grown, and traveling is in their blood. As much as we might want to lock her in her room and keep her here forever, we can't." William sighed and ran his hand through his hair before getting up from the table and grabbing his pipe off the mantle.

"Sorry, Sweets, I lost my appetite," he said and walked out of the house. As much as Saphira wanted to leave, she didn't want her dad to be angry at her for doing it.

She turned to her mother. "What do I do?"

Lily put her hand on Saphira's back. "Talk to him, sweetie. I think you're the only one who can convince him. Think of it as your first test." Saphira looked back at the door and, for the first time in her life, had no idea what to say. She took a quick gulp of her wine and walked outside.

Her father was standing in the yard by the fence that surrounded the house, his head down and his arms crossed across his big chest. The smell of his pipe smoke filled the air.

"Papa?" He sniffed and tapped his pipe on the fence where he always did. The same spot her mother always told him not to, and turned.

"Saphira, are you sure you want to do this?"

She walked next to him and nodded. "There is no job or man here for me. My destiny is out there. I know it."

He sighed and put an arm around her shoulder. "I always thought my biggest fear was you getting married to a Raventree," he said with a small smile.

Saphira giggled and hugged her father. "You don't have to worry about me marrying a Raventree, but I have to get away."

He leaned over and kissed the top of her head. "I know little sneaker. You truly are your mother's daughter, aren't you?" She looked up into her father's eyes, blue like hers, but his were a touch darker.

"I'm your daughter too."

He smiled. "You are, and I love you so much."

"I love you too. I promise I'll come back, Papa."

She felt his arms tighten around her. "You better," he said quietly.

The next morning, Saphira was packed and loaded up as she walked into the Temple of Otto to find her brother Christopher. He was easy to find, being an acolyte, he was usually in the main chamber cleaning something. Sure enough, she spied him on a ladder, changing the candles in the high lanterns. She decided to make some noise as she walked up to him. It wouldn't do any good to scare him. He might bust his head as he fell from the ladder.

After a few loud steps, Christopher looked down. "Hey, little sneaker, what brings you here so early?"

She scoffed, "Christopher, I'm eighteen years old, I am not little anymore. Well, age-wise anyway." Everyone in her family was taller than her, especially her brothers.

He laughed as he climbed down the ladder. "You'll always be little to me, sister," he said, sliding down the last half of the ladder. He turned and gave her a warm hug. "So, what can I do for you?"

"I came to say goodbye."

He tilted his head like he always did when he was confused. "Goodbye, why?"

"I'm…going to Ardenry for a while, then I'm going to find a group and put my talents to use."

Christopher clicked his tongue. "Got the bug, eh? That's not so shocking. What did Mom and Dad say?"

Saphira shrugged her shoulders and leaned against a nearby pillar. "Mom immediately gave me her blessing, and Papa, well, I had to convince him. He didn't want me to go."

Christopher chuckled. "Well, you are his little girl. But Foster may be home soon, don't you want to see him?" It was the one thing she was betting on, that Foster would get home right after she left.

"Of course I do, but it'll have to wait until I get home."

Christopher sighed and gave her another hug. "I'm glad you stopped by to say goodbye. I'll miss you, Saphy."

"I wouldn't leave without seeing you." Saphira squeezed her brother tight. Leaving him was going to be difficult. It wasn't as if they weren't close growing up, but after Foster left, all they had was each other. "Take care of Mom and Papa for me, okay?"

"I will," he kissed her forehead, and she felt Otto's blessing. "Saphira?"

"Yeah?"

Christopher backed up and took her hands. "If you happen to see our wayward brother out in the world, would you tell him I'm sorry?"

Saphira smiled. "I will, though I have a feeling he'll want to say the same to you." He sighed and cracked his knuckles, something he only did when he was thinking about their brother.

"Good luck, little sneaker. May Otto bless you on your journey, and I'll pray you come home safely."

"Thank you, Christopher. I love you."

"I love you too, Saphy." He kissed her cheek, and Saphira willed herself to keep it together as she walked out of the temple. The moment she made her way out of Raventree, she could feel what a good decision she had made. Though her family and friends were here, she knew her destiny was elsewhere.

CHAPTER 3

JUST IN TIME

A month after leaving Raventree, Saphira walked into Ardenry. Her eyes widened at the sight of so many people in one place. There was a constant buzz of noise all around her, and the smells! One sniff was roasted chicken, and the next was unwashed bodies. It threw her senses into overdrive. Raventree wasn't a small town; it was constantly growing. But it was nowhere near the size of Ardenry, and as much traveling as her family did to visit others, they never stayed in the capital. Saphira had promised her mother that the first thing she would do when she arrived was visit the temple.

It was easy to see in the distance. The large white marble building was shining in the morning sun. As she walked, she kept her eyes out for any kind of job she could get. But most of the ones she saw were waitress jobs, and she had absolutely no interest in those. Servers worked all day, or all night, and she'd have no time to learn anything.

It took her almost half an hour to reach the temple, and as she stood on the steps, she could feel the peace her mother described. It felt like love and home. This temple was the largest one in the world dedicated to Otto, and His pontiff took residence here. Saphira always felt her mother's rightful place was here in Ardenry, but she always shook her head and said her path led her to Raventree, and that's where she wanted to stay.

Saphira slowly walked in and stared at the stained-glass windows. They were the biggest she had ever seen and couldn't help but let her jaw drop at the beauty of them. The colors splashed across the inside of the hall, and everything was awash in blues, greens, and reds. She reached up and held the little seashell around her neck.

"Blessed Otto," she whispered. "I'm here, out in the world doing what I feel is right. Help me choose the right path."

"Hello, young traveler." She looked over and saw a priest waxing the pews. He seemed to be in his forties, his hair hadn't begun to gray yet, and she thought his robes looked a bit too fancy for the job he was currently doing. It had silver seashells and what looked like ocean waves stitched all around it.

"Hello Father."

He walked over and shook her hand. "Father Rayner, nice to meet you."

"Saphira Voltain, nice to meet you, too."

He smiled a little. "You're Lily's daughter, aren't you?"

"Yeah, I should probably stop introducing myself with my last name."

Rayner chuckled. "So, what brings you to Ardenry?"

"I promised Mom I'd learn about locks and traps before I head out into the world. I figured Ardenry was the place to do it."

He nodded. "It is. I happen to know of a retired adventurer looking for help at his locksmithing shop."

Saphira gasped. "Sounds perfect! Where is it?"

"It's about fifteen blocks down Rose Street on the east side of the street called 'Meet's Locksmithing'. The owner's name is Zell."

Saphira squealed and hugged him, "Thank you, thank you!"

He chuckled and patted her back. "Better hurry, young lady."

"I will, I will!" Saphira ran out of the temple and through the streets of Ardenry looking for Rose Street. When she found it, she made a sharp turn, almost running into a wheelbarrow full of cabbage. Rose Street was full of blacksmiths and armorers, and at the end of the block, she found the sign she was looking for. It said 'Meet's Locksmithing' like Rayner said it would. She quickly ran over but was just in time to see a hand take away a help-wanted sign.

"No, no, no," she whispered and walked inside as a middle-aged man with a shock of white hair was shaking hands with a boy a little older than herself. "Excuse me, but I saw you had a help-wanted sign outside. I'd like the job." She smiled widely but didn't bother introducing herself. She had to act quickly if she had any chance of getting this job.

"Sorry, miss, I gave the job to Robert here." The man with white hair, most likely Zell, motioned at the boy with the sign in his hand.

Robert smiled smugly at her. "And it's much appreciated, sir."

Saphira growled on the inside. "Do you have to train him? Cause I already know about locks."

Robert's eyes went wide while Zell scratched his chin. "I would. You know about locks?"

"Yes, sir, I do." She was only partly lying through her teeth, but it was for a worthy cause.

"Come here, young lady." Zell motioned for her, and she followed him to the back of the shop. "Most of my customers are ones needing their locks picked. He couldn't pick this door. If you can, the job's yours."

"No problem." Saphira looked at the door and knew Otto was smiling down on her. It was the same kind of lock she had on her door at home. She had locked herself out so many times she could pick it with her eyes closed. She quickly put her bag down and took out her homemade lock picking kit. After a few quick turns of her tools, the lock clicked, and Saphira opened the door. "Is the job mine, sir?"

He laid a hand on the door and nodded. "Wait here a moment if you would," he said and walked back to the store.

Suddenly, Saphira heard young Robert protesting. "But I was here first!"

"Sorry, son, she knows how." Zell didn't sound sorry. Maybe he was so desperate to have help, he gave the job to the first person who asked about it.

"But she's a girl, she doesn't know anything, she got

lucky!" Saphira scoffed and rolled her eyes as she made her way over to them. She hated boys who assumed a woman couldn't do anything because of their sex, and she loved proving them wrong. Honestly, it was more of a hubris than anything. It got her into a lot of interesting situations at home, and a few scars to prove it.

Robert glared at her. "You got lucky," he hissed at her before stomping out of the store.

"Great, I've been here less than two hours, and I'm already pissing people off," she mumbled.

Zell chuckled. "Did you get lucky, young lady?"

Saphira bit her lip. "Well, sort of. I've unlocked my own door enough times to know how, and it's the same kind."

"Ah, I see," he said, nodding. "Well, you seem more pleasant than him anyway. What's your name?"

"Saphira, sir." She didn't want to give her full name, not yet. She knew it might draw unwanted attention with her mother being so famous.

"Nice to meet you, Saphira. Let me show you around."

She smiled and picked up her bag. "Thank you for the job, sir. Are there any inns nearby I might get a room?"

He shook his head. "Call me Zell, and don't worry about that, follow me." Saphira followed him through the door she had just picked open, and he led her to another door down the hallway. "There's an extra room here, it's got a desk and a comfortable cot. You can stay here if you'd like, no charge."

She stepped inside and found the little room to be comfy. "Thank you, sir. I think I will stay here."

"It's Zell. Basically, the job is watching the shop while I go out in town. People come to get keys made and sometimes bring items in for fitting or to get unlocked. You should learn quick. You seem like a smart girl." He held out a hand, "Welcome to Ardenry, Saphira."

She happily shook his hand. "Thank you, sir. Uh, Zell." He snickered and walked out of the room while Saphira flopped on the cot, *I made it, I'm here* she thought. She could barely believe it, but thanked Otto for her quick legs and wit, without which she may not have gotten this important job. She opened her bag and began putting her meager belongings away. "I'm going to do it, Mom, I promise," she whispered to herself.

CHAPTER 4
LOCKS AND LESSONS

Over the next few weeks, Zell taught Saphira how to care for the store while he was out unlocking doors as well as installing locks and doors around town. She stayed in the store and made sure no one stole anything, sold locks, and made keys for those who wanted to buy them. Overall, it was a quiet life. In the morning, after Zell would leave, she'd walk around and pick every single lock in the store. Day after day, she did this, and every day she got better. She learned which tools would be better for each lock. The rounder locks needed thinner tools, which surprised her, and the bigger the lock, the sturdier the pick needed to be. She learned that after Zell showed her how to get a broken pick out of a particularly heavy lock.

Like Father Rayner said, Zell was an old adventurer, and when they ate dinner, he'd tell Saphira stories of his roguery days. It reminded her of being back home in the tavern, listening to the travelers tell their tales to whoever would listen. She always paid attention to anything that might help her learn how to use her abilities to their fullest potential. One night when she couldn't sleep, she began rummaging through her room. She found old files of customers and beat-up daggers. But what intrigued her most was a big wooden box. It had a brass lock on the front and was locked up tight. She decided to try her newfound skills, but the box was beyond her.

So, the next day after she unlocked every lock in the store, she set the box down on the counter in front of her and worked for hours trying to pick it. It took intense concentration, which was broken every time a customer came in. After a week, the box stayed shut, and Saphira was starting to get irritated at it. One day, she had been working on it so intently that she didn't hear when Zell came back. He cleared his throat, and she gasped as she looked up.

"Oh! Zell, sorry I didn't hear you come in." She quickly put the box under the counter and sat straight.

"Where'd you find the box?" He asked, pointing to where it once rested on the counter.

Saphira cleared her throat, "Uh, sorry, it was in my room. I'll leave it alone."

"No, no, um, bring it back up, let me show you something." Slowly, she brought it back up while Zell got out his tools. "The trick with this one is there's two latches you have to catch before you can open it." He put his lockpicks in, and after a few turns, Saphira heard two clicks and watched as he ducked to the side for some reason.

"Do you have to dance as well?" she teased.

Zell chuckled. "No, there's a trap. Did you find it?"

She leaned over and pointed at the front of the box. "I saw there was a little hole that didn't need to be there, so I figured it could be a trap."

He nodded. "A needle shoots out whether you unlock it correctly or not."

Saphira gasped. "Correctly or not?"

"Good way to kill whoever can get to your stuff. No matter how talented they are." He lifted the lid, and Saphira saw it was empty as she suspected. "Not really worth it, is it?"

She shook her head. "No." Zell shut and locked it up before handing it back to Saphira.

"Keep practicing, you'll get it," he called back. "Oh, and Saphira? As impressive as your lock picking skills are, could you please close them when you're done? Makes them harder to steal." He said with a wink.

She looked around the store and saw she had forgotten to lock them back up. "Oops, yeah, sorry!" She quickly got off the stool and began running around the store, shutting every single padlock.

Another week went by, and Saphira had mastered the box, but she was determined to find a way to open it without getting a needle in her neck. Zell had left a few hours earlier to install a door, and Saphira was sitting at the counter like normal, a big red scarf around her neck so the needle wouldn't keep piercing her skin. The door chime jingled, and the needle buried itself in her scarf. She cursed to herself and slipped the needle back in its spot as a girl about her age, wearing a dress and several pouches around her waist, made her way over to the counter.

"Morning, I was wondering if you could help me? I've been to about every other locksmith in town, and none of them could help." Saphira thought the auburn-haired mage looked a bit embarrassed. When she laid her hands on the counter with a bang, Saphira saw why. One of her wrists was locked in a large and old-looking manacle.

"Oh sure, give me a second." Saphira pulled the scarf off and put the box away. "How'd you get yourself in those, may I ask?" She got her tools out and began working on the old lock.

"Oh, you know," was all the girl said with a smile. The manacle clicked open, and the girl sighed. "Ooh, much better." She lifted her hand and rubbed at the skin around her wrist. "Say you're pretty good, what's your name?" she asked with a smile.

"Saphira." She held out her hand, and the young mage took it.

"I'm Eden McVain, and I insist on buying you dinner as thanks." Eden was a cheery one who bounced when she talked.

"Oh, not necessary, the coin will do."

Eden's gray eyes suddenly widened. "But it is!" Her hands slapped the glass counter, and Saphira jumped a little. "I went to five other locksmiths, and they couldn't help. You must eat dinner with me and my friends." Eden rested her chin in her now free hand and seemed to study Saphira. "I bet you haven't seen much of the city, have you?"

Saphira sat straight and crossed her arms. "What makes you think I'm not from Ardenry?"

Eden smiled and leaned against the desk with a look

of knowing. "You're too quiet. Most people from Ardenry are loud." Saphira snickered. Eden was right; she had been so busy with her job, she'd only seen the road to and from the temple.

Saphira uncrossed her arms and leaned on the counter. "Okay, you got me."

"You're too young to be coped up in a locksmith shop." Eden stood straight, her hands on her hips. "I'll come back at closing time, and we'll have a good dinner, okay?"

Saphira had a feeling Eden was the type of person who didn't take no for an answer. "All right, I'll go."

The pretty mage smiled and clapped her hands together. "Wonderful!" She gave Saphira ten silver for the service. "Wear something nice, there will be dancing," Eden said, practically bouncing out the door. Saphira watched as she stopped outside the shop's window and talked to a young man with dark auburn hair before they both walked away. Dinner with people her own age, she thought, could be fun.

When it was finally closing time, Saphira ran outside and locked the door as Eden walked up alone. The mage had on a very colorful, flowy dress that hugged her waist. She looked like she was ready for a fun time.

"Don't you have a dress?" Eden asked, crinkling her nose at Saphira's best shirt and leather pants. She had shined her boots, but apparently it wasn't good enough.

"Not at the moment." There was no room in her travel bag for such things, so she regretfully left all her skirts and dresses at home.

Eden shrugged. "Oh well, we can get you something pretty later. I told everyone about you, and they're all excited to meet you." She slid her arm through Saphira's and walked her a couple of blocks, chattering the entire time. "You're going to love my friend's Saphira. There's Rickert, he's working as a guard now, getting us some money. Then Iollan, he's quiet, he joined a few months ago, but he's good with a sword. Then my twin brother Edward, he's an archer."

Saphira's eyes widened. "Joined? Are you in an adventuring group?" She didn't bother hiding her excitement.

"I am," Eden said with a sly smile. "And we happen to have an opening." Saphira thought she'd have to search for a group, now one had fallen into her lap. Eden walked her into an inn called 'The Curling Smoke,' and they sat down at a table with the same auburn-haired boy she had seen outside the shop earlier. "Saphira, this is my twin brother Edward, Ed, this is Saphira." He had the same facial structure as Eden, but where her hair was more auburn brown, his was a deep red auburn.

Both of their eyes were gray, but his were lighter. It suited him nicely. "Nice to meet you, Saphira." He held out his hand, and she took it happily.

"Nice to meet you as well." She could feel the calluses on the inside of his hand, right where an archer would have them. "So, Eden said there were more of you?"

Edward smiled and nodded, spilling his long hair in his eyes. "Yeah, Iollan will be down in a moment, and Rickert is still on duty. It'll be a bit before he joins us."

Eden reached over and roughly tucked her brother's hair behind his ear. "Honestly, Ed, you ought to get your hair cut. What kind of archer has hair in their eyes?" Saphira chuckled at their behavior.

"Maybe when you stop flirting with every guy you see in front of me, I'll cut it." He took over and put his hair back the way he liked it.

"Like you don't do the same thing." Eden crossed her arms on her stomach and sat back in the chair.

"No, I don't, and you shouldn't say such things in front of a potential member, Edie. She'll think I'm some sort of hound."

Saphira giggled. "It's going to take a lot more than words to make me think ill of someone I just met."

He looked over and smiled at her. "Good, gods know what Eden already told you about me."

She shrugged her shoulders. "Only that you're an archer, but she didn't need to tell me, I could tell when I shook your hand." He sat back, his arms crossed over his chest like Eden was doing, and Saphira suppressed some giggles at the twins.

"You could? How?" His smile was part tease, part dare.

"Your hand," she reached out for him, and he leaned forward, putting his hand on the table. "You have calluses where an archer should," she touched his fingertips on his right hand. "And I bet you have one here on your other hand," she said, rubbing between his thumb and pointer finger. Saphira sat back, feeling proud of herself, but when she looked at Edward's face, she blushed. He was still staring at his hand, and his face was something Saphira had never seen before on a man and wasn't sure what to make of it. His eyes were soft as he stared where she had touched his skin, and the barest hint of a smile. "I'm sorry, Edward, did I overstep my boundary?" *Jeez, Saphira, you don't even know the guy, and you're fondling his hands,* she thought to herself as Eden leaned forward and looked at her brother's face.

"No, I think you're all right, Saphira," she said with a smile.

Finally, he sat straight and ran his hands through his long hair. "Pretty spot on. Edie was right, you have skilled hands. Do you know many archers?"

"My father and oldest brother are archers," she nodded.

Eden gasped. "You have brothers, are they cute?" She asked with a little grin.

Edward groaned. "Damn, Edie, this is what I'm talking about."

Her shoulders went up defensively. "What? It's not like I asked if they were single. Saphira may be traveling with us, and we should get to know her." A waitress came by and put five plates of food on the table, even though only three chairs were occupied.

Saphira looked around but didn't see anyone else joining them. "Are all your people usually late for dinner?"

"Not usually, oh, here comes Iollan." Edward motioned with his head. Saphira turned and suppressed a gasp as a handsome young man walked up to the table. His eyes were dark, hidden behind long dark lashes, and he had four freckles along his left cheek. Saphira could tell he was tall, but then again, most people were taller than her. He was wearing a dark shirt tucked into worn black leather pants.

"This that rogue you were talking about?" Iollan asked before digging into his food.

"Yes, Iollan, this is Saphira." Eden motioned to her with a graceful motion of her hand. "I thought I could ask Rickert if she could join our group." The fork paused at his mouth, and Saphira watched as his eyes looked down at the holy symbol around her neck and quickly looked back up to her eyes.

His gaze was so intense she felt her heart skip. "Saphira?" His voice was quiet, and as she looked at him. She realized there was something unnerving about this man.

"Yes, nice to meet you." She didn't offer him her hand. It didn't seem to want to move anyway.

"Pleasure," he said quietly. As his eyes finally looked away, she breathed a sigh of relief.

Edward's voice dragged her attention away from the confusing young man. "Where are you from, Saphira?"

She turned and picked up her fork from the table. "Raventree, how about you?" She thought she heard Iollan say something under his breath, but she ignored him as Edward smiled at her.

"Ardenry, actually. Our mom owns a magic shop in town. Not sure where Iollan's from, he never said." Ed looked over at the dark man.

"You never asked," Iollan said, keeping his face down to his plate.

"We didn't?" Eden seemed surprised, and the twins looked at each other. "Sorry about that, Iollan, where are you from?" Edward asked.

He chewed a few times before he answered. "Ral Hava."

"Isn't Ral Hava a dwarf city?" Saphira had heard of Ral Hava but didn't think many humans lived there.

"Mostly," he said without looking up. Eden was right,

Iollan didn't talk much.

"So," Eden popped a carrot in her mouth. "Saphira, do you speak any other languages?"

Saphira swallowed her drink of ale with a nod. "Yes, elvish and orcish."

The twins' eyes both went wide. "Orcish?" They echoed each other.

"How'd you learn orcish?" Edward asked.

She held in her chuckles. "It helps when their god is friends with your mother."

"Sobrei isn't their god," Iollan said, looking up from his plate. "He's just an orc." Saphira wasn't surprised Iollan doubted the orc's divine nature. Even though Sobrei had been kidnapped and banished from the throne in Dal En Val almost thirty years ago, everyone knew the story of the displaced orc god, or self-proclaimed god, as most put it.

Saphira shrugged. "Most people who have never met him believe that." She picked up her fork and speared a carrot. "But I can tell you there is an innate divine nature to him. It feels like the power my mother has, but different and…more. He's a genuinely nice orc, and I hope one day he can reclaim his throne away from those cultists."

"Nice orc," Edward shook his head. "Two words I never thought I'd hear together."

"When you say your mother," Iollan put his fork down and sat back, crossing his arms over his chest. "You mean Lily Voltain?" The twins quickly turned to her, their eyes wide once again staring at her. Saphira sat back, feeling vulnerable from the attention, and hoped they wouldn't change their minds.

"I…do. Did I not say my last name?" Eden and Edward shook their heads, still staring at her.

"No, you did not, but that's my fault," Eden put her hand on her heart. "I also didn't ask. So, you're really…"

Saphira nodded. "I am."

They stared at her for a few beats and smiled. "Amazing," Edward said as he leaned forward.

"It's not that amazing," Saphira looked back down at her dinner and hoped they'd stop staring. "She's…my mom."

"Not that amazing?" Eden shook her head, "I never thought in a million years we'd meet anyone who even *knew* Mother Lily, let alone her child! Well, you have to join now."

Saphira laughed and looked up, "Glad you didn't change your mind."

"We'd never change our minds," Edward said, laughing. Saphira returned to her dinner, relieved the twins still seemed excited about her joining them..

"She let you travel?" Iollan asked quietly. Saphira chewed her dinner and turned to him. There was an odd look on his face, a mix of curiosity and fear.

"She didn't 'let' me, but she gave me her blessing. It was my Papa I had to convince."

"He didn't want you to go?" She shook her head. "He really loves you." There was something about his tone she couldn't put her finger on. If anything, there was a tinge of awe to it.

"Of course he does, why wouldn't he?" But he didn't answer and returned to his dinner. Thankfully, Eden broke the silence.

"How old are you, Saphira?" Eden asked.

She had to quickly swallow a bite so she could answer. "Eighteen, I'll be nineteen in the fall. How about you?"

"Twenty," Edward said. "I'm the oldest," he said with a teasing smile.

"By five minutes." Eden elbowed him, and he laughed.

"Still the oldest. You're twenty-ish, right, Iollan?" The quiet man nodded and chewed his dinner without looking up. Edward shook his head and smiled at Saphira. "He's quiet, don't take offense."

"It's all right."

They continued to eat and get to know each other. The twins' mother raised them after their father died when they were young. Saphira didn't learn more about Iollan; she was fine with that.

After all the plates but one were cleared, they heard a squeal.

"Edward!" They turned and saw a girl with long blonde hair run over and hug him as he stayed seated. "I didn't know you were in town! Come on, let's dance," she pulled him to his feet and dragged him to the dance floor before he could say no.

"Who was that?" Saphira asked, holding in her laughter.

"Old girlfriend," Eden snickered. "He hates dancing." Saphira giggled and saw Eden smile as a young man walked up and held out his hand.

"Shall we?" he asked her.

"I thought you'd never ask," she said and took his hand.

"Eden?" Saphira did not want to be left alone with Iollan, but Eden smiled and twirled in the young man's arms as she left the table. Saphira sighed and turned to Iollan. He was sitting quietly in his chair, his arms resting on the arms of the chair, with his hand linked over his stomach. She thought she saw his eyes dart away from her.

"So," she was hopeless at small talk, and the way he made her nervous wasn't helping. "Eden said you were the last to join."

He nodded and turned back to her. "I was."

"What kind of weapons do you use?"

"Long sword and short sword. You really a rogue?"

She nodded, determined not to let this stranger intimidate her. "Yes, I am," she said confidently.

Iollan crossed his arms across his broad chest. "You better be. Because we can die if you don't know what you're doing."

She leaned forward. How dare he! "I'm well aware of what rests on my shoulders, but we can die if you don't know what you're doing either." *What an ass,* she thought. She knew groups could live or die if everyone didn't do their part; it wasn't all up to her.

"I never said we wouldn't, but at the moment we're talking about you." A hand slapped Iollan on the shoulder, and Saphira saw a muscular man dressed like a guard standing behind him. He looked to be in his early thirties, and his short dark hair was graying at his temples. He had kind blue eyes, and his smile seemed genuine.

"Iollan, I refuse to believe you invited this pretty young thing to dinner," the man said with a smile.

"Not hardly," Iollan breathed under his breath. "Eden found her, said she's a rogue," he said as the large man sat next to her.

"Rogue, huh? We need one, I'm Rickert Basine."

Her eyes went wide. "Oh! Eden said it was your group. I'm Saphira Voltain." She held out her hand with a smile, but jumped as Iollan slammed his arms on the table and walked off. "What's wrong with him?"

Rickert waved him off. "Oh, who knows, he's a moody one. Voltain, you say?" She nodded and wondered how many times she'd have to answer that question. Thankfully, he didn't pry. "So, how did Eden find you?" She told him of their meeting, and Rickert laughed. "Glad she found you. I lost the key to those shackles six months ago."

Saphira giggled. "Must be fate." Rickert dug into the cold food in front of him.

"Well, if you're up for the job, you're welcome to it."

"Really?" Saphira smiled. "Thank you, Rickert. I will do my absolute best, I promise." She felt like she was going to burst from excitement and fought hard not to wiggle in her chair.

"I believe you." He sat back and slapped his leg. "Well, we work like this, take any job we can while moving, and we split money equally. We also have a group fund for food, rooms, emergencies, and the like. I don't care if you mess around with anybody, in group or out, but don't bring anyone along when we leave a town."

Saphira tried not to blush. "I hadn't planned on it."

"No one does," he said and scooped some potatoes in his mouth. "But the way Iollan was looking at you before he stomped off, I wouldn't be surprised if he tried something."

Saphira's eyes widened. "Excuse me? He seemed irritated by me."

Rickert pushed his clean plate away and leaned his elbows

on the table. "I know he seems scary, but he's a nice guy."

She sighed and sat back in the chair. "I'll believe it when I see it."

Rickert chuckled and grabbed Eden's lone ale and drained the mug. "I got a few more days of my job left. I suggest you see Eden every day to stay in contact. When we leave, we'll be heading east for a while. Eden doesn't do a watch, so when we sleep outdoors, you'll do one like me and the boys. It'll make the watches shorter."

"Okay, sounds good." Rickert seemed like a happy guy, and Saphira wondered why he was adventuring with a bunch of young people instead of raising a family, but didn't pry. It was his business, and until they were close, she knew to keep her questions in check. Saphira didn't see Iollan the rest of the night, and when she was ready to head back, she let the twins walk her back to Zell's shop.

"Did you have fun dancing, Edward?" Saphira teased.

He scoffed and shook his head. "She always finds me when we're in town."

"You don't like her?" Saphira studied his face as they walked. It seemed like he was trying to find the right words.

"She's nice enough, but I'm not attracted to her. She's so perky."

"Perky?" She looked over at Eden, who was rolling her eyes.

"Meh," he shrugged his shoulders. "It's hard to explain," he said with a smile.

When they got to the shop, Eden took her hands. "So, tomorrow we're going shopping whether you want to or not. You need one dress and other things if you're coming with us." Saphira didn't like shopping much. It always took up most of her day when she'd rather be doing other things.

"All right if you say so."

"I'll see you in the morning then." Eden waved as she turned back to the inn, her hair bouncing happily behind her while her mage pouches made little jingles.

"Didn't think having another girl in the group would make her so happy." Edward turned to Saphira. "Then again, I think it'll do us all some good. See you later, Saphira." He gave her arm a little squeeze, then followed his sister down the road.

"Bye, Edward." Saphira watched him run up to Eden and put a brotherly arm around her waist. Saphira noticed Eden looked excited about something he said to her. Smiling, she unlocked the door to the shop and walked inside. When she lit her candle by the cot, she was surprised to see Zell sitting in the one chair in the room. "Good evening, Zell."

He nodded his head. "Saphira. So, found a group, did ya?"

"Yes, I did." She was beaming as she sat on the cot and told him about the other four.

"They sound like a solid group." He cleared his throat and stood. "I got something for you. You can keep the box for practice."

"Thank you." Zell walked over to a box and took its contents out. When he turned, she saw he had a well-crafted silver dagger in his hand.

"This was mine when I was young. When you throw it, it'll come back to your hand."

Saphira gasped and got to her feet. "A magical dagger? I can't—"

"You can and you will." He pressed the weapon in her hand, "There's also a little extra gold in your bag. I figured you'd want to stay with them now."

She couldn't help but think he sounded a little sad. "Zell, I can't thank you enough. You've been so kind to me since I arrived. If there's ever anything I can do for you, let me know."

He leaned down and gave her cheek a little peck. "Just stay alive out there. That's all I ask of you." He gave her arm a little squeeze, then left her alone in the room.

Saphira smiled and quickly gathered her things, and ran out of the shop. "Edward, Eden, wait up!!"

CHAPTER 5

NOT EVERYTHING GETS HEALED

Saphira left Ardenry with Rickert and his group a few days later. Eden made sure she had enough supplies and, of course, a dress. Saphira wasn't sure why she needed one so badly, but Eden told her you never know when you have to look nice for a job. They headed east, like Rickert said, and Saphira knew they were heading towards Blackridge. She had made the trip several times over the years to visit her parents' friends Ralan and Amelia, who lived a day inside the woods to the east of the town. Rickert had heard through the 'guard rumor mill' that Blackridge was looking for guards or adventurers to help with an increasing problem with the elves from the nearby woods. Saphira hoped they weren't bothering her parents' friends. They lived in peace and kept to themselves. But Ralan was an elf, and there was a lot of prejudice against them.

Blackridge was a few weeks from Ardenry, and every day of travel, Saphira got closer to the twins. She was grateful for their friendship, because Iollan continued to make her uneasy. She didn't believe he'd hurt her, but she could tell he was an intense guy and took his job seriously. He was always on guard as they walked and was the first to take watch at night. When they rested for the night, Saphira got in the habit of sleeping between the twins so she could stay away from Iollan. It was nice and warm in the middle, but Rickert would often tease her about having a thing for Edward. She'd scoff and blow him off. But she'd also catch the archer smiling at her for no reason. She'd usually return her own awkward half-grin at him, regretting it every time as Eden giggled at her.

They were a day out from Blackridge when they saw smoke rising in the distance.

"Eden, can you tell what it is?" Rickert asked as they stopped. Saphira watched her pull out a little mirror and cast a spell.

The mage's normally happy face suddenly fell. "Oh no, it looks like a carriage got hit by bandits."

Iollan put a hand up to shield his eyes from the sun. "Do you see anyone?" He asked.

Saphira watched the mage's gray eyes dart around the little mirror before she looked up.

"No one alive anyway." Edward put his hand on his sister's shoulder as she put away her mirror.

Rickert sighed and nodded his head. "Okay then. We'll get there eventually." The group walked for another hour before they came upon the scene the mage had seen earlier. The covered carriage was on its side, and they could see a lot of arrows stuck in the wood. There were no horses around, so they assumed whoever assaulted the carriage had taken them. A man was laying by the front of the carriage. His legs were pinned under it, and he was in a puddle of blood. Saphira saw a hand sticking out of the curtained window. She kneeled next to it and held the fingers; they felt cold.

"They almost made it," Rickert said. Saphira wasn't a priestess but said a little prayer to Otto anyway. "Well, there's nothing we can do. We'll let the town guard know about it when we get there in case they don't already know." Eden and Edward nodded and followed Rickert away from the wreckage.

Saphira was about to stand when her ear twitched. "Wait."

The others stopped and stared at her. "What is it?" Rickert walked up next to her as she turned her ear towards the carriage.

"I hear something."

"Saphira, I know it's hard," she could tell Rickert was trying to be understanding. "But sometimes you have to walk away." She was used to people not hearing what she did. Her father always teased her that she had fox ears. She pushed the curtain aside and crawled inside. "You're not going to like what you find in there," Rickert called out like he knew.

"No, she's right," Iollan spoke up. "I hear it too." It was dark in the carriage. Things were thrown all around. She saw a woman in the corner, her neck was clearly broken, so the noise wasn't coming from her. Saphira pulled things out of the way until the sound she heard pierced the air. A tiny baby was bawling his head off, and she didn't blame him. It must have been a jarring ride.

She could hear Rickert cry out behind her. "Bright Alar, get the baby and give me your feet, Saphira. I'll pull you out." Carefully, she picked up the naked baby, cradling him to her chest, and stuck her legs out of the window. She didn't realize how strong Rickert was and gave a little yelp as he pulled her out with one hard yank.

Eden and Edward both gasped at the sight. "Oh, Saphira, thank the gods you heard him," she said.

Rickert helped Saphira to her feet. "Ed, Eden, crawl in there and see if there's anything we can use to take care of the baby." They nodded, and Eden conjured a little ball of light to help them see, and soon disappeared inside the overturned carriage. Saphira gently jiggled the baby while Rickert patted the baby's head. "Shh, you're all right now," he cooed at the wailing boy, who slowly quieted.

"We have to take him to Blackridge Rickert," Saphira said. "We're only a day out."

Rickert nodded, but it was Iollan's voice she heard. "His family's dead, Rogue. It'd be kinder to end it." Saphira gasped and instinctively shielded the baby while Rickert walked over and grabbed Iollan by his collar.

"This is not your group, boy, and until you have one, you're never to say anything like that again. Do you understand me?" Saphira had never heard Rickert speak so forcefully before and hoped he'd start listening to what she was telling him about Iollan. The fighter stood still and stared at Rickert until he turned back to Saphira. "We'll get him to Blackridge Saphira, don't worry," he said as the twins crawled back out. They found one skin of goat's milk, several blankets, and a few diapers, which

Saphira quickly put him in. Rickert nodded his head. "That's going to have to do until we get to town. It'll only be one more night." He helped Saphira make a sling, and they gave the baby a little milk. Soon, he was fast asleep, listening to her heartbeat as they walked.

Eden stroked the baby's dark, fuzzy hair. "How old do you think he is?"

"A few weeks, maybe." Saphira had been around newborns a lot in her life since her mother doubled as Raventree's backup midwife. It truly was a miracle the little boy survived such an ordeal. While Saphira put the diaper on him, she gave him a quick once-over, but there were no broken bones or cuts. The little bruise on his back was the only clue he was in a carriage wreck. Her mother always said babies were more resilient than we give them credit for.

"He's so small." Edward sounded amazed, like he'd never seen a baby this young before. Want to hold his hand?" Saphira smiled up at him.

Edward looked a little shocked before he looked inside the little sling. "I don't want to wake him."

"You won't, he's perfectly asleep." Saphira reached in and pulled the baby's hand up, and Edward held it carefully.

"Wow." Both girls smiled at each other, and the baby twitched, putting his hand back against the warmth of Saphira's skin.

The group didn't stop until well after sundown when the baby finally woke up. He seemed like a happy baby, making silly faces and snuggling into their chests. Sapira gave him some milk while Rickert burped him like a pro. Neither of them went to sleep that night; they willingly stayed up for the baby. It was a small sacrifice in their eyes. Saphira watched Rickert play with the baby, gently blowing on his little face.

"Rickert, do you have children?" The way he was interacting with the little boy seemed like second nature to the man.

He jiggled the baby a few times, like he was trying to figure out what to say. "I had a son."

"Had? I'm so sorry."

"Thank you." The baby stuck his little hand in Rickert's mouth and laughed.

"Is that why you're traveling, you didn't want to be home anymore?"

"Partly. My wife blamed me," Saphira's eyes went wide, "it's all right, I blame me too. There was a fire, and I thought it'd be okay to sneak off to the tavern for a drink while he slept. My wife was babysitting her sister's kids, so she wasn't home either. When I heard there was a fire, it was too late." He put the baby on his chest and patted his little back. "So, now I do what I can to protect the younger generation on the road. Like my own way of trying to make up for my son's death." Saphira felt her heart break for her boss. Losing a child is never easy, but to purposefully stay on the road because of it, the guilt was probably eating him alive.

"You do a good job, boss." Rickert looked up and gave her a wink.

As the sun rose, the others woke, and they began the last leg of the trip. Saphira carried the baby like the day before, and he quickly fell asleep with the movement. Every so often, Saphira would glance behind her and see Iollan staring at her. She'd quickly look away and pretend the baby needed something. After his comment the day before, she felt protective. She didn't think Iollan would try anything, but it was disturbing to hear him say something so dark. Around noon, they walked into Blackridge. It was smaller than Raventree. Since it was on the border of the elven forest, not many people wanted to live there. Saphira and Rickert went to the local Sheriff's while the others found an inn for them to stay at. When they walked into the Sheriff's office, they saw a man sitting behind a desk.

He gave them a small wave as they entered. "Hello, what can I do for you?"

"Sir, my name is Rickert Basine. This is my associate, Saphira. While traveling, we came upon a wrecked carriage about a day from town and found this baby boy inside. He was the only survivor, and we figured maybe his parents had family here? We were wondering if there was any way to find them or get the word out to the townsfolk? We figured this would be the place to start."

The man sighed and studied the baby, still in Saphira's arms. "I suppose we could see what the church here can do. If not, it looks like you and your," he cleared his throat, "associate, have a little family." Saphira's eyebrows instantly furled in irritation. She did not like what he implied about her relationship with Rickert.

"Excuse me, you have no right to imply anything but professionalism between myself and Rickert."

The man's eyes widened, and he put his hands up. "Okay, okay, take the babe to the church. They should be able to care for him. If he's lucky, which I have a feeling he is, they'll find his family or a new one."

"Thank you, sir, it's much appreciated," Rickert said.

The Sheriff pointed out the door to the right. "It's in the middle of town, hard to miss."

Saphira nodded and walked out, trying to calm herself. "What an ass," she said as they walked through town.

Rickert laughed. "Don't piss him off too much; he may have something to do with assigning elf duty. You want to get a decent time."

"Decent time?"

"He could stick you on night duty," the way he said it told her he thought night duty was the worst thing in the world.

But she just shrugged. "It wouldn't last forever."

Rickert chuckled and shook his head. "You are optimistic, Saphira, I'll give you that," he said as he pushed the door to the church open.

An hour later, they found the rest of the group downstairs at the inn where they had separated earlier.

"How'd it go?" Eden asked with a smile.

"It went well," Rickert sat with a groan. "The church will try and find a family for him."

"Good. I hope he has a blessed life," Edward said, patting Saphira's hand.

"He will," Iollan said quietly. Saphira turned and saw he was staring into his ale. She seemed to be the only one who heard him.

Rickert sighed and patted Edward on the back. "So, I'll go get some information about the elf watch. Hopefully, it'll be good steady work for a while." They all nodded their heads, and Rickert walked back outside. Saphira turned and caught a glimpse of Iollan as his eyes moved back to his ale.

A week later, Saphira was walking the borders of the Blackridge at night. Rickert was right. Don't piss off the man who sets the schedule. She didn't really mind night duty, except he put Iollan on night watch as well. She spent a lot of her time scrabbling from rooftop to rooftop, avoiding him and most others as well. She'd look at the stars and wonder which were above Foster's head. Whenever she skulked around the taverns, she'd try not to laugh at young men's horrible attempts at wooing a pretty girl. No one ever saw her, and she learned a lot from the town by listening. At the moment, she was standing on a flat roof scanning the forest's edge when a familiar voice startled her.

"Hello, Saphira."

She jumped and saw Iollan standing silently behind her. "You scared me. How'd you get up here?"

"Same as you, probably." He walked next to her and looked down. "Have you seen anything?"

"No. Quiet night. Quiet week, I think they might have overreacted a bit."

"It's possible." It was the longest conversation they had had since she joined.

"Iollan?"

"Hmm?" He said without turning.

She licked her lips and asked what had been on her mind

for a while. "Why did you want to kill the baby?"

He stepped back and faced her. "I was wondering when you were going to ask me that."

"I wondered if I should."

He looked at the ground and sighed heavily, "It's not something I like re-living." He looked up, and his dark eyes burned into hers. "But I'll tell you." Iollan clasped his hands together. "A few years ago, I found myself in a similar situation. The child was older than the one you found and clung to me the second I picked him up. I thought I could make it to the next town in time, but he was already sick and died a few days later. I should have left him with his mother. At least they would have been together."

Saphira gave him a few moments before she spoke up. "Sounds like an awful day."

He shook his head. "Not one of my best." Iollan walked up to her, barely leaving space between them. "If that baby was already hurt or sick, I didn't think I could handle seeing you cry if he died in your arms." His words stopped the world around her, and all she could hear was her own heart thrumming in her ears.

"I didn't…think you cared," she said softly as her ear twitched. She turned to her right and, at the edge of the woods, saw several elves make their way into the city. "Look." She moved to the edge of the roof and pointed to the north. Iollan moved next to her, and they watched as several elves broke into a house. "Come on." Saphira leaped from building to building and was surprised Iollan could keep up. He didn't seem the limber type. She landed on the roof of the house, where the elves broke in and crept low. She could hear the elves causing a ruckus in the house. Silently, Saphira jumped down into an alley, her dagger already in her hand by the time her feet hit the ground. Iollan landed loudly next to her, his chain making loud jingles. "Jeez, be louder, why don't you?" she whispered.

"Pardon me for not having hollow bones," he quipped and unsheathed his sword as they walked inside. They could hear thumping and crashing upstairs, but no screams. To Saphira, it meant no one was home, and she prayed it was so. They quietly moved up the stairs, and the second they turned the corner, they came face to face with the wildest-looking elf either of them had ever seen. His clothes resembled a tree trunk. Better for hiding in the forest than the city, and he had a large tattoo of fire around his neck.

It loudly yelled out in elvish, "Guards! Kill them!" and drew his sword. It was long and had a sharp tip. Saphira had only seen one sword like that before and knew how deadly it could be. Iollan flashed his sword and engaged the elf while Saphira moved around them to find the other intruders. Two seconds later, they came running out of a nearby room, and Saphira didn't hesitate as she threw her dagger at the first one. It sank deep into his neck, and he fell to the ground. The next one trampled over his friend as Saphira's dagger flew back to her hand. She ducked away from the elf's sword and shoved her dagger into his stomach. He groaned and fell to his knees as Saphira pulled it out with a hard yank. She was poised to slit the elf's throat when an intense pain in the back of her thigh dropped her to the floor. A sound that had never escaped her lips filled the room, the intensity of it made her throat hurt. Breathing hard, she managed to turn and saw an arrow sticking deep into her upper thigh.

"Saphira!" She heard a sword pierce flesh a second before Iollan kneeled next to her. "You're going to be fine."

He gripped the arrow, and she knew what he was about to do. "No, don't! I'll bleed out!" But he was too quick and pulled it out with a sharp yank. She screamed again and watched as blood gushed from the hole. "Why did you pull it out? Are you trying to kill me?" she yelled at him. The pain radiated through her leg, and she could barely catch her breath.

Iollan pulled out a big rag and tied it around her thigh above the wound. "It could have been poisoned. I couldn't leave it in." His voice was calm as he picked her up and ran from the house. Saphira wanted to be brave, but couldn't hold in the curses as Iollan ran down the street. As it turns out, cursing like a sailor wasn't a terrible thing since it got the attention of the other guards who ran up and tried to help. Her head was laying in the curve of Iollan's neck, and she tried to ignore how wonderful he smelled by concentrating on the trail of her blood being left behind. But she had never smelled anything like him, leather, and wind. It was calming.

"Iollan, I'm bleeding too much." It was harder to say those words than she thought it should be.

Suddenly, he laid her on the ground and held her face close. "Here, drink this." He poured a liquid down her throat, and she coughed.

"What is..." her eyes closed, and everything went away.

Pain woke her, and with a groan, she opened her eyes. She was lying on her stomach in her and Eden's room at the inn, and a stabbing pain in her upper thigh was stealing her breath.

"Don't move." She watched Iollan kneel next to the bed by her head. "Drink this, it'll help with the pain." He tilted her chin and tipped the contents of a small vial in her mouth. It was bitter and made her cough.

"What is it?" She asked hoarsely.

"Painkiller from the temple. You should be able to relax soon." All temples had supplies of painkillers that were easily made from herbs they grew, but divine healing was always superior.

"Why does it hurt?" She had never felt such pain before and was surprised at how much she had to concentrate, even to speak.

Iollan sat on the bed, and she thought she felt his hand on her back. "One of the elves shot you with an arrow."

"You think I'd forget getting shot with an arrow? I mean, why am I not healed?" Her patience was quickly being tested.

"Healed?" Iollan seemed genuinely confused. "Well, the sheriffs couldn't afford the healing, and since we're employed by them, they'd have to pay. All they could afford were the vials of painkillers and clean bandages." She felt the liquid start to kick in, and everything started feeling far away.

She stopped shaking, and she could catch her breath. "Afford?"

"Not everyone gets free healing in the real world, Saphira."

"But…" The liquid was potent, and Saphira felt nothing but the wonderful floating sensation the liquid gave her.

"Rest, you'll be fine soon." She closed her eyes and thought she felt a hand stroke her hair before unconsciousness took her.

The next time she opened her eyes, the pain was better. It was more of a dull ache instead of the sharp pain it was when it first happened. But she knew she wouldn't be able to turn over without help. A chair creaked, making her ear twitch toward the noise, and she watched Iollan sit down on the bed.

"How's the pain?" She was still in a cloud of drugs, but quickly dragged herself out of it when Iollan began stroking her hair. At least the mental part. She still couldn't move very well to make him stop. Her mouth was dry, and it was hard to talk. She tried smacking her lips a few times, but nothing helped.

"Where's Eden?"

He poured her a cup of water and held it to her lips. "She's on duty." Saphira managed to drink the water and sighed as she laid her head back down.

"What day is it?"

"It's been three days." Saphira breathed deep and tried to turn, but her leg throbbed painfully, so she laid back on her stomach. "Do you want to lay on your back?" he asked gently. He was acting so odd, she didn't think he could be so nice.

"Yes."

Iollan got up and grabbed some of the bandages from the nightstand. "Let me change your dressing first, then I'll help you turn over." He moved to the end of the bed, and she felt fabric on the back of her legs. "Pardon me, Saphira, but the wound is high on your leg. Luckily, Eden lent you one of her skirts. We didn't think you'd want to be more exposed than had to be."

"She was right." Saphira could feel him gently cut away

the old bandages and spread a cool salve over the wound. He was right, the wound felt like it was just below her butt, and she was glad it wasn't her butt, that would have been embarrassing. The salve helped a little with the pain, and Saphira was able to relax. But when he wrapped the clean bandage around her leg, she gasped when she felt his knuckle brush against a particularly sensitive area between her legs. "Iollan..." she gasped and tried to move, but was still in too much pain.

"I apologize, Saphira. But like I said, the wound is high on your leg." She barely heard him as he finished wrapping the wound. Every pass around her leg, his knuckle brushed gently on the same spot, and it was incredibly distracting.

When she finally felt the skirt back on her skin, she relaxed and turned to Iollan. "Help me turn." He nodded and held her leg as still as he could while she used her arms to turn over. She felt flattened from being on her stomach for so long and breathed deep as she landed on her back.

"There's something you need to learn about being in a group," he said, still on the bed. "We see each other in many different states. Happy, sad, angry, inconsolable. When we're hurt, we rely on those we're with to help us, and sometimes that means being in...sensitive situations. Since I've been with Rickert and the twins, I think I've seen them all naked at least once. But trust me when I say I take no pleasure in it. It's part of traveling together. Seeing each other in vulnerable states. But we're a family, and we take care of each other like one."

Saphira nodded. "I understand. And thank you for getting me out of there. I'm mad I didn't see the archer." She shook her head and looked back at the window.

"He didn't last long after he shot you." She looked back at Iollan, and he gave her a little wicked grin, and she couldn't help but chuckle. "Are you in much pain?"

"Nothing unmanageable." Her hands were resting on her stomach, and sleep began to suck her under, until she felt Iollan gently slide his hand over hers. It startled her, which sent pain down her leg.

Suddenly, Iollan stood, his hand still on hers. "I'm going to get you some food. I'll be right back." As she stared at him, she felt his thumb rub gently along her skin. She had never been more nervous in her life and wished Eden was in the room.

"Okay, thank you." He nodded and walked out of the room. When the door shut, Saphira tried to calm down. Iollan had been acting so odd, since the night she was shot, if she recalled correctly. He seemed caring and kind. He seemed to worry about her, which was a whole new concept to her. From the first moment she met Iollan, Saphira accepted they wouldn't be close like she was with the others. But now he was acting as if they had been friends all along. He was sweet and gentle, but the voice in the back of her head still screamed 'stay away from him'. She always had trouble listening to that voice and wondered if she'd finally start. The doorknob turned, and she felt her nerves going haywire, but relaxed when she saw it was Rickert.

"Up and around, huh?" he said with a smile.

"Iollan's acting odd." She had never kept her opinion of the fighter from their boss before and wasn't about to start now.

He sat on the bed and chuckled. "I'll say, I've never seen him so attentive before."

"Attentive?" Rickert nodded and took her hand. It reminded her of how her father used to hold her hand when she got hurt as a little girl.

"I think he feels guilty for what happened to you. Seeing someone you care about hurt so bad is never easy."

Saphira scoffed and shook her head. "I don't know why you keep thinking that, Rickert. He can't stand me."

He clicked his tongue. "You haven't seen the way he looks at you, Saphira." His voice was quiet, and Saphira could tell how serious he was. *Well, of course I haven't,* she thought, *I try not to look at him at all if I can help it.*

"How does he look at me?" She asked slowly.

Rickert squeezed and patted her hand. "Like you're the only one in the room." That sounded a little too romantic, and she felt her heart speed from a combination of fear and excitement.

"He scares me."

He sighed. "You've never had someone's affections before, have you?"

"Not like that." She slowly shook her head. Sure, she and Miles had messed around, but he never said anything to her she would mistake for romantic feelings. Not like how Iollan apparently did.

"It can be scary," he continued. "Especially from someone as intense as Iollan." The door pushed open, and Iollan walked in with a tray of food. Rickert helped her sit up, and Iollan set the tray across her lap. It was a stew with some crusty bread and milk. When the smell hit her nose, her stomach grumbled loudly.

Rickert chuckled and patted her knee. "I'll let you eat, maybe later you can join us downstairs."

"Rickert?" He stopped at the door and turned to her. "I'm sorry I got hurt on my first job, probably doesn't give you much confidence in me."

He smiled at her. "Actually, from the guard's report, I'm more impressed than anything. Don't worry about it." He left with a wink, and when the door shut, Iollan sat next to her on the bed.

"Hope it's good," he said. "The cook's kind of hit and miss lately." Iollan sounded as if they were old friends simply catching up. Even his face seemed more relaxed, until a shadow seemed to pass in front of his eyes. "I wanted to apologize. It's my fault you got hurt. I was watching you take care of the elves instead of checking the other room. If I had done my job, you wouldn't have gotten hurt. I apologize." He truly looked sorry for what happened. His eyes were down, those thick dark lashes hiding them from her.

She decided to ignore the voice in her mind and laid her hand on his. "It's not your fault. Things like this happen." He looked up and slid his hand over hers, a small smile on his face. It was the first time she had seen him smile, and she hated to admit it, but it made him even more handsome.

"Perhaps you'll trust me at your back now."

As she thought about his words, she realized something. "I do trust you, I always did."

His eyes widened, and he studied her face. "You seemed surprised."

His fingers rubbed on her skin, and she knew her cheeks were red. "I guess I didn't realize it till now."

He shook his head and let go of her hand. "I know I made it hard for you when you joined, and I apologize. I was taken aback by your presence, and I wasn't sure how to act. But I'm over the shock. I'll be more hospitable from now on." It was like a switch was thrown in his head. Everything she knew about him seemed to be wrong now. Was he really the nice young man Rickert always said he was? She gave him a little smile and began to tear at her bread and dipped it into the stew.

"So, how goes the elf hunt?" she asked, popping the stew-soaked bread in her mouth. Seems the cook was having a good day today as the flavor exploded in her mouth. The bread was fresh and soaked up the beef juices perfectly. The carrots were soft and the onions sweet; it was a damn good stew.

"Nothing has happened since that night. No retaliation, no other raiding parties. The sheriff is hoping it was only those four elves. If so, our job here is done, and we get a bonus since we're the ones who caught them." He sounded rather proud. She didn't blame him; she was proud, too. She ate and listened to him talk about what the others had been up to. He seemed much more relaxed, but there was still something under the surface that still unnerved her.

As she took her last bite, the door opened, and the twins walked in. "Saphira!" Eden ran up and hugged her. When she got out of the way, Edward leaned down and kissed her cheek.

"You look better. Iollan's been taking care of you, huh?" he asked.

"Yes, he has." Iollan gave her another little smile and took the tray from her lap.

"Let's hope I won't have to do it again." She knew what he meant. He didn't like it when she got hurt, and Saphira hoped no one would have to look after her again.

CHAPTER 6
THE DANCE

The group stayed in Blackridge until Saphira's leg was better. At first, Iollan and Edward took turns carrying her down the stairs until she was able to get down on her own. Then she and Eden would walk slowly around town until she got her flexibility and mobility back, along with a nasty scar on the back of her leg. Iollan spent more and more time with her, talking about nothing in particular. He was like a whole different person, and she was surprised at how much she was enjoying his company. She even found herself looking forward to spending time with him, the voice in her mind getting quieter every day.

Over the next few days, they were given the bonus Iollan had talked about; no other elves had come into town, and the Sheriff thanked them for a job well done. Rickert said the group had enough scares for a while and decided they deserved a treat, but wouldn't tell them what it was. The night before they left Blackridge, the group was downstairs having dinner. A local bard was playing, and two young men came up and asked Eden and Saphira to dance. They took the young men's hands and were soon twirling around the dance floor.

No one had ever asked Saphira to dance before. At home, she was Mother Lily's daughter, and most of the boys found her intimidating and left her alone. She and Miles didn't dance; that would attract more attention than they wanted, especially from his mother. Saphira pushed her past from her mind and enjoyed dancing with this handsome young man. He was funny and spirited and didn't step on her toes as they danced. It was the most fun she'd had in a long time.

"May I cut in?" Her heart went into her throat as Iollan stood by her, holding out his hand.

Her dance partner smiled at her. "Didn't think I could hog one of the prettiest girls here all night." He gave her hand a little kiss, "Thank you for the dance." He gave her hand to Iollan, as the fighter's other hand slid around her waist.

"I didn't know you could dance."

The corner of his mouth tilted into a grin. "I'm a wonderful dancer." The next song filled the air, and soon they were moving fluidly around the floor. Her hair whipped around as Iollan twirled her with ease. He seemed to pull her closer with every step. "Does dancing hurt your leg?"

"No, it's fine, doesn't hurt at all anymore." Truthfully, it did twinge on occasion, usually in the mornings, but she figured it would go away with time.

"Good, I'm glad you're all better." As the words left his mouth, she couldn't help but notice how close his lips were.

"So, any idea where Rickert's taking us tomorrow?"

He chuckled, and the smile on his face made her stomach tighten with nerves. But there was a look in his eyes she'd never thought she'd see on him. It was a look of heat, a look that said there were things he wanted to do to her that would make a less experienced person blush.

"No, but if he says it's a treat, it will be." He stopped moving and slowly cupped her cheek. She could tell he wanted to say something, like he was working up the nerve. A steel resolve flashed in his eyes. "You're so beautiful, Saphira." She could hear the music still playing, but all she saw was his dark eyes staring into hers.

"Iollan, the things you say." She could barely speak; her heart was in her throat.

His eyes got soft as he laid his cheek against hers. "It lightens my heart to see you react to my words." Iollan's lips traced their way across her cheek, and slowly he pressed them against hers. For the first time in days, Saphira's mind screamed, *don't let him kiss you!*, it was the loudest it had ever been. But she ignored it, and her body responded positively as his hands wrapped around her. She found herself deepening the kiss and pulling him closer. She didn't know how long they had stood still on the dance floor kissing when Iollan suddenly lifted his head and sighed. "Gods, you're like a drug, Saphira," he said quietly as his lips continued to run lightly along her other cheek.

"Is that a good thing?" She was honestly surprised she could speak.

"No," his voice was quiet and deep. "It's not." Saphira's stomach flipped as his teeth gently pulled her lower lip between his. She felt his hands on her back as they pressed her against his body, her own arms did the same, seemingly against her will.

He suddenly pulled away, and Saphira saw Edward standing behind them. "Mind if I cut in?" The smile on the archer's face made her wonder if Ed knew exactly what he was interrupting. But Saphira didn't want Iollan to go; she wanted to keep kissing him.

"Be careful with her, Ed," Iollan looked back down at her. "Saphira," his hand lightly tucked some of her hair behind her ear. "I hope we can do this again." She stared after him as he walked back towards the table. Her body was suddenly screaming for him to come back and keep kissing her, but Edward stepped in front of her.

"Shall we?"

"Yeah, sure, Ed." She politely took his hand, and they began dancing around to the music. "I thought you hated dancing."

He shrugged. "Edie told me how Iollan kind of creeped you out, so I thought I'd give you an excuse to get away from him." Her eyes widened. She knew they were close, but figured what she said about Iollan was in confidence.

"She told you?"

"Edie tells me everything. I'm sorry, should I not have butted in? I saw him kissing you, and I didn't think you wanted him to. I thought I was being gallant," he sounded embarrassed.

She gave him a little smile. "No, it's all right, I understand."

"Next time I see you two dancing, I'll be sure and leave you alone." He gave her a little wink.

"Okay, and thanks for your gallantry, Edward."

"You're welcome, I think." The song ended, and he gave her a little bow before they walked back to the table where their dinner was waiting for them.

Iollan's eyes followed her as she sat back down. "Did you have a nice time dancing with the archer?"

She turned and sighed, "I did, he's good for someone who doesn't like dancing." She poked the fighter in the ribs.

Iollan chuckled and took a swig of his ale and leaned close to her ear. "I don't think it's that he hates dancing, it's that he doesn't like dancing with girls he doesn't choose. Most nights after you go to bed, the girls come over and practically beg him to dance. Ed's too nice of a guy to turn them down."

"Makes sense." She glanced over at Edward as he talked with Rickert. The young man did seem oblivious to the girls behind him, giggling and pointing. "I guess I didn't realize how coveted he was."

Iollan laughed and patted her knee. "That's one word for it."

The men always stayed down in the tavern later than the girls, so when Saphira and Eden excused themselves for the night, Iollan stood and gave her a kiss on the cheek. "Sleep well, Saphira."

She couldn't help but smile and leaned into him. "I will, don't drink too much." He put his hand over his heart like a promise. Saphira slowly walked over to the stairs as every kiss the dark fighter gave her floated through her mind.

"Saphira, wait up!" She turned and saw Eden running over, her skirt flying behind her. "Well, you've had a busier evening than I usually do," she said as she linked her arm through Saphira's as they climbed the stairs.

"I wasn't *that* busy."

The mage giggled and opened the door to their room. "So how was the kiss anyway?" Eden teased and flopped on her bed, wiggling her eyebrows in a lecherous manner. Saphira sat down and threw her pillow at Eden, who proceeded to laugh loudly. "Well?" Saphira put her feet on the bed and rested her chin on her knees. The memory of him pulling her lip between his made her stomach tight.

"Truthfully, it was the single most romantic moment of my life."

Eden hugged the pillow she threw at her and smiled. "Really? Awww."

"Honestly, I haven't had many, so unsure how it compares, but I'm...speechless."

Eden chuckled. "Not many boys at home, I take it?"

Saphira scoffed. "No, only Miles, the Lord's second son. And I think that's cause *he* made other girls nervous. But we always got along fine."

Eden was positively giddy as she smiled at her. "So, I take it you aren't creeped out by him anymore?"

Saphira sighed and laid on her side, facing Eden. "I'm not entirely sure. I liked it when he kissed me, but there's still something bugging me."

Eden shrugged. "Hmm, well, he is an intense guy, maybe that's it." She threw Saphira her pillow and grabbed a white sleeping gown. She slipped it over her head and shimmied out of her dress, not showing an inch of skin, and jumped into bed.

Saphira laid back and stared blankly at the ceiling. "I think I had him pegged all wrong." She only halfway lied; she did have him pegged all wrong, but he was more than nice. He was wonderful, and she wondered when their lips would meet again.

The next morning, Rickert set the path and walked them north. As the group traveled, Iollan walked next to Saphira all day, holding her hand. At night, he slept next to her, his fingers twirling in her hair. She enjoyed talking with the dark fighter until they fell asleep. He was wise beyond what years he had, and she was glad he finally opened up to her. When no one was looking, they'd steal kisses from each other. She swore he always looked like he felt as if he were the luckiest guy in the world. Like he couldn't believe he was kissing her.

One night, she felt his hands on her shoulder, gently

shaking her awake, and she knew it was her turn for watch.

"Saphira, wake up," Iollan whispered in her ear. As always, it twitched, and he chuckled as she opened her eyes. "Why do your ears twitch?" She sat up and ran her fingers through her hair, trying to liven it up a little.

"I don't know. My Papa used to tease me, said I had fox ears." Iollan smiled and began helping her with her hair. He had been doing that lately, so Saphira put her hands down and let him do what he wanted. It felt good having his fingers in her hair. It sent happy tingles down her body, and she smiled at him.

"I don't know about fox, bat maybe," he said, smiling.

Saphira laughed quietly. "Bat huh?" She could feel how big her smile was when suddenly Iollan buried his hand in her hair behind her neck. His face was so close she could smell that wonderful natural scent that was his alone, leather, sword oil, and wind.

"You're so beautiful when you laugh, Saphira." His fingers kneaded at her skin, and she froze.

She slowly reached up and felt his prickly chin with her fingertips. "Then you better make me laugh every day."

He pressed his lips on hers for a moment. "I'll keep that under advisement. Good night, Saphira." He laid down, his back to her, and Saphira was left wishing they were alone.

"Good night, Iollan," she whispered and took her place by the fire. But she couldn't keep her eyes focused on much. All she wanted was him, every bit of him.

The next day, Edward seemed to usurp Iollan's place by her side. He chatted happily as they walked, and Iollan was forced to walk behind them. Occasionally, she'd turn to peek at him. He was always staring at her and smiled when her eyes met his. That night, as they ate their rations, Eden asked the question that was on Saphira's mind all day.

"So, Rickert, where are we going?"

He looked over with a mischievous grin. "Can't you tell?"

"No," she said as Saphira shrugged her shoulders.

"We're heading towards Suya territory," Iollan said.

Eden gasped and turned to the rogue, "Saphira, you're in for a treat! Rickert's sister married a Suya; we visit them every so often." Saphira had heard of the Suya; they were always on the move. Their big caravans traveled across the continent as they entertained whoever they came across. They were famous for their dances and their tapestries, which could take years to make. Saphira remembered seeing one in Lord Raventree's office; it looked like every color in existence was woven into it.

She turned and smiled at her boss. "I look forward to meeting her."

Rickert was smiling widely. "I can't wait to see her. Last time we saw her, she was with child. I wonder if I'm an uncle yet."

"Rickert, isn't this around the time of the Bell Festival?" Iollan seemed nervous asking such a simple question.

"I think it is." He nodded.

"What's the Bell Festival?" Saphira looked over at Rickert.

Rickert cleared his throat. "Well, it's when—"

Iollan suddenly spoke up, interrupting their boss. "There's lots of bell ringing, very noisy, hard to sleep."

Rickert licked his lips and smiled. "Yeah, bell ringing."

Saphira looked over at Iollan and noticed he seemed tense. "Something wrong?" She laid her hand on his arm, and he turned as he covered her hand with his.

"No."

She was a little shocked at his short answer and took back her hand. "If you say so." Eden shrugged her shoulders as Edward kept flicking grass into the fire, completely ignoring everything going on around him.

The next few days, Edward resumed his place by Saphira's side. But when she looked back at Iollan, she noticed his eyes seemed worried. When he noticed her staring, he'd give her a little grin, but the troubled look would return shortly after. She'd ask him what was wrong when they stopped, and he'd say he was thinking, but not what about. Three afternoons later, they walked into the Suya camp. Big colorful tents and wagons were spread around, and some still had campfires going. A few people waved to Rickert as they walked through, and he happily waved back. He was clearly known here.

Saphira saw a large red tent in front of them and heard a woman's voice. "Rickert!" The group turned and watched a very pregnant woman running over as fast as she could while holding her big belly.

"Malia!" Rickert opened his arms and hugged the woman. "Look at you, little sister, still not an uncle yet, I see." He teased as he tickled her belly.

A tall, imposing man walked up behind her and held his hand out to their boss. "Rickert, it's good to see you. Made it just in time, I believe." His accent was different, there seemed to be a lilt to his vowels, but Saphira had no trouble understanding him. The man was tan, and his long brown hair was tied behind his head.

Rickert shook the large man's hand. "Lucien, I see you've been busy around here."

He laughed and looked at the group. "You've brought your friends again, it's wonderful to see you," his eyes landed on Saphira. "And a new one." He let go of Rickert's hand and introduced himself to her. "Lucien, this is my wife, Malia. My brother is our leader, and you shall want for nothing while here."

She happily took his big hand and gave it a hearty shake. "Saphira, nice to meet you." Lucien led them to a big green tent next to the red one, and everyone walked in. It was warm and comfortable with fur pelts covering the floor.

Everyone put their stuff down, and Lucien clapped his hands once. "So, why don't I show everyone around while Malia and Rickert visit for a while?" He held open the tent flap, and the others followed him. Lucien introduced them to his brother and wife, who were delighted to see Rickert. As Lucian showed them around, Saphira saw some of the Suya practicing acrobatics and dancing. The dancing intrigued her. She had never seen anyone move like that; it was smooth and much more sensual than she ever thought she could do. Their hips were making circles in the air or shaking fast, making their skirts jingle in the air.

"Would you like to learn?" A voice startled her, and she turned to a woman with thick curly brown hair. Saphira thought her features were very catlike with sharp angles, and her eyes even looked feline, as odd yellow irises glowed under her dark lashes.

Saphira's eyes went wide with shock. "Oh, I can't do that."

The woman smiled. "That's why you learn."

Eden excitedly grabbed Saphira's arm. "You must learn, I did the last time we were here, and I had so much fun!"

"Oh, um," she felt like she was stuck between a rock and a hard place.

"There is a festival in a few days, you'll get to show off your newly acquired skills to your friends." The yellow-eyed woman put her hands on Saphira's hips and wiggled her around. Edward laughed, and Saphira shot him a warning look. He quickly tried to hide his laugh by coughing. "Yes, you'll do fine," the woman said and held out her hand. "Come."

Saphira looked at her friends, but it was Iollan who spoke up, "Have fun, Saphira."

His words pushed her over the edge, and she took the woman's hand. "Okay, fine, fine." The woman smiled and led her over to where the other women were learning the exotic dance.

She patted Saphira's hand. "My name is Nesina. Don't worry, little one, you will have fun." As she looked at the women moving to the fast beat, she wondered how on earth she was going to move like they did and looked back at her friends. But only Iollan was still there, his dark eyes on her. "You'll never learn if you look only at your friend." Nesina's voice startled her, and she turned back around to the group. She didn't realize she had been staring so intently at him.

"Sorry."

"No need to apologize. If I had a young man to stare at, I'd do it all day long," she winked at her. Saphira scoffed; she wasn't sure what he was to her. But wondered if he'd like to watch her do this exotic dance.

Over the next few days, Rickert visited with his sister while Eden and Edward caught up with friends they made the last few times they were there. Saphira spent most of her time with the dancers and didn't see much of Iollan except at night when they slept with their arms around each other. Her mother was right, she learned quickly, and it didn't seem to matter what it was, locks or dancing. Soon she was moving with the women in time to the beating drums. She found it freeing to move her body in such a way and often found herself lost in the music.

One night, the women dressed her in traditional garb, and Saphira felt positively naked. She had never worn so little or shown so much skin before. She couldn't help but cover her bare stomach with her arms. Nesina smiled at her work and began braiding bits of Saphira's hair.

"You look wonderful, Saphira. No man dare say no to you tonight," she said with a smile.

"Say no?" The other women chuckled like hens in a hen house while they put on their skimpy outfits.

"Tonight is the Festival of Bells, Saphira. The night where the women and men of the tribe dance for their chosen lover and later, well, you know."

Her heart suddenly sped up; she knew full well what she was talking about. "Oh, I think I know.

The woman laughed, and Nesina tried to ease her mind. "You don't have to sleep with your man if you dance for him. But it is a festival of love and fertility, so to dance for a person tells them they have your heart." Saphira immediately thought about what Iollan would do if she danced for him. "So, which of your two young men are you going to dance for? Iollan or Edward?"

"Edward?" She didn't bother hiding the shock on her face at the mention of the archer.

Nesina shrugged her shoulders. "Both men look at you with different intentions, have you not noticed?"

She shook her head. "Edward's protective, that's all."

Nesina leaned down and whispered in her ear, "And what of the dark one?"

Pretty fitting, Saphira thought, and smiled. "He says the most romantic things to me," she said quietly. Her stomach tightened as she thought about kissing him and wondered if she wanted to do more.

Nesina chuckled. "Then I think you know who should enjoy your dance."

Iollan sat next to Edward at dinner that night. He had seen this festival once before, and all the women dancing was an overload to his system. Never had he encountered dancing like that of a Suya woman, and now he was about to watch Saphira participate. Half of him hoped she'd dance for him, so he could watch her hips roll to the music as her hands begged him to join her. The other half hoped she'd wiggle in a corner with the little girls. But that wasn't her way. Her way was to jump in headfirst, to experience everything she could while out in the world.

Edward leaned over and whispered, "Do you think Saphira will dance for you?"

Iollan ran his hands through his hair as his stomach fluttered with nerves. "No idea." He hadn't quite forgiven Edward for interrupting their dance the other night. But he didn't think Saphira would appreciate him acting like he had some kind of claim on her, and grudgingly handed her over.

"Do you want her to?" Iollan didn't trust his voice, so he nodded. They were sitting with all the single men and women around a semi-circle table with food from one end to the other, and as Iollan reached for his wine, the music began. Suddenly, his heart sped up. The music itself was sensual, and he knew if he saw Saphira dance, he'd lose all control.

The dancers filed out of the tent to cheers and applause of the single people at the table, and Iollan's heart leapt into his throat. Saphira was one of the first ones out. He wasn't surprised; she was the kind of girl who didn't let things pass her by. She spun around to the music, her hair flying in the wind behind her, her hips moving in time with the beat. When she stopped in front of him, he suddenly forgot how to breathe. Her beautiful blue eyes pierced his, and he vaguely heard Rickert somewhere behind them cheering. He made a mental note to hit him in the arm later.

Saphira wasn't smiling at him like some of the other dancers did for their lovers. Her face was full of heat, and he watched her chest heave up and down with every breath she took. He was barely able to tear his eyes away from hers and take in her body. Her outfit was like nothing he'd ever seen her wear. The red shirt was tight and only covered her breasts. Her bare stomach was a sight to see, smooth and long. Iollan took a long time admiring her curves before she started dancing.

Her arms flew up into the air, and as her hips began to sway with the music. The little bells on her skirt chimed in time with her movements. He wanted to reach out and play with them as she danced, but he held back, determined to watch her for as long as he could. She turned around, and her hips made little circles that ended in sharp movements to make the bells ring. She held her hands up, and Iollan watched how smooth and feminine they seemed as they danced and teased the air.

The music sped up, and her hips began swaying side to side even faster. Iollan's heart matched the tempo, and he knew he wouldn't last much longer. He had to feel her against him, underneath him. He glanced around at the other men and women around the table. They were enjoying their dances, but no one had yet stopped their dancer and taken them back to a tent. Iollan knew it was an honor to be the first dancer stopped by their choice of lover, and he suddenly wanted Saphira to have that. He found himself on his feet before he had fully made the decision to stand and stepped into the circle as everyone around hollered their encouragements.

Iollan wrapped his arms around Saphira and picked her up in one smooth motion, and carried her away from the party.

He didn't stop until they were alone in a nearby field of soft grass with trees hiding them from lookie-loos. When he finally laid her down, he hesitated. He wasn't sure where he should lay but when her hands held his hips and moved him on top of her, he sighed.

"Saphira, sweet, beautiful Saphira," he said as he stroked her cheek. "I had no idea when I first laid eyes on you that you would turn my world upside down. I've never felt this way about anyone. I didn't think it was possible."

"How do you feel about me, Iollan?" she whispered. He felt her legs move, and suddenly, he was nestled between them, and she sighed. "I want to hear it from you." He leaned down and ran his lips across her cheeks as he pushed that growing hardness between his hips against her, and she gasped.

"I love you, Saphira. Gods forgive me, I do." He moved again, and the sound that escaped her lips was one he never thought he'd hear. "I've never seen a more spirited, beautiful woman in all my life."

"Iollan, make love to me." Her voice was like a soft wind carrying his heart's desire. He brushed some of her dark hair off her forehead and looked into her eyes.

"I'd love nothing more in this world, but are you sure?"

"Iollan, I don't do anything I don't want to do, and right now," she reached up and trailed her nails down his cheek. "I want the man I love to lay with me under the stars."

He couldn't keep the smile off his face. "You love me? Truly?" She giggled and pulled him to her lips and could feel the truth of her words in her kiss.

CHAPTER 7
TOURNAMENT

Saphira woke naked in the tall grass, her arm around Iollan as the sun peeked over the horizon. The memory of the night before was immediately in her mind, and she smiled. She was in love, completely and utterly in love with Iollan, and he loved her too. She hadn't been looking for love; she thought it would distract her. But she'd heard it finds you when you least expect it. She looked up, and she saw the man in question was already awake and looking at her.

"Good morning, sweet Saphira," he whispered and kissed her gently.

"Good morning, Iollan," she whispered as her lips still touched his.

He sat them up and wrapped his arms around her. "How do you feel?"

She looked up and touched his cheek. "Wonderful."

Iollan smiled in a way she'd never seen, and it made her heart flutter. "I love it when you smile." She captured his lips and pulled him down on top of her. He chuckled the entire way down, and when she moved him between her legs, he lifted his head and laughed.

"Can't get enough of me?"

"I'll never have enough of you," she giggled. His hands ran up her sides, and he quickly tickled her bare skin. Saphira squealed and tried to wiggle away, but couldn't. "Stop that!" she shrieked with laughter.

Iollan laughed and stopped, his hands moved to her cheeks, and he pet them softly. "We should get dressed." Saphira nodded and searched for her revealing clothes from the night before. They weren't too hard to find, since they were bright red.

But she still got dressed rather slowly, letting her mind wander. She wasn't a virgin by any means, but she understood now what it meant to be with someone you genuinely cared about. And not because the two of you were curious like she and Miles had been. Iollan was a tender lover; it surprised her. Every movement of his hands or hips was slow and with purpose, and as she thought about what they did last night, she knew she wanted to do it again. Sooner rather than later. When the last piece of clothing was in place, Iollan took her hand, and they walked back to the camp.

Before the dance, Nesina told Saphira there would be a tea available the next morning for any of the young girls who wished to keep a child from her belly, and she would be welcome to have some. When they walked up to Nesina, Saphira saw many of the dancers sitting around the fire, drinking the tea, and talking about their night. Their partners were in another huddle watching them, their eyes filled with lust.

"Saphira!" She turned and saw Nesina waving her over. So, she kissed Iollan's hand and half-jogged over to the little circle. "How was your night?" she asked teasingly. Saphira tried to hide her big smile, but the women still saw and ooed and awwed at her. "Would you like some tea?" Nesina held out a small cup to her.

"Yes, please." She took the tea as the women around her laughed happily. It was a little bitter, but she could taste enough honey to make it bearable.

"How was it?" Nesina asked.

Saphira sighed and tried hard not to blush. "It was," she felt the blush on her cheeks, what they did was too much to hide. "It was wonderful."

Nesina clicked her tongue and smiled at her. "I'll have the midwife make some of this tea for you when your group leaves."

"Thank you, Nesina." Saphira knew she'd want a family someday, but certainly not now. After Saphira finished her tea, she got up and walked back to Iollan, who took her hand. "Shall we go to our tent?"

He kissed her cheek as a chorus of giggles broke out. "Yes, let's."

When Iollan held open the tent's flap, Eden was the only one there. She looked up from her spell book and smiled as they entered.

"Morning, you two."

"Good morning, Mage," Iollan said as Saphira changed back into her rogue gear. "Where is everyone?"

Eden put her book aside, a big smile on her face. "Well, Rickert became an uncle last night, so he's visiting."

"Oh how wonderful! He sure timed this trip well." Saphira sat next to her friend, and Iollan scooted behind her and wrapped his arms around her waist.

"And Edward, I assume, had a similar night," she looked over and winked at them. "Because he never came in."

Iollan chuckled, the sound radiated through her. "Good for him."

The group stayed a few more days while Rickert visited with his baby niece. Eden, Saphira, and Iollan fawned over her. Smiling as she made those silly baby faces and wonderful newborn noises. When Edward finally came back, Saphira noticed he was being rather cool towards her. Not unfriendly, just quiet, so she decided to give him some space. The day before they left, a Suya from another clan showed up in the camp and told them about a mage tournament being held in a nearby village called Buckland. Apparently, the town wanted this to be a yearly thing and invited the most well-known mages to take part. Eden begged Rickert for permission to enter the tournament. Saphira knew he couldn't say no to her, and when he finally relented, she squealed and hugged him tight.

Saphira hadn't seen Eden do much magic and was looking forward to seeing her in action. The tournament was in a week, and Buckland was only a few days away, so they said goodbye to their new friends and started the short trek. When they'd camp,

Saphira would peer over Eden's shoulder as she went through all her spell books and found the complexity of them amazing. Saphira could do a few spells, but magic usually gave her a headache, so she'd do whatever she could to avoid them. She knew of rogues who used magic a lot, but she thought it was a crutch and vowed never to get in the habit of relying on her meager magic.

When they arrived in Buckland, the town was indeed decorated for a tournament, and there was barely any room to move. People were packed along the one road the town had, and every storefront had colorful banners hanging in the windows. There were large, fenced-off areas outside of town where the mages would duel and keep any collateral damage contained.

"Boy, I hope we can find some rooms," Rickert said as they walked past a huge group of children being led by their teacher. They were all wearing red robes with a blue stripe down their back. Saphira didn't recognize it, but apparently Iollan did.

"That's Aldren Dragan, he owns the 'Dragan Mage School' in Ardenry. Looks like he brought some of his students to impress."

"Is he powerful?" Saphira asked.

"Oh yes, I've heard of him," Eden said. "His summons are where his powers are." Saphira watched the mage's hair bounce lightly as she spoke confidently about the stranger. She could see how happy being here made Eden. As it turns out, most of the mages had brought their own little tents or pavilions, so there was plenty of room at the one inn. Rickert and Edward walked up to the bartender to get some keys while Eden excitedly pointed out other mages she knew of.

"See the woman over there in the purple? Her name is Magus Blin. I heard she managed to keep a dragon confused while her group looted its horde. Oh, and the little guy over there, that's the famous gnome wizard Xoxim. They call him 'Mini McBoom'."

Saphira giggled. "Mini McBoom? Why?"

"Cause he's little and makes big booms."

The girls laughed as Edward threw a key on the table. "Come on, Edie, we got a room." He turned and walked for the stairs. Eden picked up the key and her bag, wiggling her eyebrows at Saphira, and followed her brother as Iollan sat down and handed Saphira an ale.

"Something wrong with Edward?" she asked.

Iollan took a drink of his ale and licked his lips. "I asked him if it was okay if he and his sister shared a room so we could be alone. I didn't think it'd bother him so much. It's what they did before you joined." Saphira shook her head and drank her ale. Edward was still acting weird around her, but every time she mentioned it, he'd say he was fine.

"There's definitely something going on with him."

"I think time might be the only cure for what ails him," Iollan said. "Or a pretty lady." Saphira chuckled and gave his cheek a kiss.

Eden came running back down. "Come on, Saphira, let's walk around and see who else is here before I sign up." Eden grabbed her arm, and she gave Iollan a quick kiss on the cheek before the mage dragged her out of the Inn.

Apparently, mages liked to be colorful. Every direction Saphira looked, there was a spellcaster dressed in some kind of colorful or gaudy robe. Eden looked normal by comparison. She didn't wear robes, preferring dresses or skirts and her spell component belt.

"I hope I don't have to cast against him." Saphira saw she was looking at a man in black robes. His back was to them, but her eyes went wide when she saw he was surrounded by skeletons.

"Blessed Otto." She recognized a necromancer when she saw one. "What does he think he's doing?"

Eden whispered in her ear, "At tournaments like these, allegiances are put aside so we can test our skills against those we wouldn't normally be able to. He could be a worshipper of The Shackled One for all we know. But even if he is, as long as he's here, it doesn't matter."

Saphira shuddered at the thought of Eden casting against someone with death magic. "That's a scary thought."

"It is." Eden walked them to the table where the mages signed up. There were already twenty names on the list before her, and more were behind them in line.

"Welcome to Buckland, which of you pretty young ladies will be competing for the coveted first prize?"

"She is," Saphira said, pointing at Eden as she signed her name. "What is first prize anyway?"

The man laughed. "You're entering a competition without even knowing what the prize is? You got guts, young lady." He was ignoring Saphira, so she slammed her hand on the table, and the man jumped.

"I said, what is the prize?"

He cleared his throat and straightened his collar. "A map."

Eden stood straight, confusion and disappointment apparent on her face. "A map, that's all?"

"Not just any map, young lady, a map that leads to fame and glory, riches beyond your wildest imaginations."

Eden and Saphira both scoffed and walked away from the table. "Sorry, the prize isn't better."

Eden shrugged her shoulders. "Honestly, it's the experience I'm looking for. Besides, if the prize is a map, then it's probably put up by some rich old fart who can't go themselves. We probably wouldn't get to keep much anyway."

They walked into the inn and sat next to the rest of their friends. "True." That was the life of a traveler, sometimes you'd get hired, but the riches went to those who hired you, instead of those who did the work. That's why it was good to have someone experienced in the group. They usually knew who would cheat people out of their hard-earned money.

The next few days went by slowly for Saphira. Eden was always reading her spell book, and Edward was still giving her the cold shoulder. She wanted this tournament to be over quickly so they could get out of this boring town. Though Saphira's nights were filled with Iollan and his deep kisses, it wasn't enough. The third morning arrived, and Eden bounded happily down the stairs, her brother next to her.

"You guys are going to come watch, right?" She spread jam on some toast and quickly ate it.

"When are you up? Do you know yet?" Rickert asked.

"No, they pick our names randomly. We don't know who we're casting against until it's time. We'll only fight once a day until the finals, so if I'm lucky, I'll be early today."

"Is it dangerous, not knowing who you're up against?" Iollan asked, his voice full of concern.

Eden nodded her head, but the smile never left her face. "It can be, but I'll be fine."

Edward stuffed the last of his sausage in his mouth. "Well, if you get hurt, I'm dragging you outta there, I don't care what the rules are." Saphira agreed with him but was still hurt by his cold shoulder and kept quiet.

At eight on the dot, all those who were participating in the tournament were lined up in the middle of the biggest field, while those watching gathered around the fence. The man who signed Eden up walked into the middle of the ring, and Saphira gasped as his voice seemed to carry over the din of the onlookers.

"Welcome one and all to the first-ever Buckland Mage Invitational!" Everyone clapped and cheered while a few of the mages not in the tournament sent colorful sparks into the air around the crowd. "The tournament is double elimination; those doing battle will be chosen randomly until there is only one left, and that mage will be awarded the grand prize. A map that leads to a great fortune underneath Ral Hava!"

Saphira smiled and leaned back into Iollan. "You'd get to go home if Eden wins." She looked up, and Iollan's face startled her. He looked in shock, and the color seemed to drain from his face. "Are you okay?" She turned and gently touched his cheek, "What's wrong?"

Slowly, his eyes moved down to hers. "I didn't think I'd ever go back there."

Saphira took her hand back and nodded. "Well, as much as I hope Eden wins, I doubt she will. So, you may have nothing to worry about."

He nodded and rested his head on hers. "I know, I want her to win too." When Saphira turned back towards the mages fighting, she saw it was a mage she didn't know against the one Eden dubbed, 'Mini McBoom'. They were allowed two protective spells before starting, and the one wearing the white robe took advantage. But the little gnome stood still, waiting for the other to finish.

"Mages, Battle!" The announcer cried, and suddenly, odd words filled the air, and Saphira watched as the gnome threw a glass vial across the field, while the one in white moved his hands in the air. Saphira recognized the spell; it would make the gnome stop whatever he was doing. But she had a feeling it didn't work. The glass vial broke against the white mage, and a collective gasp came from the crowd as the white mage was engulfed in a large fireball. His scream filled the air, and Saphira felt a tear roll down her cheek. *What if that had been Eden,* she thought.

The flames died as Iollan wiped the tear away. "He's fine, my sweet Saphira, see?" Her eyes studied the mage. He was on his knees, but he was moving and talking, apparently giving up.

"I wouldn't be able to handle it if Eden were swallowed up by a fireball."

His hands rubbed her arms comfortingly, and he rested his head on her shoulder. "Eden's a big girl, she'll be fine. But the thought occurred to me as well." The mage in white walked off the field, as did the little gnome, and the next two mage names were picked.

"If Mage Dragan and Mage McVain would please step into the ring!" Saphira gasped, and Edward cheered loudly for his twin.

"Cheer for her, Saphira, you'll feel better," Iollan whispered in her ear. He was right, of course. Eden needed encouragement right now, not nerves, so Saphira joined in the cheers with Edward and Rickert. As Eden walked into the ring, a lot of young men began whistling their appreciation of her beauty. Clearly, she didn't mind and began bowing and blowing kisses to the crowd.

Saphira chuckled and elbowed Edward in the ribs. "Makes it worse, doesn't it?"

He shook his head and groaned in irritation. "I know she's doing it on purpose." Saphira noticed how red his cheeks seemed and giggled. Suddenly, 'Mages Battle!' ran through the air, and when Saphira turned, she saw they were already casting. Eden knew about this man and hopefully considered his specialty. But he didn't summon an animal, and the crowd gasped as lightning streaked through the air towards Eden. She quickly rolled out of the way, and Saphira cheered loudly as Eden got to her knees and cast, but nothing happened. The group looked at Eden in disbelief, but she was smiling. They turned to her opponent, he looked like he was fighting off an invisible foe, totally forgetting about Eden, who walked closer to him. She pulled out a little feather and blew it into the air. The crowd laughed as Dragan was lifted upside down into the air by his ankles.

He began spinning in circles and the crowd laughed harder. "Ahhh! Let me down!"

"Do you give up?" Eden's voice rang clear over the crowd, who was chanting, 'faster, faster!' Eden laughed and turned back to Dragan. "Give up, or I give the crowd what they want!" She mocked the flying mage. He growled angrily, and suddenly there was a barking dog on the field, running straight at Eden. The crowd began yelling for her to turn around, but she didn't; she kept facing the dangling man. Saphira held her breath as the dog leaped for Eden, then seemingly slammed into an invisible barrier a few feet behind her. It yelped pitifully and disappeared. The crowd went wild, and the summoner fell like a pile of robes to the ground and gave up.

He was still swaying as he got to his knees. "I didn't even see you cast," he said.

She offered him her hand, which he took and got to his feet. "Hence the spinning," she said with a smile. The judges declared Eden the winner, and she smiled back to her friends.

They could see her bright smile across the field as they cheered and beat against the fence loudly for her. Saphira looked at the defeated man and saw his fingers moving closely to his body.

"Eden, look out!" She yelled, and as Eden turned, the red robed mage seemed to go up in smoke. It quickly cleared, and everyone gasped at the sight. The cheating mage had been turned into a sheep!

The crowd quieted from confusion as the announcer stepped up next to Eden. "Cheating is absolutely forbidden in this tournament. When the mages signed up, they put their names on a magical contract saying they would adhere to all the rules put forth. If they broke those rules, they would be disqualified and punished for the duration of the tournament. So, until a winner is declared, Mage Dragan will remain as you see him, a dirty animal." Some of the crowd laughed, others booed the mages' attempt, but Saphira and her friends cheered loudly as Eden ducked under the fence to join them.

Edward was the first to get hugs. "You did spectacular, Edie!"

Her brother kissed her cheek, and Rickert got the next one. "That was absolutely terrifying!" he said, laughing.

She kissed their boss's cheek. "I told you it'd be worth having us tag along."

"Never doubted it for a second."

Eden moved over to Saphira. "What'd you think?"

She wrapped her arms around Eden and squeezed tight. "It was terrifying, but I'm so proud of you!"

Iollan ruffled Eden's hair. "Did good, little mage."

"So," she turned to the group. "Want to watch more or walk around? It really is like a festival around town, there's games and food."

"I figured you'd want to watch everyone you could, Edie." Edward put a protective arm around her, and she reciprocated.

"Well, I have all day to watch them, but I don't want you to get bored."

Saphira shrugged. "I wouldn't mind walking around, but

it's interesting watching the mages battle. It's rare to actually see it in a controlled manner."

Eden smiled. "I know I can learn a lot here." Saphira noticed how she looked up at Rickert, and there was something in his smile, akin to love, and Saphira did her best to try not to notice.

CHAPTER 8

THE MAN WITH THE GREEN EYES

At the end of the day, fifteen of the original mages had been eliminated, and only one other was reduced to being a sheep. They were tied up by the entrance to the battlefields, and children took delight in throwing old food at them. The last battle of the day was taking place, and Saphira was the only one of the group still watching. The last time she saw Iollan, he was busy with a strong man game while the others were occupying themselves with members of the opposite sex.

The battle was interesting, not a lot of flashy power, mostly mind games. She watched as one of the mages screamed and fell to the ground. A flash of the elf in Blackridge she killed appeared in her mind, and she shook it away. She dreamed of that at night sometimes, waking up in a cold sweat from the dead bodies of the elves reaching for her. She knew this life meant killing, and she was right; she'd never know how she'd react until she was in the moment. But in the moment, she remembered not hesitating, not caring if she killed him. She wondered if Foster felt bad about killing. Or anyone else in their group, for that matter.

"Hello, little Voltain." Saphira turned at the familiar voice, and her eyes went wide as she saw the necromancer she and Eden had seen the day before standing peacefully behind her.

"Kaythen!" He smiled, and she hugged him. "What are you doing here? Won't Aunt Lavinia be mad at you?" She stepped back, and he shook his head. They had moved to Dal En Val several years ago. It was easier to blend in than in Buckland, and it was a 'keep your enemies closer' kind of situation.

"No, honestly, it's the safest Buckland could be at the moment." He stood up on the fence next to her. "So, what are you doing here? Did I see you walking around with one of those mages in the tournament?"

"Mm-hmm, Eden McVain, she's the mage in my group."

He smiled and gave her shoulder a nudge with his own. "Ooh, out and about, are we?"

"Yup, already got shot by an arrow." She turned to him with a smile on her face.

Kaythen turned, his eyes wide. "Excuse me?" She watched his eyes try to find where she was hit.

"You won't see it," she chuckled. "I'm fine, I healed well."

"Good." He sighed. He sounded relieved. "How's the family?" It had been a few years since they had gotten together, so there was a lot to catch up on.

"Busy, Foster's out too, haven't heard from him in four years."

His eyebrows went up in surprise. "Quite a stint. I thought he'd be the one to write long, nosey letters."

Saphira chuckled. "Not yet, anyway. I'm sure he's fine. He asked Ada to marry him, but she turned him down. He was so sad, he said he had to leave Raventree."

Kaythen turned to her, his mouth open in shock. "He asked a woman to marry him when he was eighteen?" He shook his head. "No wonder she said no."

"Oh, Kaythen, be nice," she nudged him a little. "Their ages weren't why she said no, anyway. She wanted to marry him, but you know Ada. She *knows* things."

"Mm-hmm, and did she think marrying an eighteen-year-old was a bad idea?" She could tell he was teasing, but her cousin always did have a sharp sense of humor.

She stuck her tongue out at him, and he chuckled. "Anyway, how are the twins?"

He took a deep breath, not meeting her eyes. "They're…" He sighed. "They're not good."

"What?" She reached out and laid a hand on his shoulder. "What's wrong?"

"They weren't meant for life in Dal En Val. Honestly, my mother should have taken them to Raventree when they were little and let your mother raise them." He finally turned to look at her. "Davi is part of the city guard, and he hates it; he's too… good. He does what he can and has the other men's respect, but it's crushing him. And Desi," he sighed. "She wants nothing more than to leave and never come back. But she refuses to go without Davi, and his guard duties tie him to the city, so he can't leave. She's sad, and her art is turning dark."

Saphira's heart was breaking as he told her about her cousins. "Can't he quit?"

"No. When you reach a certain age, you're conscripted. He can't leave for twenty more years."

"Gods." She was beginning to think Kaythen was right. Lavinia should have left the twins in Raventree. "Why weren't you conscripted?"

He huffed. "The son of the Shackled One is tied up in other ways, don't you worry."

"You're not his son, Kaythen," she laid a hand on his shoulder. "I refuse to believe it."

He gave her hand a pat. "Tell your mage friend good luck," he turned to walk away. "I'll see you around, cuz."

"Kaythen, you don't have to go," she turned to him. "Come with us."

He threw his head back and laughed. "Thanks, Saphy. But I think I'll keep to myself." He gave her a little salute and disappeared in the crowd. She knew her cousins were different, that the other half of her family was different, but she still loved them. Hell, sometimes she felt more like them than her own brothers. Almost like she could relax around her cousins, knowing they'd never judge her for being different.

When Saphira walked back into the inn, her friends were at a table playing cards, and she heard Eden's usual greeting, but she was so distracted about what to do for Desi and Davi, she walked past them without a glance and went up to her room. She sat on the bed and wondered what could she do? She was a nobody comparatively; there was no way she could march into the most evil city in the world and steal her cousins away.

The door opened, and Iollan walked in. "Saphira?" She watched as he sat next to her. "Something wrong?"

She shrugged. "Yeah, but there's nothing I can do about it." He hugged her, and she buried her face in the crook of his neck, breathing in his scent of wind, leather, and sword oil.

"Are you sure?"

She nodded. "Can I ask you a question?" She had to change the subject. No one could know who she was related to. At least who *else* she was related to.

He nodded. "Always." She withdrew her arms and stared down at her hands, her fingers picking at her nails.

"Do you remember the first person you killed?" She asked, not looking at him.

"I do." She was glad he answered so quickly. "I was fifteen and walking back to my room at an inn in Garythane." She looked up, but let him continue. "I think he had been following me for a while and saw me get paid. He tried to rob me, but he didn't know I could fight, and he got a stomach full of my sword for his troubles." Saphira ran through all the names of cities she could think of, but Garythane wasn't one of them.

"Where's Garythane?"

"On the northern continent, it's not a nice place." She could feel his hesitation in speaking about the town.

"Why were you in Garythane?" The question flew through her mouth before she could stop it.

His eyes went wide, and he shook his head. "Oh, um… that's where I'm originally from, my father took us to Ral Hava when I was young. Why did you want to know about my first kill?"

She could tell he was trying to change the subject. "The elf in the house, I had no qualms about killing him. I thought I would."

He reached up and held the back of her neck. "It's survival, Saphira, killing is survival. It's not evil, it's not good, it just is."

Her eyes narrowed. "How can killing not be evil?"

He took a deep breath, and she watched his eyes burn into

hers. "I look at it as if it's something you need to do to live, it's not evil. If you kill to steal, kill to make a living, sure, it's evil. But us, it's a hazard of the trade."

"So, it doesn't bother you?"

He shrugged, his hand still massaging her neck. "Sometimes, but I try not to let it. But know this, when other lives are at stake, I don't hesitate."

Saphira nodded and laid her head on his chest. "Thank you." His hands gently rubbed her back, and she could feel him slowly pushing her back against the bed.

"You're welcome, my sweet Saphira."

When she was laying back against the bed, she giggled, "Are you hinting at something?"

Iollan chuckled. "I'm not hinting at anything," he whispered as his hand snaked its way up her shirt. "I want you," he whispered in her ear before his lips got busy at her neck.

On the third day of the tournament, there were twelve mages left, and Eden was still competing. They all lined up in one of the rings and waited to be called. The announcer stepped into the ring and began pulling names out of the little black bag.

"If mages, McVain and Engeos would take their places on the field!" Saphira had remembered watching this Engeos a few days ago; he had lost his battle and seemed irritated as he left the ring. She wondered if the other two sheep would soon have a companion if he lost against Eden. The announcer got out of the ring while Eden and Mage Engeos moved to opposite ends.

"Mages Battle!" Rang through the air, and the group watched as Eden began casting, but was suddenly surrounded by thorny bushes, which tore at her dress and made it hard to concentrate. The crowd had begun to like the pretty mage, and a lot of people booed at Engeos.

But Edward and Saphira kept yelling words of encouragement to their mage. "Calm down, Edie, you can do it!" Saphira watched Eden as her twin's voice carried over the field. She seemed to stop struggling, and soon the thorns disappeared, freeing her arms. As Eden's hands moved through the air, Saphira didn't recognize the spell she was casting and gasped as she began to sink in the mud around her. Mage Engeos did to Eden what Saphira saw another mage do to him the other day.

"Oh no." Edward visibly sank. "Well, she hasn't lost one yet, so it's not a total loss, I guess." They watched as the other mage seemed to begin to celebrate his victory, but the crowd laughed as Eden seemed to miraculously crawl out of the mud and begin to cast behind his back.

Rickert smiled. "You show him Eden!" He yelled as her spell went off. Engeos turned, and his eyes widened as his skin slowly turned gray.

"What did she do?" Iollan was shielding his eyes from the sun, but Saphira saw exactly what she did.

"He's a statue," she said with a wicked little grin. Engeos stopped moving. Even his clothes stopped flapping in the breeze as he turned to stone before their eyes. The crowd cheered at her defensive move. Engeos could no longer cast, so the battle was over, and he was eliminated.

"Mage McVain is the winner!" The group was the loudest of all the spectators as the announcer declared Eden the victor and couldn't wait to celebrate. Eden dis-spelled the stone on the now eliminated mage and reached to shake his hand. But when he could finally move, he jerked his hand away from her and marched out of the ring. The crowd kept booing the mage as he walked away, but Saphira was thankful he didn't try anything worse.

CHAPTER 9
THE WINNER

The energy at the tournament the next day was intense. There were only six mages left, and today was going to be hard. By the end of the day, a winner would be declared. It didn't matter if they had already battled, what spells they used couldn't be used again, so in the beginning, they would have to be extra careful. Eden and one other mage named Zaccai Stayhnal were up first. Neither of them had lost a match, so whoever lost would still be in the running. The group watched as Eden dashed around the field, dodging lightning bolt after lightning bolt. Somehow, Zaccai was able to do more than one at a time, and they could see Eden breathing hard as she tumbled out of the way.

As she got to her feet, Saphira heard Edward gasp. "No, Edie, don't."

"What's she doing?" Saphira watched as Eden got to her feet and quickly cast at the same time, a bolt hit her and knocked her backwards.

"Eden!" Rickert yelled as she landed hard on her back. *The matches are getting more violent,* Saphira thought. Zaccai's yell pierced the air. Saphira looked over and saw a large stone golem punch the mage in the stomach. He flew through the air and landed awkwardly on his shoulder. Quickly, Saphira looked over at Eden, who was slowly getting to her knees.

"All right, Eden!"

When she finally got to her feet, the announcer stepped into the field, "Since Mage Stayhnal isn't able to continue, Mage McVain is declared the winner!" Cheers erupted, and the group could see her bright smile from across the field. A healer in blue robes ran over to both mages and healed them. Zaccai needed a bit more, but when he finally regained consciousness, he walked over and shook Eden's hand like the good sport he had been known to be. Since this was the last day, the mages left were shown to a waiting area, and unfortunately, Eden wasn't going to get much of a break. As soon as the healer declared her healthy, the announcer pulled out two more names.

"Oh my, Mages Laderic and McVain, please come forward."

Edward groaned. "Damn, she's hardly had any time to rest."

Rickert walked next to him and laid a hand on his shoulder. "Your sister's tough, she'll get through it." The two mages walked into the field, and Saphira had a bad feeling. Laderic had been eliminated once already, and Saphira thought he looked desperate.

"Mage's battle!" Both Eden and Laderic cast their two protective spells, then began their offense. Saphira recognized what Eden was doing; it was designed to make the opponent their friend, and friends don't cast against one another. But Laderic was fast, and before Eden finished speaking, she began screaming and scratching at her skin.

"What the hell?" Eden dropped to the ground and began rolling around while Laderic stayed still.

"Get them off, get them off!" She screamed while the announcer quickly came out and declared Laderic the winner since Eden couldn't cast anymore. It was so fast, Saphira had a feeling no one wanted to watch their favorite pretty mage suffer much longer, and soon Laderic ended the spell. Eden stayed on the ground, trying to catch her breath as another healer ran to her and healed her cuts.

"What happened? I don't understand?"

"I think he made her think there were spiders all over her," Edward said. "She's scared of them." Laderic projected her own fear against her, *dark stuff* she thought as she watched Eden sit down, she still looked pretty shook up.

"I wish we could go talk to her."

"Me too," Rickert said. Saphira snuck a glance at her boss.

He was losing the cool demeanor he usually had where Eden was concerned. They watched the next few battles, and they got increasingly violent and destructive. One mage won their fight by turning his opponent's flesh to ooze, which made everyone groan in disgust. When he was no longer ooze, the mage ran away. Saphira didn't blame him a bit. To the group's horror, Eden's next match was against the ooze mage. Edward was extremely nervous. Saphira watched as he stuck his dagger over and over into the wooden fence, putting many little holes into it. Rickert wasn't faring much better; he was constantly tapping his foot on the ground.

"You can do it, Eden, we believe in you!" Rickert yelled out. Soon, 'Mages Battle' rang through the air, and their eyes went wide. Eden and the other mage cast at the same time, but the crowd gasped as the other mage's spell seemed to rebound off the pretty mage. He jerked and suddenly disappeared, his clothes falling into a pile on the ground. No one was sure what to think and watched as Eden walked up and sifted through the pile. She found something and brought it out for everyone to see. It was a hunk of cheese.

The announcer walked up to her, and everyone still heard him. "Is that—"

"It is," Eden said with a big smile and handed him the cheese.

"Well, I must say I've never actually seen that before, but as your opponent is no longer able to cast, Mage McVain, you are the winner!" The crowd cheered loudly, and Eden dropped the cheese. The mage suddenly turned back into his human self and quickly gathered his clothes. Saphira thought he was mumbling to himself.

"I sure hope she doesn't make a lot of enemies here," Rickert said.

"If she does, it'll be those she's already beaten; she'll be all right," Saphira said.

The announcer walked back into the middle of the field. "Well, it seems we're down to our last two. Let's give a round of applause to those who participated over the last few days!" Everyone clapped for the eliminated mages, and Saphira watched Edward as he tried to speak with Eden. A big guard held him back, and she hoped he wouldn't cause trouble.

"I honestly didn't think she'd make it this far," she said, turning back to Iollan. He was staring at the empty battlefield. A familiar look of worry was on his face again. "Are you okay?"

He nodded and focused his eyes on hers. "I'm fine."

"Are you worried about Eden winning?"

His eyes looked around. She knew he was trying to think of something to say. "A little." She was glad he didn't try to lie. He had been a little nervous since he found out the prize map led to a treasure under Ral Hava.

It was down to Eden and the mage named Hector Nadell. Saphira remembered watching him and another mage as they pretty much tortured each other. How they did it, she'll never know, but it wasn't easy to watch. Eden was rested and whole as the announcer called out one last time.

"Mages battle!" Both of them cast their protective spells, then turned on each other. Eden's hands moved through the air, and Saphira could feel the air crackling with energy, and watched as Hector morphed himself into an exceptionally large ogre, complete with a huge piece of wood he was aiming for Eden's head.

"Do it, Eden!" Edward yelled out as the ogre ran for his twin. Saphira watched as Eden curled in on herself and suddenly transformed into a huge blue dragon.

Saphira's eyes went wide, and she gasped, "Blessed Otto, Edward, you guys are…"

"No, no, just Eden," he said, chuckling. "It's something to do with the magic in her blood." The entire crowd gasped as the ogre hit the dragon in the head with its club, but it didn't do much. Eden swiped her razor-sharp claws at the ogre, slicing its belly but not enough to put it down. It stumbled and wrapped its large arms around the dragon's body, but Eden leaped into the air, taking the ogre with her. The crowd watched as the blue dragon dipped and dived around, trying to shake the ogre off, but it wasn't working, so she decided on another tactic. Eden dived into the ground, burying them both about ten feet into the soft earth. The dragon quickly climbed out of the self-made hole and turned around. It opened its huge maw and was about to blast the ogre with its breath weapon, but instead of an ogre, the human mage crawled out, so she held, waiting for him to make his move. He looked worn out but stood and began casting. Eden didn't hesitate and swiped her large claw at him, and knocked the man back to the other end of the field. He rolled a few times and hit the fence, the crowd let out a loud 'ooooh!' as the wood cracked. The announcer walked over to the unmoving Hector, and the crowd watched as he held up his hand.

"Mage Eden McVain is the winner of the first-ever Buckland Mage Invitation!" The crowd erupted in cheers and watched as the blue dragon slowly changed back into the pretty mage. The group crawled under the fence and ran over to her, and Edward was the first to get hugs.

"You was brilliant, Edie, I knew you could do it!"

He swung her around as she laughed until the announcer walked up and handed Eden a sack of gold along with the promised map. It was tightly wrapped in a tube sealed with wax.

"You did wonderfully, and since you have won this tournament, you are invited back next year to defend your title!" The crowd cheered loudly, but Saphira noticed the group around the other mage seemed to start growing as a loud scream pierced the air.

Everyone turned and watched an angry, teary-eyed woman walk up to Eden. "You killed him! How could you, can't you control that bloody beast inside of you!" she screeched.

The announcer walked up and stopped the woman. "He knew what he was getting into; they all knew this could happen. Magic is unpredictable, madam, you must understand."

"But it wasn't magic; it was that dragon!. You didn't have to kill him!"

Edward stepped up. "Yes, she did! His ogre would have

killed her!"

Eden grabbed her brother's arm and pulled him back. "Let's go, Edward. Hector knew what he was doing when he signed up. He knew this was possible," she said softly. He turned and put an arm around her, and the group followed them back to the tavern to the cheers of everyone watching. When they reached the Tavern, word had already spread, and they walked into cheers and applause. Eden was graceful with all the attention. And despite the horrid conflict with the woman on the battlefield, she was still beaming from her victory. Everyone wanted to buy her drinks or dance with her, and she obliged as much as she could.

CHAPTER 10

HEALER AND THE BOMB

The next morning, the group gathered in the twins' room. Rickert unfolded the map and laid it on the little side table he pulled between the beds.

"So, we have a map and money." Rickert looked up at everyone. "Do we want to follow the map?" It's what Saphira had dreamed about doing. Finding a dungeon and crawling her way through to fame and riches.

"I wouldn't mind," she said, trying to keep her excitement in check. Iollan stood and scrutinized the map.

"I looked at it a little yesterday," Eden said. "There's a lot of ways to go."

Iollan put a finger on the map. "It looks like it starts in Val Shing."

"Do you know how to get there?" Rickert asked.

"Yes, but the dark elves don't particularly like outsiders unless they have something to contribute to the town."

"Dark elves?" Eden sounded a little wary, but they weren't as wild as their top-side cousins, or as evil as the ones far below, just secretive.

"I've dealt with them before," Iollan said. "But I think I know what they'd like." He turned to Saphira and smiled.

Her eyes narrowed. "What? I don't have anything."

"Of course, you do," he walked over and grabbed her hips, and jiggled them the best he could as she sat on the bed. "You can wiggle for them."

Her eyes went wide. "Wiggle?"

"I bet they've never seen a Suya dance before, and they're always looking for new ways to entertain each other. If they had a new dance, I bet it would keep them occupied for months."

Saphira thought for a moment. She honestly didn't know if she could dance without the music. It seemed to call to her, letting her know it was acceptable to move like that in front of people.

"Well—"

"I say we go," Edward spoke up. "And I bet they'll love the dance," he said quietly as he patted her hand.

Saphira looked at Eden. "It's your map, Mage. What do we do?" Eden looked at the old, weathered parchment and leaned forward. She touched the wrinkled edges lightly with her fingertips, like she was waiting for the map to tell her what to do.

"We go," she said quietly.

Rickert clapped his hands together. "All right, it's decided then. We'll make our way to Ral Hava in the morning. Let's supply up today, maybe some of the merchants will give us a discount since we're traveling with the first winner of the tournament." He leaned over and gave Eden a little nudge.

"Do you think we should ask any of the mages here if they'd like to accompany us?" Iollan asked. "We could always benefit from more power."

Eden nodded her head. "Good idea, you and Saphira gather other people. I need to be with the ones getting supplies."

Rickert nodded. "Okay then, we all have our jobs now, let's get to it."

Saphira and Iollan walked down to the tavern, looking for mages who hadn't left yet.

"How about him?" Saphira looked over to where Iollan was pointing and saw Mini McBoom sitting in a corner, eating breakfast.

"Perfect." She smiled and walked over to his table. "Pardon me, Master Mage?"

The little gnome put down his fork and looked up. "Yes, what can I do for you?"

"My name is Saphira Voltain, and this is my associate, Iollan Valare. We are traveling with Mage McVain, and we were wondering if you'd like to join us as we follow the map she recently won?" The little gnome chuckled and waved his hand at the empty chairs across from him.

"Please have a seat."

Saphira and Iollan sat down. "Thank you for at least listening to us, Mage," Iollan said.

"Oh, please call me Xoxim. So, what do you have in your group?" He kept eating as Iollan gushed about the other members. How strong Rickert was and how accurate Edward was with his arrows. "It doesn't sound like you have a healer in your group." The gnome wiped his mouth and pushed his bowl away.

"No, we don't," Saphira said. "It's the one thing we would really like to acquire before going down there."

"Well, I could suggest someone? I don't like to go treasure hunting without a healer. Nasty things can happen, you know."

"Believe me, my imagination has kept me up nights thinking what could be down there," Iollan said.

Xoxim leaned to the side and pointed across the room. "See that woman there in the corner with the long black hair? She's a priestess of Behest, her name is Levia. If you can get her to come with you, then count me in." Saphira knew Behest was a battle god and most of his followers were warriors, even the clerics.

"We shall speak with her then, thank you for the recommendation." Saphira shook his little hand. As they both walked over to the shady table, they saw Levia's eyes were already on them. Saphira smiled and held out her hand. "Levia, right?" The woman cleared her throat and shook Saphira's hand. She looked to be in her late twenties and was a classic beauty with flawless skin and bright blue eyes.

"That's me. Xoxim wants me to join up, doesn't he?" Her accent was much like a Suya's, if not a little bit more formal.

"You heard him all the way over there?" Iollan asked.

The black-haired woman nodded. "I did. You're going into Ral Hava, following the map McVain won, correct?"

"We are, and we are in need of a healer."

"I agree. What are the terms?" She motioned for them to

join her, so they obliged.

"Everyone gets a fair share, along with a party fund. Magic users don't take a watch unless they want to."

"What's fair?" She asked slowly, her eyes wandering over Iollan as her hand rested on her flawless cheek.

"No one gets more than the others." Iollan sounded like he had said it many times before.

"Hmm, I wonder if a group with Mother Lily's progeny as a member would truly be fair."

Saphira sat straight, shocked this priestess knew who she was. "So far anyway, but it's got nothing to do with me. Rickert's a good leader."

Levia nodded her head and seemed to give it some thought. "What if there is no treasure? What do we get then?" Saphira didn't realize priests of Behest were so greedy and crossed her arms over her chest.

"Any spoils you can use, divided fairly among the party. We're sure to find something down there." Levia took a big breath and seemed to give Iollan a wink before turning back to Saphira.

"All right, I'll come with you. When are you leaving?"

"Tomorrow morning, we're supplying up today."

She nodded and leaned forward gracefully. "Well then, I best get ready myself," she turned and yelled over at Xoxim. "We're going again, little gnome!"

He walked over to the table and raised his mug. "Wonderful! We shall meet you downstairs in the morning, and we'll be ready to head off." He and Levia clinked their mugs together. "You're lucky I've been there; we can circumvent a lot of traveling and teleport."

Saphira smiled. "Sounds great, it'll be nice not walking for once. Why don't we all meet down here for dinner tonight so we can get to know everyone?" she suggested.

"I'd be delighted to, Saphira, thank you," Xoxim said.

"Levia, what do you say? Nothing like a dinner with strangers." Saphira smiled at her, but the priestess chuckled.

"No, I don't think so. I have to say goodbye to a certain

yummy someone, and I plan on being in their bed all night, you understand." She got to her feet and left a few coins on the table. "I will see you in the morning, don't leave without me." She pointed at the gnome, and they turned and watched her walk out of the tavern.

"I will see you at dinner!" Xoxim walked back to his table and sat down.

"She's…different than I thought a cleric of Behest would be. But I guess it's better than nothing," Iollan said.

"I think she liked you. Did you see the way she was staring at you?" Saphira teased.

"No, I didn't actually, my eyes were all for you."

Saphira snickered, "Liar."

The dinner with Xoxim went well. He seemed to get along with everyone in the group, and since he recommended Levia, Saphira assumed they got along. As she laid in bed that night, her thoughts were of the coming adventure. It was what she had always dreamed of, crawling around an unexplored cave and finding unimaginable treasure. But what kept her up were the traps, which one usually found while crawling in said dungeons. She hadn't disarmed a trap when their lives were on the line, and prayed to Otto she'd be able to when the time came.

The next morning came too quickly for Saphira, who felt she barely gotten any sleep. Iollan dressed quickly and threw Saphira her shoes.

He ran his hand through his hair. "Excited?"

"I am." She pulled on her boots and felt him flop on the bed behind her.

He smiled and kissed her cheek. "You look tired. I was hoping what we did would have tired you out," he said with a wicked smile.

Saphira giggled. "A little, you hound. Come on, let's get downstairs before they leave without us."

"Okay." She leaned over and gave him a kiss as he helped her to her feet. They had packed the night before, so they put on their packs and walked down to the tavern to meet their group. Downstairs, they saw everyone gathered around, except Levia. Xoxim looked up as they made their way down the stairs.

"Good morning, you two. Levia will be right along," he said.

"I hope so, I'd hate to go down there without a healer," Rickert said.

"I'm sure we'd be able to find someone down there if we had to, Rickert." Iollan didn't look too concerned. Saphira assumed they could find a healer in Ral Hava if they had to.

"No need, Iollan," the group turned, and Saphira saw Levia walk in wearing black chainmail, looking like the deadly warrior of Behest most of his followers were. "I am here. We can leave whenever you're ready." She walked up to Rickert and held out her hand. "Levia, Priestess of Behest."

He took her hand and gave it a hearty shake. "Rickert Basine, this is Edward and Eden McVain. Welcome aboard. I trust Saphira explained how we work?"

"She did."

"Good, well," he turned to Xoxim. "Master Mage, shall we get going?"

"Absolutely, if we could all join hands, we'll be at the entrance to Ral Hava in no time." He held up his little hands. Rickert and Levia both took one, and the others found whatever empty hand there was. Xoxim said some odd words, and Saphira felt magic swirling around the group, pulling them away from the floor. She had never teleported before and found it to be very jarring, but worth the trouble. It would take almost two months to reach their destination by foot. When her feet finally hit solid ground, she found her stomach wasn't as happy to be there as she was. She quickly turned and heaved last night's dinner onto the ground to the chuckles of her group.

Edward rubbed her back. "Are you okay?" She straightened and wiped her mouth with her sleeve, trying not to let her embarrassment show.

"Yeah, didn't expect that." She took a swig of water and

washed her mouth out.

Levia chuckled and gave her back a few pats. "Don't worry, it happens to us all the first time." The group turned and saw the entrance to Ral Hava before them.

"Welcome home, Iollan," Saphira whispered to him. He gave her the barest of smiles but didn't say anything.

"Well, let's get going." Rickert took the lead, and the group fell in line, following quickly. There were a few Dwarven guards, mostly sentries, not anything that could hold back an invading army.

One stepped in front of Rickert. "Traveler, what business do you have here?"

"We have a map that starts in Val Shing. We need to make our way there."

The dwarf nodded and moved. "Just make sure you have something to offer those elves; they can get kind of cranky when they don't get anything."

"Don't worry, sir, we have an idea." Rickert walked past. The group followed him around one corner, and Saphira gasped at the sight. The stairs before them were huge, a good thirty feet across, and the ceiling was so high she could barely see it.

"So big," she whispered. She turned and saw Iollan staring down the stairs. "Are you all right?" He nodded and, without looking at her, started down the stairs.

Levia walked up behind her and whispered in her ear. "Is your man okay? He seems a little nervous."

Saphira nodded. "He hasn't been back here in a long time. I think it's dragging up old ghosts."

"Hmm," Levia nodded and laid a hand on Saphira's shoulder. "Old ghosts are hard to let go of." They walked down the winding stairs for what seemed like hours, but was only about half an hour. Everyone was worn out by the time they reached the bottom.

"Is there a bed nearby cause I'm about to fall flat on my face," Edward said, leaning against the stone wall.

"What's the matter, archer, a couple of stairs beat you into submission?" Levia was clearly the teasing type.

"No." He didn't sound like he knew she was teasing, and she clicked her tongue.

"Edward, you need to loosen up." She put a hand on his neck and began rubbing; he instantly began lolling his head back and forth.

"Where'd you learn to do that?" he asked lazily.

Levia chuckled and let go. "A courtesan, actually," she said and took the lead.

Saphira walked up next to Edward. "Feel good?"

He nodded. "Amazing," he said nervously. Saphira chuckled and wondered if Levia would rub her neck; it did look rather pleasant.

After passing dwarven guard after dwarven guard, they finally reached the city of Ral Hava.

"Rickert, can we please rest here tonight?" Eden asked.

"Absolutely. Iollan, do you know a good one?"

He turned and nodded. "Yeah, if it's still there." He began leading the way. Saphira's eyes tried to take in everything as they walked. Light seemed to shine out of the stalagmites and stalactites, so there was plenty of light for the humans. The buildings were built from the surrounding rocks, and Saphira bet it was comfortable year-round temperature wise and the smells! Cooking meat and spices she'd never smelled before made her mouth water, and she hoped to taste it soon. Iollan led them to a tavern called 'The Stoney Fist,' and Rickert got a few rooms for the group. That night, Iollan seemed to fall asleep quickly, like he usually did. Saphira tossed and turned. She was exhausted, but her mind wouldn't stop thinking about what lay before them. Eventually, she gave up and made her way downstairs and ordered a warm cider. Her mother always said it helped to ease a troubled mind. As she sat with her hands around the warm mug, she heard the priestess's voice.

"Saphira?" She looked up and saw Levia walk over with an ale, "Thought you went to bed." She took the empty chair across from her, and Saphira could tell she looked curious.

"I did, couldn't sleep."

"Something on your mind?" Levia took a big drink and sighed, "Gods, I love Dwarven ale. So strong you can forget all your troubles," she said with a big smile.

Saphira giggled. "It's disgusting, I don't know how you can drink it."

"Quickly," she said before chugging the rest of her drink. "Now what could possibly trouble you? Nervous about where we're going?"

Saphira shrugged. "In a way."

"Is it your young man?"

"No, it's just," she sighed. She didn't want to admit how green she was when it came to wandering around caves. But everyone had to start somewhere.

Levia reached out and laid a hand on Saphira's. "I am a priestess, no matter who I may worship, I can help. Whatever you tell me will be kept in confidence." Saphira could feel Levia's holy power radiating from her, like a comforting blanket being pulled around her. It was almost too much to bear.

"Um, well," her bottom lip quivered a bit, and she quickly bit it still. "I can't stop worrying about the group dying from a mistake I could make. I've wanted to go dungeon crawling for as long as I can remember. But now that it's actually happening, it's scary."

Levia nodded. "It is scary, no matter how many times you've gone after treasure. There's always something new around the corner waiting to pounce on you and your friends. But you are Mother Lily's daughter, you are blessed beyond most, and I know you will keep us safe. I feel lucky, such a talented young lady will be making sure our path is safe."

Saphira smiled. "Thank you, Levia, it does me good to know you have such faith in me." The priestess patted her shoulder and gave her a smile before ordering one last mug of ale.

"Why don't you go back to bed? I think you'll find sleep

will come easier now." Saphira nodded and went back up to her room. She was beginning to feel the journey of the day catching up with her and was surprised at how much better she felt after talking about her fears, and soon sleep found her and gave her wonderful dreams.

CHAPTER 11

DANCE OF A THOUSAND EYES

The group felt much better in the morning and quickly set out for Val Shing. They took a corner and Iollan froze, staring at a huge wall with thousands of little depressions, most had lit candles in them.

"What is it?" Saphira laid a hand on his arm. Rickert stopped when he heard her voice. Everyone turned and saw what he was staring at.

"Can we…stop for a moment?" Iollan asked, looking at the group as he put his pack down.

"Course we can." Levia walked over to Rickert and whispered something to him while Iollan walked closer to the wall. Saphira saw their boss's faces go from curious to sorrowful and nodded as he took his pack off and leaned back against the opposite wall. The twins looked at each other, unsure what was going on, but did the same. Levia stood next to Rickert, and Xoxim stood in front of her, her hand laid on his little bald head. Saphira watched as Iollan took a small stick and lit it from one of the candles, then lit a candle that had no flame. She walked up behind him and laid a hand on his back.

"My father was from Garythane," he said as he stood before the candle he lit. "But he hated it like most do, so he left with me in tow after my mother died, I was two. He came here because he wanted to see the marvel of the dwarven capital. He got a job with one of the many blacksmiths here, and we had a good life, but he got sick." He reached down and took her hand. "Whatever it was, worked quick, he didn't last a year. I was eight. The blacksmith who he worked for took me in, treated me like I was his own. His name was Wilfrum. When I was thirteen, one of the forges got a crack in it. He didn't notice until it was too late;

it blew up, and he didn't make it. I lost two fathers here in Ral Have. I never thought I'd be back."

Saphira laid her head on his shoulder. "I'm so sorry, Iollan, I had no idea it would be so hard for you to come here."

He breathed deeply. "It's not like I told anyone, but sometimes you have to face the ghosts." She felt him kiss her head. "When Wilfrum died, I decided to go to Garythane, see where I came from. I didn't find anything but death and disappointment."

"There was nothing to keep you there?"

He took a few breaths. "There might have been one thing. But it took me years to get out after I got back. I had to leave."

"Is it hard to leave?"

He swallowed hard. "It can be. You need a good reason, or a rich benefactor." He turned back to the group and picked up his pack. "Okay, we can go." Everyone picked up their packs, Rickert walked over and laid a hand on Iollan's shoulder, and gave him a nod before continuing down the path. Eden gave him a hug, and Edward patted his arm and followed their boss. Xoxim gave a little bow to the wall, and Levia gave his face a gentle pat before following the rest of them. Iollan took Saphira's hand, and they followed Rickert down the road. She gave his hand a squeeze, and he sighed. "I'm glad you're here with me."

"Me too."

The group continued deeper into the mountain, towards Val Shing. Saphira's eyes were on constant alert, and often she found things the others didn't see, like a deep crack in the road or a little cave mouse. It would take several days for the group to reach the dark elf city. Saphira had never been so far into the earth before, and she could feel it cooling off. She was glad she had her one wrap for when they stopped for the night. Rickert said this road was one of the safer roads to Val Shing, so they talked and continued to get to know each other. Xoxim was old for a gnome, around two hundred and fifty, but he said he didn't look a day over a hundred, and Levia said she couldn't eat cheese. That made everyone feel sorry for her.

A few hours later, the stone hallway opened up to reveal the outskirts of Val Shing. It reminded Saphira of Ral Hava in a way, carvings made into the stone, but they seemed fancier, more swirls than the ninety-degree angles in the dwarven art. The dark elves standing guard were also a dead giveaway the group had reached their destination. They were tall like elves usually were, but their skin ranged from dark purple to gray, their white hair looked like it could glow in the dark, and their armor was shining obsidian. Rickert smiled as they walked through the gateway into the big city without being asked to stop. Inside looked much like the first city they saw down here, lots of buildings made from stone, but there wasn't much light here. Val Shing may have been a dark elf city, but it was the only one that tolerated outsiders. This was the reason the other dark elf cities ignored it. No trade, no commerce from their sister cities, so Val Shing relied heavily on Ral Hava, and travelers to bring the things they needed. Hence, the warning from everyone that they needed to bring something good.

Levia took out a coin. "Behest, let me see my way." They heard her say a second before the coin shined with her god's light. There were a few dark elves walking over to them, but they didn't look like guards, more like representatives. Their clothing was dark and flowy.

"Surface travelers, what brings you to our city?" One of them asked, in common with an interesting lilting accent.

Rickert took out the map. "We are going here, and the beginning of our journey is in your fair city." He was pouring on the charm like a good leader, but the dark elf who spoke simply scoffed.

"What gives you claim on such a treasure, human?"

"Well, if we're worthy of it, we'll make it out alive, won't we?"

The elf shifted on one foot and held his chin. "Hmm, I suppose you're right, but you'll have to make it through our town first. We don't let adventurers through without some kind of boon."

Iollan moved up through the group. "We have a boon for the entire city."

The elves' eyes widened. "Entire city, huh? Well, let me lead you to some shelter." He motioned with long skinny fingers for them to follow him. They walked for about fifteen minutes. Saphira could see their dark eyes staring at them as they walked through the town. The elf reached a little lean to next to a grand house. "You may stay here until you start your journey. When you're ready to give us your boon, my man Beleg will show you to the square. I hope for your sake it's good."

The elf walked off, and Xoxim quickly set his pack down. "So, what is the boon?" he asked, sitting down.

Rickert motioned at Saphira. "Our rogue is going to do a Suya dance for them."

"A Suya dance?" The gnome and cleric echoed each other; both sounded rather shocked.

Levia's eyes were wide as she looked her over. "You know how to do a Suya dance?"

"Yeah, I learned for the Bell Festival a few weeks ago."

Levia smiled. "Oh, the Bell Festival, it's been a while since I've seen it." She slid next to Saphira, a mischievous smirk on her face. "Did you dance for Iollan?"

"I did actually." She smiled at the memory.

He took her hand and gave her a sweet kiss. "I can't wait to see it again," he whispered. She giggled and began digging through her bag for the clothes the Suya gladly let her have.

"I wish there was music, I'm not sure how well I can dance without it."

"I can help you there, Saphira," Xoxim called out. "You shall have music, don't worry."

"Thank you," she didn't bother hiding the relief in her voice. "That'll help a great deal."

She pulled out her skimpy outfit, and Levia whistled lecherously. "I think all you'll have to do is go out in that outfit and they'll give us whatever they want."

"Levia, really." Saphira could feel her cheeks blush as the

cleric laughed loudly. When she was dressed in her outfit, they found the elf named Beleg, who led them to the town square. As they walked into the middle of the square, Saphira couldn't help but think the entire town showed up; word traveled fast.

"There's so many people," she said quietly.

Rickert nodded. "Figured there would be, a boon for the entire town is rare."

"Is there anything else you need besides music, Saphira?" Xoxim asked. There was already a big bonfire going in the square; it was all she felt was missing.

"No, I think I've got everything."

Rickert held out his hand. "Let's get this over with so you can start doing things a rogue is *supposed* to do."

She smiled at him and took his hand. "Yes, please."

They both walked to the fire, and Saphira listened to Rickert speak. "City of Val Shing, my name is Rickert Basine, and this is my associate Saphira. She has something for you I think you will like." As he talked, she looked over at her friends. Iollan had a smile full of heat across his face; she knew it would help her move knowing he was watching. Edward and Eden were sitting next to each other, both smiling, encouraging her on. Xoxim was getting ready to cast, and that was when she noticed Levia was nowhere to be seen. Her eyes scanned the crowd, but when Rickert gave her hand a squeeze and walked over to Eden, Saphira knew she had to concentrate.

She took a deep breath and raised her hands above her head, and nodded at Xoxim. His little hands moved quickly, and soon sultry violin music filled the air. She smiled and closed her eyes, letting the music take her away. Her body moved slowly at first; she wanted to make sure they saw how she moved her hips. Her hands danced in the air; this part always made her feel feminine. There was something about teasing the air with her fingers that appealed to her.

Suddenly, the music sped up, and she began jingling the bells on her skirt as her hips began to wiggle back and forth, her hands slowly moving down, mimicking falling leaves. She planned on putting them on her hips, but suddenly a hand grabbed hers, and her eyes flew open. Levia was next to her, wearing her own skimpy black outfit and moving skillfully to the music. She gave Saphira a little wink and began dancing around her while the rogue tried to regain her composure. The more the elves liked the dance, the better cooperation they would get, and when Saphira noticed their dark eyes taking in their dance, she knew it would work.

Levia moved in front of her, and she heard the cleric whisper.

"Lean back." So, she raised her arms again and stepped back with one leg. As she teased the air with her fingers, she felt something soft tickling her stomach and looked down. Levia had closed the distance by leaning forward. It was the cleric's hair she felt tickling her. *Boy, if they don't like this, they're dead,* she thought as Levia leaned back up and moved behind her. They began dancing in tandem as they moved around the fire. When Saphira danced for Iollan, it was just her, but as she danced with Levia, she realized there was much more to the dance than the Suya women showed her. Levia's fingers laced with hers, so Saphira let her move them to the music; she was obviously an old pro at this sort of thing.

The cleric expertly turned Saphira and put her hands on her curvy hips. She tried to mimic her movements, but Saphira knew she was out of practice. "Saphira." She heard Levia whisper and looked up, "Keep your eyes up, it's okay if you don't match me." She gave a little nod and moved the way she knew how. Both dancers had their hands on the other's hips as the music slowed a little. "How long is this song?" Levia asked.

"No idea, maybe Xoxim will stop the spell when we stop."

"Okay, better give them a good ending then." Saphira suddenly found herself spinning around and was dipped skillfully by the cleric. The music stopped, and all she could hear was her breathing. She looked up at Levia, who suddenly laid a kiss on her neck. A collective sigh rippled through the crowd, and Saphira knew they had succeeded in their task. Levia helped her up, and they walked back to their group.

Rickert's mouth was hanging open. "Uh, well, if that doesn't work," he blew out a breath. "Uh, yeah." Levia laughed loudly, and Saphira joined her. She had never had such an effect on a man before. It made her feel powerful in a whole new way. Eden's eyes were wide, and Edward was breathing fast like Rickert, but he managed to keep his tongue in his mouth. Saphira walked over to Iollan, who quickly took her in his arms and kissed her furiously.

"The second we're alone, I'm going to show you what you did to me with that dance," he whispered and gently bit her neck where Levia had kissed her.

The dark elf they had encountered when they entered the city walked up to them. "No one has ever danced for us, especially like that." It was hard to read his face with his black eyes, but Saphira could tell his breath was coming a little quicker than before. "We accept your boon and will help anyway we can."

Saphira smiled, and Levia gave her hand a little squeeze. "I knew they couldn't resist," she whispered. The representative showed them to an actual house where they were able to spread out and relax after their walk. A lot of dark elves came by with food and wash bins so they could freshen up. Saphira was glad for the wash bin, dancing by the fire got her all sweaty, and she relaxed in the cool water as Iollan scrubbed her skin.

"So, I take it you liked the dance," she teased.

Iollan chuckled, and she heard him take his shirt off. "Even more than the first time." She turned and watched as his pants fell to the floor. His body was ready to please her, and she smiled.

"I see that." He slowly made his way in the water, and she wrapped her legs around his waist. "We're going to make an awful mess."

Iollan kissed her neck and sheathed himself inside her with a gasp. "I don't care," he whispered.

CHAPTER 12
GHOSTS OF THE PAST

The next morning, the group gathered in the common room of the house and went over the map again. It was on a table between them all, and Eden began tracing her finger down it.

"The entrance is a door through this passage here," the young mage's finger stopping at what looked like a door.

"Where did this map come from? Did they tell you, Eden?" Xoxim asked, but she shook her head and sat back.

"Unfortunately, no."

"Hmm," the little gnome held his chin, "Well, what about the treasure, any clue?" Eden leaned forward again and pointed to a little passage written on the back of the map.

"It says the bones of the past can lead to riches or death. What bones and what riches it doesn't specify."

"Foreboding, isn't it?" Edward snarked.

"Most maps lead to foreboding things, archer," Levia said, running her hands through his hair. "That's the point in being an adventurer, doing things others don't have the courage to."

"I know, I just hate going in with almost no idea what's in there. It's my least favorite part of this."

Rickert handed the map to Saphira. "Get a good look, rogue, we'll be following you after we get past the first door." Saphira took it and could see it was easy to follow one main corridor that had five offshoots. There were several rooms down those hallways, and towards the end, there was a large room, but no indication of what was inside.

She nodded and rolled it back up. "Seems pretty easy, we'll see what's changed after we get in there. Who knows how old this map is."

Everyone stood and put on their packs. Saphira took a

deep breath to calm her heart. *Here we go,* she thought.

As the group walked to the tunnel, Saphira took her place at the front of the line and watched as they passed dark elf after dark elf imitating the dance. Rickert was right, they'd be entertained for months after watching her dance for a few minutes. Saphira smiled at how she and Levia helped bring them something new, until she saw the tunnel they had to go through. It was partly blocked off by fallen stone.

"Come with me, Saphira," Xoxim said. "The rest wait here." They did as they were told, and Saphira watched the little gnome squeeze through the three-foot-wide hole with no problem. Saphira took off her pack and tossed it through before she practically flatted herself to get through.

"That was fun." She said sarcastically.

Xoxim chuckled. "Levia told me this was your first crawl, so I thought I'd show you that sometimes, only you can fit through. What would you do now?"

She put her pack back on, and her hands went to her hips. "I might ask the wonderful mage with me to make the hole bigger for everyone else."

Xoxim clapped his hands together once. "Perfect in this situation." He cast a spell, and the hole grew big enough that even Rickert wouldn't have to duck to get in. "The next question is what you do when you don't have a wonderful mage at your side."

"Be more prepared." Saphira chuckled. The group filed through the bigger hole, and Levia lit up a coin and gave it to Saphira so she could see where she was walking. Since no one lived here anymore, the torches didn't work, so the group had to rely on their own light sources. Saphira swept the coin back and forth, looking for anything out of the ordinary. She walked a good twenty feet in front of the group, making sure the route ahead was safe, but they reached the door on the map without any issues. It was made of stone, and as Saphira studied it, she realized she couldn't read the words that were carved into it. She could tell there was magic on the door, but there were no traps or locks.

"There is magic, but I can't find anything harmful about the door; it's not even locked."

Rickert stepped up and grabbed the handle. "Here we go then." He pulled, but nothing happened. "I thought you said it wasn't locked."

"It's not, it must be the magic," Xoxim said as he and Levia stepped up and cast different spells. The little gnome nodded his head. "There is blood magic holding the door shut. Can you read the words, Levia?" She stepped up and began touching the words lightly. Saphira couldn't help but notice how uneasy she seemed.

"Yes, I can. It basically says only someone of controversial birth can open the door."

"Controversial birth? What does that mean?" Saphira stepped up and wished she could read the words herself.

"Well, what's controversial?" Eden held her chin, "It could mean a unique way of being born, someone who was cut out of their mother instead of the normal way? Or I've heard of babies being stillborn who miraculously came back to life."

"Perhaps, but I don't think anyone here fits that description," Edward said.

Levia sighed and clicked her tongue. "I think what it refers to is the first controversial way of being born."

"The first?" Iollan asked.

She nodded. "One born of man and woman who aren't joined by a god in matrimony."

Saphira's eyes widened as Edward walked next to her. "What an odd way to open a door."

The cleric shrugged. "Perhaps the creator was like this and wanted to give a leg up to those who are normally shunned by their society. Rickert?"

He chuckled and shook his head. "As wild as I look, my parents were married when I was born, as were the twins. I take it doesn't describe you, Levia?"

"No, it does not, Iollan?"

He shrugged his shoulders. "I assume so, but I'll give it a try." He walked up and pulled on the door, but nothing happened. "Guess I'm more legit than I knew. Xoxim?"

He barked a little laugh. "Gnomes don't usually marry, so I'll give it a try." He moved up to the door and pulled on the handle, but it didn't budge. "Guess they didn't mean gnomes when they made this door. We could ask one of the dark elves to accompany us, at least this far."

Saphira flexed her fingers. "Good idea, Xoxim, we don't all have to go; it's safe from here back to the town." She wrapped her hand around the handle and gave it a little tug. "Rickert, why don't you and Eden go—" the door flew open and knocked her back a few feet onto her backside. "Ow! What the hell!" She looked up to find everyone staring at her. "What?"

Rickert walked over and kneeled next to her. "I think perhaps you have some explaining to do when we're done with this," he whispered and yanked her to her feet by her pack straps.

"About what?"

"About how Mother Lily's third-born was able to open a door she shouldn't have been able to."

She couldn't help but think he sounded mad. "Rickert, I don't—" but he turned and walked to the group.

"Okay, our rogue got us in, let's go." Saphira crossed her arms and watched everyone except Iollan file in.

He stopped next to her and put a hand on her back, and she whispered to him. "What's going on?"

"Rickert thinks you've been lying to him about who you are."

She gasped. "What? I would never, hell, if I did, it might make it easier to get around without everyone knowing who I am!"

He quickly gave her a soft kiss. "I know you wouldn't, but let's get through this, and later you can convince him who you are, okay? We were probably wrong about what opens the door anyway." He picked up the glowing coin, and she took it. She couldn't help but be incredibly annoyed. She didn't see any benefit to pretending to be her mother's child, especially since it attracted unwanted attention.

"Fine." The group had waited for her so she could take the lead again. Saphira noticed the twins looked at her, almost warily. *Please don't let them think I'm lying,* she prayed. Eden was her best friend. She wouldn't be able to handle it if Eden all of a sudden hated her. Saphira swept the coin back and forth, looking for telltale signs of trouble, desperately trying to keep her mind off what Rickert and the twins might think of her. When they reached the first fork, she waited for the group and inspected the entryways. To the right, it was clear, but to the left, there was a little trip wire

"Hold up, let me get this real quick." She told the group who stopped a few feet back. She got out her little tool kit and followed the trip wire into the hallway. It was attached to a torch, and she figured if it tripped, a lit torch would actually cause more trouble. She was able to attach the wire to the wall with a small fastener, and with a quick snip, the wire in the doorway fell lax, and she made her way back to the group. "Both ways are safe now. Which way do we want to go?" She tried keeping her voice as neutral as possible, but a little snark still snuck through as she crossed her arms and stared at the ground.

"Well," the gnome held his chin. "Usually, the good stuff is where the traps are, so I say left."

Rickert nodded. "I agree, left it is. We can come back and get the right after."

"All right then." Saphira held up her coin and led the way down the left hallway. A few feet down from the trapped torch was the first door, right where the map said. She couldn't see without her coin, but needed her hands free, so Saphira stuck the coin in the seashell around her neck. It worked perfectly. Slowly, she went over the door and found it was locked and rusty, but not trapped. Saphira pulled out a little bottle and poured the clear contents on the lock, and ran a tiny brush on the inside of it.

"Ugh, what smells so bad?" Edward held his nose.

"Vinegar." Saphira stood straight and put everything

away before pulling out her lock picks. "Helps dissolve rust." She quickly picked the now rust-free deadbolt and opened the door. Rickert stepped in first, his sword drawn, and Saphira followed after. Her coin lit about half of the room.

"Here, this outta help." Xoxim stepped in and cast a complicated looking spell. Suddenly, a light coalesced into the shape of a person in the middle of the room. "It'll walk around the room and let us see anything good," he said proudly.

"Great, but what if it springs a trap?" Saphira asked.

"Not to worry, Saphira; it's not corporeal." And waved the light man to walk around the room. The group stepped in and watched as it revealed another door on the other side of the room.

"Now that door isn't on the map," Saphira said.

"Hmm, shall we?" Rickert bowed and waved her forward towards the door.

"We shall." She moved over to the door, and after five minutes of looking, she turned to the group. "There's a magical trap, a mundane trap, and the door's locked," she said, getting to her feet. "It might take me a minute, so stay aware." She pulled out her kit and studied the magical one first. It was a simple trap but a powerful spell. If it went off, a fireball would fill the room in intervals and roast anyone in it. "Xoxim, want to try and get rid of the magic?" she called out behind her.

"Sure!" He walked up to the door, and they watched his hands move in complicated patterns in front of him before he huffed. "Dung beetles. It's a bit beyond me, apparently," he sounded irritated. "Eden?"

She walked up and cast the same spell, but nothing happened. "Too much for me."

"Guess I'll give it a try then," Saphira turned to the group. "Why don't you all wait in the hall in case I trip it. I don't want anyone getting hurt." Rickert nodded and moved to the hallway, as did Xoxim, Levia, and Edward, but Iollan and Eden stayed put.

"We don't want you getting hurt either," Iollan said.

"I'll be fine, but I doubt you can move fast enough in that chain shirt. Please, trust me." He sighed and ushered Eden out into the hall after she gave Saphira's arm a squeeze. Saphira cracked her neck and went to work on the door. First, she unlocked it with ease, then found the trap. If the door opened without the trap being disabled, a little door would open in the floor, and the unlucky person standing on it would fall, who knows how far, onto who knows what nasty thing.

Saphira spiked the floor trap until she was satisfied it wouldn't move, then stood before the door. The reason she asked Xoxim and Eden to try and dispel the door was because the second she found the magic trap, she knew she wouldn't be able to disable it either. For her to get rid of the fire, she needed the rune from which the spell originated. But she could tell whoever made this trap was a tricky little devil. She could feel the magic of the rune on the other side of the door. Which meant she wouldn't be able to stop it from triggering. One thing she learned by listening to old travelers was that sometimes, the only solution was to spring the trap. Saphira cracked her fingers and opened the door. Fire filled the room in intervals starting by the door, and she rolled backwards out of the way. The next spout triggered, and cut her off from the door to the hallway, and she could hear her friends yelling for her. When the fire subsided, she leaped into the hallway as the entire room filled with the fireball.

"Saphira!" Iollan wrapped his arms around her, "I thought you were dead!" He kissed her deeply before letting her go.

"I told you to trust me. I had to trip it so we could get through." He moved around her and began slapping her backside. "Hey!" She turned and covered her bum with her hands.

"You're on fire o' slippery rogue," he teased.

She gasped and took over patting out the smoke that was rising from behind her. "Well, I almost made it out."

"Is it safe now?" their boss asked.

"Yeah, all clear." Rickert pulled out his sword again and made his way into the room. It smelled like smoke, and they coughed as they made their way through the scorched door.

The hallway before them was plain stone and covered in dust. "This part isn't on the map. Is there a way we can add it?" Eden asked. Saphira brought it out and noticed the big blank spot right where they were.

"Looks like it." She took out a charcoal pencil and began drawing what she saw in the empty space. It was easy; it was only one hallway with a single door at the end. When she was done, she rolled it back up and put it in its case. "Shall we?" Rickert nodded, and the group walked up to the ornate door. It was made of sturdy wood and was decorated with silver and gold flowers. Saphira did her thing and found the door wasn't locked or trapped.

"Rickert, would you like to go in first?" With one hand, he slowly opened the door. It creaked with age, and to their delight and confusion, it opened into a room with lit candles every foot or so. The room was sweet and inviting, not musty like the rest of the tunnels. One by one they cautiously walked inside. The carpet under their feet was soft and colorful.

"Why does it look like someone lives here?" Edward asked. They were in the middle of the room when a loud bang startled them. Eden yelped as they all turned and saw a half-elven woman standing by the door. Saphira's mouth dropped when she realized the woman was see-through. Her hair was a lighter color in life and seemed to float in the air around her head.

"What are you doing here?" Her voice was quiet and sad, but when her eyes landed on Saphira, the ghost gave the group a small smile.

Levia stood in front of everyone and held her holy symbol high. "We are following a map and found this hidden room." They watched as the woman floated over to Levia, a curious look on her face. "Is that a holy symbol?" The ghost asked, pointing at the small sword the cleric held in her hand.

"Um, yes, it is, it's one of the three symbols of Behest."

"Behest? I've never heard of Behest." Everybody was a bit taken aback, everyone knew who the god of war was.

Saphira held up her seashell. "What about this one, does

it look familiar?" The ghost floated over to her, but there wasn't anything in her face that showed recognition.

"It's a shell," she said, not a hint of teasing in her voice.

Saphira fought not to roll her eyes. "It's a holy symbol for Otto, god of the sea."

"Otto? How many child gods are there now?"

Levia's eyes widened. "Child gods? How dare—"

Rickert stepped up and grabbed the cleric's arm. "Pardon our cleric, miss, she is extremely loyal to her god. Do you have a name?"

The ghost studied him as she floated around the group. "Elralia." Saphira looked to see if she had any symbols around her neck, but there was nothing.

"Elralia, I am Rickert. This is Levia, Iollan, Xoxim, Saphira, Ed, and Eden." She flew quickly over to the twins, who gasped as she stopped right in front of them.

"Twins," she smiled. "I've not seen twins in a long time." She floated closer to Edward and reached a hand out, but stopped short of touching his cheek.

"How long have you been down here, miss?" Ed asked, trying to stay calm.

"I don't know. Longer than the other one, but she has been here longer than the dragon. Everyone's eyes widened.

"Dragon? Where?" Saphira asked.

Elralia floated over to Saphira and pointed at the map case. "I can try to show you."

Quickly, Saphira took the map out and laid it on the floor. "This room isn't on the map, but we're here." She pointed to the new door she had drawn.

Elralia seemed to cross her legs and float closer to the ground. "Old map, it's been a long time since I've seen it."

"When was the last time?" Saphira asked, wondering how many other groups had come down here the same way.

The ghosts' eyes continued to scan the map. "I was still alive," she said quietly. Her hand moved over the dried parchment, and they watched as the walls on the map moved, making an entirely new map. "Better," she said with a smile. "We are here."

They all leaned in, and sure enough, the room they were in was on the map. "How did you do that?" Levia ran her fingers over the new area of the map.

"It's magical. The right spell would have done it."

Rickert looked at Xoxim, who shrugged his shoulders. "I detected no magic from it."

"Neither did I," Eden said.

"You wouldn't, you're not dead," Elralia said it like it should have been obvious. As they looked over the 'new' map, Saphira noticed the large empty area now had writing in it.

"Can you read what it says?" She asked the ghost.

Her eyes floated over to the lettering, and she read aloud. "'Bones are not always bones, treasure is not always the treasure you seek, but the treasure you already have.' This map leads to where the dragon is."

Edward's eyebrows furled in confusion. "What does it mean?"

"I think it's a warning," Saphira said. "Best to leave certain things alone and be grateful for what you have. Not many people survive against a dragon."

Elralia nodded. "Well said, blood of Vale. It's been so long, I'm sure the dragon is dead. Only the other has been in here for centuries, and she leaves the treasure alone; she has no need of it." Saphira flinched at what the ghost called her; she had never heard anyone be called Blood of Vale in her life. It worried her that Rickert would take it to mean she had indeed been lying about who she was.

"Who is this other one you speak of?" Xoxim asked. Elralia 'stood' and 'sat' down in one of the large chairs in the room.

"The other one here, it's only us, but she doesn't come to see me very often. I scare her at times. She can be skittish."

"Well, what is this other, so we know not to harm her if we come across her." Rickert sat in the chair across from her, a puff of dust floated into the air as he did.

"She is female."

Rickert waited until it was clear she wasn't going to continue. "Yes, I gathered. I guess what I meant was, what race is she? What's her name, that sort of thing." Elralia shrugged her shoulders and shook her head. "You don't know?"

"No, I don't. I've been here longer, but she is older than I. She does not speak to me."

Rickert furled his eyebrows and turned back to the group. "Well, what shall we do?"

Eden was staring at the ghost like she was a new favorite toy. "I think we should stay here and get to know Elralia."

The ghost smiled at the mage. "No one has known me for a long time; I would like it if you stayed to visit." They all looked at each other. It was an interesting prospect, Saphira thought; she'd never met a ghost before.

"I'm fine with staying here." No one argued, so they took their packs off, much to the delight of the ghost.

"I shall tell you a story of my god if you'd like to hear?"

Levia sat in front of her and nodded. "I would be interested in hearing about your god."

Elralia smiled and laid her hands in her lap. "Her name is Nyceena, and she rules over home and hearth." As she kept chattering on about her god, Saphira went through every god she had ever heard of, new, old, dead, imprisoned, and the name Nyceena wasn't among them. Either Elralia was a crazy ghost, or she was so old no one remembered her God anymore.

Elralia talked a long time about Nyceena; her aspect sort of reminded Saphira of the current goddess of the home, Etara. Whether this was the same goddess with a new name or a whole new divine aspect, she wasn't sure. Saphira leaned back against one of the other chairs while Iollan sat next to her.

"Saphira?" he whispered. "What do you think she meant by 'blood of Vale'?"

She turned and shrugged her shoulders. "Your guess is as good as mine. Elralia?"

The ghost turned and smiled at her. "Yes?"

"Earlier, you called me 'blood of Vale', why?" She tried hard not to look at Rickert.

"The blood of Vale runs through your veins, did you not know this?"

She shrugged. "My mother's maiden name was Vale, but I don't see why that's significant."

Elralia gave a ghostly sigh. "I don't understand how you humans could have lost so much of your past. Vale was a four-aspect deity; he presided over healing, battle, valor, and the sea."

"Sounds like a mix of Behest and Otto," Levia said.

Elralia nodded. "From what you've told me, I believe Behest and Otto come from Vale. In my lifetime, we lost a lot, god wise. But I believe they are alive and well in the ones you worship today."

"Okay, wait, you said *blood* of Vale, explain that part." Saphira got to her feet and began pacing as the ghost explained.

"Vale liked the flesh and would often wander the world in mortal form. It is said one day while walking in Fairwinds, he fell in love with the daughter of a fisherman and had a son by her. He had no last name to give her, so she gave her son the surname Vale, so he'd always have a connection with his father. All those with the last name Vale are believed to be of his line. I could tell it was in you because I haven't felt Vale in a long time. I immediately recognized it in you."

Saphira shook her head. "No, my father and brother are the favored ones. They have the mark of the gods on them, not me."

Elralia smiled and pulled up her sleeve. "Like this?" Saphira walked closer and saw the familiar white, crescent-shaped mark on the inside of her arm.

She gasped and tried hard not to reach out. "Yes! Exactly that!"

Elralia smiled. "That the mark is still carried on gives me great peace. It is the Mark of the Exalted. My great-grandmother was the first of our line to carry such a mark. She got it by helping defeat The Shackled One the first time." She touched the mark on her arm. "If only it were enough."

"So, those marks are passed down generationally?" Xoxim walked over and studied the ghost's birthmark.

"Yes. One in a generation will have it. My first son had it, after...I do not know, but I'm glad the line has merged with Vale's. Your family must be special indeed. I am glad to know you, Saphira."

"I'm glad to know you, too, Elralia..."

She smiled. "Eilric." Saphira gave her a nod and moved over to the mirror and stared at her reflection.

Iollan walked up behind her and put his hands on her arms. "Are you all right?"

She leaned back into his chest. "Yeah, just a lot of stories going around lately. It's hard to know what's really true or not." They stood together while Elralia talked for hours about whatever Eden asked her. It was a different start to the adventure than Saphira had pictured, speaking with a ghost she might have descended from. But Elralia had been gone so long, Saphira didn't think there'd be a way to definitively prove it. Eventually, she and Iollan sat down, and Elralia's soft, constant voice put Saphira to sleep.

CHAPTER 13

THE FIRST SAD STORY

A creaking noise made Saphira's ear twitch, and she opened her eyes. The group was asleep, scattered around Elralia's room, but no one else seemed to be awake. Iollan had fallen asleep next to her, and she could smell the leather of his armor and smiled. The squeak happened again, and Saphira jumped as Elralia popped up from the floor.

"It's the other, she is curious about you," she whispered and disappeared. Saphira's eyes focused and watched an odd-looking hand slip around the door and push it open. It was thin and yellow with odd brown marks along the fingers. Slowly, an arm came into view that matched the hand, clearly this person wasn't human. A foot slipped in, and Saphira watched as what she believed to be a Grimun walked into the room. She was clearly female; her clothes were rags that hung off her skin, not hiding much underneath. Saphira would bet if one of them touched the cloth, it would disintegrate.

The Grimun's face seemed neutral, considering Saphira thought they were a blood thirsty race. They mostly lived underground, but occasionally they'd raid a village on the surface. You could tell it was a Grimun raid because there were hardly any survivors. The other, as Elralia dubbed her, moved slowly across the room, and when she turned Saphira saw light gleaming off a large blade on her back. It was the only thing the Grimun had that was in pristine condition. Saphira watched as the woman leaned over Levia and Edward and seemed to sniff the air around them. Luckily, neither the cleric nor archer woke up. If she did, Saphira had no doubt, there would be a fight. The woman moved over a few inches and sniffed the air around Rickert and Eden. The other found nothing of note by their boss and stood straight, looking at Saphira. She could finally see the other's face, along with the horrid wound on her head. It looked like someone tried to bash in her skull, but she survived.

"Saphira?" She turned and saw Rickert was wide awake and reaching for his sword.

"It's okay, Rickert, don't make any sudden movements," she said quietly.

The Grimun turned her head at Rickert and sat down on the ground. "Regdur unshe," she said quietly.

"Levia, Xoxim, wake up," Rickert called out as he gently shook Eden awake. Quickly, all the casters woke and saw they weren't alone.

"Whoa." Iollan woke up and tried to get in front of Saphira, but the Grimun shook her head and pointed at him as she chatted in her harsh language.

"Can anybody tell what she's saying?" Rickert asked.

All the magic users cast the same spell, but Levia spoke first. "It's a form of under common, but I think she's speaking it backwards?"

"That wouldn't surprise me," Iollan said. "Look at the wound on her head, I bet it messed her up pretty good." Slowly, Levia began speaking to the woman, who instantly turned and smiled before she began talking back.

Levia quieted her and relayed to the group what she had said. "She said it's been a long time since anyone talked to her, she doesn't remember her name, but people used to call her Shortwick."

"Odd name," Edward said. Levia spoke slowly in the other language and introduced the group one by one. After she said a name, 'Shortwick' would repeat it back. Rickert became Rechert, Eden was Aden, Edward got the distinction of being called Adwin, Levia was Lavia, Xoxim got a laugh out of her, but when Levia introduced Saphira, Shortwick pointed at her.

"Vale."

"Oh, not again." She sighed and laid her head in her hands. "She must have heard Elralia or something."

She felt Iollan's hand on her shoulder. "Maybe."

"Levia, can you ask her if she knows how to get to the dragon's horde?" The cleric nodded and began chatting in the odd language again. Shortwick stood and began pointing around the room, like she was giving directions.

"She knows the way, has seen the bones of a dragon, but they scare her."

Rickert nodded. "Well, shall we try and raid a dead dragon's horde?"

"Absolutely." Edward smiled.

Iollan turned and gave Saphira a kiss. "Let's get ready to raid our first dragon horde."

She smiled. "Sounds fun."

The group did not see Elralia before they left, since she said she scared Shortwick; no one was surprised she didn't show up. Shortwick seemed more than happy to show the group how to get to the dragon's lair, so she led the way, followed closely by Saphira. Every time the group encountered some kind of trap, Shortwick would find some way of circumventing it without disabling or setting it off. It was impressive watching her leap over things or crawl along the wall. But Saphira disabled them as they passed anyway.

They walked for hours. Eden tried to keep up with the map, but there were so many twists and turns, Saphira had to get out her little charcoal pencil and made marks on the walls as they passed by. When the group grew hungry and tired, Shortwick finally stopped and sat down.

"Oh, thank the gods I'm so tired," Eden said, collapsing against Rickert. "I don't think I'd be so tired if we were above ground; it's boring looking at rocks all day." Levia sat down and was immediately joined by Shortwick, who began chatting again. Saphira didn't blame her and wondered how long it had been since she heard her own voice. They passed out some food, but they all declined as Shortwick tried to pass around a dead mouse. She didn't seem put out by the rejections and happily began eating it.

"How long do you think we walked today?" Edward asked.

"Oh, I'd say about twelve hours." Levia laid down, her head on his lap.

"Twelve, really?" Edward's eyes went wide. "Guess she's used to it."

"She'd have to be, not much else to do down here." Saphira decided to follow suit and laid down on her bedroll, soon Iollan snuggled next to her.

"Good night, Saphira," he whispered in her hair. She lifted his hand and gave it a kiss before closing her eyes for the night.

Clicking noises woke Saphira; it felt like she hadn't been asleep exceptionally long, and it was hard to open her eyes, but when she did, they flew open. Shortwick was swinging her sword in the hall, and occasionally, it would chink against the wall. When she saw Saphira was awake, she immediately stopped and sheathed her sword.

"Baeisk." She nodded her head and sat back down.

"You don't know any common?"

Shortwick clicked her tongue and picked up a rock. "Um, food," she said, moving the rock in front of her mouth. Her accent was incredibly thick, but Saphira could still understand her. She sat up and drank from her water skin. "Ah, wawter," she said, pointing at Saphira.

"Right, water." She pulled out her dagger, "Dagger."

Shortwick leaned forward and wiggled her fingers above it, "Dawgger."

"Right!" Both of them smiled as she put away her dagger and held up her seashell. "Otto."

Shortwick shook her head. "Nawt, shell, nawt owto," she said, pointing at the shell.

Saphira chuckled. "Okay, you're right, it's a shell."

Rickert groaned and stretched like he did in the mornings. "Is it time to get up?" he asked sleepily.

"I suppose so." Saphira turned and gave Iollan a kiss on the cheek. "Time to get up," she whispered. He mumbled and groaned before he suddenly wrapped his arms around her and pinned her to the ground under him. Saphira squealed and giggled before he kissed her. It woke everybody else while Shortwick giggled into her hand.

"Let's eat. Hopefully, we'll finish the journey today," Rickert said.

An hour later found the group following Shortwick like the day before, but they noticed how she seemed quieter than before.

"We must be getting close," Saphira said. Suddenly, Shortwick stopped before the tunnel curved to the right and began chatting with Levia.

"She said the treasure is around the corner, but she won't come with us. The bones scare her."

"Jittery thing," Edward said. Levia thanked her, but before the group could walk in, Shortwick began chatting quickly and touching their weapons.

"She wants us to get them out. Let's humor her for now," the cleric said. Everyone obliged and pulled out a sword, bow, or dagger and proceeded into the cave. It was monstrous inside, and Saphira was instantly impressed with the height of the ceiling. Xoxim said some magic words, and balls of light flew around the cave.

"There we go!" Everyone stood quietly for a moment, listening for movement.

"I don't hear anything," Saphira said. "Good sign."

"Into the void we go." Rickert walked deeper inside, and everyone followed. At first, they didn't find much: some rusted armor and old swords. Then they made their way around a large rock outcropping, and everyone gasped. The piles of coins stretched for what looked like miles. There were jewels, jewelry, and weapons as far as the eye could see.

"Bright Alar, would you look at it all!" Rickert said. "Eden, Xoxim, would you check for some bad magics?" They nodded and began casting their spells, and after a few moments of concentration, they both came to the same conclusion.

"There's still magic on the treasure, but I can't sense a dragon," Eden said.

"I agree with the young mage, there's magic, but I don't think it will hurt us. It's to alert the dragon of intruders."

"But if there's no dragon, it's okay, right?" Saphira asked.

"Yes!" Xoxim sounded excited and walked towards a pile of potions.

"Rickert?" she asked.

He nodded his head. "Take what you can carry, I guess." She could tell he was trying not to sound excited about the prospect of being rich, but she didn't blame him. Confidently, Levia walked over to a pile of gold and shoved her hand in and waited.

Nothing happened, and she smiled. "Wonderful." She began filling her bag with gold. Saphira and Iollan both went to a pile of weapons. He picked up a large, long sword with sapphires in the hilt.

"This is much better, I can tell." He took his old mundane sword out of its scabbard and placed the new one inside. Saphira dug around and found a black chain shirt that matched Levia's. But as she jiggled it around, it barely made a noise.

She quickly put it on and gasped, "Otto, it's so light." She couldn't help but be amazed at the flexibility it gave her.

"Oooh, look at this wand, Eden!" Xoxim called her over while Edward put jewels in his pockets. Saphira filled her bag with platinum and jewels, but after a while, she began walking around the cave, looking at all the other treasures this dragon had accumulated over its long life. Statues, armor, magical items, it was any adventurer's dream horde, and they were there. She found a comfy bedroom set with a large bed, a chest of drawers, and two side tables. Saphira's curiosity took over, and she opened the top drawer of one of the side tables. A large ruby necklace slid to the front, and Saphira gasped. It was the most gorgeous piece of jewelry she'd ever seen, set in gold with little diamonds around it. She picked it up, surprised at how light it was, and held the ruby up to one of the little lights floating nearby.

"That will look lovely on you, Saphira." She turned and saw Iollan standing behind her.

"I've never owned anything so extravagant before." He took the necklace from her and draped it around her neck. She felt goose bumps along her skin as Iollan pulled her hair free of the necklace and laid it down her back. "How do I look?" She asked nervously as she turned to him. Iollan's eyes softened as his fingers gently ran over the little diamonds surrounding the ruby.

"Beautiful, as always."

"Iollan, the things you say," she whispered as she felt her cheeks blaze.

"It's true, Saphira, you're a natural beauty. I find it hard to hold back sometimes." His hands wrapped around her hips.

"Oh, do you?"

"Yes." Saphira realized he was leaning in for a kiss and barely felt his lips when a noise made Saphira's ear twitch.

She quickly leaned back and looked around. "Did you hear that?"

"No, what?" His arms fell, and he followed as Saphira walked to the back of the cave. "What did it sound like?" he whispered.

"I don't know," she said, shaking her head. "I didn't actually hear it; my ear twitched."

"Everyone's grabbing what they can. It's bound to make some noise." He was right, but it was her job to make sure things were safe, and that's what she was going to do. They walked the border of the horde, and Saphira breathed a little easier when they didn't find anything.

"I had to check."

Iollan laid his hand on her shoulder. "I know, now come my lovely rogue, let's get rich."

She smiled and turned back to the pile of treasure. "Okay."

"Hey, Rickert," Iollan yelled out. "Have you found any—"

"Iollan, Saphira!" Levia's scream echoed in the cavern, and they burst into a run, pulling what weapons they had. They cleared a giant pile of coins, and Saphira swallowed a scream as a giant dragon made of bones swiped at Rickert. Eden quickly transformed into the same blue dragon they had seen before and rammed the other dragon back a few feet. The bone dragon was much larger than Eden, but being made of only bones meant it didn't have a lot of mass and fell with a boom onto its back.

Iollan and Rickert both ran at the stunned creature, but not before Eden was able to blast the bones with lightning from her mouth. The dragon roared and rolled onto its feet as both fighters reached it. Iollan swung his new sword at the dragon's ankle, a cracking noise filled the air, and Rickert swung his weapon at the same spot the young man did. They watched the dragon stumble as its entire left foot came away from the main body.

"I don't think there's much I can do!" Saphira yelled. Edward ran up next to her, his bow drawn, but like her, he was at a loss as to what he could do.

"There's got to be something," he said.

She watched as Eden circled down and landed next to her. "Hop on, you two, we'll find something for you to do." Eden's dragon voice was deep, but still feminine, and they quickly crawled onto the blue dragon's back. "Hang on!" Eden flapped her wings, and before Saphira could blink her eyes, she was level with the bone dragon's head.

"Go around to the spine!" she yelled. Eden dived and turned with such grace that Saphira had no trouble hanging on, and when the large spine of the dragon came into view, Saphira let her dagger fly. She couldn't take her eyes off it as it sank between two of the bones. Edward let loose an arrow, and it hit the hilt of the dagger, shoving it deeper between the bones. The dragon roared, and suddenly, Eden banked hard to the right, and Saphira felt heat on her leg. She looked over to the side and saw Xoxim had unleashed fire on the dragon. But Saphira didn't think it would do much good. She held out her hand, and her dagger flew back to her.

"Gods, if only this thing could bleed!" There was another loud cracking noise, and the bone dragon toppled over and crashed to the ground, bones spilling around them.

"Iollan!" "Rickert!" The girls yelled before Eden dived to the ground. Saphira and Edward jumped off the dragon at the same time Eden transformed back into her usual pretty self, and both ran to their friends. The men were sweaty and breathing hard, but luckily, both had gotten out of the way and stood a few feet from the pile of bones.

"Are you guys all right?" Saphira jumped into Iollan's arms.

"We're fine, a little startled."

"Guess that's why Shortwick was scared of the bones, wish she could have told us the bones were alive," Edward said.

"I doubt she knew how to put it into words." Saphira felt she had to defend the brain-damaged Grimun.

"So do we have enough?" Rickert asked the group.

"Yes, let's get out of here." Saphira put her dagger away when her ear twitched. She stood straight and listened.

"What is it?" Rickert asked.

"Sounded like bones rattling." The group turned and saw the dragon quickly putting itself back together, bone by bone.

"Everybody out now!" Levia yelled and ran for the door with Rickert and Edward beside her. Saphira watched as Eden turned back into her dragon and guarded their retreat as she and Iollan started running.

"Come on, rogue, don't let that klunker of a fighter outrun you!" Edward yelled out. They were both running as fast as they could. Saphira looked behind her and saw the dragon whipping its tail at them.

"Hurry, Iollan!" The door was fifty feet away when the dragon smacked its tail on the ground, knocking the runners off their feet.

"Saphira!" She could see Iollan reaching for her and held out her hand and felt his fingers for a second before the boned tail whipped through the air again and slammed into the ground between them. Both went airborne in opposite directions, Saphira through the door, Iollan back towards the treasure.

When she opened her eyes after the jarring impact, Saphira saw the dragon bearing down on Iollan. He was on his feet in an instant, and they watched as he ran towards the entrance.

"Claw!" It sounded like human Eden, but Saphira didn't have much time to contemplate before she watched the dragon rake its claw down Iollan's back. He screamed and stumbled to the ground. Rocks began falling from the ceiling, and Saphira could tell her love was too hurt to protect himself.

"Iollan!" Her heart was in her throat; he wasn't going to make it, and she felt tears down her face.

Saphira heard odd words come from Levia, and Iollan cried out in pain as he was jerked through the air. He landed on the ground at her feet a few seconds later. She and Rickert quickly reached down and pulled him through the doorway into the hall. Saphira looked up and saw Levia standing before the dragon. Her holy symbol was glowing as she held it high above her head.

"Levia!" Saphira screamed and tried to go to the cleric when a huge rock fell in front of the opening, trapping the cleric with the dragon. "No!" Saphira and Eden screamed. "We gotta get her out! Xoxim, there must be something you can do!" She turned and saw the little gnome shake his head. He was sweating and looked exhausted.

"I've nothing, Saphira," he leaned against the stone wall. "Believe me, if I could do something, I would."

"We can't leave her! How did she get in there anyway?"

Eden turned and hugged herself. "A spell, she switched places with Iollan. She said it was the only way to get him out." Rickert picked up Iollan, and the group ran down the hall. Saphira caught up with him and took Iollan's hand.

"You're gonna be alright." But she noticed how his blood was making a perfect trail on the ground for anyone to follow.

"No, you have to go back, we can't leave her!" Iollan screamed, his voice echoing loudly in the hallway. "You have to get her! She can't do this!"

"We can't." Saphira kissed his hand as he groaned with every step Rickert took.

"She shouldn't…" His eyes closed, and his head lolled against Rickert's chest.

A few hours later, the group was still walking. They wanted to get back to Val Shing as quickly as possible. Saphira led the way, looking behind her every so often to check on Iollan. Rickert was sweating with effort by now, but he insisted on carrying him. The shock of losing Levia had worn off, and the pain from being knocked out of the cave was kicking in, and Saphira hoped she'd make it back to the city before passing out.

"Saphira." She heard Iollan gasp, and she turned back. "It hurts."

"I'm sorry, I wish I could help," she whispered and kissed his hand.

"In my…top left pocket…a vial of pain killer." She quickly reached into his pocket and pulled it out. She tipped the little vial into his mouth, and he swallowed the bitter liquid.

"Is...everyone else okay?" he strained to say.

"Yeah, everyone else is fine."

"Thank the gods." He whispered and laid his head on Rickert's chest and let the pain medicine do its job.

They reached Val Shing the next day. The dark elves rushed to help them back to the same house they stayed in before they left. Rickert laid Iollan on his stomach in their room and stretched his back with a groan.

"We rest until he can move," he said.

Saphira boiled water while another dark elf came in with a salve. "This will help." Saphira cut away the rest of Iollan's shirt and grimaced at the state of his back. There were three deep, long cuts from his shoulders to his hips; they were still oozing blood in time with his heartbeat, and she thanked Otto he hadn't bled to death. She took the salve from the dark elf and gently spread the blue salve on his back. He didn't move the entire time.

"You're going to be okay," she whispered to him.

When Saphira opened her eyes again, it took her a moment to remember where they were. Iollan was still asleep on his stomach on a makeshift cot. Edward was asleep in a chair across the room, his arms crossed over his chest. His head was at such an awkward angle, Saphira knew his neck would be sore later. She moved over to Iollan and lifted the bandages. The slashes had stopped bleeding, but he'd need his skin stitched together.

"Ah, you are awake." A soft voice came from the door, and she turned as a small female dark elf walked in carrying a little basket. "This should help. We don't have healing like you do on the surface, but he won't be bleeding to death when you walk out of here," she whispered. Saphira assumed for Iollan's sake. She looked in the basket and found a needle and thread among a few other things.

"Thank you," she whispered.

The small elf sat on the bed and began placing leaves on Iollan's skin. "This should numb his skin so you can stitch him up. I can tell you don't wish to cause him any pain."

She tucked a loose strand of his hair behind his ear. "I love him."

"I can tell," the elf said with a smile.

"Saphira?" It was Iollan. She gasped and laid a hand on his cheek. His eyes were open. They were glassy but alert.

"We're in Val Shing, how do you feel?"

"Sore." His eyes looked a little sad around the edges.

She reached out and touched his temple. "I swear my heart stopped when I saw how badly you were hurt."

He managed a small smile. "I knew you'd take care of me."

"I'm going to start stitching you up. Let me know if it's too much." He nodded and closed his eyes.

Edward breathed in deep and stretched. "You're awake, good. How do you feel?"

"Better," he groaned. "But we'll see how I feel after getting stabbed a bunch."

Saphira got the needle and thread ready. "It's a privilege to be stabbed by me; you should be so lucky." He chuckled a little.

Edward got to his feet. "You're in good hands. I'll let everyone else know you're awake."

"Rickert said as soon as you can walk, we'll get out of here." She pierced his ruined skin with the needle, making sure to make the stitches small. He didn't react, so she assumed the leaves did their job.

"Can't Xoxim teleport us back to Buckland?"

She leaned forward and kissed his forehead. "He said he can take us as far as the entrance, then he's going his own way."

He sighed and shook his head. "He's probably upset about Levia. I think he was friends with her for a long time. Gods, why did she switch places with me?" She could hear the guilt in his voice and held back her own tears.

"Try not to think about it. What's done is done."

When Iollan was stitched up and once again fast asleep, she walked into the common room of the house. Everyone was sitting around the fire, mugs of something in their hands, but no one was drinking. Saphira sat next to Xoxim, his eyes studying the fire intently. "I'm sorry," she whispered.

Edward sniffed. "I shouldn't feel this sad," his voice was teary. "I barely knew her, but she was wonderful."

"That she was," Xoxim said, sipping whatever he had in his mug. She wrapped her arms around the little mage and squeezed. She had no idea what to say.

CHAPTER 14
NEW FAMILY

A few days later, Iollan's back was deemed fit for travel. The stitches held together well, but Saphira knew the scars would be prominent. He was moving slower but could walk without assistance. Xoxim teleported them to the entrance of Ral Hava as promised. He said his goodbyes and quickly vanished. Saphira wondered if she'd ever see the little gnome again. The nearest town was a week away, so the group started the walk, a lot richer and a lot sadder. When the town was only a few hours away, a random autumn snowstorm enveloped them, and by the time they reached the inn, they were caked with frozen snow but glad to finally have shelter.

The owner took pity on them; he didn't get many customers after the first snows, so he gave them all some brandy to warm them up. It felt wonderful being warm, and soon the bad memories were gone with a toast to the brave cleric and many free brandies. Hours after the sun set, Saphira and Iollan fell into bed, a little tipsy and happy they had a warm bed to share. The next day, Rickert was waiting outside their room, his arms crossed across his chest.

"Saphira, can I speak with you alone?"

He looked severe; it was a new look for him. She didn't like that look. "Sure, Rickert."

Iollan gave her cheek a kiss. "I'll get us some breakfast," he whispered and walked down the stairs as they walked back into their room.

Rickert shut the door and began pacing in front of her. "Normally, I don't consider myself a gullible person. I thought it was rather… extraordinary that Mother Lily's daughter had joined our group, but I was grateful. We needed a rogue, and you seemed like a nice young lady." He stopped and stared at her, "but when you opened the unopenable door, I must admit, I felt like an idiot. Now tell me the truth, are you Saphira Voltain?"

Her eyes widened. "Of course I am! Rickert, I don't know why I was able to open that door, but I swear I am who I say I am."

He stepped close. "If you're lying to me, I'm going to leave you in whatever hellhole we're in when I find out. No one lies to me." Her heart was breaking at the sound of his voice; it was like being chastised by her mother.

"I'm not lying to you, Rickert! I am Saphira Voltain, and Lily is my mother!" His eyes studied her; she could tell he was trying to see if she was lying.

"Maybe when you go home, you should have a conversation with your folks, cause magic doesn't lie, Saphira." There was a knock on the door, and Iollan walked in carrying some bowls of porridge.

"Everything okay?" He set them on the dresser by the door.

Rickert gave her one more stern look and turned to the fighter. "Yeah, so far," he said and walked out of the room.

Saphira stared after him, his last words ringing in her ears. "What did he want?" Iollan walked over and laid a hand on her arm.

"He thinks I lied about who I am, but I didn't."

"It's the door again, isn't it?" He sighed and shoved his hands in his pockets. "Listen," he stepped up close and whispered, "I don't care who you are, Saphira, if you were the daughter of the most evil man in the world, I'd," he stopped and cleared his throat. "I'd still trust you, I'd still love you."

She gave him a little smile and nodded her head. "Thank you. I wish I knew why I could open that door, but I didn't lie about who I am. I hope Rickert believes me. We had to be wrong about the magic on it; it doesn't make sense."

Iollan scoffed. "Who cares what Rickert thinks? What matters is you know who you are. Now come eat, you'll feel better." He picked up one of the bowls and handed it to her. She looked down into the bowl of porridge, *but do I really know who I am?*

It took a few weeks before the snow finally stopped, luckily the tavern had plenty of wood and food. The group helped around the Inn when they could, washing dishes and mopping the floor. It was a cozy winter, the fire warming Saphira during the day and Iollan during the night.

The first spring day finally arrived, and Saphira joined her friends around the same table they had sat at all winter. To her surprise, there was a bard playing in the corner. Winter had kept most entertainers away, so the group did their best to fill the void, but none of them were the best singers.

"I thought we might head to Salthole. How does that sit with everyone?" Rickert said as he shoved an ale at Saphira.

"Sounds good to me." But when she looked over at Eden, she saw an odd look on the girl's face. "Eden?"

Edward reached over and touched her hand. "Edie, what is it?" She didn't move and kept staring at the table.

"We don't have to go to Salthole?" Rickert suggested, but Eden took a breath and looked over at her brother.

"Mom's sick, Mathias gave me a sending, he thinks we ought to come home."

Edward's usual friendly face turned dark as he hugged his sister. "Okay, tell him we'll be there when we can."

Rickert laid his hand on Eden's shoulder and kissed her head. "All of us, we'll be there to help any way we can."

"You don't have to worry about anything, Eden." Saphira reached over and put her hand on Edward's back, and looked at Iollan, "Right?"

Iollan nodded. "Right." She couldn't help but think he looked worried.

It didn't take long for the group to get back to Ardenry. After the snow melted, the roads were clear, and with their newfound money, they all got horses and rode down to the large city. When they entered the gates, they could see it was still waking from the winter lull. Everyone followed the twins to their mother's shop on the west side of town. The door tinkled lightly as Eden opened it, and they saw a tall man with long gray hair sitting behind the counter.

"Edie, Edward, welcome home! I missed you!"

The man got up, and the twins ran over and hugged him. "We missed you, too Mathias. How is she?" Eden asked. He leaned way down and kissed her head while giving Edward a hearty handshake.

"She's anxious to see her children. She's upstairs, and I know she'll be so excited to see you."

"Thank you for looking after her," Edward said as he and his sister made their way up the stairs. Rickert waited until they were out of sight and introduced himself. "Rickert Basine, thank you for letting us know about Mayris. I know the twins appreciate it."

"It's not a problem, I assure you. I'm betting once she sees Edie and Ed, everything will be perfect." Rickert sat at a stool and began talking to the older man about helping around the shop, so Saphira decided to walk around. She had never been in a mage shop before; there was never any need. It smelled peculiar, but it reminded her of nights she slept between Eden and Edward and figured the smell must have rubbed off on them. A mix of herbs and metal. As she walked around the store, a red gem set in gold in one of the cases caught her attention. It felt wrong, like it wanted to do her harm if she touched it.

"Iollan, come here," She called out, but didn't hear any footsteps. She looked up and saw he was standing in the back of the shop. "Iollan!"

He jumped and quickly joined her. "What?"

"Look at this," she pointed at the jewel. "It feels weird, doesn't it?" When she turned to him, he was looking at the front door. "Iollan," she said in a sing-song voice.

"Hmm?" He looked back at her.

She scoffed and put her hands on her hips. "What is wrong with you?"

He shook his head. "Nothing, why?"

"Your head is in the clouds."

Iollan put his hands on her shoulders. "Sorry, a bit preoccupied. Shall we see if Eden and Edward need anything?"

"Sure." She sighed, and the two walked up the stairs to the little apartment above the shop. The door was open a crack, and when they heard Eden chuckle, they knew it would be okay to go in. The apartment was warm and inviting, with lots of deep purples and soft pillows to sit on. The sun was streaming in through the windows, and it smelled like chocolate cake.

"Saphira, Iollan, come here," Eden called out. They peeked around a corner and saw the little family around a bed in a room to their left. Both the twins were smiling so brightly it took Saphira a little off guard, then she saw why they were so happy. Their mother was sitting in bed, holding a brand-new baby, and Saphira gasped.

"I guess she wasn't sick after all?"

Eden giggled. "Nope. Mom and Mathias had a baby! Mom, this is Saphira and Iollan, they travel with us. They're sweethearts," she teased.

Mayris smiled and sat up. "Well, welcome, please come in, have a seat." Saphira excitedly took a seat next to Eden, but Iollan stayed put in the hall, leaning against the doorframe. "Would you like to hold her?" Mayris asked.

"Yes, please." Saphira held out her arms, and Mayris handed over the baby. Saphira was always surprised at how light babies were when she held them. "She's beautiful," she whispered.

Edward scooted next to her and laid a hand on her arm. "I think she likes you."

"What's not to like?" She giggled and looked over at Iollan. "Iollan would you," but he was gone. "Guess not."

"Some men are nervous around babies," Mayris said. But Saphira knew better. Iollan wasn't nervous around children; he loved them. She suddenly wondered if the scene of her holding a baby bothered him for some reason.

"Yeah, I suppose so."

Saphira enjoyed her time with the family, but after a while, Mayris got tired, and the baby got fussy, so the three of them decided to go downstairs. Iollan was right where she thought he was, downstairs in the shop, trading stories with Mathias and Rickert. "Shall we find an inn nearby?" she asked them.

"Sure." Rickert held out his hand. "Mathias, it was nice meeting you. I have a feeling we'll be seeing each other often."

"The pleasure's mine," he said, giving Rickert's hand a hearty shake. The three walked out into the sun and decided to settle into the nearest inn.

Saphira and Iollan had a room all to themselves, as did Rickert, since the twins decided to stay with their mother. Saphira ran a brush through her hair and walked back downstairs. Iollan was in the tavern, an almost empty ale in his hands.

"Iollan, would you like to come with me while I visit my friend Zell?" She laid her head on his shoulder.

"No thank you. You should see him alone." She felt him give her head a kiss.

She sat up and gave his arm a rub. "Are you sure? I think you'd like him. He has the best stories."

"Naw, you go. I'll stay here and make sure the food's good."

She sighed and shrugged her shoulders. "All right, I'll be back later." He tilted his head in acknowledgment but said nothing. She wondered if his back was bothering him or if something else was wrong.

Saphira ran to Zell's shop on the other side of town. Luckily, it was still there, so she stood outside and straightened her hair and shirt in an effort to look presentable in front of her old friend and mentor. The familiar tinkle of the door's bell filled the air, and she immediately saw Zell sitting behind the counter.

"What can I do for you?" He asked as he put a big lock away under the desk.

"Hello, Zell."

He looked up and gasped. "Saphira, you're back!" And with more dexterity than a man his age should have, he leaped over the counter and scooped her up in his arms. "I can't believe you're here!"

Saphira laughed and hugged him back. "Why not I said I'd be careful."

He set her on her feet and studied her. "You've seen some action, haven't you?" He asked as his hands gently cupped her face.

She took a deep breath and nodded. "A bit, yeah."

"Well, come on in and tell me what you've been up to." He moved to the door and locked it behind her.

"What are you doing? You never close during the day?"

Zell chuckled and led her towards the stairs. "For you I would, now don't keep me in suspense, tell me everything."

For hours, they sat at the little table in the apartment above the shop like they used to, except this time Zell was listening to her. When she got to the dragon, she didn't omit Levia's death. It was her first sad story, and she had to pass it along.

Zell sighed and shook his head. "Always a shame when a good cleric falls, but I know she felt it was worth it, Saphira. They're usually more ready to die than the rest of us."

She bit her lip and couldn't stop staring at her hands as they rested on the table. "I can't help but feel guilty, though."

Zell reached out and gently lifted her chin. "As would anyone with a good heart. It's human nature to think there's something you could have done, even when there's not," he said with a reassuring smile.

She nodded and sighed. "Yeah, I know." She reached over and laid a hand on his arm, "Zell, would you like to come have dinner with my group tonight?"

"Oh no, they don't need some old bum hanging around, keeping the young men away from you."

Saphira chuckled and sat back. "Well, you can't use that excuse, I'm already taken."

Zell smiled. "It's that fighter, isn't it? I could tell by the way you talk about him."

"It is, he's wonderful. Full of surprises," she said with a big smile.

The next morning, Saphira woke and saw Iollan packing his bag. "Morning, what are you doing?" She sat up and ran a hand through her hair.

He didn't turn as he threw a shirt into his pack. "I'm packing."

"Did Rickert say we were leaving today?"

"No." His tone wasn't harsh; it wasn't hurried or scared. He sounded sad.

She scooted to the end of the bed, keeping the covers around her. "So why are you packing?"

He put his sword on his back. His voice was soft. "I can't stay, I have to go."

"Iollan," she got to her feet and laid a hand on his back. "What is it?"

He quickly turned and wrapped his arms tight around her. "Saphira," he whispered in her hair. "Please, Saphira, please tell me you're not Mother Lily's daughter, you just happen to have the same names. Please tell me you're lying. I don't care if you are, I won't say anything to anyone, I swear, but please, if you're not her daughter, tell me." She stepped back and was shocked at how desperate he looked and sounded. His eyes were roaming over her face, waiting for a lie she couldn't tell.

Her hands brushed some hair off his forehead. "I can't."

His breath hitched as he spoke. "Can't or won't?"

"You said it didn't matter who I was, that'd you—"

"Because if you're not, I can stay!" He blurted out, pacing around the room. "If you're not her, I can stay, and all will be well."

She couldn't believe he was saying this. "Why the hell would it make a difference?"

She saw him cover his mouth before he dashed to her and

cupped her face. "Saphira, sweet, beautiful Saphira, I'm so sorry." His fingers gently caressed her face. "I love you, Saphira Voltain, I always will," he whispered before he kissed her deeply.

An odd taste filled her mouth, and she quickly broke off and touched her lips. "Don't leave Iollan, let me come with…" her eyes lost focus. "What is—" Iollan caught her as her body went limp in his arms. He gently laid her on the bed and made sure she would be comfortable.

"He'll find me, I know he will, and if you're with me, it won't end well," he whispered and slipped out the window.

Saphira woke with a pounding headache, and she felt the bed move. "Saphira, are you awake?" It was Eden.

"Gods, my head is about to explode," she groaned and turned on her side. When she finally opened her eyes, she could see Eden looked upset. The mage's eyes were sad as she reached over and took Saphira's hand.

"Saphira, what happened? I came to see if you wanted to go shopping, and you were in bed, but I couldn't wake you, and Iollan was gone. We were all so scared he did something to you."

When she said his name, Saphira remembered what happened. "He left." She could barely say the words as tears burned in her eyes. "He said he couldn't be with me."

Eden's eyes went wide. "What? He…left you? I don't understand." Their last conversation finally floated through her mind. She remembered him saying he loved her, but when he kissed her, she remembered how funny it tasted.

"He drugged me so he could leave." Her fingers went to her lips, and there was a faint sticky residue on her skin. "He drugged me."

Eden leaned forward and hugged her. "Gods! I'm glad you're okay." The mage's compassion broke her resolve, and she began sobbing on Eden's shoulder.

"He said he loved me. Why would he leave?" Her voice was barely coherent as the tears flowed freely down her cheeks.

"He's an ass, Saphira, he's not worth it."

She squeezed her friend, trying not to shake. "But he isn't Eden. I love him." The mage's hand rubbed her back while Saphira cried her frustrations on her shoulder. "Why would he leave? He said he loved me."

Eden sighed. "I knew you had something intense going on, but I never thought he'd abandon all of us."

She sniffed and sat back, rubbing the tears from her cheeks. "I don't understand why it mattered whose daughter I am?"

Eden shook her head and helped get some hair off her tear-soaked face. "I don't know, but I think he had more secrets than either of us could guess."

The door creaked, and she saw Edward walk in. "Saphira?"

She quickly turned away from him; she didn't want him to see her like this. "Ed, hi."

"What's wrong?" She cleared her throat and tried to compose herself as she turned back to him, as he sat on the bed, so she was once again sandwiched between the twins.

"Uh, Iollan drugged me and left."

His face flashed anger in an instant. "What? Drugged you? What the hell is wrong with him?" He quickly pulled her into a tight hug. "Are you okay?"

"Yeah, just a headache." She felt his hand run lightly through her hair. "And a lot heartbroken."

Saphira spent the next few days in her room, sometimes alone, sometimes with Edward. He'd tell her how Iollan was an idiot for leaving. But all she could think about was why he left. Whatever it was had to have been triggered by coming back to Ardenry. When Saphira finally went downstairs, she found Rickert eating a light lunch in the tavern.

"Hey Saphira, want something to eat?"

She shrugged her shoulders. "Not really, where are the twins?" She had a good idea where they were, but didn't want to walk over to the shop in case they weren't there.

"At their mom's fawning over their little sister," Rickert said with a smile. Saphira leaned over the back of one of the chairs and smiled at the thought of the baby.

"Have you seen her? She's the cutest little doll."

He shook his head and took a swig of his ale. "No, I figured I'd give them some time alone." He sighed and flexed his fingers. "Saphira, I'm so sorry how Iollan treated you. I know I encouraged it, but if I had any inkling he'd abandon us, I never would have suggested you give him the time of day."

She lowered her head. "Don't worry about it, you couldn't have known." She gave his arm a little punch and walked out of the inn.

When Saphira walked into the apartment above the magic shop, she only saw Edward sitting on the couch with his baby sister. "Hey, Ed."

He looked up and smiled. "Saphira finally decided to come out, huh?"

"Yeah, where's your mom?" She sat next to Edward and played with the tiny girl's little hand.

"She and Edie went to get some food for dinner. Mom wanted all of us to have dinner before we left."

"Oh, how nice." Saphira chuckled as the baby's fingers wrapped tightly around hers. "She's so pretty, Edward."

He smiled and looked down at the baby in his arms. "She is, isn't she?" Saphira watched as Edward looked up and smiled at her. "You're pretty too, Saphira."

She managed to pry her fingers from the baby's and sat back. "Thank you. I don't really feel pretty, but I'll take your word for it." She knew her eyes were red from crying, and her skin had to be splotchy. But she was never one to turn down a compliment. "I feel so stupid."

Ed shook his head. "Don't. Things like that happen every day to all kinds of people, and no one is less wise because of it."

"I had no interest in love when I left Raventree. I shouldn't have changed my mind. Maybe everything would be fine if I didn't fall for him." She looked at her arm and picked at a little scab.

"You didn't think you'd find your husband while you

adventured?"

She shook her head. "No. Probably should, no one at home has the guts to court me. But I want to travel, and sneak, and earn riches. Finding a husband is not my top priority."

Edward was quiet for a moment. "Well, you're young, we're both young, we don't need to think about marriage right now."

"True." The little girl started getting fussy, so Edward stood and gently jiggled her as he walked back and forth with her.

"You know, I think this is where mothers have the advantage over dads. They always know what's wrong," he said as the baby's cries pierced the air. Saphira watched him try to quiet his little sister, but he was right; he was in a little over his head.

"Did your mother leave any milk?"

"Oh, uh, yeah, the water skin by the bed, you think she's hungry?"

Saphira got up and brought the milk over to him. "Couldn't hurt to see." He took the skin from her, and sure enough, the little girl ate like there was no tomorrow.

"Well, what do you know," he looked up with a smile. "You were right. Want to hold her?"

"Sure." She sat on the couch, and Edward handed her the suckling babe. She made little grunting noises, and they both laughed.

"Glad you were here, Saphira. I might have let her cry until mom got home."

"Nah, you wouldn't have, you would have figured it out." Edward smiled and stared at them a moment before Saphira realized he was staring at her, not his sister. "I'm not going to break, Ed."

"I know." Footsteps on the stairs turned their heads, and they saw Eden and her mother walk in with a few baskets of food.

"Saphira, good to see you again. I was wondering if we'd

get back in time for her feeding," Mayris said.

"It's good to see you, too. She's absolutely no trouble at all."

They put the bags near the kitchen. "Edward, will you come help your sister put everything away?"

"Sure, Mom." He walked next to Eden and helped her put away various grocery items while Mayris sat next to Saphira.

"How are you?" She asked in a familiar motherly tone.

Saphira sighed and looked back at the baby. "Okay, I guess."

Mayris laid a hand on her shoulder. "Eden told me what your man did. Telling you he loved you, then left. In my experience, when someone leaves so suddenly, it means there's trouble, not that he didn't genuinely love you." She was glad their mother thought there was something else going on besides Iollan being an asshole.

"Yeah, I'm worried, but so mad at him too. Why wouldn't he just tell me? We could have figured it out.

She smiled. "If you punched him the next time you see him, he probably would agree he deserved it."

She nodded and fought back tears. "Edward's been a tremendous help; you raised a good guy there. Eden, too, she's my best friend."

Mayris smiled and snuck a glance back at her grown children. "You know," she turned back, and Saphira saw a little smile on her face, "Edward talks about you constantly."

She chuckled. "Oh yeah? Did he tell you about how I fell shoulder deep into a mud hole one time? Rickert said I did my job since no one else stepped in it."

Mayris laughed. "No, he failed to mention that. How many boyfriends have you had, Saphira?"

"Just the one." She didn't count Miles as a boyfriend since they only fooled around behind their parents' backs. "Not many boys at home could handle being with Mother Lily's daughter, too scared, I guess."

"I understand. Well, Edward's there for you."

She nodded her head. "He really is."

Saphira helped the twins make their favorite home cooked meal for the group, a cracker encrusted chicken with peppered mashed potatoes and rosemary bread. While she and Edward smashed up the crackers, Eden left to get Rickert.

"I've been dreaming of this meal all year. What's your favorite dinner, Saphira?"

"Chicken pot pie. We don't have it often cause it's a pain to make."

"Yeah, I don't think I've ever seen it at any of the taverns we've eaten at." Eden and Rickert walked in, and Saphira thought she sounded rather proud as she introduced him to their mother.

"Mom, this is Rickert Basine, Rickert, my mother, Mayris." Saphira could assume she shook the man's hand, but she was too preoccupied with the crackers to watch.

"Lovely to meet you, thank you for keeping my children safe."

"It's my pleasure, Mayris. They're a special pair. I feel lucky to have them."

Eden motioned towards the couch. "Why don't we sit down for a moment?"

The pair sat down with her on the couch. "Is Mathias coming to dinner too?" Eden asked.

"Yes, he's closing up the shop for me, and actually, we have some news for the two of you."

"Oh? Good news, I hope."

"Mm-hmm." Saphira glanced around Edward and saw a happy smile on their mother's face.

"What do you think the news is?" She whispered.

"They're probably getting married." Saphira gasped and turned to Edward. "It's the worst-kept secret that they've been in love for years. I guess having the baby finally made them realize it." Saphira chuckled and poured the crackers over the chicken.

The dinner was wonderful; it had been so long since any of them had a real family meal. The twins' mother and Mathias finally announced the baby's name, Ruby, and they were, in fact, going to get married, which made the twins incredibly happy.

Saphira elbowed Edward a little while his mother was talking with Rickert. "Guess you were right."

"I am on occasion." He gave her a wink and elbowed her back

CHAPTER 15
SECRETS AND SCARS

When Saphira woke the next morning, she was warm under the covers with Edward. His back was facing her, and he was still breathing deep with sleep. She had seen him without a shirt on a lot, but when they slept, he was usually behind her, so she never saw his back. Her eyes lingered on the big scar that ran along his spine and spread to his shoulder blades. It looked like it could have been a fatal blow, and she could tell it was old. It was whiter than his tanned skin. Slowly, she reached out and ran her hand along the soft, pale skin.

Edward twitched and turned in bed. "Morning, Saphira."

"Morning. How did you get that awful scar on your back?" She half rolled him over so she could keep playing her hand over it.

"It's not a scar, it's a birthmark." He rolled over and faced her. "Big, huh?"

"Birthmark? I've never seen one so big before."

He shrugged his shoulders. "Edie gets to turn into a dragon; I get a nasty mark on my back."

Saphira giggled. "Do you want to turn into a dragon?"

"No." He chuckled and sat up, "I like being my size, I don't know how she can stand it." Saphira watched as he got up and put his shirt back on. "Let's get some breakfast, I have a feeling mom's going to keep us busy today." She smiled and slipped her pants and boots on. The twins' mother and Mathias were having a little wedding ceremony today, and they all had their jobs.

"I bet she's so happy you guys are here to see the wedding."

"Oh yeah, that reminds me," Edward helped her to her feet, but kept her hands in his. "I was wondering if you'd be my date to the wedding?"

Her mouth formed a little smirk. "Date?"

"You wouldn't have to do much, your dance card is full of mostly me, we sit next to each other during the ceremony. Things you've done before."

She thought he seemed a little nervous. It was very endearing. "Of course I'll be your date."

He smiled and gave her a hug. "Good, I hate going stag."

"Oh, like you wouldn't be able to find someone." They chuckled and made their way out the door.

The group met and ate breakfast before helping the happy couple. Eden and Saphira took immense pride in helping Mayris get ready for her big day. Saphira curled her hair and put some of it up with flowered hairpins while Eden picked out the dress. The dressmaker knew Mayris and gave her a little gown for the baby as well for half off. Rickert supported Edward while he spoke with Mathias. Ed told him how happy he was for them and was glad his mother finally started listening to them about the older mage. Mathias practically raised the twins with Mayris after their father died, so they were happy to be an official family.

The new parents got married by a priest of Alar under a big shady tree in the park early that afternoon. Eden was holding little Ruby, standing behind her mother, while Saphira and Edward watched with a few of the couple's friends. As Mathias began to speak his vows, Saphira wondered if she was going to cry. It was an awful lot of romance mere days after Iollan tore her heart out.

"Mayris, you've been the bright jewel of my life for twenty years, you and your wonderful children. No one has made me feel as happy as you do, and when I see your beautiful smile, I know it's just for me. Now we have our own little jewel, and I can't thank you enough for her. I will love you, and care for you the rest of my life, and maybe even a few years after." Everyone chuckled a little, and Mathias kissed Mayris on the cheek. Saphira felt her eyes beginning to tear up and sniffed a little as Edward shifted and put an arm around her waist. She turned her head into his chest. She didn't want to cry because she knew it wouldn't be the happy tears one usually sees at a wedding.

Edward hugged her, and she wrapped her arms around him. "Thank you," she whispered and looked up at him.

He leaned down and kissed her head. "You're welcome, Saphy." She smiled at the term of endearment she hadn't heard in over a year.

"I now pronounce you husband and wife, Mathis, you may kiss your bride." They heard the priest say, and people clapped as the newlyweds kissed, but neither Saphira nor Edward saw it, they were still staring at each other.

"I haven't seen you smile in a few days," he said quietly.

"My family calls me Saphy. It felt nice to hear it."

He leaned down and kissed her cheek. "Then maybe I'll start calling you Saphy," he whispered, his lips lingering on her skin.

"I'd like that."

Edward stood straight as his mother and new stepfather walked up. "Did you see any of the ceremony, son, or were you staring at your pretty friend?" Mathias teased.

Edward laughed and hugged both his parents. "I did, it was beautiful."

"Thank you, Edward. Now, let's celebrate!" Mayris kissed her husband, and the two led the group to a nearby tavern owned by a mutual mage friend. It was decorated with red streamers, and there were colorful sparklers dotting the room. Magic was pouring from every corner of the tavern, and when everyone was inside, the door shut, and the party got underway.

The day was fun for Saphira; she danced with Rickert and a few other guests. She even danced with Edward and Ruby, but mostly with Edward. He was so alive, always talking about something from his childhood or where he wanted to go when they left Ardenry. Saphira found it to be very addictive. She'd ask him a simple question about something or someone, and he'd delve into a long, animated story about the subject, which usually ended up with both of them laughing.

At dinner time, the owner waved a wand and food appeared all over the room. Wonderful game birds roasted to perfection, fruits, and vegetables, along with fancy desserts and wine. Saphira didn't think she should drink, but managed to keep herself to one glass of wine. Everything was wonderful, and soon everyone was full, but after a few more dances, most would get more. Another hour passed before the newlyweds left with their little jewel, but the party continued. It was a wonderful distraction, and before Saphira realized it, the day had flown by. She and Edward were dancing to a slow song; most of the couples were doing the same thing.

"I had a wonderful time today, Edward, thank you."

"You're welcome, Saphy. I had a wonderful day too. I was actually going to ask you if I could stay in your room again tonight? I figured Mom and Mathias want some time alone."

"Sure, no problem. You don't want to stay with Edie?"

"I think she's staying in Rickert's room." He said slowly, only a hint of disgust in his tone.

"Really? Huh."When the song ended, everyone clapped for the bard. "Speaking of room, want to head back now? I don't think I can eat another bite or dance another dance." She picked up her right foot and rubbed it while Edward chuckled at her.

"Yeah, I'm a little tired myself. I think we made a good run of it." She took his hand, and they walked out of the party back to their inn.

It was late when they flopped onto the bed. "I absolutely do not feel like sleeping in my clothes tonight." Saphira picked herself up and pulled her nightshirt out of her bag, and put it on over her clothes. She had gotten good at changing without showing any skin, and when her dress was on the floor, she sighed. "Ah, much better."

Edward smiled and pulled his shirt off. "Sometimes it is nice relaxing in almost nothing." Saphira sat on the bed and watched him crawl in bed wearing only his underclothes. "What a good day." He had a little smile on his face.

Saphira giggled and took his left hand. "It was. It's been a long time since I've been to a wedding."

She rubbed her thumb into the palm of his hand, and he groaned low and long. "That feels sooo good, Saphira," his voice was lazy.

She giggled and worked around his calloused hand. "I knew it would. Has anyone rubbed your hands before?"

When she looked up, his eyes were closed, and he was shaking his head. "Nope, but I fear you'll be asked to do this again." Laughing, she let go of his hand and reached across his body for his other hand.

"Well, I like doing things for my friends. It's rare we get to relax like this, and we should enjoy our time to the fullest." Edward was right-handed, and she could feel how hard his muscles in his hands were as she rubbed.

"Ooh, gods, I'm beginning to think something's wrong with my hands."

"No, I think people overlook how nice it is to have them rubbed. They focus more on the feet and back and, well, other things," she said with a little chuckle.

"Other things? Like?" She could hear the tease in his voice and lightly slapped his muscled stomach.

"You know perfectly well what I'm talking about, Edward McVain." And with one last rub, she let go of his hand.

He sat up and cracked his knuckles with a smile. "I'm teasing. Want me to rub something for you?"

Her eyes widened at the prospect. "Oh, well, if you want."

"You rubbed my hands, the least I could do is rub something for you." He moved to the end of the bed and set her foot in his lap. When his thumb made that first little circle motion deep into the heel of her foot, she couldn't help but twitch.

"Wow." Edward chuckled and kept it up, "I think we both needed this." The exquisite pain that came from his rubbings made her relax more than she had in days. "You're such a good friend, Edward. I doubt Rickert would do this."

He chuckled. "He'd probably do it on Edie." She heard him sigh as he took her other foot in his hand. "Saphira, I got something to confess."

She opened her eyes and saw he looked rather stiff. "What is it?"

Ed looked back down at her foot as he began rubbing it. "I lied to you, and I'm sorry."

Saphira's eyebrows furled. "What? When did you lie to me?" She could tell he looked sorry, and wondered what he could have lied about.

"This morning, when you asked about the mark on my back. You're right, it's a scar."

"Why would you lie?" She wasn't angry with him. It was his business, but if he felt he had to confess, then she would listen to him.

Edward shook his head. "It's such an awful thing, and illegal." Her eyes went wide, but she let him speak. "Only Mom, Edie, and Mathias know the truth."

She sat up and rubbed his arm. "You don't have to tell me if you don't want to."

"No, it's okay. I don't mind you knowing. I think it'll feel good to get this off my chest. When I was ten, I fell out of one of the apartment windows. Mom told us to stop horsing around, and of course, I didn't want to. Mom was mopping the floors, and I slipped and fell out of the window."

Saphira's face flinched in sympathy. "Ouch, that must have been painful."

"I'm sure it was, but I don't remember. Mom said when I fell, I was speared like a fish on one of the fence posts below." Saphira gasped and laid her hands on his chest. She could feel his heart beating fast as he told her his story.

"Edward," she whispered.

He took another deep breath and held one of her hands. "It…killed me, Saphira. I died in my mother's arms a few minutes later."

She moved her hand to his face and held his cheek. "She paid to resurrect you, didn't she?"

Edward nodded. "She did, it took all her savings. She

told me she couldn't have her husband and her little boy die on her. She knew it was illegal, but she had to." It had been illegal to resurrect anyone for close to thirty years. Too many of them had come back wrong, with demons and other things attached to their souls. The havoc it created was too much, so the practice was deemed illegal. It still happened, of course, but to a lesser degree and in back alleys instead of temples.

Saphira clicked her tongue and hugged him. "She did what any mother would do if they could, and I, for one, am glad she did." He leaned forward, and his arms tightened around her. They sat still for the longest time, their arms around one another. She didn't want to let go, and she had a feeling he didn't either. Finally, she sat back, and Edward began tucking her hair behind her ear over and over; the little soft movements sent tingles through her body. It made her smile.

"Thank you for not being mad, Saphy."

She shook her head. "I'd never be mad about you being in the world."

CHAPTER 16

FATE IN SALTHOLE

The group stayed in Ardenry for a week after the wedding. The twins and Rickert enjoyed their time, but whenever Saphira walked outside, she found herself searching in the shadows for her dark love. She didn't know what she'd do if she found him, kiss him, or strangle him. But she never saw him. The night before they left, the group gathered in Saphira's room and talked about where they wanted to go.

"Rickert, you mentioned Salthole a while back. Did you still want to go?" Saphira asked.

He nodded, "I do, if no one objects, we can start making our way there."

"Why don't we take a ship?" Eden suggested. "We could go to Fairwinds, see if anything catches our fancy on the way."

"From Fairwinds, it should be easy," Saphira said. "We'd just need to find a ship willing to take on passengers."

"Okay, it's settled then. We can ride the horses to Fairwinds and sell them for passage if necessary. Doubt anybody would want such beasts on their ship anyway," Rickert said. After one last dinner with the twins' parents, the group set out the next morning after Mayris made the twins promise to visit more often. Even riding on horses, it would take a couple of weeks to get to Fairwinds. There were lots of little valleys and rivers they would have to circumvent in order to keep the horses from hurting themselves.

One night, the group found a nice glade to rest in. Rickert even dared to suggest no one take a watch, but Saphira couldn't sleep anyway and said she'd watch as long as she could. The moon was high in the sky, Saphira knew it was late, and she should get some sleep, but couldn't turn her mind off. All she could think about was Iollan. She was so angry at him. It was all she could think about. She berated herself for not listening to her instincts when she first met him. If she had, maybe she wouldn't be so heartbroken now. *Why did the bastard have to be so wonderful?*

"Saphy?" She looked over and saw Edward was awake and looking at her. "You're still up?"

She shrugged her shoulders. "I can't sleep."

He quietly got to his feet and held out his hand. "Let's go for a walk," he whispered. Saphira reached up and let Edward pull her to her feet. "Maybe I can tire you out," he teased as they walked into the surrounding woods. The grass was soft under their feet, so it kept the noise to a minimum. "So, why can't you sleep?" He stopped and leaned against a tree.

Saphira crossed her arms across her stomach. "You don't want to hear my bitching, Edward." She kicked a little rock and heard it skitter away.

"If I didn't want to know, I wouldn't ask. Clearly, you need to talk to someone, and I'm right here." He pushed away from the tree and stood close to her. "I know I lack the parts Eden has for a traditional girl talk, but you can trust me."

She struggled not to laugh. "I don't want to laugh, I'm too mad."

"At him?"

Saphira huffed and kicked another rock. "I can't stop wondering why he left. He wanted me to tell him I wasn't my mother's daughter. Like it was a big deal or something. Most are glad I'm her daughter. It doesn't make sense. But I feel like a fool for trusting him." Edward reached out and rubbed her arms; it took a little of the night's chill away from her skin.

"You are not a fool, Saphira. You're a wonderful, kind soul who sees the good in people," he bent down to meet her eyes. "And I feel blessed to know you. It's his fault if he can't get over something about you." She felt his hand slowly move from her shoulder and up her neck. It didn't stop until he cupped her cheek. He stepped close, and she looked up at him. "Saphira-" a loud crack pierced the quiet night. They both gasped and looked around. "What was that?" he whispered.

Slowly, Saphira pulled her dagger out and began scanning the night. "The camp," she whispered and began quietly running back to where Rickert and Eden were sleeping. Soon, the campfire was visible through the trees, and Saphira could see the outline of a person in the woods, watching the sleeping couple. They were kneeling in an uncomfortable position. Without a second thought, she bolted at the stranger, who turned as Saphira put her dagger to his throat. "Want to tell me why you're spying on my friends?" she asked quietly.

The man smiled, and she could see his disgusting teeth. "Just seeing if there were others before my friends showed up."

Edward ran past her into the camp and picked up his bow as he yelled. "Rickert, Eden, wake up!"

"Where are they?" Saphira asked the dirty man.

He chuckled and pressed his throat against the blade. "All over." Anger seethed through her, and she didn't hesitate as she drew her blade across the man's neck. Before he fell to the ground, she abandoned the body and ran for the camp. Everyone was awake and searching for the intruders. So, she decided to stay in the woods and search for others.

"Saphira, where are you?" Rickert yelled, but she didn't want to answer. As she ran, she could see several figures jumping through the trees towards the camp. They either didn't see her or were ignoring her because none of them stopped, and if they didn't see her, she didn't want to give her position away.

"Saphira!" Edward's yell was desperate. She hated worrying him, but she had to get a few of these people before they were surrounded. She threw her dagger at the nearest one. A grunt told her she hit true.

Another target was on the ground, and Saphira could hear him start to cast a spell. "No, you don't." She threw the dagger again, and the man screamed as it sank into his right palm. "Who are you?" she asked, walking to the injured man.

Her dagger flew out of his hand, making him yell again. "Just kill me already, stop playing with me."

"Fine." She quickly stabbed down, shoving her dagger into the man's eye. He was a quiet one, and only shuddered once before he didn't move again. Her dagger was as bloody as it had ever been when she walked slowly into the camp. So far, everyone was okay. "They're in the trees," she said calmly.

Everyone's eyes went up, and Eden gasped. "What are they doing?"

Saphira shook her head. "I don't know. Rickert, would you like to play the diplomat?"

He was standing ready with his sword out. "I guess I could try." He stepped forward a little and barely lowered his sword. "This doesn't have to be an ugly confrontation!" he called out.

"But it does," a voice from the trees called out. "You're in our glade without our permission." When Saphira heard the voice, she could see the outline of another man high in a nearby tree and quickly flung her dagger at him. Another satisfying grunt told her she hit, and soon they heard the man crashing through the tree as he fell. Edward's bow was aimed high, scanning the trees as she walked over to the still man. His eyes were wide, and he was holding his hand over the bleeding wound on his neck.

"This glade does not belong to you. How dare you threaten us!" Saphira hissed at him. The man reached into his coat and pulled out a rock. She expected him to throw it at her, but instead, he squeezed it in his hand, and a flare went off. Soon, the woods were alive with yells and arrows all aimed at her. Saphira ducked and rolled the best she could, but there were so many. Edward grabbed her hand and pulled her close, and she heard Eden cast a spell. When she looked back, Saphira saw arrows bouncing off some invisible barrier around them.

"Ed, how many are there?" Rickert asked as his eyes squinted at the darkness around them.

"Six, I think." He knocked an arrow and quickly stepped out of the barrier and fired into the trees. As he hopped back in, they heard another body falling through the branches.

"Rickert, I could take them all out, but it'd leave us all vulnerable," Eden said.

"Do it," he said without hesitation, and stood defensively in front of her as Eden took the barrier down and pointed at one of the trees. Lightning shot from her fingers and leaped from tree to tree. Men screamed, and the night air was filled with the sound of breaking branches. Rickert looked down at her. "Saphira." Quickly, she and Rickert checked the bodies. "If they aren't dead, finish it," he said. She had no problem with his orders, but everybody she found was dead.

"All these are dead." Her ear twitched at the sound of a bow firing, and she looked back at the twins as Eden fell to the ground.

"Edie!" Edward yelled and fell to her side.

Saphira's eyes went wide, and she ran as fast as she could to her friend, "Edie!" she echoed Edward's yell, letting her know she was coming and everything would be all right. Rickert smashed through the trees, and they all heard the sound of his sword piercing flesh. Apparently, the mage missed one. Saphira slid next to Eden, her head was cradled in her brother's lap, and Saphira could see an arrow sticking high in her shoulder. Eden was breathing hard, and her face was a mask of pain.

"It's going to be okay, Edie, I promise." She wanted to pull the arrow out, but knew the mage might bleed to death if she did.

Rickert ran back and rifled through Eden's bag. "What color is it, Eden?" he asked as bottles began popping out of her bag.

"Blue, it's blue," she said through the pain, writhing in her brother's lap.

"What's blue?" Edward asked. Saphira looked over at the archer, his eyes were teary, but she knew he wouldn't cry. *How fast things change*, she thought, less than five minutes ago we were talking in the woods, now he's holding his wounded sister in his lap.

"Got it." Rickert pulled out a small blue bottle and popped the cork off before he sat next to Eden. All gentleness was lost as he pulled the arrow out, and Eden screamed as it was yanked from her body. "Drink Eden." He poured the liquid into her mouth, and Saphira watched as the wound stopped bleeding but didn't close all the way. "She won't bleed to death, but we don't have anymore healing potions." Saphira quickly got into her own bag and pulled out the last of the bandages from when she was shot.

"Here we'll use these, it'll help keep it clean." Edward helped his sister sit up straight; she groaned with every movement.

"Hey Saphira," she said weakly. "We're twins." She chuckled lightly, and Saphira smiled.

"If you're joking, then I know you're going to be fine."

"I will be, but gods does it hurt." Both Saphira and Edward wrapped up the mage's shoulder and made sure she had limited mobility with her arm.

Saphira turned to Rickert, "Should we move on for today?" Rickert was staring at Eden as she wiggled her fingers back and forth, seeing if any of her dexterity had been compromised, it didn't seem like it.

Saphira laid a hand on his arm, and he looked up. "Yeah, we should if you can manage Edie?"

She nodded. "I can get up, but I might have trouble steering my horse."

"You can ride with me." Rickert cupped her cheek. "I'm so sorry you got hurt."

"Hey, hazard of the trade, now get me on a horse so we can get out of here." He nodded and picked her up while Saphira and Edward cleaned up the camp. When the fire was out, they got on their horses and followed Rickert towards Fairwinds.

The group rode until they got to Fairwinds; their horses were exhausted, so were they. Eden's wound opened a few hours from town, and when they arrived, her dress was covered in blood, and she was woozy.

"Take her to the Temple!" Saphira yelled, "I'll make sure she gets healing, payment be damned." Their horses stopped with a jerk outside the temple, and Saphira led them up the stairs. Rickert was carrying Eden, and her brother was close behind.

The doors were open, and when the first acolyte came into view, Saphira ran to them. "I need help, please. I need a healer for my friend."

The young girl looked up and saw the group walk in. "Goodness, wait right here, I'll get someone." And she dashed away behind some curtains. Rickert set Eden on one of the pews, and she laid her head on his shoulder.

"Just a few more minutes, right?" Eden asked, her eyes closed tight.

Edward sat next to her and took her hand. "Right, you'll be feeling fine soon."

Saphira paced until Father Leif came running up to them. "Don't worry, young lady," he laid his hands on Eden. "You're going to be right as rain." Saphira felt the familiar warmth of Otto coming from the priest, and when Eden sighed, she knew her friend was healed. "There, feeling better?"

He stepped back while Eden moved her arm up and down. "Feels perfect, thank you, Father."

"You're most welcome. I'm Father Leif. Are you passing through today?" He turned, smiling at the others, and gasped when his eyes landed on the rogue. "Saphira! I'm sorry I didn't see you standing there. How's your mum doing? I trust Lily is still giving Lord Giles a run for his money?" He opened his arms wide, and Saphira hugged the priests who had married her parents.

"Hello, Father Leif. You know, Mom. We were hoping to catch a boat when our mage was feeling better, looks like she does."

Eden stood and elbowed Rickert in the stomach. "Told you," she hissed at him. "Yes, I'm much better." Saphira gave her a little wink as thanks. If what Leif wasn't proof enough for Rickert, there was no hope he'd ever believe Saphira was who she said she was.

Leif chuckled and clasped his hands in front of him. "Good, so where are you four headed?"

"Salthole," Edward said. Saphira couldn't help but see

how relieved he looked now Eden was healthy.

"Really? Might the church ask a favor of you then?"

"Absolutely, Father, name it," Rickert said with a smile on his face as he rubbed his stomach. Leif leaned against the pews, and the light glinted off the seashell around his neck for a moment.

"I have a young acolyte who wishes to take his vows in Salthole. Would it be too much of an inconvenience if he tagged along with you?"

"No, not at all." Saphira smiled and relished the idea of an acolyte traveling with them, especially one so close to taking their vows.

Father Leif clapped his hands together. "Wonderful! I'll let Andros know he'll be leaving soon."

"I think we'll go peruse the docks and see what's available to us. We won't leave without him, Father," Saphira said as Rickert shook the priest's hand before they watched him quickly make his way back into the temple.

"Another healer, hope he fares better," Edward said.

"As long as we don't run into any pirates, we should be fine, Ed. Come on," Saphira linked her arm through his. "Let's go look for ships." He let her pull him from the temple, and she walked the familiar route to the docks. They could see several ships in port, and Saphira hoped one of them was headed towards Salthole.

"So, you knew that Priest, Leif?" He asked as they walked down the wooden planks.

"Yeah, Mom is from Fairwinds, and she and Leif grew up in the church together. He actually married my parents after the Battle of Raventree."

"Oh, how nice. Does she ever think about moving back here?"

Saphira shook her head. "No, she'd never leave Raventree. It means too much to her now. She and Lord Giles are best friends; we were all born there."

They stopped on the dock and looked at the ships around

them. "I've never been that far west." Edward looked down at her. "We should visit."

"Yes, we should. I'd love my family to meet my other family."

She felt her ear twitch as she heard a voice above them. "Ho there! Care for a trip abroad?" Saphira snickered and looked around for the owner of the loud voice and found a man leaning over the railing of the ship they were standing next to.

"Actually, we are looking for passage for five to Salthole, going that way by chance?" she called up.

The man smiled and leaped onto the dock, walking over to them. "We can be, if you got the coin." He was younger than Saphira first thought; he couldn't have been more than thirty. His black hair was slicked back, and he had the oddest facial hair she'd ever seen. It almost looked like octopus arms on his cheeks, and his goatee came to a point an inch away from his face.

"Coin isn't a problem," she held out her hand. "Saphira, this is Edward; there are three others."

He took her hand and laid a kiss on her skin. "Wonderful to meet you. I am Captain Nightingale. This is my ship, The Double D, and if you have the coin, I will take you wherever you desire."

Saphira snickered and took her hand back. "Thanks, we can be ready to leave later today, if that's good with you?"

"Absolutely, my men are ready and anxious to get to sea. We will await your return."

"Good, we'll be back, then."

Edward took her hand, and they headed back to the temple. "I'm not sure I like him."

Saphira laughed. "You're annoyed because he kissed my hand." He scoffed but didn't correct her.

They walked up the steps of the temple, and Saphira could see a tall young man in white robes shaking hands with Rickert. *He's quite handsome,* she thought. He had shaggy blonde hair, and his face was kind. He turned as she walked inside, his face was already smiling, but when his eyes landed on her, she could see it brighten even more.

"Hello, you must be Saphira. I'm Andros." He held out his hand, and his divine nature flowed over her, and she felt comforted for the first time in months.

"I am, it's nice to meet you."

"I must say it will be a pleasure traveling with Mother Lily's daughter. I know Otto will bless our journey." She smiled. It reminded her so much of being around her family, she knew this trip would be a treat.

"He will. Why don't we make our way to the docks? I have a feeling the Captain is itching to get out of port." Everyone got their packs, and they found a man to buy their horses, and like Saphira thought he would be, Captain Nightingale was waiting for them as they walked up the plank.

His arms were crossed, and a smile spread on his face. "A priest of Otto? You didn't say you had a priest in your ranks. This will definitely be a fortuitous trip," he said, welcoming them on board. The rest of the group introduced themselves, and the Captain was nice enough to show them the room they would stay in. There were no cots, but they could hang hammocks or lay on the blankets they had.

"Looks like enough room for everybody," Andros said happily. He took Saphira's hand. "It's been ages since I've been on a boat, let's go watch it pull out." She laughed as he pulled her out of the room and up the stairs. Andros was so upbeat, it was refreshing. So much drama and tough times had been a part of her life recently. She almost forgot how comforting Otto could be. They walked back on deck, and Saphira saw the rest of her group file out after them. Edward stopped next to her.

"Ready to get going?"

He looked over and smiled at her. "Yes, Rickert paid the Captain, and we're about to get underway." He slid an arm around her. "Are you feeling better?"

She shrugged her shoulders. "I think being around Andros will be good for me. Honestly, it'll be good for all of us." She laid her head on his chest and felt the boat give a little jolt.

"Let Otto bless us on our journey." She heard Andros say and smiled at him.

"He will."

Andros turned and smiled a dazzling smile at her. "Perhaps we can pray together later, Saphira?"

"I'd like that, Andros, thank you." He nodded and made his way below deck.

Saphira felt Edward's fingers under her chin, and she looked up at him. "You've missed Otto, haven't you?"

"I have, he reminds me of home. I was never as pious as Christopher, and maybe not even Foster. But the familiarity is comforting."

"Then I'm glad we said we'd take him along. I want you to be happy, Saphira."

She chuckled. "I want to be happy too, Ed, believe me."

The trip took a little longer than usual; early autumn storms greatly slowed the ship, and the group spent a good deal of time in their room out of the rain. Andros and Saphira prayed every day, and she felt her old self coming back. At night, she would sleep next to Edward, his arms wrapped tightly around her. It was comforting, but not the same. One day, the clouds were daring to rain on them, and Saphira was on deck, letting the cool air whip her hair around her head.

"Saphira?"

She turned at the almost cleric's voice and smiled. "Good afternoon, Andros."

He walked next to her and laid his arms on the railing. "Clouds are busy today," he said.

"They are, guess we'll see if they go into overtime."

Andros smiled and laced his hands together. "Saphira, may I ask you something?"

"Of course, anything."

He stood straight and faced her, looking just a tinge embarrassed. "What was it like growing up with your mother?"

Saphira chuckled and licked her lips. "It was wonderful,

Otto was always present in our home. I didn't realize how much I'd miss it when I left."

"Why did you leave?" He leaned against the boat.

She shrugged her shoulders. "I wanted to travel, make my own fortune. What about you? Why do you want to take your vows in Salthole?"

"My father's from Salthole. I was ten when he died and was sent to live with my grandparents in Fairwinds. But when they died, the church took me in. I always knew I wanted to go back to Salthole, try to bring some light to such a dark town. I'm grateful you're letting me tag along."

She waved her hand and looked out to sea. "It's no problem, but I doubt you'd have trouble finding a boat. A good Captain would easily accept a cleric of Otto on their ship, most for free." She smiled, and he laughed and took her hand.

"You're right, I know, but I'm glad to be with your group." She squeezed his hand, begging for Otto's comfort, but as the days passed, she realized it felt different than before. "Is there something weighing on your heart, Saphira?" *Of course, he could tell,* she thought, a good priest could see a troubled soul a mile away.

"I've appreciated praying with you, Andros, but I'm wondering something." He didn't speak, just focused on her, letting her say what she needed to say. "It feels familiar and comforting, but I'm wondering if it's comforting because it's familiar, and that…maybe my heart doesn't see Otto."

He patted the hand he held. "That's a hard place to be."

"Especially for me. It's not like I don't love Otto, he's a wonderful god, but," she sighed. "I don't think I feel it the same as the rest of my family."

"Your relationship with the gods is a personal one, something only you can decide how you wish to fulfill it."

"I know. But I worry…" she couldn't believe she was able to say it. "I worry Otto doesn't favor me. No," she shook her head. "Andros, there's something in me that's different from the rest of my family."

"Different how?" She was glad he hadn't let go of her hand and squeezed. Her other hand pulled out her dagger, and she gave it a little flip.

"I've killed men, I'm sure you know it's part of this life," she sheathed her blade. "But when I do…I feel satisfied. I worry it means I'm—"

"Shh," he reached up and cupped her cheek. "You are not evil, Saphira, I can tell. And you're right, killing is part of this life. Perhaps the feeling you get is the satisfaction of a job well done, or knowing this person isn't going to hurt anyone else. There are those who take pleasure in killing, but they usually seek it out. You don't seek it out, I'm thinking?" She shook her head. "You are Mother Lily's third-born, and I know Otto sees you. Maybe in a different light, but there is no way he would abandon you." Saphira closed her eyes and tilted her head to the sky. She tried hard to keep the tears from falling, but they fell anyway.

"Thank you, Andros." She let the sea wind whip around her and dry her tears. "You're going to make a wonderful priest." She opened her eyes and looked back at the young acolyte.

"Thank you, that means a lot."

Saphira felt his divine nature flow around her and smiled. "So, are you devoting your entire life to Otto, or will you marry one day?" she asked, desperately trying to change the subject.

He chuckled. "A lot of girls ask me the same question," he finally let go of her hand and rested his arms on the edge of the boat. "I'm devoting my service for the moment."

She nodded her head and smiled. "My brother is devoting his entire life. I can't imagine not loving someone or having children. I tried to talk him out of it, but he wouldn't hear of it."

Andros gave her a playful nudge. "I see you and your friend Edward are rather close."

She sighed and looked back out to sea. "We're just friends, touch is his love language, I think. Besides, I think my heart needs a rest." She told him what happened with Iollan, and he shook his head.

"What a dumb move. Perhaps this is one of those things

that only time can fix." She felt his hand on her back. Time was supposed to fix things, but so far, she wasn't sure.

"Perhaps."

She turned and saw Edward walking over. "Andros, there you are. Would you like to play cards with us?"

Andros moved, and she felt his hand slip off her back. "I would, if that's okay?"

She nodded. "Far be it from me to keep you from losing coin."

Andros laughed. "I'll meet you down there."

The acolyte walked away, and Edward took his place by her side. "You seem to be getting along with Andros."

Saphira shrugged. "I grew up with clerics; it's natural to me."

He reached out and held her hand. "I had been wondering if you liked him."

"Oh no," she shook her head. "I'm not ready for any of that."

He squeezed her hand and let go. "I didn't think so, but you take all the time you need to heal." She watched him go back below and wished she'd have stuck to her original plan and not bothered falling for anything while out in the world.

CHAPTER 17
ROGUE KING

After a month at sea, The Double D finally made port in Salthole. Capt. Nightingale thanked them for their patronage and said anytime they saw his ship, they would be welcome aboard. The group decided to walk Andros to the temple; he was sort of their charge after all. Saphira had been to Salthole once and vaguely remembered how to get there, so she led the way. After a few twists and turns, they could see the roof of the temple gleaming in the distance.

"There it is!" Andros pointed at it, and Saphira couldn't help but smile at his enthusiasm. Inside, the temple looked much like the one in Ardenry, but there were more shells decorating the dais. Being on the coast, it was much easier to acquire them. Andros turned to the group, his face was all smiles. "Thank you so much for letting me tag along. I shall say a prayer for you each night." He walked up to Saphira and took her hands. "It was an immense pleasure meeting you, Saphira. I wish you all the happiness in the world." He leaned down and kissed her cheek, and she felt Otto's blessing.

"Thank you, Andros, your prayers are most appreciated." She gave his hands one last squeeze, and he walked down the aisle towards a few of the priests who were talking by the confessional booths.

"Well, shall we find some work?" she heard her boss ask.

Saphira turned. "Sounds good. How long did you want to stay, Rickert?" The group walked out of the temple and into the dirty streets of Salthole.

"Maybe we could stay through the winter? There are not too many places we could get to before then, unless you're itching to get home, Saphira."

She knew he was teasing, but indulged him anyway. "Not a chance."

He chuckled. "I didn't think so."

The group found work easily enough. Saphira and Rickert got jobs as town guards. She vied for night duty again, especially since the nights were cooling off. She knew the cool air would keep her awake. Eden got a job helping a local mage make potions and look after the shop. Saphira could tell she looked forward to it every day, and Edward found work helping a blacksmith while his apprentice was out with a broken foot.

They got rooms at a local inn and quickly settled into their lives. During her night watch, Saphira would sneak around town and do what she did in Blackridge; she'd watch. There were a lot of dirty dealings that happened in this port town, and her mornings were spent reporting what she heard from the thieves on the streets or petty criminals she'd run across. She only killed while on duty once. She found a man trying to force himself on a woman, and she sank her dagger in the man's back before he had his way with her. Saphira helped the woman home and gasped when she saw the three little ones waiting by the fire for their mother. They all smiled and squealed as she walked through the door. The last thing this woman needed was another child. Saphira left some coins on the table by the door when she left. The little family needed it more than she did.

When she wasn't sneaking up on people, Saphira would stand on the rooftops and think about her dark fighter. She didn't know why she thought about him; maybe it was the chilly air reminding her of Blackridge. But it was clear he wasn't coming back.

The threat of winter was upon Salthole, and Saphira had to go on duty with her heavy cloak now. One night, she was standing on one of the highest roofs in town, the wind was blowing in from the sea, and the smell of salt and fish permeated the air. It had been a slow night so far when an unfamiliar voice spoke behind her.

"You know you're pretty sneaky." She turned, her dagger already in her hand, but she kept it behind her back. Her ear hadn't even twitched; it worried her.

"Not as sneaky as you are apparently." The man looked around her age and was smiling at her. He was the most handsome man she'd ever seen, with dark hair and a short beard on his face.

"Honesty, I like that. I'm Gareth Quinn." Her eyes widened. From all the nights she had spent sneaking around Salthole, this man's name was on many a thief's lips.

"You're head of the thieves' guild? You're so young." He chuckled as he paced back and forth. Saphira watched as he flipped his dagger over and over, catching it by the handle every time.

"Age has nothing to do with it, skills, connections, they help more than how old a person is." He turned, and she could see his gray eyes looking her over. "You've caused a lot of problems for us lately."

"Whatever do you mean?" She feigned ignorance, and he laughed; it was hearty and happy. He was still flipping his dagger end over end in his hand, catching it lightly. Saphira was waiting for him to throw it at her.

"You've been spilling our secrets to the local guard, and our livelihood has been disrupted. Our coin flow has lessened immensely, and I intend to do something about that."

Saphira started pacing with him. "What did you intend to do?"

Gareth stopped and pointed his dagger at her. "Recruit you," he said with a dazzling smile she had to fight not to react to.

Saphira blinked a few times. She did not expect to hear those words. "Recruit me? How would that help?"

"Well, you'd be one of us," he whipped his dagger around as he talked. "I'm sure the secrets you learn could benefit us. Plus, you wouldn't be stopping my men from getting the coin they're used to getting from the public. You'd get a fair share, of course, more if you've got more to offer." Saphira stared at him. Never in her life had she been given such an opportunity.

"You do know who I am, right?"

He smiled, his arms behind his back. "Saphira Voltain, only daughter and youngest child of Mother Lily of Raventree. You're traveling with Rickert Basine and the twins, Eden and Edward McVain. I know full well who you are and what I ask." He took a few steps closer. "And I think you're more interested than you let on."

She crossed her arms and tried not to meet his eyes. "Maybe."

Gareth chuckled and scratched the side of his face with his dagger. "What do you say, Voltain? Want to join?"

"Is the only reason you want me to join is so I'll stop turning in your thieves?"

He laughed. "Oh no, I've watched you the last few weeks, and you're a talented rogue. The way you leap from rooftop to rooftop is otherworldly. Your knife work is neat and accurate, and I'd be honored to teach you everything I know and make you one of the best thieves in the world. Keeping you from stopping my men is a pleasant side effect." He sounded so proud, Saphira didn't know if she should be flattered or not.

"What if I say no?"

"Hmm," she felt his eyes roam over her as he licked his bottom lip. "I don't think you will." Gareth walked close, and she could smell the spicy cologne on his skin mixed with his leathers. It was ambrosial.

She cleared her throat to try to put it from her mind. "Don't you think wearing cologne is kind of a no-no if you're sneaking around?"

He chuckled, and she swore she felt it rumble through her. "I do, as a matter of fact," he leaned close. "But I'm not sneaking, I'm recruiting. What do you say?" She swore his voice got quieter with every word.

She rolled her eyes. "You expect me to say yes or no right here?" His dagger flashed, and Saphira quickly blocked and rolled out of the way. "What the hell?" Gareth jumped for her, and she managed to get out of the way. When she turned, he was gone. "I know you're still here, I'm not an idiot."

His sly chuckle bounced off the air, and she couldn't tell where it was coming from. "Of course you're not an idiot. I don't hire idiots." Saphira's ear twitched, and without looking, she thrust her dagger out. When she turned, she saw the point of her dagger touching Gareth's throat while the flat of his blade lay against hers. "You heard me, impressive Voltain. You know, most of my men want me to kill you. They say you're bad for business, but I say otherwise." Slowly, he took his dagger off her neck and backed up.

Saphira got to her feet, keeping her weapon in her hand. "Who's to say they won't kill me anyway, or you for asking me to join?"

The chilly wind picked up, and his dark hair ruffled in the breeze. "They wouldn't, they do what I say, and if I say not to kill you, they won't. So, what do you say, Voltain?" Truthfully, he had her from the moment he said he'd teach her everything he knew, but she didn't want to seem too eager.

"You'll teach me what you know?"

He smiled and put an arm around her shoulders. "Everything."

She crossed her arms over her stomach. "You better."

Chuckling, he withdrew his arm and sheathed his dagger. "I may be a thief, but I always keep my word. Meet me at The Roasted Orc tomorrow night, unless you have something better to do?"

"Tomorrow night?" It was actually her night off, and she knew Edward was planning something fun for them to do. But she couldn't resist this once-in-a-lifetime opportunity. "I'll be there."

"Splendid." He gave her a little salute and hopped off the roof. Saphira ran over to the edge and watched as Gareth walked calmly down the street, like he owned it, and she couldn't help but smile. The things she'd learn from him could make her rich and well known; tomorrow night couldn't come fast enough.

When the sun rose, Saphira walked over to the blacksmith's shop where Edward was working. She had to catch him before he finalized the plans he wanted to make that night. She knew he was already at work when she heard the familiar clink clink of metal on metal. When she could finally see him, he was shirtless, even though it had to be fifty degrees outside, but he was already dripping with sweat and had smudges of soot on his chest.

"Edward!" He looked up and smiled; it made her feel guilty about what she was about to do.

"Have a good night?" He asked as he hammered against a sword.

"I did, it was interesting. I wanted to talk to you about tonight." Edward smiled and put his hammer down and quenched the blade in a nearby water barrel.

"I'm really looking forward to spending some time with you."

Saphira bit her lip. "Is there any chance we could do something earlier in the day? Something came up tonight."

He sighed. "They making you work again? We don't need money that bad, tell them no."

She shook her head and clasped her hands together. "No, it's not work, it's something else."

He pushed his dark auburn hair back into a ponytail. "Oh, what is it?"

Edward crossed his arms, and she could tell he was trying not to sound as upset as he was.

She pulled him close and whispered, "Gareth Quinn came to me last night. He wants to teach me."

He pulled back, and she could plainly see how upset he looked. "Gareth Quinn? He's a criminal, Saphira. Why would you want to hang around him?"

"I know he's a criminal, but he can teach me a lot. That asshole actually snuck up on me!"

His eyes went wide. "Damn, he did?" She nodded, and

he went back to hammering whatever it was he was working on. "Okay, I guess I get it. Rain check?"

"Yeah, for sure." She patted him on the back and ran to the sheriff's office to report what had happened last night. Sans her meeting the Thief King.

Saphira had been trying to sleep for hours, but the excitement about learning from the thief king was keeping her awake. She tossed and turned until a knock on her window made her sit up. Gareth was waving at her through the window. The sun was shining behind him; it had to be around one in the afternoon. Saphira threw the covers off, glad she didn't undress for bed, and opened the window a crack.

"What are you doing here?" His nimble fingers slid through the crack and opened the window all the way.

"Well," he sat on the windowsill and held his hands in his lap. "I heard the little conversation you had with your man, and I thought, far be it from me to cause discord in your life. So, this asshole thought I'd come by and offer to teach you right now, instead of tonight." She stared at him for a few moments. He seemed genuine, and learning what he had to teach sounded a lot more fun than sleeping.

"Were you following me?" She crossed her arms over her stomach and watched his face. He seemed highly amused.

"Of course I was," he said with an irritating smile.

Saphira rolled her eyes and sat back on the bed to pull her boots on. "Of course you were," she mumbled to herself.

Gareth chuckled and hopped into the room. "By the time I'm through with you, you'll be able to see me coming, guaranteed."

"I better," she stood and pulled her cloak and boots on. "And he's not my man."

"Apologies." He gave her a little bow, and she fought hard not to smile.

"So where do we start?"

"The Roasted Orc." He motioned to the window.

"You know we could just walk out the front door," she said as she leaned down and crawled onto the roof.

"Yeah, but where's the fun in that?" He had a point.

As they walked to the 'Orc', Saphira noticed how some people gave Gareth a wide berth, while others smiled happily at him.

"Some people seem afraid of you," she said quietly.

He shrugged his shoulders. "I imagine I must have done some kind of business with them that they didn't exactly find fair."

She raised an eyebrow at him. "Fair? Like you cheated them?"

Gareth scoffed and put his arm around her shoulder. "I don't cheat Saphira," he whispered in her ear.

"Uh-huh." She didn't believe that for a second. The Roasted Orc was in the roughest part of town, the furthest from the ocean, and the closer they got, the more familiar the faces were. "I've arrested almost half of the people we're walking by," she whispered.

Gareth snickered. "I know, and they're embarrassed. Part of the reason why they don't want you to join."

"Embarrassed they were caught or embarrassed they were caught by a girl?"

Gareth laughed loudly as he opened the door to the seedy tavern. "Both most like." The Orc was dark inside. Lit candles were placed at every table, but Saphira would have preferred it to be a bit brighter. Gareth led her up the stairs while the entire room stared at her.

She decided not to let it bother her and turned to everyone. "Good morning, all! Gareth and I have some important business to discuss, so I'd appreciate it if you gave us some time alone." She winked and slapped Gareth on the butt before walking into the second story hallway.

Gareth was laughing as he joined her. "That really woke them up." He unlocked the door at the end of the hall and waved her in. It was bright from the afternoon sun, and everything was neat and in its place. Gareth sat on a large trunk by the foot of his bed. "Now, where shall we start?"

Saphira shook her head. "Wherever you want, you're the expert."

Smiling, he stood and drew his dagger. "Let's see you in action then."

As the sun went down, Saphira walked into her room and saw Edward pulling on his nice red shirt. "Ed?"

He turned at the sound of her voice. "There you are, I was worried when I didn't see you in bed."

Saphira hung up her cloak and sat on the bed. "I'm fine."

He sat beside her, his hands clasped. "If you're not too tired now, we could still spend some time together?"

Saphira smiled. She was bone tired, but decided to tough it out for a few more hours. "I'd like that." Edward smiled and whisked her out the door. They walked around town and talked about their days. Admittedly, Saphira had trouble concentrating. All she could think about was what Gareth had taught her, and it was already paying off. There were things about the town she didn't notice before that were painfully obvious now, and her eyes darted back and forth, keeping watch while Edward talked away.

Gareth showed her a way to walk on slanted roofs so you wouldn't fall off, how to trail a person when you have to duck into an alley to avoid suspicion. She wanted to know more, but he said a little at a time was best. But when they went back to the Orc to eat, he showed her how to see if there was poison in your food. Because, according to him, 'your nose might be stuffy, but your eyes will always work'. She asked him what you do if you're blind. He said don't eat soup. That advice brought the first genuine smile out of her all day.

"What do you think about that, Saphy?" Edwards' voice woke her from her thoughts.

"Sorry, I thought I saw something. What did you say?"

He smiled. "I said, since we're going to be here for so long, we should try to find a house to stay in. We'd probably save some money."

Saphira nodded. "Yeah, good idea. I'll look around tomorrow night if it's quiet."

"Good. So, tell me about your day. I feel I've been talking non-stop."

She smiled. "You have been," she teased and pinched his cheek. "Gareth showed me some tricks of the trade. It's already paying off." Edward stood straight; she could tell it bothered him that she spent time with the rogue.

"Gareth, huh? Well, I hope it's worth it, guys like him are dangerous."

She laced her arm through his. "It will be, but you don't have to worry. I'll be fine."

"I can't help but worry about you, Saphira," he said as he led them towards the docks. "I don't know what I'd do if I lost you." His words made her feel guilty; it seemed like he cared for her more than she cared for him. It wasn't as if she wasn't attached to him; she was attached to everyone in the group. But Edward was just Ed, he was too…she could never put her finger on it. But he seemed too pure for her. Like he belonged in the sunlight, and she belonged in the shadows.

They walked towards the end of the docks before he spoke. "Surprise," he said as she read 'The Double D' on the side of the ship.

"Are we going for a ride?" She followed Edward up the plank and gasped when she saw the little candlelit picnic on the deck. "Oh, Ed." There were a few fire pits around a blanket to keep them warm as they'd sit and eat.

Captain Nightingale walked over and bowed to them. "That's a right thoughtful man you have there, miss. You two enjoy your dinner," he said and left the two alone.

Edward walked over to the blanket. "Come join me," he held out his hand.

"This must have cost a pretty penny." She slowly made her way over.

"It's okay, it's a special occasion."

The corner of her lip tilted in a smile. "What occasion?"

"First picnic on a boat," he teased.

Saphira snorted and took his hand. "I've never had a picnic on a ship before." They both sat down on the blanket. The firepits kept everything comfortably warm. She'd feel a cool breeze from the sea every so often.

"I wanted us to have a nice private dinner, but it's hard to come by when you're living in an inn."

"That is so true." It had been a long time since dinner wasn't interrupted by some fight or disagreement somewhere in the tavern. It was nice having a quiet dinner for once.

The food was wonderful and private, like Edward said it would be. He brought fried chicken, potatoes, and corn, and to her delight, the amazing sweet cornbread from a bakery down the road from the inn. After a day of sneaking around, she was starving and ate her fill and wondered if Edward would have to roll her off the ship.

"Saphira, can I ask you something?"

She nodded. "Sure." He looked almost hesitant, and he was reaching for her hand when a voice rang out.

"Well, look at this." They both turned, and Saphira saw Gareth walking up the plank to them.

"Gareth? What are you doing here?" He walked over to them, a slick smile on his face.

"Gareth Quinn?" Edward looked at Saphira; she could see he looked a little worried.

"The one and only," he held out his hand to Edward.

Being ever the gentleman, Edward took it and gave it a shake. "Edward McVain."

"Pleasure." He looked down, "Oh, fried chicken."

Edward motioned to it, "Please have a piece."

Gareth sat down gracefully and picked up a drumstick. "Thank you."

Saphira crossed her arms and stared at the thief. "What are you doing here?"

He took a big bite and closed his eyes. "Mmm, good." He opened them and pointed to the fires around them. "I was walking down the docks and saw the fires. I wanted to make sure the ship wasn't on fire, but instead I found you." He looked between them and took another bite.

"Aren't you just the most upright citizen?" Saphira teased.

He gave her a wink. "So," he swallowed another bite, "how long is your group staying in Salthole?"

"Least through the winter," Edward said.

"If you're staying that long, it might be more comfortable in a house."

"Edward had mentioned finding a house earlier," Saphira motioned towards the archer. "It was a good idea."

"I agree," he nodded at the archer. "I think I know the perfect place."

"Oh?" Saphira sat back and crossed her arms.

"I can show you tomorrow night," he said around the big bite of chicken in his mouth.

"Why at night?" Edward asked.

"Gotta break in, don't want to catch too many eyes. Plus, Voltain works at night, the timing is right."

Saphira huffed. "We don't need a stolen house, Gareth."

"It's not stolen," he waved the chicken around. "No one lives there, and the owners died a long time ago. No one wants to live there."

"Why not?" Edward looked warily over at Saphira, who shrugged.

"The town thinks it's haunted."

Saphira laughed. "No such thing." Then she remembered Elralia and wondered if the rumors might indeed be true.

"You're right, but that unfounded fear has kept this house empty for nigh on thirty years. So, it'll be dusty, but free."

Saphira looked over at Edward, who shrugged and nodded. "Okay, show me tomorrow."

Gareth got to his feet in one smooth move, still eating the chicken. "Wonderful, I'll see you tomorrow. Nice to meet you,

McVain. Thanks for the chicken." He turned and walked down the plank. After one more big bite, he threw the bone into the water and walked back onto the dock.

"Odd, but at least we have a lead on a house." She leaned forward and took a sip of the sweet wine. "What did you want to ask me?"

Ed finally turned back to her and smiled. "I forget, it must not have been important."

"I'm sure you'll remember later."

When they got back to their room, Saphira had been up for almost twenty-four hours, and she was exhausted. She slipped into her nightgown and moaned happily as she slid under the covers. "So tired."

Edward chuckled, "Yeah, you've been up for a while, haven't you?"

"Mm-hmm." Her back was facing him, but she could hear him undressing and felt him get into bed. She felt his arms around her, and he pulled her against his chest. "So warm."

He chuckled, "Sleep well, Saphira."

"Okay. Thank you for the lovely dinner." She wasn't sure if she said it or thought it before sleep sucked her under.

After some well-deserved sleep, Saphira woke alone in bed but found a note from Edward on the vanity.

Saphira, I hope you had fun last night. I can't wait until we have a night together where you aren't exhausted.

She smiled and folded the letter before putting it in her bag. When she was ready and her stomach full, it was still a few hours before her guard shift, so she decided to see if going outside would conjure the thief king. She wanted to see the house he told them about. As she walked towards the older part of town a voice caught her attention.

"Voltain!"

Saphira whirled with a smile and saw Gareth walking over to her. "My Lord, what can I do for you?" she teased.

He stopped in front of her, chuckling. "I've come to show

you the house, My Lady." He motioned for her to follow, and they walked down a block with big old houses. He stopped in front of a dark, two-story house. "Here we are." Saphira studied the empty structure. There was wood over the numerous windows, and she hoped they weren't broken. Glass could be expensive to replace.

"No one lives here?"

Gareth shook his head. "Nope, thieves honor."

Saphira scoffed. "Who owned it last?" They walked up the stairs, and she watched Gareth pick the lock with ease.

"The last family was named Eli, and no one's lived here permanently in over thirty years."

Her ears picked up at the name that was almost as familiar as her own. "Eli?"

The thief nodded as the door swung open with a loud groan. "I believe you're familiar?" he said with a brilliant smile. Carefully, Saphira stepped inside. It smelled musty, and dust covered everything like Gareth said it would. But she knew this house. Her mother had spoken of it often when she was a girl. She, her first husband Henri, and her friend Taren Eli had stayed here one winter in Salthole. It was Taren's family's home.

"Gareth, I don't believe it." She was in awe. She could almost hear her mother's stories as she looked around. The living room where she would brush their hair dry. The staircase where she cried about the little girl who was murdered. Saphira pulled the dust-coated cover off one of the chairs and was happy to see it was in good condition. "It's exactly like she said." Saphira turned and saw him smiling at her in the doorway. "How did you know about this?" He pushed away from the wall and walked around the living room.

"Everybody in town knows about this house. How forty-some-odd years ago, the family who lived here experienced a great deal of tragedy. The father was killed in the woods, and a month later, the mother was eviscerated in her son's bedroom. He was found covered in blood in the kitchen, but survived. Then one day he just left. No one ever saw him again until he brought a few friends to stay the winter." Gareth stopped in front of her. Once again, he was so close she could smell his cologne. "Your mother was one of those friends," he said wistfully.

Saphira snickered and crossed her arms over her stomach. "How the hell do you know so much?"

He shrugged and walked over to the cold fireplace. "It's my job to know. Plus, this house is sort of an urban legend. Ask anyone around here, they'll tell you the same thing."

"Oh, so it isn't your preternatural senses that knew about the house then, noted." She teased, and he put a hand on his heart and feigned disappointment.

"My lady, you wound me! Everything about me is preternatural, I'll have you know."

She laughed. She never thought she would tease the rogue king of Salthole.

"Everything?" He closed the distance between them in two strides, and his scent, that heavenly scent of cedar and leather that was all him, filled her nose.

"Everything." His voice was low, and she couldn't help but notice how close his lips were. "Come, let me show you around." He linked his arm with hers and walked her from room to room.

As they walked, she thought about what her mother told her about her time in Salthole. She, Henri, and Taren settled into his childhood home one winter. Her mother knew Taren was a werewolf by then. That part fit into the story about the house's sad history, but Saphira didn't know he had accidentally killed his mother. Whether he kept it to himself or her mother omitted it, Saphira wasn't sure, but wouldn't blame Taren for not sharing everything.

"So, Mr. preternatural," they walked into the kitchen, and she took her arm back from him and put her hands on her hips. "Do you know everyone who stayed here that winter?"

Gareth made odd marks on the dust covering the windows as he talked. "Well, your mother and her love Henri, the owner, I think his name was Taren or some such, and a priest of Otto."

A priest? Her mother never mentioned a priest had traveled with the three of them.

"Are you sure there were four of them?"

Gareth turned and nodded his head. "Oh yeah, they made a big impact at the temple while they were here." Saphira turned and stared at the stairway. Who was this man, and why didn't her mother mention him? The voice in her head screamed at her to leave it alone. But she didn't know why it bothered; she never listened to it. Iollan was proof of that.

She walked back into the front room and leaned against the stair railing. "Do you know anything else about this priest?"

"Hmm, well, he was older than the others, but not his name. Did she not tell you any of this?"

She shook her head. "I knew about Taren, and Henri, of course, but she never mentioned a priest." Why had her mother never mentioned this other man. Was he dead? No, Taren was dead, and her mother always talked about him. Had this priest asked her not to speak of him? Seemed like an odd thing to ask for. Was he an old boyfriend? No, her mother told them about all her boyfriends, though it wasn't many. Why leave this one out, a priest of all people?

Slowly, she walked towards the door, but Gareth stepped in front of her. "What is it?"

She shook her head. "Nothing, Gareth, thank you for showing me the house." She tried to sidestep him, but he caught her arm and pulled her close.

"I can tell something's wrong, Saphira. Is it the house?" It was the first time he had called her Saphira, instead of Voltain. As much as she wanted to hear it again, she had to leave.

"It's nothing. My mind's wandering to places it shouldn't." Gareth closed the already short distance between them and wrapped his arms around her.

"I thought you'd like to see this house."

She slid her arms around him and held him tight against her. "I am glad you showed me, Gareth. I feel closer to my mother than ever." She laid her head on his chest and could hear how fast his heart was beating.

He lifted her head with a gentle touch of his hand. "I'm glad I could help." Again, she couldn't help but notice how close his lips were to hers. They looked soft, and she felt her stomach tighten at the thought.

"Thank you, Gareth. I'll let everyone else know about the house."

He smiled. "You're welcome." She stared into his lovely gray eyes for a moment before she reached up and ran her fingertips along his jawline. "You know that man of yours is a nice guy," he whispered. "But he doesn't fit you." Gareth leaned down, and she felt his lips speak against her cheek. "You need someone more intense, less sunshine, and more darkness."

She turned so her lips grazed the corner of his. "Like you?"

He smiled. "Maybe." She slowly raised a dagger between them and touched the tip against his lower lip. "You wicked little thing." Gareth chuckled and looked down. "You nicked my dagger," he sounded impressed.

Saphira shrugged and pocketed it. "It's mine now. And he's not my man." She started for the door again, and he leaned against the side of the stairs, a hungry smile on his face.

"No?" She shook her head and heard him laugh as she ran down the road. Flirting with Gareth was fun, but he had revealed something about her mother's past she didn't know, and despite the voice in her mind telling her to leave it alone, she had to know.

Saphira was out of breath as she reached the top of the stairs of the temple and heard a cheerful voice call out to her.

"Saphira!" Andros jogged over to her. He was wearing the robes of a fully ordained priest of Otto, pure white with silver shells stitched into the collar. Saphira admitted his new robes made him even more handsome.

"Hello Andros, I see the life suits you." He gave her a hug, and with a kiss on her forehead, she felt Otto's blessing surround her.

"It does, more than I ever thought. Did you come to see

me, or is this an official visit?" he asked with a smile.

"It is nice to see you, but I have an odd question. Maybe you can help me."

"Absolutely, what do you need?" He crossed his hands in front of him in his robes.

"Who has been here the longest? I'm trying to find a priest or priestess who was here when my mother was, about thirty years ago, or maybe during the Battle of Salthole?"

Andros nodded and gave it some thought. "I believe the head priest was here back then; his name is Sanvan. Would you like me to take you to his office?"

"If he's not too busy."

Andros held out his arm. "I think for you, he could spare a few minutes."

Saphira sighed with relief and linked her arm with his. "Hope you're right." He led her up the stairs to the third floor. As they walked down the stone hallway, she could hear her footsteps bounce off the walls. It was so quiet here, in Ardenry, there would be people moving through the temple at all hours of the day and night; it made for a loud temple. Salthole's temple reminded her a great deal of the temple in Raventree, busy during certain times, but generally a quiet place to contemplate.

"So, may I ask why you need to see our head priest?"

She sighed. "I'd like to know more about my mom when she was younger. I know she spent a winter here when she traveled."

"Did she not tell you about it?"

Saphira shrugged. "Some."

Andros stopped them in front of a wooden door and gave it a knock. "Yes?" They heard a man call out and stepped inside.

"Pardon me, Father Sanvan?"

The older priest looked up and gave them both a friendly smile. "Andros, who do you have there?"

"This is my friend Saphira. Would you happen to have a few moments to speak with her? She had some questions about her mother."

Sanvan's eyes widened. "Well, if I know her mother, I'd be glad to help, thank you, Andros." He bowed and gave Saphira's hand a little squeeze before leaving them alone. Sanvan stood and held out his hand. "Saphira, it's good to meet you. I hope I can help."

She reached over to his desk and shook his hand. "Thank you, Father. I hope so too. My mother's name is Lily Voltain, and she was here in Salthole about thirty years ago, and then again later when the cultists attacked the temple."

His eyes slowly widened. "Lily Voltain is your mother?"

She nodded. "Yes."

Sanvan sat back and sighed heavily with a smile. "I don't believe it. It has been a long time since I've thought of Lily. I did know her when she was here. I was, but an acolyte, and she helped a family discover what happened to their poor little girl." He sat back, and she could see the familiar haunted look in his eyes. Her mother had it when she would tell her certain stories. "A man had kidnapped the little girl and done horrific things. The family thought it was a wolf of some kind, but your mother was able to determine the killer was human."

"That must have been hard for everyone."

Sanvan nodded. "It was, poor child went through more than the average soldier. It was disturbing to say the least. Unfortunately, the family decided to thank your mother and her friends by trying to kill them."

Saphira gasped. "What?" She knew of the little girl and her fate, but her mother never mentioned that anyone tried to kill them while they were here.

"Oh yes, the family locked them in a barn and tried to set it on fire. Luckily, Otto was with them, and some passersby were able to save them. Her friends almost died; there was so much smoke in their lungs, we wondered if they would make it."

At the mention of Lily's friend, Saphira sat up. "Actually, it's her friends I had a question about."

"Certainty, which one?"

Saphira nervously licked her lips. "Um, the priest?"

Sanvan smiled. "Dante Foss, yes, I remember him. Your mother was in love with Henri at the time, but we could tell Dante loved her as well."

"He did?" *Oh shit,* she thought. Things were starting to come together.

"Oh yes, did she not tell you about him?" She shook her head. "Hmm," Sanvan clicked his tongue. "Dante was older than your mother. Perhaps something bad happened to him? If I were you, I'd ask your mother when you get home. I don't know why she never told you about him, but they were a special pair. They touched a lot of lives while they were here. When she was here during the assault, I knew Henri had already passed, but there was no sign of Taren or Dante." Saphira sat quietly, wondering why her mother had left out this important man in her life.

"Mom said Taren died a few months after they left Salthole, a cultist. But she never mentioned the priest."

Sanvan's eyes turned sad. "I'm sorry about Taren's loss. He was a good man. I wish I had more information on Dante." Truthfully, it raised even more questions, but she feared only her mother could answer them.

"Well, thank you for your time." She stood and shook his hand again and walked out of his office, where Andros was waiting for her.

"Was he able to help you?"

She sighed heavily and walked back down the stairs. "Yes and no. I guess I have to keep it from my mind until I get home."

"Perhaps that's for the best."

"Perhaps." She walked out into the sunshine, or what was left of it. "I better get on duty," she turned, and Andros was still behind her. "It was nice seeing you again, Andros."

"And you, Saphira, be safe tonight."

"Thank you, I will." She walked down the stairs and headed towards the rougher part of town to start her rounds. Her mother loved telling her and her brothers' stories about her travels, and she wondered why she left out this man, Dante. He sounded like an important person in her life, and it made Saphira wonder what else her mother may not have told them.

CHAPTER 18

A HOT NIGHT

The next morning, Saphira walked into the inn after her shift and found Eden and Rickert eating breakfast.

She ran over and joined them. "Guys, I think I found us a house to stay in this winter."

Eden smiled. "Thank goodness I'm tired of this tavern. How much will it cost?"

"Not a cent, no one has lived there in thirty years, so it's going to need a little work. I figured I could quit my guard job and work on it before we moved in."

Rickert put down his fork and took a swig of whatever he was drinking. "Are you sure? I know how much you like it."

She shrugged her shoulders. "We need a clean house. Plus, I think I've found something else to occupy my time that will be more lucrative."

He nodded his head. "Well, if you're sure about the house, I think it sounds like a promising idea. It'd be nice not paying for a room every week."

Saphira smiled. "Great, I'll go put in my resignation and get to working on the house."

The Sheriff was sad to see her go, but Saphira knew she couldn't do her job and work on the house enough for it to be livable before winter came. It took weeks for her to get all the dust and grime out of the house. Every once in a while, Rickert, Eden, or Edward would help. Sometimes she'd get there in the morning, and there would be more cleaning supplies or food. Once there was a red flower, it was called The Gods Passion. When she picked it up, she could smell Gareth's cologne on the stem and smiled. She hadn't seen him since he'd shown her the house, but figured she could start learning from him again when the house was fit for occupancy.

The day the group moved in, the house was clean and smelled like flowers. The wooden floors were dark and shiny, and all the furniture had been beaten into submission to get the dust out. Edward's room was the first on the left at the top of the stairs. From what she remembered from her mom's stories, it was Taren's old room. She picked the room that would have been her mother's. It looked exactly as she described it. Big four corner bed, fireplace, and heavy red curtains.

Edward's blacksmithing job ended, so he took up Saphira's old guard position to keep bringing in the gold. She told him all she remembered about the dangerous parts of town and how to avoid them; she didn't want him getting hurt. When the sun went down, Saphira finally decided to find Gareth, and much to her dismay, it was bitterly cold outside. All day, people were saying it was going to snow, but it wasn't winter yet, so she didn't hold out much hope. She hopped down the stairs and could hear Rickert talking in the sitting room.

"Rickert, I'm going out!" she called out. When she reached the bottom of the stairs, she almost slipped when she saw Gareth drinking tea with the couple.

"Saphira, you never told me you made a friend," Eden teased as she walked in.

Gareth chuckled and put his cup down. "Oh, I'm not surprised she didn't mention me; most don't." He stood and smiled. "Would you like to continue our lessons?"

"Lessons?" Rickert looked between them. "What's he teaching you?"

She grabbed Gareth's hand and dragged him out of the house. "He's teaching me to accentuate my natural adroit self," she yelled back as the door closed.

Gareth laughed. "They seem like nice people," he said as she dragged him down the street.

"They are, they're wonderful. What were you doing there?" They walked into the alley between the houses and made their way to the middle of town.

"It's been a while since I've seen you, and I thought you might want to learn more."

"I was just leaving to find you. What did you have in mind?"

"The docks."

She looked over at him and could tell he was serious. "The docks?"

"You'll see," he said with an irritating smile.

Since late autumn storms were particularly violent around Salthole, there were a lot of ships docked at the moment.

"So, what are we doing here?"

Gareth dragged her behind a tall stack of barrels and took off his cloak. "We're going to see which ship has the best stuff," he whispered and began peeling her cloak off.

"It's freezing out here, Gareth!" She hissed quietly at him as he began to take his boots off.

"I know, it's so cold, most of the sailors will be in the inns keeping warm. There'll hardly be anybody on board."

He pointed at her shoes, and she scoffed before taking them off. "If I catch my death, I'm coming back and killing you, I hope you know."

He chuckled and took his shirt off, exposing his pale, muscular chest. "If you catch your death out here, it'll be from a knife, not the cold. Now quit bitching and strip." He lifted her shirt over her head and flung it into a pile of their clothes. She had an undershirt that was tight on her breasts and folded her arms so he wouldn't be tempted to take it off as well.

"I'm not taking this off."

"Nor would I ask you to." He took a step towards her and stopped a breath away from her lips. "Not yet anyway." She scoffed and pushed him back while he chuckled. "The other clothes are heavy. It'll be too hard to swim in them."

Her eyes widened. "Swim? You really are crazy." Saphira kept her dagger on her belt as they made their way through the shadows and slipped into the water. "Good gods!" she hissed and felt satisfied as Gareth began chattering in the water as well.

Her pants soaked up the freezing water like a dying man in the desert, and she felt the cold sink into her skin. She had never been so cold in her entire life.

"Trust me, Voltain, this'll be worth it." They swam to the nearest ship, and Saphira watched as Gareth used some odd-looking clawed daggers to climb up the side of the ship to the nearest porthole. His wet muscles were shining in the moonlight, and she let herself appreciate his physique as he fiddled with a porthole window. He opened it and poked his head in before calling back down to her. "All clear." He climbed inside and threw down the claws to her. Thankfully, they floated, and she crawled her way out of the freezing water into the bowels of the dark ship.

"See how much harder the climb would have been if we had all our clothes on?" He gave her a wink and started going through the ship's cargo.

"So, it wasn't just a ploy to get me half-naked?" It was cold in the bottom of the ship, but since she wasn't in the water, she was able to warm up a little.

He chuckled. "That was a perk." She looked over at him. Gareth was like a shining ghost, moving from box to box, quickly inspecting the contents. "Hmm, a lot of food."

"I don't think they'd survive the swim well," Saphira said as the smell of different cheeses filled the air.

"Depends on what it is. Most cheeses do fine, since they're sealed in wax. But I don't recommend the leeks." He lifted one of the lids and whistled, "Voltain, look at this." She walked over and peered into the box. It looked like uniforms, orcish ones, and not the orcs who supported Sobrei.

"Blessed Otto, they're supplying the Empire!" Gareth began opening all the boxes, and they found more uniforms and weapons that were much too big for humans.

"Well," Gareth twirled his dagger between his fingers. "I say we give this ship a little Salthole hospitality." He walked over to one of the unlit lamps and lit it with a flick from his dagger, and smashed it against the uniform box. It went up like kindling, and Gareth took Saphira's hand. "Time to go."

They took one step towards the porthole when they heard a voice yell out in orcish. "You little bugs!" Saphira turned and watched an orc with an exceptionally large sword begin to charge them. She ducked out of the way and watched Gareth sink his dagger into the Orc's chest, but his leather armor kept most of the damage at bay.

As she got to her feet, Gareth took her hand again, "Run!" As they dashed up the stairs, she swore he was laughing. They didn't see anybody else until they got on deck and had to stop themselves from running into a man as they tried to run down the plank. "Time to go swimming." They ran to the other side of the boat and jumped into the freezing waters of the ocean as more guards appeared on the deck of the ship. Saphira and Gareth swam as fast as they could, to the next boat. Using the boat's shadow for cover, they waded in the water, listening for more yells.

"Did you know they had orc supplies?"

He shook his head. "Not a hint, actually. I'm afraid my preternatural senses have failed me this one time." He smiled, and she noticed his eyes dart up before his arms pulled her against him. "Shh," he whispered. Slowly, she looked up and saw a young boy crawling along the ship's moorings. She doubted he'd seen them, but after what just happened, she was all for caution. They watched the young boy disappear back into the ship, and they both sighed with relief.

"Well, that was an adventure," she said. It surprised her how warm Gareth was, even though the water was freezing.

"What say we get our clothes back on, and we head to my place," Gareth said. "I got the perfect thing to warm us up."

Saphira could feel her lips starting to tremble from the cold. "What, no more ships?" she teased. Her hands splayed against his back. She could feel little scars on his skin. Gareth chuckled as his hand slowly slid up her back until it was buried in her wet hair behind her neck.

"I figured setting fire to one ship would be exciting

enough for you, My Lady." He leaned forward and pressed his lips against hers. They were so warm against her freezing lips, she couldn't help but deepen it and sucked his lower lip between hers. The moan from his throat rippled through her body, and suddenly she wished they were dry and in his room at the 'Orc'. Her hands moved down his back, her nails lightly scratching his skin. "We need to get out of the water." His voice was breathy and chattering; the cold must have caught up with him. Saphira nodded, and they both swam for the shore under the dock.

As they ran for their clothes, they could see the ship on fire in the distance. Other ships were moving away for fear of catching fire themselves, despite the cold. Their teeth were chattering as they pulled on their thankfully dry, albeit cold, clothes.

Gareth picked up Saphira's cloak and wrapped it around her shoulders. "Come, let's warm up properly." He kissed her again, and Saphira could feel him steering her backwards, hardly parting from her lips. Saphira giggled as his hands guided her to where she should walk, and a few backwards blocks later, he opened a door and steered her into a house.

There was already a fire going, and the warmth hit her cheeks immediately. "So how does one 'warm up properly'?" Her fingers were pulling on his belt as he kept walking her back towards a large couch.

"Well, this is a good start." He flopped them both down on the soft cushions. Gareth's hands began peeling her cloak off, stealing little touches of her body as he did so.

Laughing, Saphira kicked his boots off with her feet. "Don't tell me this is how you warm up all your thieves?"

He laughed. "Gods no." He nibbled on her neck, his lips were slow and attentive as he gently sucked the most sensitive spot of her skin. All she could hear was her heartbeat and her breathing as his hands slowly worked their way under her shirt. He cupped her breast with his nimble fingers, and she couldn't keep quiet.

"Gods, Gareth." Suddenly, a tapping noise made her ear twitch, and she opened her eyes. A young woman with long blonde hair was staring down at them, her arms crossed over her stomach. Saphira gasped and pushed him off. "Gareth, if you're married, I'm going to kill you!"

He laughed and pulled Saphira to her feet. "No, I'm not married. This is my sister Elyse. Elyse, this is Saphira. Nice timing by the way."

Saphira felt her shoulders relax and held out her hand. "Oh, thank goodness. It's nice to meet you." Elyse smiled and shook her hand while moving the other one in unfamiliar gestures toward Gareth. "Yes, the same Saphira," he said as only a brother could to their nosy sister.

"Um," Saphira had never seen a more confusing interaction between two people.

"Sorry, Elyse can't talk, so she uses her hands and writes to me."

"Oh, I've never seen such a thing before; it must come in handy." Elyse smiled and gently hit her shoulder before turning back towards the fire. "What?"

Gareth was holding in chuckles and whispered. "Handy, it's a joke," he said as he wiggled his hand in the air in front of her.

"Oh, okay." Her head felt a little fuzzy from the cold and the sudden attention Gareth had given her, so she figured she'd get the joke later.

Gareth finally took off his cloak and laid it along the couch. "Come, let's warm up." He picked up a blanket, and they both sat in front of the fire as Elyse handed them both a mug of some kind of warm liquid.

"What's in it?"

"What I normally give my thieves to warm up," he took a drink and sighed. "Apple cider with brandy and cinnamon works wonders."

"Brandy?" Saphira sniffed it and could smell the alcohol in it, but could tell it wasn't very much.

"Something wrong?"

"Um, no. Brandy kind of gets me loopy, that's all." She

had a little drink and could feel her insides warming as the liquid made its way into her stomach. "Good stuff though."

Gareth smiled and nearly drained his mug. "Our mother's recipe, practically raised me on the stuff."

Elyse smacked him on the head and made some more gestures. "She did too, Elyse, you just don't remember," he said, laughing.

Saphira smiled at the exchange. "Were you born in Salthole?" she asked the siblings.

Gareth nodded and finished his drink. "Born and bred. I saw Edward on duty earlier." Gareth said as Elyse handed him his second mug of the miracle concoction. "He'd make an excellent guard, in any town but Salthole."

Saphira sat up, surprised at what he said. "Why not Salthole?"

"He's too nice."

Saphira scoffed and took a drink. "You can't be nice and be a guard?"

"Not in Salthole, it'll get you killed."

She put her mug down and turned to him. "So, I'm not nice?"

Gareth sighed and wrapped the blanket around them tighter. "Not when it matters." He reached up and slicked his wet hair back from his face. "You know, when I heard Mother Lily's daughter was in Salthole, I was intrigued. When I heard it was *her* sneaking around my town at night, turning in my men, I became obsessed. I had to meet you." He reached up and cupped her cheek. "That night we met, I watched you for hours." He ran his lips over her cheek as he spoke, "You were fucking ethereal as you moved from rooftop to rooftop. It was impressive, and I wanted to show you more, so I introduced myself. It was the first time I got a good look at you, and I was unprepared."

"Unprepared?" She turned and kissed the palm of his hand. "For what?"

He smiled and brought her closer. "Your beauty shocked me. Your bright blue eyes were like the most precious jewels

I'd ever seen, and your dark hair," he buried his left hand in it behind her neck. "I wanted to bury my hands in it and kiss you right there." His right hand held her face. "You can't believe how happy I was when you said you wanted to learn more. That I was going to get to spend time with you. There's something special in you, Saphira, something calling to me, and I want it all." Saphira listened to him pour his heart out to her; her own heart sped up with every word he said. There was something about this rogue that ignited something in her she thought she had lost.

"I want you too." It was the easiest thing she ever admitted and kissed him.

CHAPTER 19
MEMORABLE PARTY

"Saphira?" A voice dragged her from her dream, and she felt fingers lightly brush her cheek. When she finally opened her eyes, she saw Edward smiling at her. "Good morning, birthday girl."

Saphira chuckled and sat up. "Gods, I forgot." She looked around, and her eyes widened when she realized she was still in Elyse's house and Gareth was standing behind Edward, a sly smile on his face. "Oh, gosh, I'm sorry, I must have fallen asleep." There was no way she was going to sleep with Gareth while his sister was there, but they did end up kissing for a long time on the couch. She remembered snuggling up next to him, his arms around her, before she fell asleep. She couldn't think of anywhere else that she felt so safe, without being at home.

Edward helped her to her feet. "Don't worry about it, Gareth said you two were out late doing whatever it is you do. Besides, I wouldn't want you to walk home alone while it was snowing."

Her jaw dropped at the mention of snow. "Are you serious?" She ran over to the door and flung it open. She was greeted by bright white light as the morning sun glistened off the freshly fallen snow. "But it's still fall."

Gareth laughed. "Welcome to Salthole, Voltain."

She turned as Edward wrapped her cloak around her shoulders. "Gareth, you, and your sister should come by the house tonight. We're having a little party for Saphira's birthday."

Gareth smiled and nodded. "Sounds like fun, we'll be there." Saphira had forgotten about her birthday, let alone the party the group had planned for her. As she stood between the men, she could feel how much she wanted Gareth. It was as if whatever had died in her when Iollan left was suddenly fanned back to life, and it wanted the rogue king.

She gave Gareth a little wink, then turned to Edward. "Let's get going."

Edward put a hand on her back as they walked towards the door. "Okay," he looked back up at Gareth, "Thanks for looking after her."

"Not a problem." She looked back and saw the wink Gareth gave her. She smiled and easily admitted she couldn't wait to see him tonight.

The snow was crunching under their feet as they walked. "I've never had snow on my birthday."

"Neither have I, but our birthday is in the summer." Saphira laughed and patted his back.

When the house was in view, he gave her hand a little tap. "I have to pick up a few hours at work today, so I have the party off. I'll see you later."

"All right, see you later." She practically ran up the stairs and closed the door as Eden came walking in from the living room, wearing Saphira's smock.

"There you are, where were you?" Saphira hung her cloak behind the door and quickly shucked her boots off.

"I fell asleep at Gareth's sister's house. We were out late."

"Oh, good," Eden sighed in relief. "I was afraid you'd get caught in the snow. Did you hear a boat caught fire last night? It was kind of scary; we could see the smoke from here."

"Yeah." She pulled Eden into the living room, it was already rearranged for the party tonight with the chairs around the edge of the room and a table by the window. "That was us."

Eden's eyes went wide. "Us? You and Gareth?"

Saphira nodded with a smile. "They were supplying orcs from the Empire, so we burned it all."

Eden gasped, covering her mouth. "How did you get away?" Saphira pulled her to some chairs and told her everything, from the swim up to the boat, to jumping off to escape.

"You got lucky, next time bring us," Eden said, clearly annoyed that Saphira was doing something dangerous without them.

"That's not all."

"Good gods, what?" She crossed her arms over her stomach, and Saphira laughed.

"It's a good thing, I promise. Gareth kissed me."

Eden's eyes narrowed, and she looked at Saphira for a moment. "You aren't with Ed?"

Saphira sat up in shock, "Ed?"

"Yes, Ed, he's crazy about you!"

Saphira waved her off. "No, he's never said anything, never made a move on me."

Eden's eyes went wide. "Seriously? Never?" Saphira shook her head. Eden groaned, "Men."

"Did he say something to you?" She almost didn't want to ask.

Eden shook her head and brushed some flour off the apron. "No, but I could tell. He was always gentle with you, so open. I saw you dancing after mom's wedding, and when he'd lay his head on yours during a slow song, his eyes were always closed, and there was a little smile on his face. I've never seen him look like that, not even with his girlfriends." Saphira almost felt her heart break. Like there was another future that would no longer be. Because the things she felt for Edward were not romantic. He was not someone she would kiss and make love to; he was a friend.

"I had no idea."

Eden reached out and laid a hand on her knee. "Well, he clearly waited too long; that's on him. Maybe next time he won't wait.

"You're not mad?"

She chuckled. "Why would I be mad? I'll admit I liked the idea of you being my sister one day, but the heart wants what the heart wants. If anything, I'm mad at Ed for not being more straight-forward." She sat back and shook her head.

Saphira snickered. "I do wish Ed the best. I don't want to ruin things between the group because of this. But something clicked with Gareth. I haven't felt like this since before Iollan left."

Eden stood and pulled Saphira to her feet. "I'm glad you're happy, but be careful, okay?"

"I will. And I am your sister, Eden, just a different kind." She gave the mage a hug and quickly ran up to her room. Saphira threw open the curtains and saw Salthole covered in snow. It was beautiful, like it covered all the bad bits.

She turned to start a fire as Rickert walked in.

"There you are, interesting night?" He leaned on the doorframe, his arms crossed.

"The most interesting one I've had in a while," she said, a smile on her face.

"Did you see the fire?"

She nodded. "Yeah, that was me and Gareth. We found imperial uniforms and orcish weapons in the hold, so we set them on fire."

Rickert laughed and patted her on the back. "Well done."

"It was the most fucking insane night ever, but I had so much fun." They laughed, and he helped her put some logs in the fireplace. "Oh shit, Edward invited Gareth and his sister to the party. I forgot to tell Eden."

"Don't worry, the more the merrier, I always say."

Saphira lit the fire before she heard footsteps and saw Eden walk in with a beautiful gown. "Happy Birthday, Saphira." Ricker and Eden said together.

"Oh, it's beautiful." She petted the soft fabric and smiled. Eden certainly knew how to pick a dress. Saphira was never one for dressing like a lady, so she relied on Eden for the fashion tips. The dress was red with a lace bodice and a flowy skirt. The fabric had lots of colors swirling around it, and Saphira knew it would spin well as she danced. She suddenly wondered if Gareth danced.

When it was time for the party, Saphira put on her new dress and made her way downstairs. Her hair was up in a bun with a few curly wisps around her face; she felt beautiful. A few of the friends they had made over the weeks were already in the sitting room, and when Saphira walked in, Eden yelled out.

"Happy birthday, Saphira!" She couldn't help but smile as her friends yelled out their good wishes.

"Thanks, everyone, I'm glad you're here." There was food and a cake set out, and everyone tucked in. Andros walked up to her, wearing a regular tunic and pants instead of his vestments, and kissed her forehead.

"Happy birthday, Saphira."

She felt Otto's blessing and smiled. "Thank you, Andros, I see they let you out for the night," she teased.

He laughed and nodded. "Yes, occasionally we can act like a normal person. I'm glad you invited me."

"Well, you are technically the first person we knew in Salthole."

Andros chuckled and laid a hand on her shoulder. "Will you save a dance for me?"

"Wild orcs couldn't chase me away." He flashed her one of his flawless smiles and walked over to the food. Saphira noticed how a few of the girls there were staring at him and chuckled. There was a knock at the door, and Rickert rushed across the room to get it. Saphira felt her heart speed up as she watched Gareth and Elyse walk in. He was wearing a nice red shirt, and Elyse was wearing a white dress with spring flowers stitched into the skirt.

"Happy birthday, My Lady, you look ravishing." Gareth leaned down and gave her a little kiss, and handed her the box he was carrying.

"Gareth, you didn't have to do this."

"Nonsense, now open your gift." He stood in front of her as she cut the string with her dagger and chuckled when she saw what was inside.

"Gareth, you really know how to shop for a girl, don't you?" She picked up her own pair of clawed daggers; they looked new.

"You need your own pair, you can't be borrowing mine all

the time," he teased.

Saphira smiled at him and put the box on the little side table behind her. "Thank you, Gareth."

"You're most welcome. Save me a dance?" He kissed her hand and made his way over to his sister, who was studying the food on the table. Saphira watched as Andros put down a cracker and walked over to Elyse. Saphira couldn't help but chuckle to herself and wondered how Gareth would take a priest flirting with his sister. Their friend Xander started playing his accordion, and soon everyone was dancing around the room.

Another hour passed, and Saphira was eating a piece of her cake when Edward finally walked in. Saphira watched as he gave Eden a quick hug before he walked over to her.

"Happy birthday, Saphira." She suddenly felt guilty. After what Eden had told her, she wondered if she should accept the gift.

"Edward, you didn't have to do this."

He shrugged his shoulders. "I ordered it a few weeks ago. I wanted it to be ready in time for your birthday." He handed her a little box and kissed her cheek. When she lifted the lid, she saw a gold locket laying on soft cotton, a seashell engraved on the front of it.

"It's lovely, thank you." She opened the locket and gasped; a small picture of her mother was on one side, and one of herself was on the other. "Oh, Edward," she whispered as she stared at her mother's face. It had been so long since she'd seen her, she felt tears in her eyes, but looked up anyway. "Gods, what a wonderful gift." Who else but Edward would even think of giving her such a present.

He leaned down to her ear and whispered, "I thought you'd like it." Before walking over to the punch bowl.

Saphira turned to Eden and showed her. "Did you know?"

She shook her head as a few of the other girls came over to ogle the gift. "No idea." She thought Eden sounded sad.

Her ear twitched, and she looked over to see Gareth standing next to her. "That is a lovely gift, Voltain." He took it from her and put it over her head. She felt him lift her hair and lay the necklace against the back of her neck. "I know you'll treasure it forever."

"How could I not?" He held out his hand, and she took it before he twirled her to the dance floor. "I wondered if you could dance," she teased him.

He chuckled, and she could feel him vibrate against her. "A king must know how to dance; I am proficient in several."

"Oh, are you, what ones?"

"There's the Asyik," he twirled her around and dipped her. She felt his hand behind her head before he brought her back up. "The quickstep." He moved her quicker around the floor, her skirt flying behind her. "And of course, the Sarabande." His feet moved in a different time than the music, but he still made it work.

"I shall never doubt you again," she said through giggles.

"Good. So, what do you normally do on your birthday in Raventree?"

Saphira felt a little homesick, thinking about her birthdays with her family. "My Mom makes my favorite dinner, chicken pot pie, and we have a cobbler for dessert. My Papa will sing, and we'll dance, then he'll tell the story of how I was born. He does that with all our birthdays."

Gareth smiled. "And how did you grace the world with your presence?"

Saphira chuckled. "Quickly, it seems. Mom said I was three weeks early, and I came so fast they didn't have time to get the midwife, and my Papa delivered me."

"Your father delivered you?" His eyebrows went up in question.

"Hmm-mm. Mom said she woke up and it was almost three am, and she was hungry."

The house was quiet, and Lily managed to get out of bed without waking William and snuck to the kitchen. The moment her eyes opened, she had a terrible craving for the cornbread he had made earlier. Lily took the kitchen towel off the cornbread and sighed at the smell. It was lovely and sweet, and she put a piece on a little plate and poured honey over it.

She got a fork and quickly took a bite. "Mmmm." It tasted so good she could cry.

"Baby hungry?" She jumped a little at William's voice and chuckled.

She hadn't totally swallowed her bite and covered her mouth as she spoke. "She wanted cornbread."

William chuckled and got her something to drink. "Ah, yes, the *baby* wanted cornbread, not you."

"Exactly." Lily stood in the kitchen, eating her cornbread while William lovingly ran his hands over her belly, a peaceful smile on his face. "What are you doing?" she teased.

"Memorizing you like this," he kissed his fingertips and laid them on her stomach.

Lily put her plate down and gasped as her water broke. She had suffered in pain for hours with both Foster and Christopher before her water broke. This was the first time it broke before any pain had started. "Good thing I memorized when I did." William kissed her cheek and grabbed a kitchen towel.

"Good—" Pressure like she had never felt blasted through her, and she leaned against the counter, trying to catch her breath. "William," she reached out, and he took her hand. "The baby's coming."

"I know, let's get you in bed."

He tried helping her towards the bedroom, but she could barely walk. "No, I mean right now!"

"Now, now?" His eyes went wide as Lily tried to catch her breath. She swore she could feel the head already.

"Now, now."

"Oh shit," he picked her up and walked as fast as he could to the bedroom and laid her down. She immediately rolled onto her side, and the urge to push was overwhelming. "What do I do?" William pushed the blankets off the bed and rubbed her back.

"Can you see the baby?" William got by her feet and moved her nightgown out of the way.

"You weren't kidding, Sweets. She's coming, I see her." Lily reached down and could feel the top of the baby's head as she pushed.

She groaned, "Why is it happening so fast!"

"Third baby, Sweets, I heard this can happen."

"Yeah, but this is ridiculous!" She pushed and felt the head come out. "Catch her, William, catch her. I can't stop pushing." It was like her body had taken over and wouldn't give her a break, and with the next push, the baby was in William's arms, her big blue eyes just looking at the world. "Is she okay?"

Lily sat up and saw tears streaming down William's face. "Oh, Sweets, she's beautiful." Lily put her finger in the baby's mouth and cleared her airway, but she seemed perfect. "Look at all that dark hair." Lily's fingers gently ran over her daughter's cheek, and it twitched as she made those wonderful newborn noises. "I don't think I've ever loved someone so much so fast." William wiped his eyes. "Want me to get the midwife?" He handed her the baby, and she sat back, admiring the perfect little girl in her arms.

"Yes, please."

As the sun came up, the door to their bedroom crashed open like it did every morning as Foster and Christopher ran inside. But instead of jumping onto the bed and crawling under the covers, they stopped when they saw their mother in bed with a baby.

Christopher pointed at her. "That's a baby!"

William chuckled, laying next to Lily as he pet the baby's head. "It is. Would you like to meet your baby sister?"

"A sister!" Foster jumped for joy and then lept onto the bed like he normally did. Christopher ran over, and William helped him onto the bed, and he crawled over next to Lily. The boys cuddled next to each other, staring at the baby.

"She's little." Foster slowly reached out and held her hand.

"She is." Lily smiled. "Her name is Saphira."

"Saf-i," Christopher tried out.

Foster laid his head next to his sister's. "Hi, Saphira, I'm Foster, your big brother." She squealed, and the boys laughed. Lily looked over at William, his eyes full of love as he looked upon his children.

"Papa would pretend to hold a baby me, and say, 'You were the most beautiful thing I'd ever seen, and I felt honored I got to bring you into the world'."

Gareth smiled wistfully and pressed his cheek against hers. "He sounds like a good man."

"He is, he's amazing." She gave his cheek a kiss. "What about you? Did you come into the world holding a dagger?"

He threw his head back and laughed. "Oh, nothing so dramatic, I imagine, but honestly, I have no idea, I never asked."

"Where are your parents?"

He gave her forehead a kiss. "They're gone, but at least they're together."

"I'm sorry." She meant it, too, she'd be lost without her parents.

"Thank you, Voltain." He took a breath like a palate cleanser, "So, how old are you?"

"Twenty. You?"

"Turned Twenty-One a month ago."

"Oh, younger than I thought," she teased. "I'm sorry I missed your birthday."

He chuckled. "I can think of a few ways you can make it up to me." He kissed her lips and twirled her around. "You know your story was wonderful, and I feel lucky you shared it with me, but something is making my mind twitch about it."

"Because of how fast it happened?"

He shook his head. "No, you said you were early, but they never mentioned it in the story." Saphira gave it some thought as he twirled her around. He was right, her parents told her she was early, but never said so in the story.

"Huh, you're right. Weird."

For hours, people danced in the sitting room, and one by one, their friends left. Andros got a dance as well, but she noticed how most of the time he spent with Elyse. They were writing notes back and forth, and she was showing him some hand signals, a smile on his face the entire time. Edward also got a dance; it was the least she could do after he gave her such a wonderful gift. Gareth danced with her for hours; a minute hardly passed between the kisses he gave her. She had never felt such a kinship with anyone like she felt with Gareth. It felt like there was something in their souls calling out for each other.

When the music stopped, Saphira and Gareth were the only ones dancing in the room. Xander congratulated them on their stamina and teased Gareth he had worn Sahira out for any fun later. They thanked him for playing and made sure to pay him handsomely for his time, although he didn't ask for payment. Saphira didn't notice when the other guests had left, especially Andros and Elyse, but she figured he offered to walk her home. She picked up some of the napkins off the floor when Gareth suddenly picked her up.

"It'll still be there in the morning," he said before whisking her up the stairs. She giggled the whole way. "Which is your room?"

She gasped, feigning displeasure, "You mean you don't know?" He smiled wickedly and slowly walked to the doors on the second floor and stopped in front of her room.

"I knew," he whispered and opened the door, pressing her against him so as not to drop her as they walked inside. The door closed behind them, and the room had a chill to it, so Saphira hopped down and started a fire in the hearth.

When it was blazing, she sat in front of it on the fur rug and let it warm her. "Thank you for coming tonight, Gareth. I had a wonderful time. I know a birthday party is rather mundane compared to what you usually do."

He sat on the rug in front of her and cupped her cheek. "Not at all, my sneaky love, we have birthday parties at the Orc all the time. They usually end a little differently, though."

"Do tell." She couldn't keep the smile off her face as she studied his handsome face. His sharp jawline and nose that had clearly been broken one too many times. There was a scar on his cheek, where his facial hair wouldn't grow anymore, and she reached up and touched it.

"Well, after the party, someone is usually naked in the streets, locked out of their room." They laughed, and he leaned forward and kissed her. "I can't wait to try out our claws together."

"Me either." She smiled and pulled him against her, making sure to kiss him slow and steady as his hands moved around her waist. Saphira leaned back and pulled him down on top of her. The fire crackled next to them as their slow, steady kiss became deeper and deeper. Saphira could hear his breathing getting faster and faster as one of his hands moved from her hip to her breast. Over the fabric of the dress, she could barely feel him, but it was enough her body tingled at his touch.

"Gods, I want you, I've never wanted anyone more," he whispered and slipped between her legs.

"I want you too, but I don't have any moon tea." She chastised herself for not looking for any this afternoon.

"We don't need any. I have something." He quickly got to his knees and reached into his pocket. "I made sure to get some, just in case."

She took the little paper container from him and looked inside. "What is it?"

"I put it on, and it catches my seed. We'll be fine."

She turned it over in her hand. "Catches?"

Gareth sighed. He seemed to be searching for the right word. "Keeps it from getting inside of you." He took it out, and she could see how it would work; it was so simple yet genius.

"Why doesn't everyone know about these?"

He shook his head. "Don't know, the important thing is we do." He set it on the rug and began unlacing the front of her dress. She reached her hand down between them and squeezed him. She could feel him swell at her touch and rubbed her hand along him. He moaned as the laces of her dress finally freed her, and she let out an unexpected sigh of relief.

"Damn, I didn't realize I was so constricted."

Gareth laughed and pulled her into his lap. "Well, if you are disinclined to be constricted so soon, maybe you should be on top." He nipped at her ear, and her heart flipped as he picked her up and laid them both on the bed. His hands worked quick as his shirt and pants were lost in the darkness of the room. Saphira took the opportunity and pushed him on his back. "You have such a nice chest," she said quietly as she straddled his hips. He chuckled and relaxed as her hands softly pet his well-defined chest. There were a few scars dotting his perfect skin, so she leaned down and kissed each one tenderly.

"Please, you think I have a nice chest." He reached up and slid the top of her dress down to her waist, and she sat up. It was the first time she'd been this naked in front of anyone in a while, and she watched his eyes roam over her naked flesh. "You beat me any day." Saphira sighed as his hands slowly moved up her stomach and cupped her breasts. His hands were warm, and as his fingers began playing with her nipples, they soon turned hard and extra sensitive. Wonderful, deep pressure grew between her legs as soft moans escaped her lips. "I love that sound, Voltain." Suddenly, he sat up and took one of her nipples between his lips. She gasped and found herself holding him against her as his tongue rolled the sensitive peak in his mouth.

"Gods, Gareth," she whispered and could feel him between her legs. He was hard and ready to please her. "I want you, now please." She shimmied the rest of the dress off, their lips met. She almost melted when she could feel the heat of his sex so near to hers. His fingers massaged her thighs, and she felt them get closer and closer to her.

"Can I touch you?" he whispered.

She looked up into his darkened, gray eyes and wanted nothing more. "Yes." She gasped, and her head flew back as he slipped a finger inside and stayed motionless for a moment.

"Feel good?" She couldn't speak, only nod as his fingertip

began to rub on some hidden spot inside, even she didn't know about. The noise that escaped her lips was something she'd never heard herself make. She looked down and met his eyes; they were almost feral as he moved his finger inside her. He gave her another wicked smile before lowering down to her breast and began rolling a hardened skin between his teeth.

"Fuck Gareth." His thumb found her clit, and she bucked in his lap. The pressure inside was building so quickly she thought she might actually explode. "Oh, gods, Gareth, I'm—" she couldn't even finish before her body erupted in pleasure she had forgotten existed. She moaned loudly and wrapped her arms around him, not trusting her legs to hold her up. Gareth's chuckle was low and seductive; she could feel it rumbling through her as she sat back, glassy-eyed and relaxed. "Your turn," she whispered. He groaned and put the finger that was inside her in his mouth, licking her off his skin.

"Gods, I almost forgot." He got out of the bed and picked up the little contraption that would catch his seed. She watched as he took it out of the little paper container and rolled it onto his thick shaft. "Now, where were we?" He crawled onto the bed, in between her legs, and without thought or hesitation, entered her. Saphira gasped, he was wide and filled her completely, it took her breath away as he slowly moved in and out of her. "Blessed gods, Saphira, I've never felt such bliss." He thrust deep inside, and finally, it hit a spot that made her cry out. She looked down and watched his hips moving and matched his rhythm, but it only made him speed up. With every movement, that spot deep inside was getting teased. Saphira closed her eyes and couldn't stop her moans. It was such a relief to feel him inside of her; it surprised her. Like she had been waiting for him, like she'd never find anyone who would love her more. Suddenly, he flipped, and she was on top. The change was intense, and for a moment, Saphira sat still, her head flung back as he penetrated her deeper and deeper. "Is that too much?" he asked. She finally caught her breath and decided to try it out, and moved slowly around him.

"No, no, it's fine." When she looked back down, his eyes

met hers.

"Gods, you're the most beautiful creature in existence. How did I get so lucky?" She smiled and deepened their already intimate embrace until he cried out. Her hips moved steadily on him, and she could feel the pleasurable pressure start to build so deep inside. Gareth's hands laid on her hips and encouraged her on as she flung her head back and moved faster. "Oh, gods, Saphira," he whispered, but Saphira was never a quiet one in bed and cried out as blissful pressure broke inside her once again. Quickly, he flipped her on her back, his lips found hers, and she slipped her tongue in his mouth, and they kissed deeply as he slowly moved inside her. Saphira broke away from his lips, laughed happily, and locked her ankles around his waist.

"Faster," she whispered.

Gareth chuckled darkly, and she bit her lip, "As my love commands." And began moving in and out with renewed vigor. The feeling was almost too much; her body was still reeling from his last assault, and she fought not to cry out with every thrust of his hips. Suddenly, his rhythm changed, and she could tell he was fighting his body that wanted to finish, but he didn't. Little spasms were firing inside of her as she and Gareth both cried out at the same time. He lay still on her, for a moment, his head in the crook of her neck, his hands running down her arms. Finally, he lifted himself off her chest, doing a half push-up, and she could see his heart racing at the pulse in his neck while she felt him pulse inside of her. "Gods, Saphira, I never imagined such a thing." He took a deep breath in and laid back against her chilled skin.

Saphira smiled and kissed his cheek. "That was wonderful." Her voice was lazy and satisfied. He chuckled and covered her neck and chest in slow little kisses before he looked up, his eyes locked with hers. "I've never slept with someone on the third time I've ever seen them," she teased.

He laughed and gave her a kiss. "First date, I taught you about sneaking around town, second date, torched a ship," she snickered. "Third date, birthday party, then sex. Seems normal to me."

Saphira laughed as he slipped off her and pulled her close. "Those were dates, huh?"

"Mm-hmm." He gave her another kiss. "Happy birthday, my sneaky love." She smiled and hugged him close. Saphira saw how happy yet sleepy he looked from their activity.

"Thank you, My Lord."

CHAPTER 20
CURIOUS MIRACLE

A few weeks after her party, Saphira was sneaking around during a frigid winter night. Gareth was doing whatever he did, so she decided to occupy herself by leaping from shadow to shadow, hoping to get a good bit of gossip for him. Over the weeks, she had gotten the best information, and Gareth had paid her well for it. She was about a block away from the house when she heard the familiar call of the rogue king.

"Voltain!" But he didn't sound like his usual jovial self.

When she turned, she saw Gareth running towards her, and he looked worried. "What's wrong?"

He barely stopped before grabbing her hand. "You need to come quickly." And began pulling her towards his sister's house.

"What is it? Is Elyse okay?" He didn't answer and kept running. "Gareth, tell me what's wrong!" When they reached the house, he opened the door, and Saphira could see Elyse pacing in front of an open bedroom door, her eyes were red, and she was wringing her hands together.

"How is he, Elyse?" Gareth asked, and she moved her hands in response, but Saphira didn't understand what she said.

"He who Gareth?" Elyse's eyes widened, and she began moving her hands furiously at her brother before she took Saphira's hand and pulling her into the bedroom. It was well lit, and she saw Andros sitting on the edge of the bed, fussing with someone. "Andros?"

The priest turned when he heard her voice. "Saphira, good you're here." Andros stood, and she felt her heart skip a beat as she saw Andros' patient.

"Edward." His eyes were closed, and his breathing was erratic. His chest was bandaged, and blood was seeping through.

"Edward, oh shit!" She ran over and held his hand, "Edward, open your eyes!" But they stayed closed, and the hand she held stayed motionless. "What happened!" Saphira turned and saw Gareth walking in as Andros sat across from her. The rogue looked nervous as he rubbed his face. She didn't think anything would make him nervous.

"His route was in the rougher part of town; one of my men did this to him. I came across him soon after, laying in the snow, and brought him here because I knew Andros was visiting my sister. Did you figure out why you couldn't heal the wound?" Saphira lifted the bandages, the wound wasn't deep, but looked terrible. It was blackened around the edges, and she could smell something sweet coming from the wound.

"Yes, it's poisoned," the priest said. "I've never seen anything like this before. It doesn't respond to healing at all."

Tears dared to fall, but Saphira was far too angry to let them. "Who did this?"

Gareth leaned close and sniffed the wound. "Strayson, I recognize the poison," Gareth said. "Only he has the antidote."

Saphira unsheathed her dagger and marched for the door. "Well, what are we waiting for? Let's go get it." She stomped out of the door and could hear Gareth behind her.

As they walked into the 'Orc', she saw Strayson sitting in the back, laughing about something. The mere sight of him enraged her. "Strayson!" The tavern went quiet at her voice.

The big man froze and got to his feet. "Saphira, Gareth, join me." He opened his arms in welcome as Saphira threw her dagger at him. Everyone gasped as Strayson was flung back against the wall, her dagger sunk deep into the man's arm. His screams made her smile. Both Gareth and Saphira ran over and grabbed the big man. She pulled her dagger out of him, and they both shoved him out into the street, his blood trailing behind him.

"You're going to give me the antidote to your poison, or so help me I'll make sure you suffer long before you die," she hissed at him. But he wasn't interested in helping and swung his fist at her head. It connected, and a searing pain ripped through her left cheek, but she didn't let it get to her and slashed at his throat. He backed up out of the way, but not far enough, and she saw a thin line of red spread along his neck. "Give me the antidote!" She screamed and rammed her shoulder into his stomach. He toppled over, and she quickly stabbed her dagger into his thigh.

Strayson screamed, and Gareth stood ominously over him. "Do what the lady says, Stray."

"Aargh, all right, all right, it's in my room. The trunk under the bed, it's a vial with purple liquid in it," he said through gritted teeth. Saphira pulled the dagger out of his leg and pointed it at him, his blood dripping on the ground.

"You're coming with us," and walked back towards the 'Orc', Gareth half carrying, half dragging the big man up the stairs to his room, while everyone else stared at the scene. Saphira kicked open the door. It was a mess inside. There were clothes everywhere and half-eaten food on the table next to the bed. "Drag the trunk out," she ordered him. Strayson growled but complied. The trunk was black with silver locks and hinges, and Strayson searched his pockets. "Hurry up!" She kicked him in the back, and he groaned.

"I need my key."

"Well, get it," Gareth said dangerously through bared teeth.

He reached into his pockets again, but his hands came back empty. "I think it fell out in the street."

Gareth hit him in the head. "Stop stalling and pick it open, I know you can!" He gave Strayson a pick, and Saphira felt ages pass as he picked the lock. When it clicked, she flung open the trunk; it was like being in an apothecary shop. Vials filled with odd liquids lined the bottom of the trunk. There were leaves stuffed into jars, and Saphira thought she could see some kind of animal head at the bottom. "What the hell is this, Stray?"

"My side business," he leaned in and picked up a vial with purple liquid. "This is the antidote, pour it down his throat, he'll be fine by the morning."

Saphira pocketed it and nodded at Gareth, who picked up Strayson. "What are you doing? I gave you the antidote!"

They roughly walked him out of the tavern. "You did, but I never said I'd let you go," Saphira said as she began running.

She burst into Elyse's house, leaving Gareth far behind. Eden and Rickert were there now. His twin was sitting next to him on the bed, holding his hand with tears down her face. Saphira ran to the bed. "Here, drink this, and you'll be fine, I promise," she said, even though he couldn't hear her.

"Antidote?" Eden asked. Saphira nodded and took out the little cork and poured the liquid into his mouth, and made sure he swallowed it.

"Blessed Otto, what happened?" Andros reached out, and she felt her cheek sting again. "You're injured."

She reached up and remembered what Strayson had done. "It's nothing, Andros."

He scooted closer and touched it. "Blessed Otto, heal your servant of her injury so she may care for her friend." She felt Otto's love, and the pain in her cheek slowly ebbed away.

"Thank you, you didn't need to do that."

Andros sat back and changed Edward's bandages. "I feel it's about the only useful thing I've been able to do all night."

"We're grateful for your help, Andros," Rickert said, his hand on Eden's shoulder.

Saphira leaned down and gently laid her head on Edward's chest and held his hand. "I told you not to go to that part of town," she whispered and brushed his long auburn hair away from his closed eyes. "You're going to be fine, Edward, you hear me, you're going to be just fine." She sat up, her left hand was resting on his chest, feeling it move up and down erratically with every breath he took, while she laid her head in her right hand. "Just fine," she whispered.

"Come on, Ed," Eden begged. "Wake up." Saphira closed her eyes to pray when she felt his body shake. Her eyes flew open, and she saw he was jerking from side to side.

"Edward?" Andros stood and tried to hold him down, but

Saphira could see his muscles were tight and wouldn't give in.

"Edward!" Eden yelled as he suddenly fell against the bed and didn't move.

Saphira's eyes moved quickly to his chest. It wasn't moving. "No, no, Edward, please breathe!" She shook him, and his head lolled from side to side. "Breathe!" She screamed, but his chest didn't move. "Breathe, I beg you!" Eden was sobbing as she laid her head on her brother's chest. Tears streamed down Saphira's face as Andros checked for signs of life.

After what seemed to be forever, he finally lifted his hand off Edward's pulse. "I'm so sorry, he's gone."

Saphira's world shattered around her. "No!" she screamed, a sound that had never crossed her lips filled the air. Andros wrapped his arms around her, and she squeezed him tight.

"You can't leave me!" Eden cried, inconsolable as Rickert kneeled next to her, hiding his face in one hand, the other on Eden's back.

Saphira felt Andros rock her in his arms. *He can't be gone, please.* "I'm sorry, Ed, I'm sorry!" Andros let her go, and a second later, Gareth's arms wrapped around her and hugged her tight from behind. When she turned, she saw his face was sad but steady as ever. "We were too late." She wrapped her arms around him, and he squeezed her. She held onto her rogue king tight while she cried. "He didn't deserve..."

"No, he didn't," Gareth whispered to her, and she felt him pet her head. "Edward was a good guy; he's at peace now, Saphira." She felt a hand on her shoulder, and the familiar love of Otto surrounded her. She knew it was Andros.

"Gareth is right, Edward feels only Otto's love now; there's no more pain." Usually, such words would give her comfort, but at the moment, she was too angry to hear them.

Gareth gently lifted her chin. "Strayson will pay for taking your friend from you, Saphira, count on it."

"Saphira," she felt Andros' hand on her shoulder, "revenge isn't the answer. The gods will punish the man who did this to Edward; have faith, he will have vengeance."

Gareth scoffed. "Sometimes the gods help those who help themselves, priest. I think this is one of those occasions." At the moment, she agreed with the rogue king, Strayson deserved whatever she was going to do to him, and she would enjoy it.

"Saphira," she could hear how irritated Andros sounded. "Don't stoop to this dishonest man's level. You're better than him."

She sniffed and wiped her eyes. "No, Andros, I'm not." Elyse walked into the bedroom, red-eyed and silent. Saphira watched her unfold the sheet and gently lay it over Edward before her eyes teared up, and she couldn't see anything. She cried and sank back into Gareth's chest as he gently rubbed her back.

Suddenly, Andros' voice startled her. "What?" she heard him say. Saphira looked up and saw Elyse was crying, almost smiling, and moving her hands at them.

"What's she saying?" She asked through the tears.

Gareth looked over at Edward, his eyes in shock. "She said he's breathing."

Saphira's eyes widened as Eden sat up like lightning. "What?" The mage ripped the sheet back, and they saw his chest was moving up and down like it should.

Relief and happiness filled Saphira like nothing she had ever felt. "Edward?" He still didn't move, but his breathing was normal now. Everyone stared at him, not wanting to hope but praying he kept breathing.

Andros quickly laid a hand on Edward's neck. "He's alive, his heart is strong, and his breathing is fine. I don't understand."

Eden's laugh was filled with tears as she laid her head on his chest. "I knew you couldn't leave me," she cried. Rickert wiped his face, his eyes red, and he laid a hand on Ed's head.

Saphira sniffed and wiped her cheeks before taking Edward's hand. "We aren't meant to know the will of the gods," she said as happy tears fell down her cheeks.

Saphira and Eden kept watch through the night, but there was no change in Edward. She thanked Otto for whatever miracle had happened over and over. When Gareth told her he was keeping Strayson alive for her, she thanked him. She wanted to be the one to punish him. Andros once again tried to talk her out of it, but she knew it was in vain. He had to be punished. Saphira stayed up all night but lost her valiant fight with sleep as the sun was rising and fell asleep next to Edward, his twin, on the other side. A few hours later, the smell of food woke Saphira, and to her dismay, Edward was still unconscious. She sat up and laid a hand on his cheek.

"Edward, you need to wake up, please."

The door creaked open, and Saphira heard Gareth's boots on the floor. "He's still not up?" He asked and sat on the end of the bed. Saphira could see he looked worried.

"Not yet."

He reached out and laid a hand on her shoulder. "Don't worry, Saphira, he's strong. It just took a while for the antidote to get to him. He'll be fine."

Saphira nodded. "I've never watched anybody linger like this; it hurts."

"He lingers because you're here. I know he can hear you, and it keeps his heart beating."

She looked back at Gareth, surprised at his soft words. "Does it?"

He nodded. "I'd linger for you."

She turned back to Edward and put his hand down. "Thank you, Gareth, for everything." A few minutes passed, and she saw Edwards' eyes flutter. She quickly leaned forward, "Edward, can you hear me?" His head turned, and he moaned. "Gareth, he could be in pain. Do you have anything?"

"Just liquor," he turned toward the door. "Andros, he's waking!" He yelled out, and Andros came running in and sat across from Saphira.

Eden woke with a start at the sudden yelling. "Ed?" Eden gasped and took his hand. "Edward, we're here."

"He might be a little disoriented," Andros warned them.

"Saphira, be careful," Edward moaned and thrashed in

bed. "Get away, he's coming!"

Saphira leaned close and petted his cheeks. "Shh shh shh, Edward, open your eyes. I'm fine."

Slowly, they opened, and he seemed to think about what he was going to say. "Where am I?"

"Elyse's house, do you remember what happened?"

He tried to sit up, but the wound in his chest kept him still. "A big guy, never seen him before. He said he was going to kill us, then go after Gareth because he was getting soft." His left hand slowly made its way to Saphira's cheek. "Did he hurt you?"

She shook her head as tears of relief fell down her cheeks. "Not as bad as he got you. How do you feel?"

He licked his lips and took a few slow breaths. "Tired, weak." He turned and saw his sister, "Edie, I'm okay, I promise."

She cried happy tears and threw her arms around him, the best she could. "Never do that again, it was horrifying!"

He smiled. "I'll try. What happened?"

"Strayson stabbed you with a poison blade; it almost took you from us," Saphira could barely say the words without crying.

Andros reached out and laid his hand over the stab wound. "Let's see if this works now." He prayed, and Saphira watched as the wound closed.

Edward sighed, and she could tell he relaxed a great deal. "Thank you, Andros. I feel much better."

Gareth cleared his throat and got to his feet. "I'll see if Elyse has any food; all of you need to eat." He pointed at them and left the room.

Andros stood and laid a hand on Saphira's shoulder. "I think the patient will be fine in your hands now, ladies. I'll head back to the temple now. But, Saphira, please think before you do anything to the one responsible." Saphira stared at Andros as he walked out and left her and Eden alone with Edward. "What does he mean by that?" Edward asked.

She turned and took his hand in hers. "He worries about me."

Gareth walked in carrying a tray of bread with some butter

and jam. "Eat up, Elyse's strawberry jam does wonders," he said with a little smile. Eden sat up and spread some jam and butter on a piece of bread for her brother while Gareth gave Saphira a look that meant 'I need to speak with you,' so she followed the thief out of the room. When the door shut, he turned but kept his voice down. "Now that the archer is going to live, and the priest is gone, I have something to show you." He motioned for her to follow, and he led her to a warehouse a few blocks away. Inside, a few of his trusted men were guarding Strayson. Of course, he didn't need the guards. Strayson was chained to the floor and could barely move.

Saphira walked around the chained man and pulled out her dagger. "I wondered what you did with him."

"I figured I would leave it up to you or Edward to decide his punishment," Gareth crossed his arms as he stood in front of the prisoner. "But then I realized Ed's a softy and might let him go. I knew better about you, Voltain." Gareth looked up at the men surrounding Strayson. "You can leave us now." They left without a word, leaving the three of them alone. Strayson's eyes followed Saphira as much as he could while she stalked around him.

"I'm soft when I need to be, but this isn't one of those times."

The big man snickered, "You gonna kill me, little girl? I don't think you can. Think how your mother would feel if you killed a defenseless man." His smile enraged her more with every breath he took.

"You don't get to speak about my mother," she said calmly while Gareth punched him in the mouth. His head flew back as blood dripped from the corner of his mouth.

"Did you notice how I didn't help her fight you, Stray? Cause I knew she could take you. I knew she'd win, and I've never been prouder of her than when she sank that dagger into your fucking leg." Gareth stepped where she stabbed Strayson hours earlier. He yelled out as blood seeped from the wound and Gareth wiped the bottom of his boot on Strayson's back.

"Fuck the both of ya!" He yelled, but they ignored his words.

Saphira walked around Strayson, picking her nails with the tip of her blade. "Once, I was worried that killing made me into someone I wouldn't like. Someone the gods would shun, but I was assured, since I didn't seek out those I killed, it was fine. Otto would forgive me. But now…" she laid her dagger against his neck. "Now I don't fucking care." She slowly pushed her dagger into his neck, his gurgles filled the air. With one swipe, the dagger exploded out the other side of his throat. "You don't get to hurt my friends and live." Saphira watched as he slumped over as much as his bonds allowed, his blood spilling on the floor.

Gareth walked up to her and wrapped his arms around her. She looked up at him; his lips were so close she swore she could feel his words on her skin.

"Well done, My Dark Lady." Gareth's hand trailed up her back to her neck, burying itself in her hair. "We're the same, you and I, there's a darkness in us. It calls to one another," he whispered. "I felt it the moment I saw you, something I'd never felt in anyone else."

"I know." It was that feeling that Edward never gave her, the reason she never fell for him. He was all light and happiness. But she had something dark in her; she knew that now and had never felt it in anyone else but Gareth. He'd always understand her, never hold her back, and would love her for who she was, no matter what.

He kissed her furiously for a moment before letting her go. "Feel better?"

She nodded. "Much."

CHAPTER 21
THE SEER

It took Edward a few days to get the poison out of his system to where he could work again. Gareth showed his men what Saphira had done to Strayson and said if anyone stepped out of line again, worse things would happen, and if they wanted to leave, they should. No one did. Saphira continued her lessons with Gareth all through winter, and she became one of the best rogues in the city, after their king, of course. It took her less time to pick locks; no one ever heard her when she followed them, and she heard the best gossip from the dark corners of all the taverns. Saphira spent most nights with Gareth at the 'Orc', but when he stayed at the house, Eden made sure to have a nice dinner waiting for them. Surprisingly, Edward thanked Saphira for getting rid of Strayson. He told her Strayson was dirt Salthole didn't need.

The four of them had decided to go back to Ardenry when the snow melted, so when the weather warmed up, they got everything ready for another sea voyage. The night before they left, Gareth took Saphira out for one last sneak fest. They climbed all over Salthole but didn't see or hear anything of use, so they ended up at Elyse's house drinking the brandy and apple cider drink.

"Gareth, come with us." Saphira had been wanting to ask him for weeks, but it never seemed like the time.

He took a big drink and smiled at her. "Stay here."

Her eyebrows furled. "What? I can't stay here."

Gareth chuckled and set his mug down. "Of course, you can. You can stay with me, and we'll rule Salthole," he said as he slowly laid her down on the fur rug. She couldn't believe what she was hearing; he sounded absolutely serious at the prospect of her staying.

"What King and Queen of Salthole?"

He nodded. "Sounds good to me."

"What about my group?"

He shrugged his shoulders. "I never said they couldn't stay. We can always use more mages and fighters."

Saphira sighed and shook her head. "I can't, I still got the wanderlust, you know that. Why couldn't you come with us?"

He put his elbow on the rug and laid his head in his hand. "Why do you want me to come with you?"

"We could use you for one. You could get rich, famous, all those things I bet you want." She wrapped her arms around him and pulled him on top of her. "We could cut a swath through cities, showing them what it means to be a rogue. And I could keep kissing you every night."

Gareth chuckled and traced her face with a finger. "I agree you could use me, but you know everything I do. Besides, I'm rich here, everyone here knows me, and I'm happy with my life. Plus," he sighed, "I can't leave Elyse. We're all we got." Admittedly, Saphira had forgotten about Elyse; she depended on Gareth for so much.

"I understand, but I had to ask."

"Me too. I think I knew you'd say no, but I'll miss you when you go." He kissed her neck, and she wrapped her arms around him.

"I'll miss you too, Gareth." He looked up and gave her one of those endearing half smiles he was so good at.

"We're kindred souls, Saphira, you and I, we'll always find each other."

Saphira ran her hands through his hair. "I love you, you know that, right?"

"And I love you, My Dark Lady."

When the sun rose, the group was already up and headed towards the docks. Saphira found a blue flower on the porch when they left. It smelled like Gareth. The flower was a 'Blue Alar' named after the sun god. It was given at sad occasions as a reminder that the gods are always with us. It wasn't the Double D that took them back to Fairwinds, but a brand-new ship making its maiden voyage called 'The Squealing Whelp'. They could still smell the tar and fresh pine resin as they put their things in the room the captain said they could use. Saphira sat on one of the few boxes in the room and twirled the flower in between her hands.

Edward sat on the floor in front of her. "Pretty flower, where did you get it?"

"Found it on the porch this morning."

He took it from her and put it in her dark hair. "There, beautiful." Saphira smiled and felt the boat jerk a little, which usually meant they had cast off.

"Are you excited about seeing your mother again?" she asked.

Edward smiled and hugged her legs. "I am, I can't wait to see little Ruby either. I bet she's gotten so big by now." Saphira smiled and laid her head on his, wrapping her arms around him the best she could. She still thanked Otto for whatever miracle brought him back to them. She hated how close they were to losing him forever.

"A few months on a child can do wonders, and it's almost been a full year. She's probably running all over the place."

Edward chuckled. "Probably."

The trip was smooth but cold, and they reached Fairwinds two weeks later. It was cheaper to get off at the port town instead of riding on the boat all the way to Ardenry through the tributaries. They bought horses and made the trip to Ardenry. The further south they rode, the warmer it got. When they rode into the large city a few weeks later, it looked like the busy town they knew it to be. But it took a little longer to get to Mayris's shop this time because the streets were crowded with people.

"Seems like an awful lot of people, even for Ardenry," Rickert noted.

"Guess we'll find out what's going on when we get to 'Mom's." Edward tried to get his horse to go faster, but there were too many people. When their mom's shop finally came into view, Edward handed Saphira his reins while he jumped off and ran inside, while everybody else found a handler to buy their horses. When they finally entered the shop, there were a few people wandering around, and Mathias was behind the counter.

"There you are, Ed's upstairs with Mayris and Ruby, go on up!" Eden gave him a quick hug, and the three walked upstairs.

"Mom!" Eden called out, and Mayris stepped into the living room with an almost year-old Ruby on her hip.

"Eden!" She opened her one free arm, and they hugged while Ruby played with her sister's hair.

"Where's Edward? Mathias said he was up here?" Rickert asked.

Soon after, he came walking in. "I'm here. Doesn't she look big?" He tweaked the baby's cheeks, but little Ruby stared at him with her big brown eyes, like she had no idea who he was. "Mom was telling me why there are so many people here." They all moved to the couch, and Ruby began walking around the newcomers, pulling at this or that.

"Another town was devastated by the Empire," Mayris said gravely. "There's so many refugees we weren't prepared for them. It'll be okay in a few weeks, it's just kind of a madhouse right now."

"Guess we picked a bad time to come back," Eden said.

"Oh, nonsense, it's never a bad time to come home." Mayris ran her hand through Eden's auburn hair and kissed her cheek. "So, what brings you back? Anything specific, or did you want to see your old mom?"

"We wanted to see you and Ruby, see how things were going," Eden said with a smile.

Little Ruby climbed over into Saphira's lap, pulling on the strings of her cloak, happily babbling while the twins caught up with their mother. Saphira took one of the strings and put it in her mouth, then pushed it out with her tongue while making a silly noise. Ruby giggled like it was the funniest thing she'd ever seen and kept putting the string back in Saphira's mouth to the best of her ability so she could do it over and over. Edward reached around, and Saphira could tell he was trying to tickle her little cheeks, but she kept dodging out of the way.

"I can't get over how big she is now," he said.

"You miss a lot on the road." Saphira managed to say around the string.

The rest of the day, she and Edward looked after Ruby while Eden and their mother cooked a feast. It was such a different day from what she was used to, stabbing men or running from monsters, but she found she liked it. It was peaceful and happy, and as Saphira watched Edward play with his baby sister, she began to wonder what it would be like to settle down. Living in Salthole, ruling the city with Gareth. It brought a smile to her face.

The next day, Edward said he wanted to take a walk, so they wandered, arm in arm, to a side of the city Saphira had never been to before. "What shops are over here?" Saphira asked as she began reading all the signs.

"You know, for a rogue, you didn't explore Ardenry much," he teased.

She shook her head. "No, I was busy learning, figured I'd have time to sneak around later." They passed a sign that was made from a thick piece of wood, which was decorated with carved stars and swirls. It made her smile.

"What an interesting sign." Edward stopped, and they both read, 'Adelaide, seer extraordinaire.' "Oh, sounds fun, let's see if she'll read for us." Saphira wasn't particularly excited about getting a reading; most seers were charlatans. Well, except one.

"If you want." They walked up and knocked on the door, and waited a minute before a man with a sword on his back answered.

"Good afternoon, is Adelaide available for a reading?" Edward asked.

The man nodded. "She is. Please come in." The man stepped aside, and they walked in. Saphira could smell the incense in the air; it smelled of flowery herbs and fire. The man with the sword led them to a doorway covered with a curtain of gold beads. "Please go on in." Saphira gave him a small smile and moved the beads out of her way. A woman was sitting at a large oak table, shuffling cards, but Saphira recognized her immediately.

"Ada!"

The woman looked up and smiled brightly. "Saphy! Oh, my gods, I thought I'd see you soon!" She got up, and they ran around the table and hugged each other tightly.

"Ada, I never thought I'd see you again. I don't believe it." Ada was as tall as she was when Saphira saw her six years ago. Luckily, she had grown and was now a good head taller than the small half-elf. Saphira was never tall, but Ada was practically miniature.

"How are you? Sit, sit, tell me everything." Ada ushered the two into some chairs and held Saphira's hands.

"Aren't you the seer? You should know all this already," Saphira teased.

Ada laughed and nodded. "I know, but I find most people like to talk about themselves rather than me talking for them."

Saphira turned and motioned to Edward. "This is Edward McVain, he's the archer in my group. This is Ada, my family used to travel to visit her parents every other year. We practically grew up together."

"How fortuitous."

Ada shook his hand. "It's nice to meet you, Edward. So did you two want a reading?"

He rubbed Saphira's arms and smiled. "Sounds good." Ada nodded and moved back over to her cards.

"What do you want to know? Anything specific, or should I see what pops up?"

Saphira looked over at the archer. "What do you think?"

He shrugged. "Let's see what pops up."

She nodded and turned back to Ada. "You heard the man." Ada giggled and began spreading the cards in front of her.

Saphira watched Ada's elven eyes scan the cards when a baby's cry pierced the air. Saphira gasped, "You have a baby?"

Ada smiled. "I do, I think River's hungry. Come, you can meet her." Ada got up, and the two followed the small half-elf into the living room. It looked like the typical living room, with bookcases and a fireplace. Sitting in one of the many chairs was the man who answered the door. He was smiling down at the baby in his arms as she ate from a bottle. Saphira leaned down and touched the little tuft of white hair on the child's head.

"Oh, Ada, she's beautiful!"

The man looked up at River. "Didn't want to interrupt your session, so I gave her a bottle."

Ada sat next to him and patted the couch next to her. "Come sit, this is my husband Dryn and our daughter River."

He lifted the fingers that were under the baby, and Saphira gently shook them. "Nice to meet you." Saphira sat down next to Ada.

"And you. I take it Ada knows you more than her usual clients?" He teased.

Ada reached out and laid a hand on his arm. "Saphira is Foster's younger sister." Saphira thought Ada sounded proud to know her. It felt nice.

The man's eyebrows went wide. "Foster's sister? No kidding, it's nice to meet you."

"Do you know my brother?" The bottle made squeaking noises as River emptied it, and Dryn handed her to Ada.

"I do, met him a few weeks ago, actually."

Saphira gasped. "He was here? Is he still here?"

"No, he's heading back towards Raventree now," Ada said.

Saphira was practically bouncing in her seat. "Well, how is he? What's he been doing? I haven't heard a thing since he left."

Ada smiled. "Are you sure you don't want to be surprised?"

Saphira scoffed, "No."

Ada laughed. "He's good, taller if you can believe it. In love and expecting a child."

Saphira gasped so hard she almost choked. "What?"

Ada laughed and nodded her head. "You're going to be an aunt! Sunette is his wife's name, and I will not spoil the story of how they met. It's too good for them not to tell you."

Saphira sat back and thought about her oldest brother. "I miss him so much." Edward gently rubbed her neck.

"Do you want to go home and see him?" he asked. She looked over and seriously considered it, but she still wanted to be out in the world.

"Not yet, but I'm glad he's going home. Christopher's never really forgiven himself for what happened between them when Foster left." Ada rocked her daughter in her arms until she fell asleep.

"Foster feels bad, too. I'm sure they'll mend their ways in no time." The seer sighed, "Well, it's much more comfortable here anyway. What do you say to having your reading in here?"

Saphira nodded. "Sounds fine." Ada closed her eyes and began breathing slow and steady. Saphira watched her eyes dart back and forth behind her eyelids and wondered what she was seeing. She sighed deeply, and Saphira saw a tear fall from Ada's eyes. "Ada, are you okay?"

She reached out and held Saphira's hand. "I see you are marked, little girl."

Edward gasped. "Marked? Is she in danger?" She could feel his hands tightening on her arms.

"I'll be fine, Edward." She patted his hands and watched Ada.

The seer sighed. "I see great hardships with your friend, Saphira; he's already warned you. But it hides from me," she said slowly. Ada's eyes stayed closed, but she looked confused before she chuckled, "You're so talented now. A king holds you in his heart and eagerly awaits your return. You will see him again, but at a time of crisis. He'll follow you to the abyss and back if you ask it of him. I see a time of great turmoil for you." She opened her eyes, "Saphira, may I speak with you in private?"

Edward sat up. "In private?"

"Some things are for her ears alone." Ada said, not unkindly.

Dryn got to his feet. "Let's go over to the tavern across the way. I'll buy you a drink."

Slowly, Edward got to his feet. "I guess we'll be back in a little bit."

"All right, have fun."

"Don't worry, she does this a lot." She heard Dryn tell Edward as they walked out of the house.

When the door shut, she turned back to Ada. "What did you see?"

"The one who marks you, I could only see he had salt and pepper hair. He hides himself well," she sounded annoyed.

"Why did he mark me?" Saphira thought about it, but didn't know anyone with salt and pepper hair.

"To claim you."

Her eyes went wide. "Claim me? That's disgusting."

"I agree. I saw your old love, the one who left." Saphira's eyes went wide. "He was hired by the one who marks you; he left because he was afraid, he'd lead the man right to you in the city."

"Iollan?"

Ada nodded. "I have a feeling you will see your dark fighter again, but it won't be a happy reunion." Saphira sat for a long time thinking about how she felt. She knew she wasn't in love with Iollan anymore; though the pain was still there, the betrayal. But she felt a bit of closure, knowing why he left. Whoever this man was that hired him, must have be dangerous.

Saphira picked at her thumbnail. "Maybe that's why my guts were always telling me to stay away from him."

"Possibly, but young love is hard to ignore." Ada patted her knee.

Saphira sighed. "What friend were you talking about? What's hiding from you?"

Ada motioned to the empty chair next to her. "Edward, there is something unnatural in him. But it's hiding in him, slowly poisoning him. Does he seem different?"

She sat back. "What? No, he seems fine."

Ada reached over and laid a hand on hers. "Saphira, the truth, was he raised recently?" Her eyes went wide as the memory of him lying dead in the bed filled her mind.

Again, she shook her head. "No, not recently. He… a priest said he was dead, but clearly, he wasn't."

"What do you mean by recently?" She sighed and told Ada about what happened in Salthole and how he was killed as a boy. "Hmm, tricky." Saphira slumped in the chair Dryn was in earlier. "You need a little peace, Saphira. Would you like to hold River?" She gave Ada a little smile, and the seer put her infant daughter in her arms.

"Did you see what we found outside of Blackridge?" she asked Ada.

"I did, it was good of you to take him."

"I thanked Otto that I could hear him; he was so quiet under all that stuff." Saphira stared at River as she made little sucking noises in her sleep. "Why did you name her River?"

"We named her after Dryn's sister. She died when she was a child." Saphira smiled and stared at the baby. Lately, she'd been wondering what it would have been like to have children. To be home with her family, to see them every day, and feel her mother's prayers at dinner again. "Part of me wants to go home now, but it doesn't feel right yet."

Ada closed her eyes again. "You will go home with your love, I've seen it. It may not happen for reasons you think, but it will."

When the sun set, Saphira walked over to Zell's shop, alone. Before she could knock, she heard rushed footsteps a moment before the door opened.

"I thought I saw you walking down the street," Zell laughed and opened his arms, and she hugged him. "I'm so glad you're back."

"Me too."

"Come in, tell me what brings you by." They walked up

the stairs, and she sat at his little table while he pulled out some brown liquor and two glasses.

"Wanted to check in on you," she said with a smile.

Zell chuckled and set down the glasses. "Oh, I'm fine, business is good." There was one reason she wanted to visit Zell; if anyone could answer this question for her, he could.

"Can I ask you something?" He nodded. "Have you ever encountered someone who was raised from the dead and came back wrong?"

He poured them some liquor and quickly downed it. "Once. We were hired to bring home a woman who had run away from home. We found her in Salthole, hiding among the thieves. We told her we were there to bring her home, and she went," he thought for a moment. "Feral almost. It took all five of us to bring her down. One of the thieves there said she was odd, and a few of them wondered if she was possessed because of her bloodlust and ruthlessness. We took her to the temple, and they confirmed it; she had a devil in her. It wasn't her fault, back then it wasn't illegal to bring people back. It was before we knew something was wrong. But we couldn't bring her home and left her with the church to deal with; we assume they killed her. I've never known anyone to be saved from possession. I guess it depends on what gets stuck with ya, but most of the time it's bad news." She downed her drink as well, thinking on his words. "Did you bring someone back?" he asked.

"No," she didn't meet his eyes. "But he came back anyway."

"Is he acting different?"

She shook her head. "No, I was wondering if there were signs I could watch out for?" She finally looked up and met his eyes. He looked sad, not judgy, like she thought he might.

"Mostly a change in character, doing and saying things you know they wouldn't normally. But usually by then it's too late." She nodded and poured herself more to drink. "Did Iollan come with you?" he asked.

She shook her head. "No, he ran off."

"What?" He jerked in surprise, "Why'd he do something dumb like that?"

Saphira shrugged and took another shot. "He thought if he stayed, he'd lead a bad man to me." She shook her head and swirled the liquor in her glass.

Zell slowly sat up. "What bad man?" Saphira fought a little smile as his protective tone reminded her of her father.

Saphira shrugged. "Don't know, someone with salt and pepper hair wants to claim me, according to a family friend."

He leaned forward, looking more serious than she'd ever seen him. "Are you safe, Saphira?"

She nodded and finished her drink. "As safe as I can be. I promise."

Zell sighed and crossed his arms. "I'm sorry there's such intrigue in your life."

"It's all right," Saphira ran her hands through her hair. "I have a new love, he taught me to be the best of myself, and I know he isn't going anywhere."

Zell poured her another drink and smiled. "Do tell." She spent the rest of the night telling him about Gareth, what they did around Salthole, and how she loved that Gareth let her be herself.

"Sounds perfect," Zell said softly.

"We are."

CHAPTER 22
SHADOW VS. SHADOW

Saphira had enjoyed seeing Ada, despite the ominous messages she told her. She spent almost every day at her house, talking or cuddling with River. She wrote a letter to Gareth, telling him everything that happened since they got to Ardenry, and the things she would do to him when she came back to Salthole. She didn't know if they'd still be in Ardenry when he wrote back, but she wanted him to have something of her while she was away.

A few weeks later, Rickert decided he wanted to visit his sister, so they made off for Suya territory, Ada's warning in her mind the entire time. When they reached the summer camps, it was afternoon. Children were running around playing, while most of the women were skinning different animals. They could see the big red and green tents in the distance, and Rickert took off running.

"Malia!" The green tent flap opened, and the group saw Rickert's sister smile and run over to him.

"Rickert!" The closer she got, it was evident Malia was with child again, but not as big as she was the last time they saw her.

"Oh! Little sister, I'm going to be an uncle again?" They heard the families' happy laughter as they walked up. Malia's husband, Lucien, walked out of the tent carrying their two-year-old daughter.

"Rickert, good to see you!" The men shook hands, and Rickert fawned over his niece. She had curly brown hair and blue eyes and seemed to love the attention her uncle was giving her. "I'm so glad you are all here. We've been discussing hiring some people, but we didn't know how much we could trust them. But I know we can trust you," Lucien said.

"What is it?" Lucien motioned for them to follow him into his tent. It didn't surprise Saphira how Lucien was behaving. The Suya could be secretive. But she wondered what had them so scared.

When they were all inside, Malia gave them all some tea she had made. "Something's stalking our camp, but we can't find it," Lucien said.

"Is it killing your livestock?" Rickert asked.

Lucien sat down and let his daughter walk over to Rickert, who sat in his lap. "No, it's killing our children."

Everyone gasped. "What would do such a thing?" Eden sounded horrified.

The large man shook his head, and Saphira could see he looked sad. "Something evil, no doubt. My brother's youngest child was the first victim. We found his little body about a mile from camp; it was barely recognizable." He shook his head as Malia laid her hand on her husband's shoulder.

"It was awful, and a child has died every night since. It's been this way for two weeks. We have sentries every night, but no one has seen anything. We're at our 'wits' end, Rickert. I know you can help, please?"

Rickert leaned forward and took his sister's hand. "We'll do everything we can, Malia, I promise." He looked back at the group. "Won't we?"

Everyone nodded their heads. "Of course we will," Eden said. "We'll find this thing and make sure it doesn't bother you again."

That night, Saphira took an odd place to keep watch, under a cart parked in the middle of the camp. From there, she could see every tent in the camp and stayed as quiet as she could. At the moment, everyone was asleep for the night, and Saphira's ears were listening to every sound. Her hardened eyes searched for the barest of movement, and her fingers twitched at the excitement of plunging her dagger into whatever was killing these children. A cricket chirped, and she heard a dog scratch behind its ear, all perfectly normal sounds. Rickert was watching the perimeter of the camp, and she could hear his familiar footsteps making another round.

Edward and Eden were spread apart as well, one was in a tent to her left, the other in a tent to her right, both had children in them, and their parents welcomed the extra muscle. As Rickert walked to Saphira's back, she noticed the shadows the surrounding campfires cast on the ground. They were happy, moving about on the grass like shadows do, but one shadow caught her attention.

It was darker than the others if that was possible, and the fire didn't make it dance like the others; it was utterly still. Saphira moved from her hiding place and crept towards the shadow, it still didn't move. She cast a little spell as a tiny ball of light zoomed over to the shadow, but all it did was swallow the light up.

"Rickert!" She yelled as the shadow wrapped around her ankle and jerked her to the ground. Her head hit a rock, and the shock froze her body as she watched the shadow snake its way up her legs.

"Saphira!" She heard Rickert's running footsteps, and the shadow quickly dashed out of the camp.

"Fucking hell," she whispered and got to her feet as Rickert reached her.

"Are you okay? What happened?"

She winced as she felt the lump on her head. "There's a shadow. It could be the thing taking the children, it went this way."

She ran to the edge of camp, Rickert close behind as he yelled to everyone. "Wake up, intruder!" People began coming out of their tents, weapons already drawn, but Saphira wished they would stay inside. The more shadows on the ground there were, the harder it was to see the one she needed to see.

"Please! Go back inside, let us look for the shadow, but be wary inside your own tent!" She yelled and scanned the shadows. Luckily, they listened to her and began filling back in their tents.

Edward and Eden walked over, and Saphira told them what to look for. "It's darker than a normal shadow. You can see it in light, it doesn't disappear like a normal shadow either, and be careful, it's strong." The twins nodded and headed off in opposite directions while Saphira ran to the edge of the camp. She stood in the quiet of the field and saw the offending shadow making its way to the north through the tall grass.

"Found you," she whispered and took out her magical dagger as she ran after it. The moon was high in the sky and gave off plenty of light, but as Saphira ran into a clump of flowers, her eyes scanned the darkness over and over, but realized she had lost it. "Damn." She berated herself for being too slow and headed back to the camp in case it doubled back. As she turned, hands grabbed her throat, dragging her hard to the ground.

A hissing laugh filled her ears. "Gullible human, you're a little older than I like, but you'll do for now." All she could see was the shadow above her; it had a human shape to it, so she did what she would do if it were a person: she stabbed it. Her dagger struck true, and she could feel the magic tingling in her hand before it started to burn. A pain in her chest stole her breath, but she managed to keep twisting the knife into the shadow.

It began screaming, the sound made Saphira want to scream as well, but her chest hurt too much to take a good breath. Her vision lightened, and she realized it had flown away, leaving her alone in the flowers as she desperately tried to catch her breath. It felt as if her heart was struggling to beat. For a moment, she saw the stars above her head twinkling. They were a little different from the ones above Raventree, but she recognized them enough to feel homesick.

After her heart finally felt normal again, she managed to catch her breath and get to her feet. She wasn't as steady as she usually was, but didn't fall as she walked slowly back into the camp. Her body felt funny, like your foot when it falls asleep. Rickert, Eden, and Edward were still in the middle of the camp, keeping watch.

Edward was the first to see her. "Saphira, there you

are." He walked over to meet her, and she could see he looked increasingly scared the closer they got to each other. "Pippa's bouncing tits, what happened to you?" His arm wrapped around her waist, and she fell to her knees. She watched as his other hand moved to her chest. When she looked down, she saw her chest was covered in a huge blue and yellow bruise.

"I didn't realize." She touched it lightly and could feel how sensitive it was as pain shot through her body. "Aah," she gasped. "That shadow must have done it to me."

"You caught up with it?" Rickert walked over and studied her bruise.

"Yeah, I think I stabbed it," she raised her hand, and saw it was covered in blisters. "It screamed and ran off, but it's going to be tough to get rid of."

Eden clicked her tongue and gently held Saphira's hand. "Come, let's see if Malia has something for your hand." Eden helped her up and led her into the big green tent.

Lucien and Malia were awake, watching over their little girl. "Did you get it?" she asked fearfully.

"Not yet, but we know what it is," Eden said. "It's some kind of shadow; it seems to have taken a liking to your camp." Saphira sat down, and Malia began studying her wounds.

"Do you have anything?" Ed asked.

She nodded. "For the burn, yes, I'm afraid the bruise will have to heal on its own." Malia got out a small jar and began rubbing the white contents on Saphira's hand; the pain instantly subsided.

"Thanks."

"It's no problem. Do you think it'll come back tonight?"

"Hard to say, definitely tomorrow night, though," she managed to say.

Malia nodded and moved back to her sleeping child. "We'll stay vigilant then." Edward carried Saphira back to their tent while Edie went to get Rickert. He laid her on the blanket, and all she wanted to do was sleep for a thousand years.

"How's your hand?" Edward took it and gave it a little

kiss.

"It'll be fine, doesn't hurt at all." He smiled as his hand made its way to the bruise covering her chest. His fingers trailed lightly over her skin. Saphira watched his eyes stare at her neck. He looked entranced for some reason, and she felt his fingers slowly move up to her neck. She closed her eyes as his fingers began kneading at her muscles. "That feels good." Saphira swore she was almost asleep when Edward's hand brushed her bruise hard enough it made her gasp. Her eyes flew open, and Edward was staring at her. "Why did you do that?"

His eyes blinked rapidly as he shook his head. "I'm sorry, Saphy, I didn't realize I touched you so hard." He looked upset and sat back on his bedroll. "I'd better not sleep next to you, I don't want to squish you." Edward did tend to squish her and agreed.

"Okay," she whispered and laid down. Her head hit the pillow perfectly, and as her eyes closed, she knew the pain wouldn't keep sleep away.

The next night, her bruise looked and felt worse, but her hand was perfectly fine. Saphira had slept the entire day away and still felt tired. The moon was even bigger tonight, and everyone hoped it would aid them in seeing the misplaced shadow. Saphira did her best to ignore the pain as she walked around the camp like Rickert had done the night before, when a scream pierced the air. It came from across the camp and Saphira began running faster than she ever had towards the sound. People were coming out of their tents to see what was happening when she realized it was Rickert's scream. *Not Rickert, not him,* she thought as she reached the scene. The big man was on his knees, and the shadow had its hand plunged into his chest.

"Let him go!" Saphira screamed and sliced her dagger in the air. The shadow screamed and took its hand out of Rickert, who slumped on the ground.

The shadow growled, and its eyes started to glow red. "You've interrupted me enough," it hissed at her, and she watched as its left arm turned into a solid black sword. It swung it at her with unnatural speed. Saphira ducked but felt a stinging pain on the side of her neck. She tried to ignore it as she whirled around and raked her dagger along the shadow's chest. It let out an unholy scream. The shadow lunged forward and surrounded her, dragging her to the ground.

"He's not the same anymore," it hissed in her ear. "He'll never be the same." It hissed a horrible giggle in her ear before lightning surrounded them. The shadow screamed and let her go. Saphira looked behind her and saw Eden cast another spell at the creature while Edward helped her up.

"Get away from them!" Eden screamed as fire erupted from her fingertips. They watched as the shadow caught on fire. It flailed around, screaming and tried tried to run, but with every step, its fiery legs crumbled before their eyes. Saphira scrambled over and began stabbing it with her dagger, tearing it into little pieces while it screamed.

"Saphira!" A hand grabbed hers, and she turned. It was Edward. "It's dead, you can stop."

Saphira took a breath and relaxed her arm as he let go. "Sorry." She looked behind them and saw Eden talking softly to Rickert. He had a bruise like hers on his chest. "It was trying to crush our hearts," she said quietly.

Lucien came running over and leaned next to Rickert. "Are you okay?"

Thankfully, he nodded. "Yeah, we got it, it's dead." Lucien smiled and helped Rickert to his feet.

"We'll forever be in your debt, Rickert. We can't thank you enough." Edward helped Saphira up and followed Lucien as he helped their boss into their tent.

"I will tell my brother what you did for us. For now, sleep. You deserve it." When the flap closed, Eden hugged Rickert, and Saphira could hear her crying softly.

"I thought—" Saphira heard her whisper.

"I'm fine, Eden, I'm all right." Saphira smiled at their exchange as Edward lay down behind her and pulled her close.

"How are you?" he asked.

She took a deep, painful breath and sighed. "I'm okay, a little confused. The shadow said, 'he's different'. I don't understand what it meant," she whispered.

"Different?" She shrugged her shoulders and closed her eyes. "Who did it mean?" Edward asked.

Saphira licked her dry lips. "I assumed Rickert," she whispered. "But then I would be different, too, but I feel fine."

"Hm, weird." Edward ran his fingers through her hair, and the gentle motion quickly put her to sleep.

It was almost night once again when Saphira woke. Rickert spent all day asleep as well. Apparently, having your heart squeezed by a shadow took a lot out of you. The Suya celebrated when they finally woke up, thanking the group for all their work. Saphira wanted to dance and celebrate, but her chest hurt so much she could barely move, so she happily sat by the fire while everyone celebrated around her.

CHAPTER 23
GOTHRIN

The group stayed with the Suya until Saphira and Rickert were healed. It took a few weeks until their bruises finally disappeared. Since they were close to Buckland, Rickert suggested they head there so Eden could defend her title. But to everyone's surprise, Eden said she'd rather not. She wasn't interested in defending her title and would rather not risk herself, but they could go and watch. Saphira understood. She'd rather not have Eden risk herself either.

Saphira was on duty the first night away from the camp, Rickert and Eden were sleeping a few yards away, but Edward was still awake for some reason. Her hand absentmindedly petted her chest where her bruise used to be. It didn't hurt anymore, but she realized how close she had come to dying. *Maybe I should get back to Salthole,* she thought, *everything seems to be getting more dangerous.*

"Saphira?" Edward's voice made her ear twitch, but she didn't turn.

"Yes?" She heard him sit up and felt his arms around her.

"You look troubled," he whispered.

Saphira leaned back into his arms. "Probably because I am," she chuckled lightly.

"What's wrong? Maybe I can help."

She sighed. "I keep thinking about going back to Salthole, to stay."

"Ah, I see. Is this something you want to do soon?"

She shrugged. "Not *too* soon."

His hands ran lightly along her arms. It always gave her goosebumps. "Do you want me to come with you?"

She turned and smiled at him. "Well, you're welcome too.

I know Gareth said they could always use more fighters."

"Gareth?" He looked confused.

"Yeah, he could get you all jobs if you wanted to stay."

He scoffed. "You can't marry him, he'll never leave Salthole, and you don't want to live there."

She crossed her arms. The nerve of him to say what she could or couldn't do! "You don't know what I want, Edward."

"Maybe I know better than you think." She couldn't believe what she was hearing as he kept talking. "Salthole is no place to raise a family." Saphira stared at him like she didn't know who he was. How dare he assume to know her heart?

"Why don't you start your watch now?" She picked up her sleeping bag and moved it closer to Eden.

"Saphira," he sounded irritated. "You don't have to move."

"Good night," she said curtly and turned away from the fire. The shadow's voice was screaming in her head, *he's different now.*

The next day, Saphira took point, mainly to stay away from Edward. What he said got under her skin. The way he told her Salthole was no place for a family, or how she couldn't marry Gareth. How dare he! What did he know anyway? She grumbled to herself for the millionth time that day as they tromped over a hill. In the distance, they saw an orc fighting a group of men.

"Hard to tell who's in the right from here, shall we?" Rickert asked. Edward drew his bow, Eden readied a spell, and Rickert unsheathed his sword. The group quickly made its way down the hill. The closer they got, they could tell it was the orc in need of help. The men he was fighting were Korites, and the ground was littered with dead orcs. Edward let loose an arrow, and one man fell to the ground.

The fight stalled as the group ran up. "You picked the wrong day for a fight!" Rickert yelled as he engaged the nearest man in red armor. Eden covered one with flames, and he quickly fell to the ground, screaming. Rickert and the orc ganged up on one while Edward shot the last one to the ground. Saphira drew her dagger and moved behind the distracted Korite, and when he raised his sword to block, she struck. Her dagger went deep into his back as she twisted it. He froze and slipped limply off the dagger.

The orc stared at the body before he looked up at her. "Thank you, but I had it handled." He put his blade against his worn leather pants and wiped the blood away.

"You're welcome." Saphira saw the scars on his arm and knew this was an old orc. He was bald, and his leather armor was worn. As she knelt by one of the men Edward shot, she could tell he was still alive. She grabbed him by his collar when he twisted in her grip, his bloody hand wrapping around her wrist and pulled her close.

"Water sprite bitch!" He hissed and tried to smash his hand into her eyes, but his bloody hand made it easy to twist from his grasp and sink her dagger into his throat.

"Rot in hell, you piece of shit," she muttered to no one. Saphira got to her feet and saw the orc was walking off. "Hey, wait."

He stopped and turned to them. "What?"

Saphira jogged over and sheathed her dagger. "We're going to Buckland, want to come with us?"

She thought he looked a bit surprised at the offer. "With you?"

Rickert came over and held out his hand. "I'm Rickert. This is my group. We could always use some more muscle if you're interested."

The orc took Rickert's hand and gave it a hearty shake. "Gothrin. You'd hire me?"

"Sure, why not? You seem to still have some fight left in you," Rickert said with a smile.

"Hmm, your group is young," he said as he studied everyone.

Saphira gave the orc a tap on his arm. "But talented, I assure you." She looked back at Eden who was smiling brightly. When

Saphira saw Edward, her heart skipped a beat. He looked angry at the prospect of this orc joining and was staring at Gothrin like the orc had drowned his kitten. "Edward?"

Suddenly, his face lit up, and he smiled at her. "Huh?"

"Are you okay?"

"Yeah, I'm fine, why?"

"You looked like you didn't want Gothrin coming with us."

Edward looked up at the others. "I did? I was reeling from the fight, you know how it is." He walked over to her and laced his hand with hers. "I'm fine."

"If you say so." Saphira patted his hand and took her hand back.

She turned and saw Rickert and Gothrin were shaking hands. "Thank you for inviting me." The old orc nodded at them. "I wanted a glorious death. Clearly, I wasn't going to find it here, but perhaps I'll find it with your group."

Rickert chuckled. "We try to keep everyone alive as long as possible, truth be told. But we'll be glad to have you for as long as we can." After the group helped Gothrin bury his friends, the old orc took point as they made their way to Buckland. They were a few miles away, and they could already see the town dressed up for the tournament. Colorful tents and flags lines the road, it looked much like it did last year. But there were more tents this year. Seems the tournament was doing exactly what the town hoped, and was bringing in more people. The group walked to the only inn in town and got some rooms. Saphira couldn't help but notice the looks they were getting and knew it was because of Gothrin.

Not all orcs were imperial orcs, but he did a respectable job at ignoring the stares. The owner recognized Eden and said if she was competing, they could get their rooms for free. But she told him she wasn't and would happily pay. Rickert passed out some keys, and Edward picked up Saphira's bag and carried it upstairs.

Eden snickered, "Guess you're bunking with Ed."

"Guess so." Saphira knew Rickert wouldn't let Eden stay alone or with their new member because he was so new. But Gothrin said he didn't mind being alone, apparently it had been a long time since he slept by himself, and he wondered how he'd sleep without the snores of his brethren around.

The morning of the tournament found everyone downstairs eating breakfast. Eden was excited to watch the mages, and Saphira knew Rickert would watch with her. She only watched because Eden was participating. Since the mage decided not to this year, Saphira figured she'd take part in the festival with Edward.

Eden got up and pulled Rickert to his feet. "Come on, we don't want to miss any of it!" Rickert laughed and let her pull him from the tavern, and Saphira laid her hand on Edward's.

"Feel like playing a few games?"

He wiped his mouth and shrugged his shoulders. "I don't know, I kind of feel like not doing anything today."

Her heart dropped a little. "You don't want to impress all the pretty girls with your talent?" she teased him.

He turned and kissed her cheek. "I'll see you tonight, Saphira." And got to his feet.

"Edward!" But he didn't stop and walked up the stairs to their room. She huffed and crossed her arms over her stomach. "Ass," she whispered.

Gothrin finished his drink and cleared his throat. "Your man is a grumpy one, and that's saying something coming from me."

She snickered. "He's not my man, but yeah, he's been grumpier lately."

"If you are not busy perhaps, I could impart some knowledge on you."

She turned, keeping her arms crossed. "Knowledge?"

He nodded and got to his feet. "I take it you are well versed in your dagger, but where swords are concerned, you know little."

Saphira shrugged. "Swords are heavy. I'm not extraordinarily strong. My strength is in my legs." She gave her thighs a slap.

Suddenly, the orc pulled her to her feet. "You would do well with a rapier, little one," and started walking outside. Truthfully, she'd never been good with a sword. The closer she was to her target, the more accurate she was.

"I've never owned a rapier." She called out and quickly followed him out the door.

Gothrin stopped at the first clear field they could find.

"Buy one." He pulled out his swords and handed Saphira his short sword. "You have coin I know. If you get one, I'll teach you." She scoffed and held the sword unceremoniously in her hand as she put them on her hips.

"You don't look like a finesse fighter." Suddenly, he charged, his sword raised high, and Saphira spun out of the way and pointed the sword at him. "Are you crazy?" He charged again, but this time he hit her sword. She felt her arms shaking from the vibrations.

Gothrin gave her a toothy grin. "Some have said, now hit me."

Saphira shook her hands and raised her sword. "It's awkward."

"That's because you're not used to it," he swung and hit her sword again. "And because you are a woman."

Now her blood was really boiling. "A woman? So, because I'm a woman, I can't swing a sword? I've known plenty of girls who could fight with a sword!" She pressed forward and clanged her little sword against his big one, but didn't think it did much.

"There are stories of great women fighters," Gothrin said, "they had to cut off a breast so she could properly swing a sword."

"Bullshit! Why should we have to be less feminine to match a man in battle? You made that up." Saphira used her youth and agility and moved quickly around the orc. He was old, but still fast, and managed to keep up with her. "Come on, old man, keep up!" She watched him move his feet and could anticipate his movements, and with one last turn, she whacked him on the back with the flat part of her blade. "Ha! Gotcha!"

Gothrin stopped, and she could hear him breathing hard. "I knew you could do it." He turned, and she could see an orcish smile on his face. "Now, again."

CHAPTER 24

UNEXPECTED VIOLENCE AND CALM

It was night when Saphira and Gothrin walked back into the inn for dinner. They had been swinging swords at each other all day, and Saphira never felt so good. She had learned so much and couldn't wait to talk about her day to her friends. When they walked in, she only saw Eden and Rickert at the table.

"Hey, where's Edward?"

Eden rolled her eyes and crossed her arms over her stomach. "In your room. He wouldn't come down to eat."

"Why not?"

The mage waved her hand. "Oh, who knows, he's been acting so weird lately, I don't know what's wrong with him. Maybe you can get him down."

"I'll try." She made her way up the stairs and found the door to their room was unlocked. "Edward, are you in here?" It was dark, but Saphira could see him sitting on the edge of the bed, staring out of the window.

"Finally done playing with that orc?" he asked quietly.

"Well, you didn't leave me much choice." She walked in and shut the door. "Come down to dinner."

"No." Saphira stared at him. He had bags under his eyes, making him look exhausted, and when she reached out to touch him, he flinched a little.

"Edward, what's wrong? Are you sick?"

He scoffed. "Sick, no, I'm not sick." He suddenly grabbed her hand and flung her on the bed. "I feel fine, Saphira." His voice was low, and it was hard to hear him over the squeaking of the bed.

"Edward, what the hell are you doing? Get off me." She snaked her leg between his and twisted out of his grasp, but he was quick and pinned her shoulders to the bed.

"You know you want me, Saphira." His voice was so low he was practically growling at her.

"Get the fuck off me!" She screamed at him, but he only laughed.

"You are a hellcat, aren't you? Gareth was right," and pressed his lips to hers. His teeth pulled her bottom lip between his, but she resisted and tasted blood a second later. Edward lifted his head and sighed. "Gods, you taste good, Saphira." Saphira took advantage of his distraction and rammed her palm into his chin. He yelled out and fell to the floor. She could see a little trickle of blood on the side of his mouth.

Saphira got up and ran for the door, but felt a hand around her ankle. It jerked her backwards, and she fell face-first to the floor. Her cheek was stinging, and she kicked furiously and connected with something. Edward yelled out again, and she was able to get to her feet. She wrenched open the door and heard him still on the floor. "Saphy?" She turned, and for a second, she saw him on his knees. He looked confused and beaten. "Saphy, what's going on?" But she didn't want to hear it and ran from the room. She could hear Edward behind her. "Wait, Saphy, I'm sorry, come back!" but she didn't stop. She ran out of the inn and didn't stop until she was on the outskirts of Buckland, on a little bridge over a stream. Her heart was racing, and she was having trouble catching her breath, *'Otto, please don't let it be true,'* she prayed over and over as she tried to regain her composure.

"Saphira?" Her cousin's voice startled her, and she turned. Kaythen's face turned angry when he saw her wounds. "Who did that to you?" He hugged her tight, and she did the same. "Who hurt you?" She could feel him shaking with anger. "I'll kill them."

"No, you won't," she looked up, and Kaythen touched her cheek. She felt the pain go away, and she stepped back. "I... I don't think it's his fault."

He laid his head on hers. "Saphira, it's always their fault."

"No," she stepped back and held up her hands. "It's not

like that. I think he might be possessed."

He sighed and shook his head. "You didn't."

"No, I didn't, his mother did, when he was a boy."

Confusion flashed on his face, something she'd never seen before. "Which one, the young man, right? I saw him earlier when you arrived. I could see the darkness in him, but I didn't think it meant he was carrying something."

She leaned on the railing and put her head in her hands. "He died," she rubbed her face. "He died this past winter. A priest declared him dead, but he started breathing again, so we thought it was going to be okay. It was a miracle."

"Hmm, true miracles are hard to come by, Saphy." He leaned on the railing next to her, "getting rid of those unwelcomed attachments usually takes one."

She licked her lips and looked over at him. "Do you think you could get it out of him?"

He was quiet for a long time. "If I did, it would break your friend."

"Yeah, I'd like to avoid breaking him."

He put an arm around her. "I'm sorry." She shook her head. It wasn't his fault that his magic was different.

Saphira ran her hands through her hair. "I guess I'll have to take him to the best."

"I'm sure Lily can get it out of him, if she can't, well…" He turned so his back was against the railing. "Do the others in your group know?"

"I don't think so. This is the first time he's been like this."

"Hmm, maybe that's a good thing. Perhaps its grip on him isn't permanent yet."

Saphira rubbed her once stinging cheek. "Maybe."

Kaythen turned back around and patted her back. "Besides the current setback, how are you?"

She poked Kaythen in the arm. "How are you, cousin? You hardly ever talk about yourself." She shot back.

He smirked. "I am fine as always, nothing bad in my life."

Saphira scoffed. "I don't believe you."

He barked out a laugh. "Smart of you."

Saphira hugged herself and kicked a rock off the bridge. "I have a love, I have friends, and I'm out in the world. It's everything I've wanted."

"A love?" he teased, and she snickered. "Do tell."

She looked up and smiled as she said his name. "Gareth Quinn of Salthole."

His eyes went wide. "The Thief King? You share a bed with the thief king of Salthole?"

Saphira's jaw dropped. "You know him?"

He shook his head. "Of. But he's well known in certain crowds." She looked over and could see he was studying her. "You seem different. You seem more free of yourself." She smiled as he leaned close. "There's something almost dark in you." Her eyes softened as he spoke. "You have the spirit of a dragon, wise yet vicious when need be." Saphira liked being compared to a dragon and didn't think he was wrong.

"You…feel that?" Gareth had been the only other person to say she was different than others. It helped her understand why she felt almost mismatched from her family, why sometimes she felt closer to her cousins than her brothers.

He nodded. "I do, I always have. It's nothing to be ashamed of."

"I'm not. Ashamed, I mean."

"Good." She cleared her throat and turned back to the little stream that ran under the bridge.

"Foster is going home. He's in love and having a baby."

She'd never seen Kaythen's eyes go so wide. "What!" Saphira laughed at his reaction. "I should visit, it's been too long."

"I think everyone would like to see you. You could mention the twins' predicament to Mom. She might be able to do something?"

"Hmmm," he growled. "Their situation has irrevocably changed, and while I'm glad for them, it's made things more difficult for the rest of us."

She could see he seemed a little annoyed, but not bad at

his siblings. "What happened?"

He shook his head. "Not here." He turned to her, "But they're safe and…happy. So be at peace knowing they're safe." He took a deep breath. "Are you all right? Do you need me to do anything?"

"No, I'll try to get him to my mom. I'd like to free him without killing him."

"I'm sure he'd want the same." They smiled, but Saphira noticed his smile disappear in a flash. "I need to go, do me a favor." She nodded. "Head back to your inn now."

"Okay, is everything—"

"Is it ever?" She moved to hug him. "Not now." His sharp tone shocked her. Something was wrong. "Go."

"Love you." She didn't wait to hear if he replied. Clearly something was putting him on edge. She walked calmly through the people, trying not to draw attention to herself. *Love you too* she heard in her head and smiled. The closer she got to the inn, she felt as if there were eyes on her. She prayed it was her cousin, making sure she made it back safely.

Saphira walked inside the inn, and thankfully, the feeling of being watched went away. Eden, Rickert, and Gothrin were still sitting at the table and made her way over. Eden looked up, and Saphira could see her worried face from across the room.

"Saphira, what happened?" Eden sounded as worried as Kaythen had. "Where did you go?"

"There's something wrong with Edward. He…" She couldn't bring herself to say everything that happened, "he got violent with me." Eden and Rickert gasped. "I think…I think when he came back, something came back with him."

Gothrin leaned forward and stared at Rickert, "You raised him?" He sounded as angry as she'd expect him to.

Eden shook her head. "No, we didn't, I swear."

"But he was Eden," Saphira reached out and laid a hand on Eden's, "when he was a kid."

Realization slowly crept into Eden's mind, and she covered her mouth in shock. "After all this time?"

"When was he raised?" Gothrin mumbled towards Eden.

Eden sniffed and quickly wiped away a tear. "We were ten."

"That's a long time." Gothrin sat back and rubbed his chin. "He's never acted like this before?"

"No, he's always been wonderful," Saphira looked over at Rickert. "Right?"

Their boss nodded. "He's never been violent before. If he's possessed, I don't want anyone alone with him. Saphira, you and Eden can bunk together. I don't want you sleeping next to Edward."

"Okay." Saphira watched her quickly wipe away a tear.

Rickert nodded. "Gothrin and I will have a talk with him, if he seems not himself, then Eden," he turned to her and gently brushed her cheek with his thumb. "I'm afraid we'd have to leave him behind."

She sniffed and shook her head. "No, we're not leaving him behind. We're going to find him help."

"I agree," Saphira spoke up. "I say we take him to my mother."

Eden's eyes went wide as she smiled. "Yes! If anyone can help him, it's Mother Lily."

Rickert sighed. "No one's been able to help that kind of condition." Eden's smile slowly faded, and Rickert sighed. "But we'll see what we can do, okay?"

"Would you speak to him now?" Eden's voice was jittery. Saphira didn't blame her. "I don't want to drag this out longer than it has to."

Rickert nodded and motioned for Gothrin to follow him. Saphira and Eden watched as they climbed the stairs and disappeared into the darkness.

Eden sighed loudly, "I think I'm going to go to lay down, I can't take this." She quickly got up and followed them, leaving Saphira alone at the table.

"Otto, let me be paranoid, let me be a worrier, but please, don't let him be possessed." Saphira made her way to the bartender and got the last available room.

An hour later, Saphira was lying on the bed, staring at the ceiling. Eden was laying in the bed across the room. Neither of them could sleep at the moment. Rickert hadn't had come to talk to them, so she figured they were still dealing with Edward. Saphira's mind wandered and kept her from sleep. She was too worried about her little group. There was a light knock on the door, and her heart leapt into her throat. Both of them sat up, and Saphira called out. "Yes?"

"Saphira, it's me, can I come in?"

It was Edward. Slowly, she crawled off the bed and walked over to the door. "What do you want?" She stopped against the door and laid her ear against it. She could hear his feet shuffling on the wooden floor.

"I wanted to apologize." He sounded calm, so she opened the door a crack. Edward was standing as close to the door as she was, he seemed a lot calmer than the last time she saw him. "Hi," he said quietly. "Rickert and Gothrin thought since Eden was with you, it'd be okay to let me talk to you without them." Saphira looked back at Eden, who nodded.

"Want to come in?" He nodded, and she moved aside, letting him in the room. Eden sprang from the bed and hugged her brother.

"Please tell me it isn't true." She cried into his chest. "Tell me you're just you, please."

Saphira walked over to the bed and sat down, tucking her knees under her chin. "What did Rickert say to you?"

He spoke as his sister kept him in her arms. "He asked me what happened, and I told him what I remembered."

"What do you remember?" Saphira had never seen him so sad. His eyes were red, and she could see tear stains on his shirt.

"I remember being on the floor, and you were trying to get away from me. Saphy, you looked so scared." He gently pried himself from Eden's arms and sat on the far edge of Saphira's bed. She noticed he was careful not to touch her. "Then I realized

I had no idea what I had done, and I thought the worst. What did I do?" Her hand moved to her cheek. His eyes widened and his shoulders dropped. "Gods no, I didn't hit you, did I?"

"No, Edward, you didn't hit me." His eyes were misty, and he was clearly still upset. "You seemed to want to…force yourself on me." It was harder than she thought it would be to say those words.

Edward seemed to deflate before her eyes. "I what? Why would, but I'd never," tears fell down his cheeks as his breath shuddered out. Eden once again wrapped her arms around her brother, and he hugged her back. "I'm so sorry, Saphy, I don't know how you can ever forgive me." Her eyes watered as she watched Edward try to come to terms with what he had done.

"Edward." She crawled next to him. "Do you honestly not remember what happened?"

He sniffed and turned to her as Eden crawled on the bed behind him. "No, I remember you saying you wanted to go to the festival today, then we were in the room. I don't know what I did today." Saphira studied him as he talked, the way he moved his body, the way his eyes looked, and she could tell he was telling the truth.

"Edward, look at me." His eyes slowly moved up and met hers. "You really scared me today, but I believe you when you say you don't remember." His eyes squeezed shut, and he nodded his head before his breath shuddered out. She knew he was trying hard to compose himself.

"You can't trust me, Saphira," he whispered. She couldn't keep the tears from her voice and ran her hand through his thick auburn hair.

"I know."

"Rickert thinks as long as we can stay apart, I should be fine. He wants to find a cleric to figure out what's wrong with me."

Saphira nodded and could feel her heart break a little. "If we're going to a cleric, then we're going to get the best, Edward. We're going to see my mother."

His arms wrapped around her, and she could feel his trembling. "I didn't want this to be the way I met your mother."

Saphira couldn't help it and cried on his shoulder. "Me either."

CHAPTER 25

ALMOST HOME

Everyone agreed that Saphira's mother might be Edward's best bet to get rid of whatever was making him lose his mind. But the twins were desperate and wanted to see all the clerics they could as they made their way to Raventree. The first stop was Ardenry. The twins didn't tell their mother they were in town. Edward didn't want her to know why they were there.

For a month, he saw many different clerics, but none of them had a solution. They said there was a presence inside of him, and they couldn't get it out. Saphira begged to see the Pontiff, but all the priests said he was too busy to see some random boy whose friends were reckless enough to bring him back, and they were lucky they didn't arrest them. Saphira had never been so angry with the church in all her life and screamed at them.

"I am Lily Voltain's daughter, and when she gets rid of this entity, you are going to feel how inadequate and useless you really are!" As the group walked out of the temple, one of the priests kept trying to get them back, apologizing for their attitude, saying they never would have turned away Mother Lily's daughter. But the group didn't stop. They all had enough of what was supposed to be the beacon of light for Otto in the world.

They then traveled to Fairwinds, where they saw Father Leif, but he said the entity was a nasty piece of work, and if anyone could get it out of Edward, it would be Lily, so they got passage on the next boat for Salthole. It was getting into autumn, and Saphira wondered if they would make it to Raventree before winter hit. During the voyage, they could all see a change come over Edward. Almost like the entity inside him knew they were getting close to getting rid of it and would act out. Edward was quiet and barely talked to anyone. He spent most of his time drinking with the crew and came back smelling of rum and sweat. Once, he tried to kiss Saphira, but she shoved him away. It was then she realized the Edward she knew was gone and felt her heart break for them all.

The autumn storms delayed them so much, it was snowing when they pulled into Salthole. Saphira knew unless they could get someone to teleport them to Raventree, they would have to wait out the winter in the port town with their steadily declining archer. The group decided to see if their house was still empty. Thankfully, the haunted stories were still going strong, and the group happily found it was still unoccupied. They cleaned the dust and cobwebs away and settled in.

The first night Saphira was able to get out of the house, she made her way over to the 'Orc' to find Gareth. She took the back way and was almost there when she heard the familiar voice of the rogue king.

"Voltain!" The sound of his voice made her heart speed up, and she smiled just as Gareth landed in front of her. He looked the same, a little older but no worse for wear.

"My Lord." She teased as he wrapped his arms around her, and they hugged tightly.

"I'm glad to see you back, My Dark Lady." His arms were warm in the chilly air like they always were.

"I was coming to see you." Gareth stepped back and let his fingers trail on her cheek before he kissed her deeply. It felt as if they had spent no time apart.

He leaned down, and she could feel his words on her cheek. "So, what brings you back to my little kingdom? You missed me, didn't you? Decided to stay and be my queen?"

Saphira chuckled and caught his lips again. "I wish it were for a nice visit, but we were trying to get to Raventree. Unfortunately, we didn't make it before the snow, and we can't get a teleport."

Gareth's happy eyes slowly turned to worry as she talked. "You're not trying to get home to stay, are you?" He asked like he knew something was wrong.

"No, it's Edward." Gareth leaned back against the nearest building while she told him what had happened.

"I thought it was odd he came back, but you were happy, so I didn't press the issue. If you want, I can put him up at the 'Orc', it might be safer for you."

She shook her head. "Thanks, but we're fine for now. He's hopeless at picking locks." They told him they would be locking his door at night. Thankfully, he didn't argue, but Saphira swore she heard the clinking of metal in the lock the night before.

Gareth chuckled. "Well, I'm going to keep an extra eye on your place, Voltain. You can't trust people like Edward. They could snap at any moment." He closed the distance between them. "So, I have some brandy and apple cider at my place, interested?"

She nodded and wrapped her arms around him. "Sounds good, I was going to go see Elyse later anyway."

Gareth smiled and led them back down the alley, their arms around each other. "Well, you wouldn't have found her. My sweet sister is now married and traveling with her husband."

Saphira smiled. "How wonderful! Who did she marry?"

Gareth snickered and shook his head. "That priest friend of yours, Andros. They married this summer and then caught a boat to travel the world."

Saphira giggled. "So, you might be an uncle someday."

He smiled brightly. "And gods willing, I'll know my nieces and nephews. So, how about it, Voltain? Are you up for a little gathering? Or brandy-cider?" He always called his sneaking 'gathering' because of all the knowledge he gathered, and she smiled.

"As long as we end up in bed, I'm good with either."

"Oh well fuck gathering, we're gonna go break in my new bed at home." They laughed as they ran towards the house by the docks.

For weeks, the two rogues sneaked around Salthole together. It was just like old times. One night, while they were in his room writing down what they had heard a rich merchant say about a shipment of weapons, Gareth pulled a letter out of a pile of papers.

"I got your letter, Saphira, the one you sent from Ardenry. Did you get my reply?"

She shook her head. "No, I think we left before it got a chance to get there."

He sat on the bed and ran his finger along the folded edge. "I read this letter so many times I wore a hole in it." Saphira laughed. "Did you think of me, out there this year?"

She stopped pacing and faced him. "I thought about you all the time, Gareth," she giggled and sat on the bed. "But in what way do you mean?"

He sat up and held her face before he kissed her deeply. "I don't have to stay here anymore, Saphira. I could follow you anywhere you went," he whispered.

She pulled him down on top of her, kissing as they fell. "I've been waiting for you to say those words." She whispered and felt her heart speed up as his skillful tongue slipped into her mouth. They made love all night, and as the sun peeked over the rooftops, they laid breathless and sweaty next to each other.

"Gods, Saphira, I should have gone with you. What was I thinking?" he chuckled.

Saphira laughed. "Oh, now Gareth, I wouldn't have wanted you to miss your sister's wedding."

Gareth laughed and half rolled onto her. "Trust me, Voltain." His hand lightly ran over her breast. "It would have been worth it." The rogues stayed busy keeping an eye on Salthole and each other. Saphira hardly stayed at the house with her group, preferring to stay with Gareth at the 'Orc'. Saphira began wondering if she should stay in Salthole and rule with him. But she also remembered what Ada said, *'he'd follow you into the abyss if you asked.'*

CHAPTER 26
HAUNTING PAST

It was one of those rare days when Gareth was in their house. He and Saphira were having some tea with Eden, Rickert, and Gothrin. Edward hadn't come home the night before, and Eden was worried about her brother and asked Saphira to bring Gareth by. He happily obliged and followed her into the warm sitting room.

"I understand your concern, Eden, but I have some of my men tailing him when he walks about the town." Gareth set down his teacup. "I don't trust him around anybody right now."

Eden sighed and rubbed her temples. "I know he's dangerous, but he's my brother. I worry about him."

Gareth nodded. "I empathize, I still worry about my sister even though she's older than I. Last my men said, your archer was holed up in the basement in 'The Broken Limb'. They have illegal fights down there, so most likely he got himself whupped good and is resting it off."

"Illegal fights?" Saphira sighed, "He hates fighting."

"Apparently, that thing in him likes to," Gareth said quietly.

Rickert rubbed his face vigorously. "He's letting it take over more and more recently. I wonder if there will be anything left of him before we have a chance to get to Raventree."

"Maybe the fights are good for him," Gothrin suggested. "Keeps him out of trouble elsewhere."

"Perhaps, until he gets too violent," Gareth said. Saphira had been wondering the same thing over the weeks and prayed that he would be able to hang on until they reached her mother.

There was a knock at the door, and Eden gasped. "Edward?" She quickly got to her feet, and Saphira heard the door fly open, but she knew it wouldn't be him. Edward wouldn't knock.

Eden walked back in with their friend Xander. "Good morning, everyone," he said, a big smile on his face.

"Hello, Xander, what brings you by?" Rickert asked.

"I am throwing a party next week, and I want you all to come." Normally, Eden would gasp and immediately start planning what she would wear, but the situation with her brother was stealing her normally happy demeanor.

"A party? Sounds like fun, Xander, we'll be there," she said.

"It's a masked ball, so wear a costume!" He said happily as he made his way out the front door. They met Xander the last time they were in Salthole while he played his accordion in one of the taverns. As it turned out, his father was one of the richer men in town, but instead of focusing on the family business, he let his son focus on his music. Saphira always liked that about his father.

"I wonder if he meant 'all of us,' all of us," Gareth said with a smirk.

"I don't see why you wouldn't be invited." Saphira reached over and laid a hand on his arm.

The rogue king shrugged a little. "His father and I don't get along, seeing as how he still lives with him, I don't know if I'll be welcome."

"He did say it was a masked ball. He may not recognize you," Rickert said.

Saphira watched realization dawn on her lover's face. "Ahh, perhaps I will be welcome after all." He had a wicked little smile on his face.

"Even if you weren't, you would be my guest, Gareth. He'd have to accept you." She leaned over the arm of her chair for a kiss, which he readily supplied.

"Thank you." The door slammed shut, and everyone but Gareth and Gothrin jumped as Edward came walking in. Eden gasped at the sight of her brother. The rogue was right. Edward had a terrible black eye, and they could see a handprint bruise on his neck, like someone tried to strangle him.

"Edward, are you okay!" Eden rushed over and hugged him gently. To Saphira's relief, he hugged her back. One time, he shoved his sister away, and Eden cried so hard no one could calm her down.

"I'm fine, Edie. Did I see Xander leave?"

She stepped back and fussed with his hair. "Yes, he invited us to a party. It's a good thing it's next week because you look dreadful. What happened?"

"Nothing, I'm fine." He gently moved her hands when his eyes landed on Gareth. "What's he doing here?" Saphira felt her heart speed up. The last thing she wanted was a confrontation between him and Gareth in the house.

"He's a guest, Edward, be cordial." Gothrin was always the first to scold or hold Edward back. Being the biggest and strongest of the group, it made sense. Edward visibly shrank and turned back to his sister.

"We were worried about you, Ed," she rubbed a hand on his arm. "Gareth told us where you were." Edward's nostrils flared as he huffed out an angry breath, his jaw set hard like he was grinding his teeth.

"How did he know?" he finally asked.

"Some of my men told me, I didn't see you personally," he said casually. Gareth was patient when dealing with Edward. He always said Ed could snap any minute, so he always did his best not to be the one who made him snap, even though he knew his very presence could do it.

"Hmm. I'm going to wash up," he said quietly and walked up the stairs.

"I'll make you something to eat," Eden called up after him.

"No thanks, Edie." And disappeared around the corner. She stood still for a moment. Saphira knew she was trying to compose herself before turning around.

"He'll be hungry later," she said quietly as she turned around and sat down next to Rickert.

"Yes, he will." Rickert reached over and ran his hand

down her long hair. "As will we all, as a matter of fact, Gareth, care to join us?"

The thief got to his feet. "I think I've overstayed my welcome here." He reached out for Saphira's hand, and she took it. "Come, my sneaky love, let's go find something to gather."

She stood and followed him to the door. "I'll be back for dinner, Eden, I promise," she called out before the door shut. As they walked down the street, Saphira couldn't help but feel the back of her head burning, as if Edward were staring out of his bedroom window at her, but she never turned to see if it was true.

A week later, the group, including Edward and Gareth, was walking up to a big house at the edge of town. It was a white, two-story house with huge columns lining the front of it. Saphira tried to get Gothrin to come, but the old orc said parties like that were for youngsters. Gareth joked that Gothrin could win best costume, but he still declined with a smile. Candles lit the walkway, and they could hear music and laughter floating out of the door towards them.

She felt Gareth kiss her head. "Sounds like a real fun party." Saphira looked up at him. The black mask he wore covered the top right side of his face and down his cheek. There was a long, thin feather sticking out of the top. She'd never seen Gareth dressed so fine before; his black jacket was trimmed with silver, which accentuated his slim physique.

"You know, I bet you could pass for an honest gentleman tonight," she teased him.

Gareth chuckled and squeezed her hand as it rested on his arm. "I bet I could." She looked over at Eden, her golden dress made her hair redder, but the usual smile was absent from her face, even though her brother was walking next to her.

"Eden, are you okay?"

She startled like her mind was on something else. "Yes, I'm fine, just thinking," she said with a little smile.

Edward wrapped an arm around his sister's waist. "Cheer

up, Edie, this party is going to be fun! People will be talking about it for weeks." He almost sounded like his old self, happy and excited, but everyone knew it would be short-lived.

"It will be, Xander always throws the best parties," Eden said. The music could be heard through the fancy double doors in front of them, and Saphira felt Gareth lean close to her ear.

"I can't wait to twirl you around for all to see, Voltain."

She smiled as the doors opened. "Me either.""Good evening, please come in," the doorman said with a bow.

"Thank you, Smith," Gareth said with a smile as they all walked inside. Saphira wasn't surprised he knew the man's name. Gareth took pride in knowing the names of those who served, rather than the ones who ruled. The ballroom was grand for Salthole, with tall ceilings and candle-lit chandeliers every few feet. There was holly wrapped around the dark wooden columns, and a huge pine tree in the corner made the entire room smell like a forest.

Eden gasped. "It's gorgeous." Saphira heard her say.

Gareth stepped in front of her and held out his hand. "Shall we?"

She laid her hand in his. "Absolutely." He put his arm around her waist and began dancing her towards the dance floor. Gareth twirled her with ease, but when the group dancing began, he led them towards a table covered with food.

"I'm starving," he said, looking at the different pies and sweets offered. Saphira watched Rickert and Eden dance and smile at each other. But Edward was nowhere to be found.

"So far, it seems like a success." She turned to Gareth, who had a bit of cream on his lip. She giggled and got to her tiptoes. "You've got cream on you," she whispered and quickly nipped it away.

"I know, I put it there just for you." Saphira laughed and picked up a glass of champagne. It was crisp and cold the way she liked it, and she downed it quickly. She chuckled to herself when she thought of what her mother would say as she reached up and laid a hand on the locket around her neck, *'Saphira, you needn't drink it down like a drowning fish.'*

"Saphira, Gareth, I'm so glad you came!" Xander's voice woke her from the memory, and she turned as their friend came walking over. He gave Saphira a hug while shaking her partner's hand.

"It's a lovely party, Xander, thank you for the invite."

"You're most welcome, Saphira. I was wondering if you might honor me with a dance?" He bowed a little and held out his arm.

"Of course, I'd be happy to." She turned to Gareth, "You don't mind, do you?"

He leaned down and kissed her cheek. "Not at all, have fun while I take a little nip around," he said with a wink and walked off. Saphira took her friend's arm, and he led her back to the dance floor. Xander was a good-looking guy with short brown hair and kind brown eyes. Saphira wondered if he was courting anyone. Out of all their friends in Salthole, Xander was the most mysterious to her. He didn't talk about himself as much as the others, preferring to focus on his music. What they knew of him, they learned from others.

"So, Xander, is your date going to be jealous you're dancing with another girl?" she asked with a little smile.

Xander chuckled. "I didn't bring a date, I wanted to keep my night open for anything."

"Ah, I see."

"Plus, if I got to play, I wouldn't want her to think I was ignoring her."

Saphira chuckled. "Planning ahead, well done."

He licked his lips and seemed a bit nervous as he bent down to her ear. "You look lovely tonight, Saphira."

"Thank you," she said with a smile. "I think we all cleaned up rather nicely."

He flashed her a dazzling smile. "That we did." He twirled her around until she was laughing and dizzy. "Sorry, would you like some air? It seems like you've been dancing non-stop since you got here."

She nodded. "Sure, I could use some fresh air." She let him lead her out the door into the back garden. The fir trees were decorated like they were inside, and the music was quiet once the door closed.

She shivered a little but could feel a nearby fire keeping the worst of it away. "Are you okay? Should I get your wrap?"

"No, I'm fine, thank you." She didn't mind being cold. It was the heat that bothered her.

He reached out and gently touched her forehead, near the part on her hairline. "I like the little bit of gray in your hair, it looks sophisticated."

Her eyes went wide. "What?" She reached up to where he was touching, not like she'd be able to tell by touch, but she didn't notice any gray hair last she looked.

"You didn't realize?" He was trying to hold back a laugh.

"I'm twenty-one, I should not be going gray." She growled to herself. "Eden did my hair. I can't believe she didn't say anything."

He laid a hand on her shoulder. "It's not a lot. Besides, maybe you'll get a badass streak in a few months."

"Pippa's tits, I do not want gray hair, badass streak or not!" She tried to look at her reflection in a window, but it was too bright inside.

Xander laughed and patted her back. "It's okay, it looks good on you."

She was so annoyed at her hair that she forgot all about the cold. "Thanks, I guess."

"You're welcome. So," he leaned against a nearby waist-high wall. "Wintering in Salthole for a second time, I guess that means you like the town?"

She turned to him, her arms crossed over her chest. "I do. Despite what my talents lean towards, there's a lot of good one can do here."

He smiled. "You sound like you might want to stay."

The corner of her lips tilted up as she thought of Gareth. "I've been thinking about it."

"Ah, young Xander, who's your friend?" They both looked up as a tall man wearing Otto's robes came walking over. It was a bit chilly, so she didn't blame him for having his hood on. She hadn't seen him in the temple before, so she assumed he was a traveling priest. Otto had a lot of them. She looked over at Xander, and his happy demeanor was faltering. His smile seemed to be wilting around the edges.

"Father, this is Saphira Voltain. Saphira, this is Dante Foss. He's a traveling priest of Otto."

Her eyes went wide with recognition. "Dante Foss? The priest who traveled with my mother?"

He smiled, and she swore there was something peaceful in his face. "I am. Xander's father said he was friends with you. I had hoped you would come tonight." He held out his hand, and Saphira shook it. "It's nice to meet you, young lady."

"Nice to meet you as well."

He motioned to the short, cement wall behind them. "Shall we have a seat? I'd love to hear all about you."

"Sure." She hopped up on the wall while he leaned against it. "So, you knew my mother when she was young."

"I did. Even before she was a priestess, she was so powerful. I knew she was favored even then."

Saphira chuckled. "That doesn't surprise me."

"Tell me about yourself, young lady. What brings you to Salthole?"

Saphira sighed and looked back at the party through the glass doors, "Just out in the world. Salthole turned into a kind of second home to my group. We have friends, jobs, and love," she smiled a little and turned back to him. "I've learned how to be the best of myself here."

The priest nodded. "Some towns hold the key to our true selves, a lesson I learned over the years."

Saphira looked down at her feet. "She never talked about you."

"She didn't? How did you know my name?"

She shrugged, keeping her eyes down. "Urban legend,

and the high priest here remembered you."

He gave a little chuckle. "We did make waves while we were here. But I'm not surprised she didn't talk about me. I take no offense either. Why bring up a painful past?"

She looked up at him. "What was so painful?"

Dante breathed out a breath and hopped up on the wall next to her. "We were together for a bit. Then the incident with her sister happened, and Lily decided to stay in Fairwinds." He looked down at his hands as he spoke. "A year later, Taren and I went back to Fairwinds, and I had my heart set on winning her back, but with my love came bad memories. So, when she met Henri, I wasn't surprised she fell for him. He gave her something I could not."

"Which was?"

He looked up and met her eyes. "Peace. There was something about me that made her relive the awful night at her sister's manor. No matter what I did, or how she tried, all I reminded her of was the horrible night Lavinia almost killed her." Saphira could hear pain in his voice, but didn't blame her mother for choosing Henri. You want to be at peace with your love, not fight bad memories. She also knew what story he was talking about. Her mother told them when they were older that she and her sister didn't always get along. Saphira remembered being afraid of her aunt for a bit after hearing the story. But after a warm hug from Lavinia, her fear went away.

"Sounds rough."

"My god helped me through it, but I'll always love her. I was glad to hear she remarried after Henri died. She deserves to be happy."

Saphira nodded. "She is." The nearby bushes rustled a bit, and Saphira watched as Edward came walking over, his eyes scrutinizing the priest.

He crossed his arms, and he looked angry. "Who the fuck are you?"

"Edward!" Saphira snapped at him. "Be respectful."

Dante smirked. "It's okay, Saphira. I'm Dante Foss."

Edward studied him a bit before he turned to Saphira. "You okay?"

"I'm fine, Ed, he's a priest. He knew my mother." It was then she realized Xander was gone. She didn't even realize he'd slipped away.

"What?" Ed looked around as well.

"Where did Xander go?"

Edward scoffed and shook his head. "Xander? I thought you were fucking Gareth."

Her eyes went wide as she turned back to him. "Ed!"

But he clearly didn't care. "Maybe that's your plan all along, to have them both at the same time."

"Edward, please go." She did not want to fight with him in front of the priest and wondered what triggered him.

"No. I don't know him, priest or not. I'm not leaving you alone with a stranger." She crossed her arms and felt one of the hidden daggers in her dress and hoped she wouldn't need it.

"He's not a stranger, Ed, please!"

"He is," he got in Dante's face, and Saphira felt her heart go into her throat. "Who knows why he's really here." Dante reached up and gently touched Ed's cheek, but the archer flinched back. His eyes were wide, and he finally walked away, watching them.

She turned to Dante. "What did you do?"

"Blessed him. It seemed to bother him?"

She sighed and shook her head. "He's not himself lately."

"He seemed to be protective of you."

Saphira shrugged. She didn't want to think about what Eden told her last year. "He's in my group, we're protective of each other."

"Seems more to me, but what do I know? I'm just an old priest."

Saphira chuckled and lowered her arms. "Are you staying in Salthole for a while?"

"No, I'm leaving in the morning," he hopped off the wall. "But thank you for sitting with me. I'm so glad I finally got to meet you." He had a great priest voice, soft and comforting, and she could hear how much it meant to him that he got to meet her.

"I'm glad I met you, too." He gave her a little bow and walked back into the party.

Gareth walked over from the shadows and put an arm around her. "I take it, you know him?" She felt his lips on her forehead.

She smiled and closed her eyes at the feeling. "Remember the priest who was with my mother's group? That's him."

"Still alive, eh? Doesn't look as old as I thought he would."

"Oh, right, the head priest did say he was a bit older than the rest in the group. I forgot." She laid her head on his shoulder. "I want to leave," she said. She didn't want to risk running into Edward again, not if he was being rude for no reason.

He laid his lips against her hair. "Stay with me tonight?"

"There's nowhere else I'd rather be."

CHAPTER 27
SELFISH

Gareth and Saphira walked to his sister's house. It was dark inside as usual. "Let me start a fire." He made his way over to the fireplace and managed to get the wood crackling and warm. Saphira sighed. She could see her reflection in the mirror above the fireplace. Her hair, which Eden had lovingly put up in curls, was coming down in messy waves.

Gareth wiped his hands on his pants and walked behind her. His head poked up behind hers perfectly, and he wrapped his arms around her waist as he leaned down. "My Sweet Saphira." She heard in her ear, the way it fell from his lips always made her shudder.

She turned and wrapped her hands around the back of his neck. "Kiss me." He quickly complied, pulling her bottom lip between his as his hands pressed her to him. Every kiss they shared reminded her of the first time he kissed her in the freezing waters of Salthole last winter. The excitement and thrill coursed through her body as she reached up and pulled his coat off. She felt him unlacing the back of her dress. Her fingers worked at the buttons on his shirt, and it quickly fell to the floor. The ribbon holding her dress together made a little noise as he ripped it out of the last little hole.

"Sorry," he chuckled as her dress slid down her body.

"I don't care." She pushed his pants down while he worked his way out of his shoes. When they finally stood naked before each other, she watched as Gareth's nimble hands slowly made their way around every inch of her body. His calloused fingers ran gently along her hip, and she felt his scratchy skin as he made his way up her stomach and cupped her breasts. Her nipples instantly hardened, and she gasped as his knuckles ran over them. Warm tingles spread through her body, and her stomach tightened in anticipation of feeling him inside her.

Suddenly, he turned her around and pressed her back to his chest as his hands kept up their assault. She arched her back as his lips kissed and bit her neck. Her hands buried themselves in his hair and held him still. Her breath caught in her throat as she felt his hand slowly make its way down her stomach.

"God's touch me, Gareth," she whispered a second before his finger found that most intimate of spots. Her knees threatened to buckle as he made achingly slow circles around that bundle of nerves while his knuckle still ran over her nipple.

Waves of pleasure radiated through her body; she could barely take the double assault. She jerked ever so slightly with each pass, and her breath came in time with each wave. She could feel the hardness of his that she loved with every movement and made sure to brush up against him. She may have been helpless at the moment, but she still wanted to tease him as much as she could. Gareth pulled them both down on the couch, keeping Saphira on top. She sat quietly for a moment while her hands slowly pet his chest. Gareth was a skinny man but muscular. She loved how his pelvic muscles formed against his hips, a perfect V that showed her the way to his pleasure. He was hard and ready to please her, if not fit to burst, when she laid her head down on his chest. His heartbeat always seemed so fast to her. His hands moved up and down her back with the perfect amount of pressure.

"I love you, Gareth," she whispered. His hands didn't skip a beat as they continued rubbing on her back.

"I love you, too, Saphira Voltain. From now until my last day, I will love you." She sat up, relieved at his words as he smiled that endearing half smile as his right hand slowly moved around to her front and cupped her breast. She scooted down his body and lowered her face over the hardness she found. She could feel the heat of it on her lips and licked it with a quick flick of her tongue. He gasped and chuckled. "Fuck Voltain." She looked up and melted at the way he was looking at her, like she was a goddess in her own right. Slowly, she slipped her lips over him as his breath shuddered out. "Saphira." It was so quiet she barely heard it. She wrapped her lips around as much of him as she could and moved up and down his hard length. His hands reached back and gripped the arm of the couch; it creaked under the strain of his fingers, and she smiled. The effect she had on him always amazed her. She loved the feeling of having such power over someone, especially Gareth, who was always the epitome of order and power.

She held his hips down as she worked him, feeling that favorite muscle group of hers under her fingers until she couldn't take it anymore. She lifted her head, and his eyes met hers.

"You are gonna get it, Voltain," he growled playfully.

"Oh yeah? What are you going to do to me?" She crawled close to his face and slowly ran the tip of her tongue against his lower lip. "My Lord?"

He grabbed her arms and pulled her closer. "I am going to fuck you so hard you're gonna feel it tomorrow."

She laughed and quickly straddled his hips. "Try it." She lowered herself onto him. His back bowed as his hands reached out for something to hold. At first, she moved slowly on him, making sure he was all the way in. Gareth always hit the end of her. Sometimes it was too much, but tonight she didn't care. She wanted every bit of him, everything he could give her. Her hips found their rhythm, and he relaxed back onto the couch. Saphira had never been with a man who was so vocal before. Usually, it was her making the noise, but with Gareth, she was often outdone. Especially lately, when they were totally alone. It was part of the reason she preferred staying with him at the 'Orc' rather than in her house. The tavern was always busy and noisy; they were less likely to be heard there than in a quiet house.

Saphira made little circles around him that got the noises started; every movement brought a groan from him. He reached out and held her hips as she moved.

His rough hands scratched softly against her stomach as she moved. "Gods, you're so soft, Saphira." He leaned forward and flicked her nipple with his tongue. It sent a shock of pleasure through her. His tongue slowly licked her hardened skin while his teeth gently scraped, pulling more of her breast in his mouth. She gasped and held his head still, and not a second later, she began her assault again with renewed vigor, moving faster and deeper on him.

He cried out and leaned back. "Gods!" She loved making him yell out like that, but what he did next surprised her. He brought his knees up high behind her, then quickly pushed her down onto her back and took over. Most of the times they made love, Saphira had been on top, and she only wondered for a second why he changed his mind. He was so light on top of her, like he weighed nothing despite his muscles. She locked her ankles around his back, and he laughed as he pushed himself deep inside of her. The change was so sudden she lost control and dug her nails into his back.

"Fuck Saphira!" But he didn't sound angry. She knew he liked it. He looked down, and their eyes met. She thought there was something there she hadn't seen before, but didn't have long to contemplate it before her body exploded with pleasure; she yelled out his name as her back bowed underneath him. "Gods, I love that," he growled and thrust deep one last time before he echoed her and threw his head back. Saphira saw his pulse thudding quickly at his neck. She reached up and touched his cheek as he looked down and laid on her slightly chilly skin.

"I want to do that for the rest of our lives." He kissed her cheek. "I want to bring you pleasure and hear my name on your lips every day."

Saphira chuckled and ran her hands through his hair. "Deal."

His lips ran lightly against hers. "Shall we go to bed?" He slid off her and picked her up.

"Sure." Gareth carried her into his bedroom, and she crawled under the covers. It was cold, and she felt goose bumps on her skin.

"Gods, it's cold in here," she said, chattering her teeth.

He smiled softly and crawled in after. “I’ll warm you, my sneaky little love,” he whispered against her neck.

CHAPTER 28

HE'S GONE

Spring was a week away, but winter was stubborn this year. There were still a few inches of snow on the ground, keeping the group in Salthole. Traveling when there was snow on the ground could be dangerous for them and the horses, so they were stuck waiting. They still couldn't get a teleport, and Eden couldn't quite get this one spell right that would make a little cabin for them to stay in. Eden blamed herself for not getting Edward the help he needed, but Rickert and Saphira reminded her if a spell was beyond her, it was best not to push herself because they wouldn't want her to get hurt. Saphira remembered seeing a mage in the temple's healing room when she was a child. He had tried to cast a spell beyond his ability, and something popped in his head. Blood had poured from the man's nose for hours. Saphira had never seen anyone so pale before.

One night, Saphira was taking a shortcut through the cemetery after a successful gathering session. There weren't many traders during the winter, but when they made their way through, the information was always juicy. She had to make it back to Gareth and tell him about the shipment of potions making its way through town the next week. They would make a killing selling them to their contact later.

As she walked around a big oak tree, she heard a voice call out. "Saphira?" She gasped and looked up. Edward was standing a few feet away with a little box in his hand.

"Edward, what are you doing here?" The last time she saw Edward was weeks ago. He was fighting with his sister, and he smacked Eden across her face before any of them could intervene. He moved into the 'Orc' after that incident, and none of them had seen much of Edward since. Saphira thanked Otto for Rickert that night; he was the only one who could calm Eden when she realized her brother was gone.

"I realized I missed your birthday, and I wanted to give you something." He slowly walked over to her. "I know I'm not myself most of the time, but I want you to know when I am, I appreciate what you're doing for me. Trying to get me to Raventree and helping Edie out when I'm an ass. I still haven't forgiven myself for what I did to her." His eyes looked sad as he spoke about the incident. "Happy birthday, Saphira." He was standing in front of her, holding the little box out for her.

She crossed her arms over her stomach. "You didn't have to get me a gift, Ed."

He shrugged. "It's all right, I wanted to."

"Edward, I—" She reached for the box, but he sighed, and his hands flew down to his sides, clearly irritated.

"You know, just because you're sleeping with Gareth doesn't mean you can't take gifts from others."

She instantly frowned at his words and took her hand back. "I *was* going to take it. And why do you have to be rude? He's not some random guy I let into my bed. He's my partner. I've known him a long time."

Edward shook his head. "I don't know why you bother with him. You expect your parents to be happy about you being with a man like that?"

"A man like what?" They both looked over at a large mausoleum and saw Gareth leaning against the cold marble building. "What kind of man do you think they would let her marry, Edward?" Gareth walked over to her. His hands were hidden in his cloak, but Saphira knew there were knives between his fingers. "Would they let her marry a man who's always been there for her, taught her how to be the best of herself, and is willing to share a kingdom with her? Or a man who tried to force himself on her and beat his sister."

"Those things aren't my fault!" Edward yelled, pointing a shaking finger at the rogue, but Gareth continued as if he didn't speak.

"A man who has loved her from the very first kiss and prays to the gods that there will be more in the years to come, or a man whose jealousy almost broke a group apart."

"Shut up, you piece of shit!"

"Gareth, what are you doing?" Saphira whispered. He was usually calm when it came to interacting with Edward. Gareth stepped up next to Saphira and loomed over Edward, ignoring her question.

"But I wonder why you think Saphira needs her parents' permission to marry anybody. She has a mind of her own and will marry the man she wants, if she wants to marry at all." Edward was breathing hard, and Saphira knew Gareth was pushing him over the edge with his words.

"You do not deserve her," Ed said slowly.

"I never said I did. But I love her, and I feel lucky to have her love in return. But you need to realize it was never going to be you."

"Gareth." She gasped at his words, but they were drowned out by Edward's angry growl. He threw the gift on the ground and tried to push Gareth with his chest, but the rogue king didn't move.

"You should be rotting in a hole somewhere!" Edward sounded irate, and Saphira knew he was letting the entity take over.

"Edward, stop it!" Saphira begged. "Get a hold of yourself before it's too late."

He huffed and picked up the gift; one corner was now wet with melted snow. "Tell him to stop throwing things in my face! I can't help this!"

"They are your fault, Edward, that's part of your problem." Saphira could feel her heart in her throat as Gareth kept talking. "I've known others afflicted like you, and it took years for them to finally succumb. I held my tongue for too long when it came to you, hoping you'd come to your senses. But when you hit Eden, I knew you were lost. It's praying on your insecurities, and you need to start taking responsibility and stop blaming 'it' and

Saphira for your current situation."

"But it is, it's all her fault!" He threw the box at Gareth's head, and he ducked out of the way as Edward tackled him to the ground. "I chose to come back!" Edward yelled as he tried to hit the rogue in the face, but Gareth was faster, and Edward's hand slammed into the frozen ground. He didn't seem to notice, though, and kept up his assault. "I could hear her crying over me, and I didn't want to leave!" He threw a punch at Gareth's ribs, and Saphira heard the rogue's breath catch in his throat. "It told me it could bring me back, so I accepted! I didn't know it was going to be like this!"

"Edward, stop it!" Saphira reached down and pulled on his arm, but he flew up and punched her in the face. It was so unexpected, Saphira slipped on the snow and flew backwards, hitting her head on a small grave marker. When she opened her eyes, things were spinning.

"Saphira!" She could tell it was Gareth, but wasn't sure where it was coming from. She heard Edward yell in pain, and suddenly, there were hands on her face, and she could smell Gareth's cologne.

"Voltain, you okay?"

She looked up and saw three blurry faces. "There's three of you," she moaned and felt a cold stinging on the back of her head.

"Keep your eyes open, okay?" Gareth reached in his coat, but before he took whatever it was out, Edward began his assault again.

"You're dead, you piece of shit!" He yelled and kicked at Gareth, but the rogue rolled out of the way, landing on his left knee with his right leg out for stability. Saphira saw a glint of silver in his hand.

"Leave Edward, or you'll force my hand."

"Are you going to throw your little dagger at me? Go ahead, let's see—" Gareth threw the dagger with the speed of a god, and Edward fell to the ground with a cry.

"I didn't want to do it, Ed." Gareth got to his feet and

slowly walked to the unmoving figure. "You hurt Saphira, you hurt Eden, you're too dangerous." Saphira slowly sat up. The spinning was better, but her head hurt something fierce. Gareth knelt next to Edward. "We're gonna put you somewhere where you won't hurt anybody anymore." He reached out for Edward when the still man suddenly sat up and ran his own dagger into Gareth's stomach. The rogue grabbed his stomach and stumbled away from Edward before falling to his knees.

"Gareth!" Saphira screamed, but the pain made her wretch on the ground, and everything started spinning again.

"It's bad enough you had to shack up with that piece of shit," she heard Edward say. "Did you not think that would kill me, Saphira? Seeing you with a worthless thief who only wanted to add you to the notches on his bedpost!" The snow crunched as he walked over, and Saphira couldn't fight back as he lifted her to her feet. "Did I mean nothing to you, you succubus?" She tried to look behind Edward to check on Gareth, but the pain and nausea were all she could focus on.

"Edward, please, let me get to Gareth," she managed to say. The smell of blood hit her nose, and she forced her eyes to focus. Edward was bleeding profusely from his arm, but acted as if he didn't feel a thing. He was well and truly gone.

"You're a whore," he said as he shook her violently, and a burning pain in her head stole her breath. "You play with men's hearts until you make them believe you love them. May the abyss swallow you whole while the Shackled One plays with your soul for all eternity." He threw her down, and she could hear footsteps walking away. When she was finally able to open her eyes, she saw Gareth slowly crawling over to her, staining the snow with his blood.

"Saphira," he was breathing hard and holding his stomach. "Saphira, are you okay?" He groaned and collapsed back to the snow as everything went black.

Warm hands touched her face, and a familiar smell made her open her eyes. Gareth's gray eyes were looking into hers as he breathed a sigh of relief.

"There you are. Gods, I was scared you'd never wake up." He gently pressed his lips to hers, and she could taste the salt from the tears he had wiped away. The bed moved, and as Gareth sat back, Saphira saw Andros next to her. It took her a second to realize she was in her room at the group's house.

"You're going to be all right, Saphira," Andros ran his thumb on her cheek. "You had a bad concussion, but you're healing just fine."

"Concussion?" She looked around and saw Eden and Rickert standing in the corner, both looking incredibly sad. "Edie."

The mage walked over and took Saphira's hand. "How do you feel?" Eden gave her hand a kiss.

"Confused, what's going on?"

"Gareth brought you in last night. You were so cold, and your head was bleeding," she heard Rickert say. "Thankfully, Elyse and Andros happened to be in town."

"They said Edward did it. Is it true?" Eden asked. Saphira could hear her holding the tears back. At the mention of her brother, the memory of that awful night came flooding back.

"He…punched me, and I slipped. I think I hit my head on a grave marker." Eden lowered her head and covered her face as she sobbed. Saphira tried to sit up and hug her, but she was so stiff it was hard to move.

"Try not to move much, Saphira," Andros said and laid his hand on her head. "You might hurt yourself more." She felt a sleep spell working its way through her body, and she quickly took Gareth's hand.

"Don't leave me." She could feel her eyelids closing against her will as he scooted close and kissed her cheek.

"Never My Lady," he whispered, and she let sleep take her away.

When she woke the next morning, Gareth was still by her side, sleeping next to her in a chair. She looked over to the window and saw Gothrin was there, also asleep, his arms crossed over his big chest. She leaned over, feeling much less stiff, and touched Gareth's knee. He breathed in and opened his eyes.

"Morning," she whispered.

"Morning." Gothrin stretched and opened his eyes. When he saw they were awake, he walked over to them.

"How are you feeling, little one?" He gave her foot a squeeze.

"Better."

"We have a surprise for you," Gothrin said with a wink. She heard the door open and managed to turn her head. Familiar blonde hair and white robes made tears instantly fall from her eyes.

"Mom." Lily smiled and sat on the bed across from Gareth. Saphira struggled to sit up to hug her, but Lily quickly wrapped her arms around her and held her still.

"Hello, my little sneaker."

Saphira couldn't hold it in anymore and sobbed against her mother. "I missed you so much."

She felt her mother run her hand down her hair and rock her gently. "I missed you, too. Your friend Andros is a talented healer. When I got here, there wasn't anything left for me to do but wait for you to wake up."

Saphira sat back, and her mother wiped the tears from her cheeks. "How did you get here? We haven't been able to get a teleport for months."

"Perk of having a mage for a daughter-in-law. Sunette teleported us in last night. She's waiting downstairs now."

"Sunette," Saphira thought for a moment, her mind still a little fuzzy. "That's Foster's wife, Ada told me her name."

Lily smiled. "You saw Ada? She's been a tremendous help lately." Saphira snuggled harder against her mother. "You're going to be alright, no lasting damage." She noticed Gareth and Gothrin were gone, having quietly snuck out of the room.

"Mom," she whispered.

"Hmm." She felt her mother lay her head on hers.

"I met Dante." Her mother suddenly sat up, and Saphira was shocked at her mother's face, how worried, almost scared it was.

"What?" She stared at her mother for a moment, wondering if the concussion was still making her head fuzzy. Saphira didn't think her mother would have such a visceral reaction to such news. "How did he find you?" she asked slowly.

"He was at a party a friend of ours had, I think he was a guest of his father." Her mother took her hand, she could feel her shaking. "Mom, what's wrong?"

A look of betrayal crossed her face for a moment. "What did he say?" Saphira looked down at their hands, gripping each other like her mother was afraid something would drag them away from each other.

"He heard I was in Salthole and wanted to meet me." She watched as her mother took a few calming breaths, but she swore her hands were still shaking.

"What else did he say?"

"Just that Henri gave you peace when he couldn't. We didn't talk long. Mom, what's wrong?"

She heard her mother's breath hitch before she spoke. "Dante is not to be trusted, Saphira." Pain flared in her neck, and Saphira gasped. *Not to be trusted?* Lily quickly laid her hand on her neck, healing her.

Saphira sighed at the relief. "Why not? He seemed like a normal priest to me." It wasn't as if she didn't trust her mother; she believed her, but there was always a reason for her actions.

Lily took a deep breath and ran her hand over Saphira's hair. "When you come home, we'll sit and have a talk, okay?"

"All right." She snuggled against her mother again. "It's bad, isn't it?"

Lily sniffed. "It is, baby."

"I'm sorry, I shouldn't have said anything."

Her mother quickly moved and held her chin. "No, you did the right thing, little sneaker, I promise." Her mother was always a source of comfort and love for her, and Saphira hoped whatever she wanted to talk to her about wasn't painful. The last thing she wanted to do was have her mother relive something awful in her past to satisfy her ridiculous curiosity.

"If you say so."

After an hour, Saphira finally got out of bed and let her mother brush her hair. They walked down the stairs, hand in hand. Saphira could hear the others talking quietly in the kitchen, along with another unfamiliar voice. They turned into the kitchen, and Saphira saw a woman in colorful robes with long dark hair talking with her friends. Her accent was exotic, and she was the loveliest woman with kind eyes and a friendly laugh. It had to be Sunette.

Gareth was the first to notice them. "Saphira." He looked relieved as he walked over, and she felt her mother let go of her hand so she could hug him. "Are you feeling better?"

She nodded, keeping her arms around him, then remembered. "Shit, are *you* okay?" She touched his stomach, but he was intact.

"I'm fine, it wasn't as bad as I first thought." She knew he was lying, but was glad he was fine.

Sunette walked over and laid a hand on her shoulder. "Saphira, it's so nice to meet you. I'm Sunette, your sister-in-law." Saphira slid a hand from around Gareth and gave her a hug. Sunette was good at them, nice, tight, and full of love.

"It's nice to meet you. Ada said you have a child?"

Sunette smiled. "Yes, little William. Your mother tells me he's as rollie poly as you were when you were a baby."

Saphira laughed. She loved that her mother compared her to the baby. "I can't wait to meet him."

"Saphira," she felt her mother's hand on her back. "If you feel well enough, Sunette and I can head back to Raventree. I think your friends will take care of you."

She turned and hugged her mother. "All right, thank you for coming."

"Anytime, little sneaker." Saphira moved back, and Gareth

quickly hugged her mother. Saphira could see how tight a grip he had on her.

"Thank you so much, Mother, I can't begin to tell you how much it means that you came."

Her mother chuckled and hugged him back. "It's never any trouble, son." She rubbed his back before he stood back with Saphira.

Rickert stepped up and shook Lily's hand. "Hopefully, Saphira won't need such healings again. Thank you."

"It's absolutely no trouble." Lily patted his hand. "You are all welcome in Raventree if you ever decide to make the trek. I'm sure Saphira would love to show you around." Eden stepped and shook her hand. "If you find your brother, bring him to me. I'll see if there's anything I can do."

"Thank you, we will." Saphira heard footsteps behind them and saw Gothrin walking up.

"Would you like to come back with us?" Lily asked him. "I'm sure Sobrei would love to meet you."

He gave her a slightly crooked smile. "I appreciate the offer, My lady, but I feel my place is still with them. Maybe one day."

Lily nodded, a smile on her face. "Thank you all for being such good friends with Saphira. I will add you to my prayers." She held out her hand, and Sunette took it.

"Love you, Mom."

Her smile was full of love as she looked at Saphira. "Love you too, my little sneaker."

"I look forward to seeing you again, Saphira," Sunette said, and they watched as they teleported back to Raventree.

Saphira sighed and turned to Eden. "Is he here?" Saphira asked quietly as she moved into the living room. Eden and Rickert sat across from her, and Gothrin took a seat by the window. Saphira couldn't help but see how scared Eden looked; she was pale, and her hands were shaking.

"No, he ran inside the night it happened, muttering about a…whore, then packed what he didn't take to the 'Orc' and left before we could figure out what was wrong," she said. "When Gareth brought you in, I thought Edward had killed you."

"I had never seen the young man so angry before," the old orc said.

"What happened, Saphira?" Rickert asked.

Saphira leaned closer to Gareth, who put an arm around her. "He found me in the cemetery. He wanted to give me a birthday gift, but when I didn't take it quick enough, he got angry. I think he let the entity take over. He said the most awful things."

Gareth kissed her head. "That wasn't Ed, Saphira," he said quietly. "Your Edward wouldn't say such things."

"I know." She turned into his chest and hugged her sneaky love.

Gothrin stood and laid a hand on Eden's shoulder. "We knew it was a matter of time before this happened. If we had made it before the snow, maybe the young man would have had a chance." Saphira sighed and silently cursed the snow.

"When you were visiting with your mother," Saphira looked over up Gareth. His eyes were full of worry. "I went to check the 'Orc' to see if Ed was there, but he wasn't." Gareth tightened his arms around her. "Bale said he left with some man, older, salt and pepper hair, but he didn't know him." Saphira slowly sat up, her eyes going wide. "What?"

"Salt and pepper?"

Gareth nodded. "Is his hair color significant?" She took a few calming breaths and tried to gather her thoughts, but everything Ada told her was flying through her mind.

"When I, we, saw Ada in Ardenry, she told me I was marked."

Gothrin sat down and put his elbows on his knees. "Marked how?"

"Not sure, she said a man with salt and pepper hair wanted to claim me."

"The fuck?" Gareth laid a hand on her back. "Claim you? No one's going to claim you." The passion in his voice made her feel better.

"No, they won't." Gothrin sat back and crossed his big arms as he looked at Eden and Rickert.

"Do you know anything else about this man?" Eden asked. Saphira sighed and sat back, hoping her friends wouldn't be mad for keeping this to herself.

"He's why Iollan left, the salt and pepper man hired him to kidnap me from Raventree." Everyone's eyes went wide. "Iollan left because he was worried being in Ardenry again would lead the man right to me. He left because he knew the salt and pepper man is dangerous, and Iollan was trying to keep me safe."

"Oh, Saphira," the mage whispered.

"You don't think it's the same man, do you?" Rickert asked Saphira, but he looked around at the group.

"I hope not," she held Gareth's hand. "But I don't think the stars are in my favor."

A week later, the group was still in Salthole, hoping Edward would make his way back. But Saphira knew in her heart, he'd never come back. Eden had never been so morose. Everyone was doing whatever they could to try to cheer her up, but nothing worked. The five of them were in the living room, trying to decide what to do now the snow was gone, hoping a change of scenery would help the mage's mood.

"I dread telling Mom what happened to Edward," Eden rested her head in her hand. "I think I want to go anywhere but Ardenry."

"Would you be joining us, young man?" Gothrin turned to Gareth, who was sitting next to Saphira, her hand in his.

"Perhaps, it depends on a few things."

Saphira turned to him. "What few things?"

Gareth smiled at her and kissed her hand. "I was thinking, while my sister and her husband are here, you and I could take advantage of Andros's affinity with Otto and marry us." Saphira's eyes went wide as everyone else in the room gasped. Gareth got down on one knee in front of her, still holding her hand. "Saphira, my beautiful dark lady, I swear I have loved you from the moment you laid your dagger against my neck." A little giggle slipped from her lips. "I have never met another woman I want to share my kingdom with, so it's not only your hand I'm asking for, I'm asking that you help me rule this town from the shadows. Your love makes me stronger, and there is nothing more in the world that I want to do than share my life, share my love, and share my town with you. Saphira Voltain, will you marry me?"

"Yes," she whispered and slipped to the floor in front of him. "Yes, Gareth, I'll marry you." She kissed him deeply as the other three in the room clapped for the couple. When she finally parted from his lips, she felt Eden's arms around her.

She had also knelt on the floor. "Oh, Saphira, I'm so happy for you!" She turned and hugged Eden who had been the sister she never had.

"Will you stand up with me?"

Eden gave a little happy squeak, "Yes! Of course, I'll help you find a dress, and I can do your hair," she sat back, a smile on her face that Saphira hadn't seen in a while. "You'll be the most beautiful bride." It was the first time in a week Eden had smiled, and Saphira thanked Otto for that.

"Well, you got seven days to plan, on the eighth they're leaving again," Gareth said with a smile.

Eden gasped and pulled Saphira to her feet. "Oh my gosh, you're right. Dress first!" Saphira laughed as Rickert came over and shook Gareth's hand before giving her a hug.

"I wish you all the best in this new endeavor."

"Thanks, Rickert."

Gothrin came over and gave her a hug, "I'm glad you have found happiness, little one, even with such a rogue." Saphira giggled and squeezed his hands before Gareth laid his forehead on hers.

"Do you think your family can make it?" He asked.

She held his face and gave him a kiss. "I want to get married with this family here, we can have a party later for my family. But this is for us."

"As you like, My Dark Lady." He sighed heavily and kissed her cheek. "I never thought Mother fucking Lily Voltain would be my mother-in-law."

Saphira laughed. "Just don't call her that to her face."

"Oh, gods no, never," he chuckled.

Saphira didn't dream much about her wedding day growing up, but with Eden helping her get ready, she could see why so many thought about it. They had fun finding a dress; it was a lovely copper color that laced up in the back, and the skirt went down to her knees. It had a few layers, making it a little poofy. It was the opposite of every dress she ever wore growing up, and she absolutely loved it.

One of the bakers nearby said they'd make her a cake for the little party afterwards. Saphira knew she wanted to keep it small, only her group and her new in-laws. Standing in front of a bunch of people, pouring her heart out sounded like a nightmare.

The night before the ceremony, she was walking around the living room. The wooden floor was cold on her bare feet. She walked from the table where the cake would go; it had a big green tablecloth on it. Then, she walked over to the lovely arch made of flowers that Elyse and Eden put together. A mix of black roses and orange lilies, she never thought they'd go together, but they were gorgeous.

"Hello there, little one." Saphira turned and saw Gothrin standing in the doorway. Seems he had a late night. If she wasn't sneaking around with Gareth this winter, she was working with Gothrin on her swordplay. She wasn't strong enough for a full blade yet, but the rapier she'd been practicing with was quickly becoming a favorite weapon.

"Hey Gothrin, glad I caught you. I had a question for you."

He chuckled and walked over to her, "What can I do for the bride-to-be?"

"Will you walk me down the aisle, or rather the stairs?" She chuckled.

His eyes went wide, and he blinked a few times. "You

want me to give you away?"

"Of course I do, I can think of no one better." She spoke in orcish, which she hadn't done in front of him before.

His jaw dropped and turned into a smile as he responded back in orcish. "You know my mother tongue?"

"Sobrei taught me."

His hand went to his chest. "You honor me, little one. I would love to walk you down the aisle."

"Great!" She walked over, and they hugged. "Meet me in my room at noon."

He chuckled. "I will see you there, little one. You better get some sleep, you want to be well rested tomorrow."

"I will, I had to make sure everything was done down here first or I'd never get to sleep." He ran his hand down her hair and walked to his room; it was the only one on the first floor. Saphira ran up the stairs and snuck into her room. The fire was almost dead as she slipped under the covers and wrapped her arms around Gareth. He breathed in deep and kissed her head. "Good night, My Lord," she whispered.

"Good night, My Dark Lady."

Saphira was sitting at her vanity, watching Eden curl her hair. A few strands were pinned up with pearled pins, the curls cascading down her back.

"I feel a bit too fancy."

Eden chuckled. "It's your wedding, you're supposed to be fancy." Saphira wasn't going to argue, but it was something to get used to. But she could easily admit she felt beautiful. "One last thing." Eden handed her a jewelry box. "Gareth gave it to me for you last night. A little gift from a King to his Queen, he said."

"Aww," she opened the little white box and saw a string of copper-colored pearls. "Oh gods." She held it up, and Eden gasped. "That's the most beautiful necklace I've ever seen."

Eden held up her hair, and Saphira put it around her neck. "Must have cost a fortune."

Saphira scoffed, "Wouldn't surprise me if he stole it."

Eden snickered and laid her hair down. It looked perfect with her dress.

"You are a vision, Saphira," Eden smiled behind her. "Are you excited?"

"I am, I love Gareth so much I want to do everything with him, live, steal, rule, have children, everything."

"I understand. Well, except the stealing part." Saphira laughed and slipped into her black flats. "Well, you look beautiful if I do say so, I'll let Gothrin know you're ready."

"Thanks, and thank you for standing up with me and helping with absolutely everything else."

Eden gave her a hug. "You are most welcome, Saphira, anything for my best friend." She gave her hands one last squeeze, then left the room. Saphira sat back down at her vanity and looked at herself. She couldn't believe she was about to get married. To the Thief King of Salthole, no less. The thought made her smile and brought her peace. She had never felt so like herself when she was with Gareth, sneaking around town.

When she woke from her reverie, she realized Gothrin wasn't there. She got up and opened her door, but didn't hear anything.

"Gothrin! I'm ready!" Nothing. She walked down the hall and down the stairs. "Gothrin, you're gonna make me la—" She looked up and stopped when she saw someone at the bottom of the stairs. "Edward?" He was standing with one hand on the railing, smiling up at her. It had been so long since she'd seen him smile like that. It was pure happiness. He was dressed in a nice black tunic and pants, like he knew what was happening today and dressed for the occasion.

"Hi Saphy," he held his hand out.

"How do you feel, Ed?"

"Better, much better." She ran down and took his hand, a smile on her face. "You look so beautiful, Saphy."

"Thanks, Ed, I'm glad you made it."

"Me too." She turned towards the living room, and it took a minute for her eyes to register what she was seeing. Standing under the flower arch was a man in black robes, not white, but before she saw his face, her eyes noticed the bodies on the floor by the window.

Her hand slid out of Edward's as she slowly walked into the room. The smell of blood hit her nose, and her brain finally let her understand the carnage that lay before her. Eden was on her back. She was lying in a large puddle of blood. But Saphira couldn't tell if it was hers or Rickert's because he was lying protectively on top of her. His back was a ruined mess of red. Saphira felt her heart break as she tried desperately to catch her breath.

"Eden?" She fell to her knees beside them and shook her boss. "Rickert?" Neither responded. "Eden!" Saphira pulled on her friend's arm, and Rickert slid onto the floor. Saphira screamed when she saw Eden's heart was gone. "No!" She screamed, pulling her friend into her lap, covering her legs in blood. "No, no, no!" Tears streamed down her face. This couldn't be happening, not now!

"Gothrin!" Saphira turned towards the stairs and saw the old orc on the floor in the hallway, unmoving. "Gothrin!" Saphira slipped in a pool of blood getting to her feet, but managed to make it across the room. Gothrin's open eyes were unmoving, and a sob escaped her lips. "Edward, what's going on!" She turned to him as Edward stopped in front of her. "Please tell me you didn't do this." Saphira slowly got to her feet, pulling the dagger from her thigh sheath. "Where's Gareth!" She screamed and pressed the dagger against Edward's chest.

He looked so calm it was unnerving. "Gareth is fine, Saphy, don't worry, he won't interrupt us."

"What do you mean, interrupt us?" She heard footsteps and remembered the other person in the room. She turned, and her heart leapt into her throat. "Dante." Her voice was barely a whisper as she remembered what her mother told her. He smiled and clasped his hands in front of him. His salt and pepper hair was evident now; he hid it under the hood of his cloak at the party. She believed her mother when she said Dante wasn't to be trusted, but she never believed *he* could be the one who marked her.

"Saphira, my dear, you look absolutely beautiful."

Tears betrayed her as they ran down her cheeks. "What do you want?"

"I only want to officiate my daughter's wedding."

His words made no sense. "I feel sorry for your daughter." She sneered.

"Saphy," Edward took a step closer, but she took a step back. "Don't you see?" She looked between the two men. They looked like nothing was wrong, like there weren't three dead bodies less than ten feet away from them. That one of them wasn't Edward's twin. "You're his daughter," Edward said with a smile. Saphira shook her head as she backed into the wall. "Haven't you ever wondered why you felt different from the rest of your family?" She kept shaking her head as her dagger pierced Edward's chest. Blood welled up from the wound, but he ignored it.

"I know this must be a shock, Saphira," Dante kept using his calming priest voice, but she wasn't buying it. "But it's true. You are of my blood."

"My mother would *never* cheat on my father, you lie!" She pointed her dagger at the priest.

Dante nodded. "You're correct, she would never cheat on her husband, not willingly."

His words rang in her mind, *willingly*. "You fucking bastard!" She lunged at Dante, but Edward wrapped his arms around her, and with a wave of the priest's hand, her dagger flew from her hand and sank deep into the wall. "I'll kill you! How fucking dare you do that to my mother!" Without her dagger, she had nothing, so she swung her arms and legs, trying to hit anything. "How fucking dare you!" She screamed so loud her throat hurt, and Edward put a hand around her mouth, holding her tight against his chest.

"I know it wasn't the best beginning, Saphy," Edward whispered in her ear. "But it's true, remember the door in Val

Shing?" She stopped thrashing. She hadn't thought of Val Shing in years; that damn door only she could open. "You know it's true."

She reached up and moved his hand. "No." She looked over at Dante, seeing her light blue eyes on him, the familiar nose.

"I'm sorry you had to find out this way." Dante's calm voice enraged her more. "I had hoped giving your mother the beautiful little girl she wished for would have turned her heart back to me. Unfortunately, it did not work, but I don't regret my actions, Saphira, because they brought you into the world." She squeezed her eyes tight as more tears betrayed her. "Now, how about we get on with the wedding?"

She jerked, trying to get out of Edward's hands, but he was too strong. "What wedding?"

"Ours, Saphy." She looked back at Edward, still smiling happily. "Your father will marry us, and then you'll be where you belong. With us in Dal En Val." Her eyes went wide, and she tried dashing for the door, but Edward's arms clamped down around her. She screamed, but Dante touched her cheek, and her scream was silenced. "Don't worry, Saphy," Edward's calm voice enraged her. "Everything will be fine." He turned her towards him, and she felt something wrapped tightly around her wrists. She looked down and saw a magical rope digging into her skin.

Edward, please, she said, but no sound came out. *Please don't do this.* But the smile on his face never faltered.

"I promise I'll treat you like the queen you are," he kissed her forehead as she held her hand out for her dagger, but it didn't move.

"Oh, I dispelled your dagger. You won't need it anymore," Dante said with a lazy wave of his hand as Edward dragged her into the living room, her feet sliding over the wooden floor. Her heart broke all over again; that was the dagger Zell gave her. Her eyes landed on her friends, but she realized neither Gareth, Elyse, nor Andros was there. Maybe there was hope.

Please, Otto, help me she prayed. Dante was standing under the arch, and the smell of death hit her nose. But not recent death, rotting, old death, and she gagged, putting her hand up to her mouth.

"I apologize about the smell, but you'll get used to it, dear." She pulled against Edward, but his hands gripped her arms so hard she knew they were bruising. She tried stomping on his feet, but Dante cast a spell, and she suddenly stood straight, and couldn't move. "This is for the best, my dear," Dante brushed some hair off her cheek, and she hated she couldn't get away from him. "I can't wait to show my daughter and her new husband off when we get home."

No, please, no, anything but that, Otto, please, she prayed as Dante looked between them.

"I think we'll make this quick. We don't want the bride under more stress than she has to be." He cleared his throat, "Oh, the rings, I almost forgot." He waved his hand, and from the shadows a body shuffled forward; it was where the smell of death was emanating. The body was emaciated and decayed, but Saphira felt like her heart was about to burst out of her chest when she saw him.

Iollan.

Tears once again streaked down her face as she saw him. "Thank you, Iollan." Dante held out his hand, and the zombie put two rings in it. "I hired Iollan to bring you to me years ago, but he decided to run off instead. I thought it fitting you two ended up in the same group years later. I do wonder how he managed to pull himself from you; he was deeply in love with you. But he wasn't good enough for my daughter." She didn't think she could take much more heartache and felt sick. "Now, Edward, do you take Saphira to be your wife, to cherish and protect, and do you promise to teach her the ways of The Shackled One so that you may both flourish in his dark power for all the days to come."

He smiled down at her and ran a hand down her hair. "I do."

"Saphira, do you take Edward to be your husband, to obey and love so that you both may flourish in the power of

The Shackled One for all the days to come." She couldn't move, couldn't speak; she hoped he would take this spell off her so she could move, but he didn't. "I'll take your silence as acceptance."

No! She screamed in her head as he gave Edward the rings. The archer put one on his left hand and reached for Saphira's when a knife flew at Dante's head. He dodged it, and Edward pulled her against him, but she couldn't turn her head to see who was there.

"Let her go you fucking bastards!"

Gareth! Her voice screamed in her head before she heard several footsteps walking into the room.

"She is *mine,* you fucking thief, I loved her first!" Ed's comforting tone of voice was gone, and the demon in him was at the front now.

"She never loved you!" Saphira would have gasped if she could have, as she heard her cousin Kaythen's voice.

"What the fuck are you doing here, *Vale*?" Dante sneered at the newcomers.

Saphira heard a familiar feminine voice. "We were invited by the *actual* groom, *Foss.*" It was her Aunt Lavinia, Kaythen's mother. She heard metal tinkling to her right, and Dante gasped. "You've fucked with my family enough over the years," Lavinia said. The sound of heels on the wooden floor made Saphira's ears twitch. "I'm going to enjoy this."

"Boy, if you want to marry my daughter, you'll fight!" Dante screamed at Edward and flung a spell somewhere, but no one yelled out, so he must have missed. Edward let her go and drew his sword, but Kaythen was there in an instant before it was fully out of its scabbard. Her cousin pressed his own sword against Edward's neck.

"Move, and you die," he growled, and she felt hands around her; it was Gareth.

"I got you, My Lady, I got you." The relief she felt was like a wave crashing into her as he pulled her away from the archway and untied her hands.

"Damn it, boy!" Dante raised his hand but stopped when

he saw what Lavinia held. Four necklace vials, thrumming with death magic, dangled from her outstretched hand.

Her mouth tilted into a wicked smile. "Bye." She smashed the vials against the nearby table, and Dante screamed as black wisps of smoke flew back into his body.

"Blessed Otto, destroy this abomination!" It was Andros. Holy fire erupted where Dante stood, and he screamed as it burned him into nothing. The fire stopped. The only thing it left was a pile of ash on the ground. The Iollan zombie collapsed to the ground, and Saphira found she could move again. She quickly wrapped her arms around Gareth.

Andros walked over and healed her wrists. "Are you hurt, Saphira?" She felt his hand on the back of her head.

"I'm not hurt, but everyone else," she couldn't finish. She watched as Andros kneeled next to Eden and Rickert, confirming what she already knew. Lavinia walked over to her, and Saphira gave her a hug. "Not that I'm not grateful, but what are you doing here?" Lavinia chuckled and hugged her tight. If it weren't for the faint smell of death around her, it'd be just like hugging her mother.

"Kaythen looked your man up last summer; he wanted to make sure he was good enough for you. Seems they had a rather enjoyable conversation since your man slyly invited us today. But when we got here, we saw your friends were dead, so we had to act quickly. I'm sorry we didn't get here sooner." Saphira kept her arms around her aunt and looked over at Kaythen, his sword pressed on Edward's neck. Her cousin's face was as angry as she'd ever seen.

"What do we do with him?" Kaythen pressed the sword a little harder, and a line of blood ran down his neck.

"You can't do this," Edward said. "We all follow The Shackled One. You should *want* me to marry Saphira!"

"Saphira will marry who she chooses," Kaythen growled at him. "And it clearly isn't you."

Lavinia passed Saphira to Gareth, who held her tight. The priestess walked over to Edward and laid a hand on his head. His body began shaking, making the wound in his neck bleed more.

"That thing in him is buried deep. I've never felt an entity so entangled in a soul before." She turned back to Saphira. "I fear no one will be able to help him, not even your mother."

"It's been over a decade since he died." Lavinia's eyes widened when she said that. "I'm not surprised."

"You heard the ladies." Kaythen pushed his sword into Edward's neck. A horrible gurgle filled the air before he dropped to his knees. Saphira covered her face and couldn't stop the mournful cries. This was supposed to be her wedding day, but now all her friends were dead.

Gareth hugged her tight; she heard him sniffing and felt his tears on her shoulder. "I'm so sorry, Saphira, I'm so sorry." His voice was thick with tears.

Saphira sat in the living room, holding Lavinia's hand while priests from the temple came and took all the bodies, even Iollan's. Kaythen cast a spell to get rid of the blood, and the room looked like nothing had happened.

"Is what he said true?" Saphira turned to her aunt, "Is he my…" she couldn't bring herself to say it. Lavinia ran her hand down Saphira's hair. She could tell her aunt was trying to find the right words.

"Yes. When I learned what he had done, I wanted to kill him, but your mother told me it was too dangerous, and that if I did kill him, I needed to find his phylacteries first."

"He was a litch?" Her aunt nodded. "Well, then how? I don't understand."

"Magic made you, sweet girl. Him being a litch he couldn't truly have children, but he found a way through magical means. I suggest you have a nice long talk with your mom when you get home."

"She told me he wasn't to be trusted, and we'd talk when I got home. I didn't think in a million years this is what she meant." Saphira looked up at her aunt. "Thank you for coming, even if I didn't get married."

"You're welcome. I felt honored to be invited."

Kaythen sat next to her and put an arm around her. "How are you feeling?" She looked over at the door. Gareth was talking with the guards. No matter how sneaky you are, you can't hide five bodies from being taken to the temple at noon.

"I have never been so sad in my life." She turned to him. "But thank you for everything."

He laid his forehead on hers. "Think nothing of it, cuz."

Gareth closed the door and walked over to them. "Okay, the guards believed we were randomly attacked, so they won't bother us again. Andros is overseeing the bodies. He'll cremate them so we can take them when we leave for Raventree."

Saphira sat up straight at his words. "Raventree?"

Gareth kneeled in front of her and took her hands. "Dante may be gone for now, but he might have more phylacteries. I think we'd be safer in Raventree with your family."

Her eyes narrowed. "But Salthole is your home."

He reached up and cupped her cheek. "You are my home, Saphira, and I want you safe, damn my kingdom here."

She could hear the passion in his voice as he talked about wanting her safe. "Are you sure?"

"I've never been surer about anything."

"He's willing to give up a kingdom for you," Lavinia laid a hand on her back. "I'd listen to him." Saphira looked over at her aunt, who gave her a little hug. "We'll leave you two alone to figure things out. I am so happy you have love, sweet girl. Gareth seems like a good man."

"He is." Lavinia stood, and Kaythen hugged her next. "Thank you."

"You're welcome. Anything for you."

That night, Saphira was sitting in a room in the temple with Gareth, Andros, and Elyse. The five boxes of ashes were on a table in front of her.

"I'm the only one left." Her voice hitched. "I started traveling with them three years ago in Ardenry, and now…"

"I am so sorry for your loss, Saphira," Andros laid a hand on her shoulder. "They were great people."

"I have to tell their families." The thought made her sick. Rickert's sister, the twins' parents, how could she do such a thing?

"I'll be with you the whole time, My Lady." Gareth kissed her hand. "You won't be alone."

She turned to him. "Thank you." She laid her forehead on his for a moment. "Andros?"

"Yes?"

"Will you marry us now?"

He sat up, "Right now?" She nodded. "I will," he said softly and stood in front of them as they stayed seated. Elyse scooted next to Saphira, and she turned, giving the quiet woman a hug. She turned back to Gareth, and they held hands. "We are gathered here to not only say goodbye to dear friends, but to bring Saphira Voltain and Gareth Quinn together, heart and soul. I have known them both for years and have seen how much they love each other. I wish everyone could find such fierce love." Saphira leaned into a kiss Gareth gave her on her cheek.. "Gareth, do you wish to say your own vows?"

He nodded, "Yes." He cleared his throat and kissed Saphira's hands again. "Well, I didn't write any vows. I knew if I tried, they'd end up being eighteen pages long, and I wouldn't be able to cut anything out. So, I decided to let the words flow from my mouth on the day, and as you can tell, I'm not doing any better." She managed to smile at his sincerity. "I'm never one to pray; I think you can count on one hand how many times I have, but I am grateful to the gods who let me meet you. I am grateful I will get to see your beautiful face every day for the rest of my life, that we will continue our lives in Raventree, and see what kind of gathering we can do." He gave her a wink, and it drew a little chuckle from her. "My beautiful, sneaky love, I cannot begin to tell you how much I cherish you, and I will spend the rest of my life showing you how much I love you. You make me stronger, Saphira, and for that I thank you. To the abyss and back."

"To the abyss and back," she echoed him.

"Saphira, did you want to say your own vows?"

She nodded and kissed Gareth's hands, took a deep breath, and sighed. "Yeah, I didn't write any either." Gareth chuckled and kissed her cheek. "I remember the first time I saw you on the rooftop behind me. It was bone-chillingly cold, and I could smell the sea air, and somehow you actually got the drop on me." Andros dipped his head to hide his own little chuckle. "You were the most handsome man I had ever seen, and I knew you were trouble." Gareth smiled and shrugged his shoulders. "But sometimes trouble is worth it. You have been with me through some of the best and worst moments of my life. We have tended to each other's wounds, we have celebrated and mourned together, and I think those experiences created an unbreakable bond. I have loved you from our first kiss after we torched the Imperial ship, and I will love you till the last. To the abyss and back."

"To the abyss and back," he whispered.

"Otto has heard your love and knows that together you can do a lot of good in the world. Together you will be stronger, and together you will create a life of love and friendship. In Otto's name, I declare you husband and wife. Gareth, you may kiss your love and know you are blessed." Gareth leaned forward, and she kissed him, holding him there until she felt she wouldn't cry.

When they finally parted, Gareth cupped her cheek. "I want to take your name, Saphira."

She managed a little smile. "You don't have to. We can keep our own names."

He shook his head. "I want everyone to know how impressive you are, that your husband took your name, not the other way around."

"Gareth Voltain," she ran her hand through his hair. "I suppose it has a ring to it."

"Then may I present, Saphira and Gareth Voltain," Andros motioned to them as they kissed one more time.

CHAPTER 29

HARD TRIP

A month after Rickert, Eden, Edward, Iollan, and Gothrin were cremated, Saphira felt up to traveling and put the boxes gently into her pack. She felt responsible for their remains and didn't want any harm to happen to them while they traveled. She and Gareth packed all they could and began the hardest trip she'd ever had to take. The first thing they looked for was a Suya camp; it took another month before they found the right one. Saphira had hoped to find them before she and Gareth hit Buckland. The camp looked much like it did the last time, big colorful tents rustling in the breeze of the plains.

Saphira stopped at the edge of the nearest tree line. "Here." Gareth watched her take Iollan's ashes and spread them on the ground. "I hope wherever you are, you're not in pain," she whispered and said a silent prayer to Otto, asking him to keep Iollan's soul safe. She got to her feet and cleared her throat. "All right, let's go." Gareth took her hand, and they walked into the camp. A few people waved to her as they walked towards the middle of the camp. She spied Malia at a cauldron, making some food, a baby in a sling on her back.

"How do I do this? What do I even say?" she said quietly to Gareth.

She felt his hand on her back. "Honestly, I think if she sees you without Rickert, she's going to know."

"You think?" She looked over at him, searching his face for answers.

He nodded. "That's how it usually happens when I do it." She imagined over the years, Gareth had to break the news to a family more times than he wanted. Malia looked up and saw Saphira before she reached her. She waved and heard her call for her husband, Lucian, as they walked over.

"Saphira, it's good to see you. How are you?" She leaned down and hugged her; the baby stayed asleep on her back.

"I've been better. I see you have a new little one."

Malia stood straight. "The little boy Lucien has been dreaming of," she laughed as her husband joined them.

"Lucien, this is Gareth." The men shook hands. "Can we talk in your tent?" Malia nodded and turned to the tent, but Lucien stayed still, the smile gone from his face.

"It's Rickert, isn't it?" Saphira nodded. Lucien closed his eyes and took a breath before joining his wife in the tent.

That night, they slept under the stars, away from the Suya camp. Saphira didn't want to be around them; it was heartbreaking. She gave Malia her brother's ashes as she cried. Lucien had thanked her for that kindness, tears falling down his face as well.

"Despite how you feel, it went well," Gareth said. Malia's cries would haunt her for nights to come, she knew.

"This is the worst part of traveling," she said, wrapping her arms around her love.

He laid his chin on her head. "It is."

They made their way to Buckland the next day. It was the last town before they'd turn towards Ardenry. After Gareth had been snoring lightly for an hour, she slipped out and walked to the bridge at the end of town. The night was cool, a nice respite from the summer days as they traveled. The little stream running under the bridge was loud compared to the silent night around her.

Her ear twitched as she leaned on the bridge. "I had hoped you'd come," she said without turning.

Kaythen's chuckle filled the air as he stepped next to her. "I figured you'd make your way through at least once more. How are you?"

"Still reeling." She turned to him. He wasn't wearing robes tonight, only a simple dark shirt and pants. "Thank you for your help."

He shook his head. "Don't mention it, we've been trying to get rid of him for years. Took Mother eight of those years to find four phylacteries; there are probably more. I wouldn't put it past him."

"Me either," she sighed heavily. "Did you know about Dante?"

He nodded again; this time, she could tell he seemed more solemn. "That was the number one reason my mother hated him: that he dared to defile her sister. She never liked him, even before he changed. But he didn't pose a threat, so she let him be. When he came to Dal En Val, powered up by our god, she knew she should have killed him years ago. But we waited. When she found out what he had done to your mother, she was livid. I'd never seen her so mad."

"I'm glad she found those phylacteries. If he has more, will you be in trouble?"

Kaythen shrugged. "There's always power grabs between litches in Dal En Val. If he comes back, it'll show people he's harder to get rid of than they thought, and my parents might lose some favor, but not all."

"I hope you'll all be all right. Could you thank her for me?"

He nodded. "Absolutely. You know, I think you look more like your mother, in spirit anyway." He gave her a wink and turned to walk away.

"Wait," she called out, and he turned back to her. Saphira rushed over and hugged him. He quickly wrapped his arms around her, reciprocating the tight hug. She swore he was shaking, a little.

"Thank you for not treating me differently."

He chuckled. "Likewise," he whispered and slid his arms from her and continued down the bridge.

"See you later."

He turned on his heels, a sad smile on his face. "We'll see, but it was an honor." Saphira saw a woman at the end of the bridge, smiling at him. She was tall and wearing a blue skirt with a green shirt. Her long brown hair was blowing gently in the wind. "Marilla," he took the woman's hand and turned back to Saphira. "Meet my cousin, Saphira."

"It's nice to meet you," she said. Her voice was kind and sounded a bit like Sunette's.

"And you." Kaythen gave her a little salute, then teleported them away. Saphira turned back to the bridge, letting the sound of the little stream fill the air once more.

Two weeks later, they walked into Ardenry, hand in hand, and without a word, Saphira led them to Mayris's shop. There seemed to be even more people than the last time they were here, and they wondered if the Empire hit another town. They checked into an Inn across the street from the shop and Saphira sat in the window all day, waiting for the sun to go down. When the shop was closed for an hour, she got to her feet.

She put the pack with her friends ashes on her back. "I feel like my heart is about to burst from my chest."

Gareth took her hand. "I'll be there to keep it in, don't worry." They walked across the street and knocked on the door in the alley that led to the apartment above the shop. They heard footsteps running down, and Mathias opened the door.

"Saphira! Hi, welcome," she saw he was looking behind her for the twins. "Are Ed and Edie with you?" He ushered them inside, and they stood at the bottom of the stairs.

"No," she whispered, and she could see the light in Mathias' eyes go out.

"I see." He cleared his throat and rubbed his face. "Mayris and Ruby are upstairs." They slowly walked up the stairs, and he opened the door for them.

Mayris looked up and smiled as Saphira entered. "Saphira! Hello, are you all back in Ardenry? The twins with you?" She turned and put some vegetables on Ruby's plate, who quickly gobbeled them down.

"Mayris." Mathias walked up behind them, and she looked up.

Saphira watched her eyes go from curious to worry, to grief. "No," she whispered and collapsed into her chair. Mathias went to her, wrapping his arms around her.

Tears fell from Saphira's eyes as she set down her pack. "I'm so sorry, I wish I could take it back, I wish I could..." She felt herself getting hysterical, so she took a few calming breaths, Gareth's arms on hers. "We had to let you know." She pulled the containers of their ashes from her pack and, with a shaky hand, laid them on the table. "They're both there."

Ruby looked over at her mother. Worry filled the toddler's face. "Mama?" Mayris sniffed and put the little girl on her lap and rocked her.

"What happened?" Mayris asked through the tears as Mathias slowly picked up the boxes and held them to his chest. There was no way Saphira wanted to tell her exactly what happened. No mother wants to hear such atrocities.

"Cultists." Usually, that was enough for people to fill in the blanks.

"Damn cultists," Mathias said, his lower lip trembling. "Ruining the world."

"We had a little funeral for them in Salthole," Gareth said. "It was lovely. We've been taking their ashes where they deserve to be, Rickert, Gothrin, Iollan, Eden, and Edward." As he spoke, the names came out slower and slower, like the grief was catching up with him.

"Five of you?" Mathias shook his head, "You must have gotten away by the skin of your teeth."

"It was a challenging day," Saphira said. She opened her backpack and pulled out a holding bag. "All the twins' belongings are in here. It's mostly clothes and jewelry." She set it on the table and took Gareth's hand. "Again, I can't tell you how sorry I am. Eden was my best friend, and Ed was a good guy. The world is darker without them in it." She could taste tears on her lips as she spoke. She gave Gareth's hand a squeeze and turned towards the stairs.

"Wait!" Mayris called out and ran over to Saphira and

gave her a tight hug. "Thank you for letting us know. Thank you for being their friend and bringing them home."

"It was my pleasure, Mayris." They walked out into the night air, quickly drying their tears. "There's one more place I want to stop by," Saphira said.

"Lead the way." They walked down Rose Street until they got to 'Meet's Locksmith'. Saphira knocked on the door and waited a few minutes. She could hear footsteps, and when the door opened, it was harder than she thought it would be to hold back the tears as she saw Zell.

"Saphira!" He pulled her into a hug. "I'm glad you're back. Come in." He looked up and saw Gareth. "Both of you come in. I was about to eat dinner. Join me." They walked inside, and the moment he shut the door, Saphira broke down and hugged Zell as she cried, Gareth's hand on her back. "Saphira, what is it?"

"I failed them all, Zell, it was my fault, they're all gone, every one of them!" She cried into his chest. She felt his arms squeeze her tight as she cried; she knew if anyone would understand, it was Zell.

"I'm so sorry." He stood there and let her cry until she finally felt able to let go. "Let's get something to eat?"

"Good idea," Gareth said as Saphira nodded. They followed him up to his little kitchen and took seats around the table. He had stew on the table, and thankfully, it was still warm. Zell put some in three bowls for them and sat down.

"I don't believe we've met. I'm Zell." He held out his hand to Gareth.

"Gareth, nice to meet you.

"Oh, you're Gareth, Saphira told me about you," he said with a smile.

"She did?" He turned, and he wiggled his eyebrows at her. Surprisingly, it made her laugh. "When did she tell you about me?"

"Last summer when they were in the city," Zell took a bite of his stew. "I had a feeling about you."

"Gareth is my husband."

Zell smiled peacefully and held her hands. "All my heartfelt congratulations to you both. I'm so glad you found love."

"Thank you, sir. She told me about you as well, how she hustled her way into a job." They laughed, and Saphira finally took a bite of stew.

"She certainly did." Zell sighed, "I'm sorry about your group, Saphira, but I'm glad you made it. But don't think it was your fault, sometimes the stars are against us."

She sighed and closed her eyes. "I think the stars hate me right now."

"We just came from telling the twins' mother about them," Gareth said.

Zell looked sympathetic as he clicked his tongue. "Never a fun job."

"You ever do it?" she asked him, finally looking up.

"We got lucky, only had to do it twice. The last time was about a year before I opened the shop. Had to tell our bard's wife he wasn't coming back. It was awful. She yelled and threw things at us, told us it was our fault he went out at all. We stood there and took it. Cause that's what you do with grieving people, you take it, so they don't have to feel it for one moment."

"Their mother hugged me and thanked me for being their friend. I don't deserve that hug."

"You'll forgive yourself in time. I promise." They all ate, and Saphira felt a little better by the end of the night. She told Zell if he ever wanted a quieter life, he'd be welcome in Raventree.

CHAPTER 30

HOME AT LAST

It was almost fall when Saphira and Gareth walked into Raventree. The first stop they made was to the temple. The two of them walked in, and Saphira saw her mother standing at the end of the aisle, speaking with someone who looked like a paladin. Raventree had no paladins, so whoever they were must have been traveling through. Her mother turned as they were halfway down the aisle, and her eyes went wide.

"Saphira!" At the sound of her mother's voice, Saphira started running. Lily ran as well, and they wrapped their arms around each other when they met. "Oh, my little sneaker, you're home."

"Yeah, Mom, we're home." She hugged her mother for a good long while. "I know," she whispered.

Lily stepped back and held her face. "Shall we talk now?" Saphira nodded and held her hand out for Gareth, who walked up and took it. "Let's go upstairs."

Half an hour later, Saphira was on the couch with her mother and father, the three of them hugging while Gareth stood by the fireplace, his head down and arms crossed. Listening to her mother talk about how, when Christopher was two years old, Dante tricked her into coming to Ardenry under the guise of becoming Otto's Pontiff. It was heartbreaking. She told Saphira how he kept her locked up for two months, before, by the grace of Otto, she was able to get free and ran to Lavinia's home. It made Saphira shake with rage. If she ever saw Dante again, she'd kill him. Lily told her that she wasn't early like everyone believed, but was in fact a little late. They had told everyone that William had visited her in Ardenry, and that's when she was conceived.

Everyone believed the lie without question.

William held her hands between both of his. "You are *my* daughter, you've always been my daughter, and I loved you from the moment I knew you existed."

"I love you too, Papa."

Saphira turned and gave her mother another hug, as Lily gave her forehead a kiss. "Do you want your brothers to know?"

She thought for a moment. "No, let's keep it between us."

Her parents nodded. "If you want," William patted her knee. "But I know they won't love you any less or treat you differently if they knew."

"I know, I just…not now anyway."

Lily tucked some hair behind her ear. "All right, little sneaker."

William sat back. "So, a married woman now, huh?" Saphira smiled over at Gareth, who gave her a wink. She told her parents about the awful, almost wedding, but she didn't feel like telling anyone else about it. To say they eloped was good enough.

"Yeah, he took my last name."

Her parents turned to Gareth. "Really?" Lily smiled, and Gareth nodded.

"I figured Voltain was a better name to have in Raventree than Quinn. Gives us a little more respect in whatever we end up doing."

"I'm glad you're both home and well," Lily looked between them. "Welcome to the family, Gareth." He gave her a little bow and smiled at Saphira. She felt a little better, now that everything had been said. She was surprised she didn't feel different, like she thought she might, knowing the truth of her parentage. But her father was right, she was *his* daughter, and always would be.

The next day, Saphira was sitting under the tree her mother planted outside the temple, the box with Gothrin's ashes in her lap. It was the last one.

"I hope you like it here. It's peaceful. Sobrei is here, Gothrin, as are the Burned Hand, so you won't be alone."

"He won't be." She looked up and saw the orc god standing behind her, leaning against the tree. "I heard you were finally home, *Sma'Ni*." His hair was white now, but there were no signs of age around his eyes. He looked to be the same, strong orc god Saphira knew as a child.

Saphira closed her eyes as tears fell from her eyes. "That's what Gothrin would call me, 'little one.'" Sobrei sat next to her. "He was loyal, and strong, and I knew I could trust him with anything." She opened the box and got to her feet. Sobrei followed. "Thank you for your friendship and your knowledge. I'll never forget you." She lifted the box, and the wind swirled around them, taking the ashes up and away into the tree above them. "I hope I'll never have to do that again." She turned to Sobrei and hugged him.

"As do I, *Sma'Ni*. It is a different kind of devastation to be the only one to survive. Trust me."

She wiped her eyes. "It really is."

When she felt she wouldn't cry anymore, Saphira walked home, her group on her mind. She and Gareth had moved into her childhood home with Foster and Sunette. They said she and her husband could stay until they found a place of their own. Being home helped a great deal. She and Christopher would pray in the temple, and after the first time she snuck up on Foster, his scream made her laugh so much she knew everything would be okay. She saw Foster and his little family outside, sitting on the grass. Sunette looked up and waved at her. Saphira walked through the fence and sat down with them. Her nephew William was eating a piece of bread with one hand and running his hand through the grass with the other. She hated that she missed his first year but vowed to be there for the rest.

Sunette reached out and held her hand. "How are you?"

She nodded and gave her hand a squeeze. "Better. Glad it's over." She turned to Foster, who was trying to keep the baby from eating grass. "So…" she leaned over to him. "What did you bring me?" Foster smiled and laughed as he got to his feet and ran into the house. Sunette watched him with amused eyes and put William in her ever-shrinking lap.

"Where's he going?" Sunette asked with a chuckle.

"He promised when he left that he'd bring me back something."

Sunette laughed. "I see."

Foster came back outside and sat next to her. "Here." He handed her a white rectangular box. It felt light in her hands, and when she opened it, she gasped. "That is a unique dagger," he said. Saphira picked it up, it was indeed light as she twirled it around. "All you do is snap your fingers, and it'll hover wherever it is, snap again, and it'll come to your hands. I hear it's a favorite of sneaky types."

Saphira snapped her fingers, and the dagger floated in the air. "Gods, Foster, this must have cost a fortune." She snapped again, and it flew back to her hand.

"Not a gold piece, found it in a trunk in Ardenry. I figured it'd do more good in your hands."

She put it back in the box and hugged him. "Thank you so much. I'm glad we're all home now."

"Me too."

Gareth walked out of the house and sat next to her, giving her cheek a kiss. "How did it go?" Little William got up and sat in the thief's lap. He had been the little boy's new favorite person since they got home, and Gareth loved every minute of it.

"It went well," she ran her fingers through her nephew's blonde hair. "Sobrei showed up."

"Good, I was hoping he would." Little William held up a piece of his bread for Gareth, who ate it with a growl, filling the air with the toddler's high-pitch laugh. "What shall we do now, my sneaky love?" She leaned over, and William gave her a little bite of his bread as well.

"We live."

Karen Thrower was born in Tulsa, OK, and still resides there with her husband, daughter, and cat. She graduated from The University of Tulsa with a BA in Deaf Education in 2005. She is a member of Oklahoma Science Fiction Writers and has served in several capacities, such as President, VP, and is currently Facebook Wizard. She has been published in various genres since 2018 and was included in the bestselling anthology 'Secret Stairs: A Tribute to Urban Legend' in 2019.

www.ingramcontent.com/pod-product-compliance
Lightning Source LLC
LaVergne TN
LVHW090554110826
845146LV00001B/126